WHAT WE ARE

PETER NATHANIEL MALAE

WHAT WE ARE

Grove Press
New York

For Kevin —
Bellua clestema who's
down for the blota — Wishing I'm and you the
very best, and the work, too — With hope and gratitude PNM

early July '11

Published simultaneously in Canada
Printed in the United States of America

ISBN-13: 978-0-8021-4522-2

Grove Press
an imprint of Grove/Atlantic, Inc.
841 Broadway
New York, NY 10003

Distributed by Publishers Group West

www.groveatlantic.com

11 12 13 14   10 9 8 7 6 5 4 3 2 1

Alas it is delusion all.
The future robs us from afar,
nor can we be what we recall,
nor dare we look on what we are.

—*Byron*

Contents

WHAT WE ARE

I

I Try to Figure Out My American Life

I TRY TO FIGURE OUT my American life on a lightless corner of a four-stop-sign intersection in a rainstorm, 3:42 A.M., Friday. I could go forward, backward, right, left; it doesn't matter. I have nowhere to go, really, but around the city, and have wandered along on foot all night.

I dropped into a dive bar called Blinky's Can't Say Lounge for a drink and a Johnny Cash tune on the juke, ducked past the flashing neon signs of the Blue Noodle Cabaret Club to watch the beautiful Maxine do acrobatic flips on the pole, smiled my way to a table surrounded by fake bamboo and ceramic dragons and ate kimchi and kalbi and poke sashimi and drank Hite beer and Japanese sake in a Korean-owned sushi bar called Ga Bo Ja, hustled down the aisles of a twenty-four-hour Longs Drugs and bought candy and condoms and a discount umbrella with Pokémon dancing on the latex, and am now peering up beyond the BBs of rain to the mad gray mass of clouds above, not in wonderment or gratitude or even some momentary bout of depression, not in any poor man's version of self-condemnation, neither contentment nor elation nor anything within that emotional range, but in a strange kind of nothingness that sat somewhere between my head and my heart and had bothered me for much of the day, like a facial tick you're conscious of but that won't go away.

I sit down on the curb and try to chill a bit; no melodrama in this empty hollow of the city. The rain morphs into silver glitter. It looks like the mist of a late-night horror flic on the tube, the haze of a northernmost California lumberjack town. The sheen on the street is oily smooth, black like the shine of leather, slick like a duck's wet back on the pond. I can see the streetlights flickering past Lawrence Expressway and through the little borough of Cupertino and shrinking into dots at De Anza College.

I'm big and brown enough not to have problems on the streets that I don't create myself. I could be Mexican or Brazilian or Creole or Persian or mulatto or Afghan, or of darker Mediterranean blood, like Sicilian, Moroccan, Greek, or maybe Serb, and I'm tough to peg with this black and logoless beanie on my head pulled down to the brow, the stalker's knee-length jacket, blue jeans, and slippers. People can't figure me out on sight and I'm not sure I could either in a first-ever mirror shot.

What I am, by blood anyway, is half Samoan—I'm certain of that—and half American white, which means (if it means anything) that my mother is of your typically mixed brew of Euro descent: English, Irish, Pennsylvania Dutch, Italian, and a smattering of French.

My father used to take my sister and me to the Samoan churches up at Hunter's Point, a fifty-minute drive from our house in San Jo. This was just before he left for the islands, when my folks were staking cultural claims on their children, like Soviets and Americans planting flags on the moon. I remember one funeral, a big gala affair. Five days long with hordes of big silent men in black polyester ie lavalavas standing stoic and strong, their mitts crossed just under their bellies. I remember the acreage of carnations and roses in the aisles, right out of a *Godfather* movie. Whenever someone with your own last name would die, you had the responsibility to prepare your cousin or uncle or sister-in-law for the outer realm with the Good Lord. I remember wondering who would send me or my sister off sixty years in the future, if the event would die out first. If Samoans would even be around.

I always felt alone in those churches. I knew that the kids my age and the parents who paid me any attention thought I was diluted, watered down by my mother, too much white blood, an *afakasi*, a half one. Certain things you can't reverse, and genetic inheritance is one of them. I couldn't do much anyway, except be a follower, which I wasn't about to do, even then. I only knew rudimentary greetings like *Talofa, fa'a fe mai oi?* and bad words like *ufa kefe*, and any time I'd hear some elocutory wisdom kicked off in formal Samoan by a visiting high-talking chief *matai*, his deep, husky, oracular Polynesian voice somehow gentle in its tone, the pews full of three-hundred-pound ladies cooling themselves with woven palm fans, bone-thick youngsters leaning against the walls in red sweaters with red hoods and red picks and red bandannas stuck to their wild black wiry 'fros, my mind would go to my mother, the one person who was more outside this scene than me. The pure foreigner, slight 140-pound white woman from the Northern California suburb of Campbell, California, lost in the unknowable zone of natives. But she was already long gone by then, had bugged out.

My sister, a year older, looked Samoan as a girl, still does now as a woman. She even got a Samoan name, Tali. I remember her making fun of me: "Paul! Paul! What a white name!" She used to blend right into those occasions. I remember thinking the obvious back then: They like her because she looks like them. Deep down, and maybe not that deep, we're all phrenologists who fear the albino chimp. How much of Tali's simple and predictable personality developed in response to their acceptance? Because she had a group to claim in her formative years, and vice versa? At twelve she was wearing T-shirts that read PROUD TO BE SAMOAN, and I always felt embarrassed at her obviousness. How she could wear something like that around our mother, who had entered those churches with the restless yet timid face of a dog seeing the doors of the vet.

Being a half-breed must be part of my problem. When I applied to college out of high school, I didn't know what to fill in under the category of race. Long distance from American Samoa, my father said over the phone, "Mark Polynesian," but I couldn't. Neither could I mark white. I just left the damned thing blank. And that's exactly how I felt about it: blank. Still do, actually, don't care either way. By now I know that every culture in the world is equally beautiful, equally ugly. The few years of college I could stand convinced me of that. The few years of prison, too. In either place I was an English major with lots of reading time, lots of watching time.

I quit the daydreaming. I see him spot me from a bus stop across the street, posted up like a light pole. His hightops are out of the 1980s, Velcro straps around the ankle, big Nike swoosh on the tongue. He's got a hood pulled up over his head, and I can't find his eyes until he pulls it back and shakes his pointy head in the sprinkling rain. The red and green hair stands out on the ends like a dandelion. From the shoulders up, he looks like a miniature Christmas tree. He looks off and then back at me. He's on his way over and I don't move. The distance doesn't matter; I know what I see way before he reaches me: another suburban zombie on crystal meth.

He's violently itching one hand and then violently switching to the other. He's gonna rip through his own damned hand, insane. Sort of sad. Not even within five yards he says, "Wassup, brother? Wassup, brother? Wassup?"

I say, still not moving, "Wassup, man."

He looks around again. I shake my head. I've never used the shit, but I've known more than my share of cranksters. Suburb, city, high hills, country, plains, it's just standard American protocol to see, know, love but never trust your average tweeker. These cats'll steal from their own mothers, and even if you know one who won't, he's still looking over his shoulder like he already did. Always peeking out blinds, hiding behind dumpsters, hanging up the phone in the middle of a conversation. Hooked on an injection of paranoia. He can't even lie down in the familiarity of his own bed, close himself off from the world, and trust the blackness behind his eyelids.

I say, "You want something, dog?"

He hunches his shoulders, plays the mendicant. "Can you help me with some cash? I'm dying over here, brother, I'm dying."

He's husky-necked, sufficiently fat in the cheeks. Early into his journey to the pit. He smiles humbly and has all his teeth. Cauliflower ears, former high school wrestler. A car drives by and he whips around and then back again. In the glare of a struggling moon, his eyes are spinning like a top, but he's focusing the best he can to press the sincerity of the issue.

"Come on, bro," I say. "You ain't dying."

"I'm dying, brother."

"Yeah, dying for a fuckin' fix."

"No no no no." He grabs his balls, as if he's forgotten they were there. He thinks I said *fixed*. "No, no, brother. It's okay. I'm all there, man. Right there, that's right, all there. Everything's cool, brother."

"Then you don't need me."

"Trust me, brother, I'm dying. I hear the tinny chimes. Help me! I see the reaper, brother."

"It's in your head, dog."

"No, no, no, brother. I'm dying!"

I sniff in some air, indicating a step back from the conversation. Somehow he reads the insinuation and does just that: one step back, though he doesn't leave. He's balancing on the curb, heel to toe, and I'm waiting for him to spill over, then jump up and go sprinting down the street. This is the point where anyone else would leave. Not him. Me.

"What the hell," I say. "I'll get you some food, man. Come on."

He thinks it over, as if he has a better offer. Then he says, "Okay, brother. Okay. Where do you live?"

I laugh out loud, it feels good. The rain comes again, in one big orgasmic gust. As it is, I'm probably broker than this cat. "Hey, bro," I say. "Gimme your money."

He steps back again.

"Nah. Just kidding, man. Let's get to Jack in the Crack, dog. I'll buy you a burger."

"So you got money then?" he says, and right there I know that unless this crankster has a midnight revelation, we'll be fighting soon enough over the $3.68 in my pocket.

I say, "Follow me," and he does, staying a half step to my rear.

We walk through the rain toward El Camino Real. I remember the Pokémon umbrella, pull it out of my jacket, and hand it to the crankster. I don't think about why it's taken me this long to use it. He doesn't say thank you, doesn't grunt, nod. Doesn't pop it. He jams the umbrella into the pocket of his pants, a future tradeable good, and looks behind him for the ghosts of the past. All he finds is the Vuong Vu Video Outlet, an Afghan grocery store called House of Khan, and an Exxon station patched with the lights of skyrocketing prices. Each one closed, each empty of bodies. On the horizon the stars glisten behind the blur of the clouds, and if anything opens up tonight, I will welcome whatever comes.

He pulls out a bottle of good vodka from his pocket, takes a shot, repockets it.

I don't think on his hoarding selfishness. Ravished by greed and cowardice, a man of the streets gets villainous with needs. Breathing in the cool wet air, I drift into the warm realm of remembrance. The earth water seems to stimulate the senses: sky water, ocean water, river water. The Ohlone, I learned in fourth grade, call it the blood of the mother. I always thought that accurate. Just to be there with her, or inside her, at the tips of life's fingers. Back then, at nine, I used to stand under the apricot tree in our yard and ask the big questions of God. I'd let the rain mix in with my tears. I'd address to the vast angry hanging sky those problems which my Sunday School teacher couldn't ever answer in front of the class. She'd always wait for the good kids to leave and then take me aside ("Now listen here, young man"), max out on the intimidation of adulthood, buttress her arguments with size and force and a mysterious alliance with my parents. When my folks split and my mother started taking us to the grand old Catholic Church, I addressed those same problems again at confession with Father McFadden, Papa Mac, a real gentleman, cool cat. He'd cleverly reverse the burden of doubt into ten assigned Hail Marys ("Salvation comes from within, lad"). But the core of every question I had was the rational position that I didn't believe.

My namesake, Paul, had died alone, sanctified in a Roman dungeon, and I, at nine, was certain to the point of excommunication that one either sank or swam when traversing water and that if five thousand people were fed by five fish, four thousand nine hundred and ninety-five people had lied and been left hungry and that dead was dead, however you looked at it and that some people who still lived in grass huts and sat naked around a savage fire at night had never even heard of Jesus. And I'd felt self-pity over this, over my fakery in the face of God.

When I wasn't struck down by lightning for my lie, the internal lie, the worst kind of lie, my living in itself was the true indictment of holy scripture, tangible proof of my doubt. Though I didn't know it, I was beginning a fifteen-year journey whose days began and ended with the same longing. The minute you eliminate God, everything else comes down like dominoes. I can see tonight without the haze of zealotry, yes. But I'm not thankful or stupidly proud. The cost for clairvoyance is high and personal and ironical: I yearn to harness the pure, blurred, blood-rushing ecstasy of my species. I desire belief, faith. But I feel nothing worthy of a golden book chalice to save us. My psyche is fine and undaunted. I'm an anti-epiphany, ultra-knowing yet ultra-nothing, the new American.

We reach Hamsun Park and quiet desolation. Streetlights dwindle in number. I imagine them from above: little matchsticks in the ocean waves of darkness. We cut across the grass and beneath the conical pines and through the piles of needles collecting in the puddles. Sand in the playground clumps like cafeteria oatmeal. At the barbecue pits is a scattering of empty Budweiser boxes, some intact and tossed to the side, others torn in half and smashed, a few shredded into strips, red and white tiger stripes on the lawn. Broken glass crunches under our feet. I slap at a piñata dangling from the branch of a dead birch tree. It's been split down the middle in one swift Caesarian whack, barren inner wall lined with newspaper. I remember a line from Hemingway: *The deer hung stiff and heavy and empty*. Little piles of streamers are spread across the grass: red, green, white. A few egg-shells pool in dried yolk. Popped balloons, colorful scraps of rubber, all kinds of fiesta debris. There will be ample labor in the morning for the green-T'd park worker with a generic tree on the pocket.

The crankster speeds up so that we're side by side, and as I say, "What's your name, dog?" he shows me the blade, his hand jerking worse than his face.

I shrug, half smile. The tempests are loose. He's picked the wrong night, the wrong knife, the wrong person. A box cutter the size of a Pez dispenser won't break leathery skin like mine. And even if it does, who cares? I won't die on site. And even if I do, it'll be long after the fight is finished. And then the question is: What will I lose? It's not bravado; it's a desperate longing for happening: something, anything. I almost want him to stab me, just to see how the thing turns out. Just to act without the restrictions of conscious thought. Just to act.

His one eyebrow which still has nerves rises in apprehension. If he was hard-core or hard up, he would have stabbed me in the back to take my wallet. In fact, he would've done it before we'd ever talked. That he shows me the weapon means he doesn't want to use it, and it's that simple. He sees I've done the math, and suddenly his other eyebrow comes to life.

By now, at twenty-eight, I've been in a dozen situations twice as perilous. He couldn't know this, but he should've guessed. It's always best to keep wild cards like me in the public eye so that the mind, facile in darkness, doesn't wander into the isolated quandary of justified self-defense. Isolated, violated, I now have the right to kill this crankster, to leave his corpse to that same park worker for a life-changing discovery at dawn.

I say, "You're gonna get your burger, bro. Just take it easy."

I turn around and start to walk. From behind, I hear, "Hey, hey. You. Hey." I stop. He's poised like a half-ass wrestler, the knife loose and limp in his hand, not sure if he should get down any lower.

I spit into the ash of a barbecue pit. "So you wanna do something, homie? You wanna go there, you Christmas-tree looking mutherfucker?"

He doesn't move, but looks over one shoulder, then the other. This kind of language he understands, a simple proposition grounded in threat. He pockets the knife and his shoulders rise: the friendly beggar again. Walks over to me, stops at three yards, leans away as if he's about to race in the other direction and is waiting for the starting gun to fire, asks, "Is it okay?"

All huff and all puff but no blow.

"Yeah, man," I say, reassuringly. "Just quit with all that stupid shit, man. Let's get you a burger so you can be on your fucked-up way."

"Okay, brother. Whatever you say, man. Anything you say, brother."

2

The Teenage Boys Are Shooting Blanks

THE TEENAGE BOYS are shooting blanks against the wall, spit wads that dribble out their straws. The happy crankster and I are at the Jack in the Box on El Camino and Lafayette. I'm watching him eat his three-dollar burger. I didn't have enough cash for both of us, but it's cool. I may be doing myself a favor being broke. Saving my gut the unenviable job of processing dressed-up shit. When I get back to the motel room, I'll cook some Korean top ramen.

Two of the kids are blue-eyed blonds, the other a black-haired Southeast Asian, all in football jerseys big as gowns, sagging jeans with pockets down the leg, black and powder-blue baseball caps crooked on their heads. Gangstas without street cred, hard as steel out their two-story cribs with the four-car garages, a phat ride bought with Mommy's credit card. One girl emerges from the bathroom—one girl—and all three boys get immediately elbowy with one another. As she slides into the booth, paying none of them any attention, it's easy to understand why women are taking over the western world. Suddenly they just look dumb, these boys, court jesters kept around to entertain the queen.

I am worried about our boys. They have identity crises worse than domesticated lions. My sister is raising one now, poor little Toby.

He may be the only person on the planet more confused than me. But he's just four, man, not enough mileage or damage to wonder why *cogito ergo sum*. He's supposed to be reckless and intrusive, bold and free with his body and mouth, but he just sits there, hungry or not, will wait till he's a teenager to eat, even talk. It's like he was lobotomized at birth. Tali looms over his wet little ass, and the kid keeps looking over, under, and through her for his father.

Where is the man I come from? he wants to say.

I want the damned kid to crash into walls and hang from bars on the swing set. I want him to take his tricycle to the creek and pedal right to the edge of the water, a narcissistic peek at his image, then howls of laughter as he jumps in feet first. I want him to climb the eucalyptus in the yard and scratch his elbows and knees on the bark and throw footballs in the rain, resist the peace of dryness. None of it will happen. His father is probably the very crankster sitting across from me now who masturbated into a test tube in a sterile white-walled room with a stack of *Penthouse* for forty lousy bucks and a red, white, and blue I JUST GAVE SPERM button. Poor little Toby doesn't have a father, and nobody, not even the father, cares.

In a lobby of after-hours drifters, the fifteen- to nineteen-year-old Helen in high heels has got everyone under her spell. Even the crank-impaired. If I cared and if I could, I'd die in a big epic war to reclaim her from the hostile shores of the enemy. How refreshing it would be to play a role with absolute clarity like my Aegean homie Achilles, to know exactly what you get from the king if you live: forego the harems and cities and treasure chests of gold. I'll take this Jack-in-the-Box vixen in the white cotton form-fitting sweater-skirt with a blue stripe at the turtleneck, the tight hem at the thighs, thick- and plump-hipped, clean- and supple-faced, long blond hair to the bosom, aware of so much more than we adults give her credit for. The smartest person in this room, too, by far: she knows what she wants and can get it.

The crankster interrupts my thoughts. Of course. He doesn't like the silence between us; it implies threat, even though he's eating on me. He's way past being concerned about implied judgment. The crankster looks over at the kids in the corner, back at me, thinks he knows what I'm thinking, risks it, and slaps my shoulder. "You ever hit a vrank shot, brother?"

Got no clue what it is, but I don't say so or shake my head. I'm about ready to go. Did my good deed for the day.

"Viagra and crank. You hit 'em both. Fuck for five hours straight, brother. Rub your shit raw."

This time I shake my head.

"I'd love to take that into a stall right there." He's pointing at the restroom. "Fuck that sweet little thing right up the ass, brother."

"'Ey," I say. "'Ey."

He's got a frown on his face, gritting his teeth, as if he's in the act. "I'd drill that bitch for half a day spun on a vrank shot. Beat it up, brother, beat it up. Stretch that bitch out so bad she never take a shit again."

"'Ey, man. 'Ey." He looks up at me, breathing hard, face still in mid-frown. "Watch your fucking mouth, man."

He takes a casual bite from his jalapeño burger, as if I didn't say a word. Just like that, I'm up on my feet, reaching across the table, an index finger in the wrinkles of his dirt-encrusted neck. I snag the burger out of his hand.

He doesn't say anything. Not with his mouth, anyway. He says something with his eyes, though—*Not afraid of you, brother*—and I slap it right off his face. He falls off the chair and catches himself. The vodka bottle flies out and rings dull through the restaurant. One of the boys at the other table shouts, "You see that, Bojeezie!" The crankster twists and looks up from the napkins and splattered ketchup.

"Hey, brother," he whispers. "I'm sorry, man, I'm sorry."

I throw the half-eaten burger at his face. "You *are* sorry, you punk-ass mutherfucker."

"All right, brother. All right."

"Don't call me brother, you fucking crankster."

"All right, all right."

I turn around, wipe the smiles off the faces of the boys. Scan for any adults I've missed. At the corner table, there's a paisa in a black-and-tan cowboy hat, dark green flannel, and a Pancho Villa mustache thick as undergrowth. He's chewing on his fries, as if this is just what he's expected out of us all along. Either that or he knows it may soon be time to take his green-cardless flight from this once-safe spot. I don't know why, but I love the hell out of the guy—or I love, any-way, what's on his face: silent immigrant in the silent corner who's seen worse, probably done worse, and knows a ten-cent sideshow like this ain't worth his time. He's got real business to worry about. The hombre intrigues me.

I reach down, grab the vodka bottle, say, "You gonna go for your little Swiss Army knife, you piece of shit?"

He's coming down off the crank, talking to himself in our mess. I'm already turning away, as he utters, "No, no, brother," and then, calling out after me, "It's cool, man! It's cool! God bless you, brother! You can have the liquor! It's okay, okay?"

I'm walking right toward the table of boys and not one of them can look me in the eye. For once, it's exactly what I want: it's how it should be. All I get from the paisa is the top of his hat. The girl watches me—I can feel it—out the exit and back again into the darkness of night. If I hear the whining sirens of authority, I'll run. But if she sheds the boys and follows me down the street, then for the sake of her courage, or her lunacy, we'll split a free bottle of blue-berry Stolichnaya as I escort her highness wherever she wants to go through the shadows of this valley.

3

I Can See Through the Fuzziness

I CAN SEE THROUGH the fuzziness of hangover a sliver of light behind the morning clouds. The Stoli is right there beside me, and I wince at the thought of my liver, heavy with labor this morning. I guess it's good that the empty bottle is upright, uncracked, but it still feels like someone busted it over my buzzing head. The girl's nowhere to be found. She may have never made it here, I don't know; she may have been shy about drinking in the heart of a Christian mission. I remember saying, "It's a school now, don't worry, been a university for a hundred and fifty years, I know, I went here for a while, trust me," and her insisting, "You did not have to hit that guy in the Jack in the Box."

I look up at the bottom of Jesus' palms, his forearms laced in flowers and rosaries. In the midnight hour my freshman year at the University of Alviso, I used to sit at the feet of this chiseled statue. The courtyard would be drowned in the kind of layered silence that seems to let out the tiniest of sounds, a soft whistle, beaded in the center of your ear. Now I push up to my elbows to see why I hear Spanish everywhere, Mexican Spanish, mixing in with the symphony of blackbirds and finches.

About twenty paisas are standing, hands in pockets, at the base of the mission steps. They're wearing variations of the same threads:

Pendletons, paisley flannels, L.A. Dodgers baseball caps with little
Mexican flags in the mesh. A couple in cheap rodeo gallon hats. All
with breath clouds coming up before them, a few sipping coffee, their
long mustaches steaming at the wet ends.

I gather up the last thread of spittle in my mouth, aim it at the
bushes, and let it fly. It's like I sucked on cotton all night. I hear from
behind, "This is going to be a beautiful day."

I rub the crusty sleep from my eyes and find Father McFadden,
my old priest, standing above me. Been almost ten years. He's got
those same clover-green eyes, a little tired now, but still alive and
jovial behind the thick black-framed militaristic glasses. He's completely bald, pink and beige sunspots mottling his scalp. He's reaching down, lightly clapping my shoulder, almost with felicity, saying,
"Paul. Paul."

There's a young student in the gathering, model-thin, almost-white-
haired blonde. She's very clearly undamaged and clean, healthy-pored.
On her hands and knees etching into a cardboard sign with a big black
marker. She hasn't done a thing to me, but I already know I don't want
to talk to her, and that I may soon, and that she'll do most of the talking, and at length.

This must be a march: they're about to take to the streets, starting
here at the Alviso Mission. The blonde is nearing. You can see it in
her eyes: she's a believer. Nothing else in the world matters at the
moment. She's probably a poli-sci major, minoring in sociology. Maybe
a leader here, an organizer.

Father McFadden says, "I'm proud of you, Paul. You've done the
right thing."

I say, "I was trying to pray at the shrine last night. I fell asleep I
guess."

He puts his hand up to stop me from self-indictment. He wants to
believe in me with the same desperation that I'd wanted to believe in
God as a kid. I feel bad for him, for his calling, for the sadness he must

feel every Sunday when his master's beatific house of stained-glass splendor is four-fifths empty. I can see the refracting light of blue and red tickling his trembling cheeks at the altar, the imported marble saints collecting dust in the crevices of nostrils and armpits, in the four corners of the crucifix.

But he must be used to the faithless by now, to his flock being daily lost to tech and science and genetic manipulation, MTV and the Internet. An electric ocean of amorality. I can see the struggle in his face as he's retrieving for the first time in many years certain failures in faith that I'd had as one of his lambs. Things that seemed harmless then, perhaps even endearing and precocious, but blasphemous now, as a man. I'm not the prodigal son this father's looking for.

Still, he gives it a shot. "God watched over you."

I smile.

"You're a lucky young man."

"Yes," I say, "I believe that, Father. But it doesn't help."

"Hungry?"

I don't want an allusion to the bread of the Lord. "Well."

"Here." He hands me a Sausage McMuffin. "Don't be so hard on yourself, Paul."

I don't say anything. Like, for instance, that the first thing out of my mouth this morning was a lie. Passing out drunk and delusional doesn't pass for devotion at the shrine.

Shit, man, I wish a drop of the old demon water was all I needed. If I could find God in liquor or weed or any other hallucinogen necessary, I'd be the first to volunteer at whatever Monte Cassino the paltry handful of priests of this valley begin their training, AA and NA be damned, the health of my body temple be damned. I'd be just like that crankster, wandering the streets for my next fix. I'd be a son of Jameson's whiskey just like I know the good Father is, or I'd be a reefer like a Rastafarian. I'd make premium boc in the Belgian lowlands, a monk's brown hood and brown frock and how to brew good German beer my only earthly possessions.

But any altered state I've tried just seems to induce sleep. It's temporal, flighty, and I become an eyesore to myself, can't look in the mirror at the broken-down man. And I don't forget a thing about this life, and the dreams—even as I'm dreaming them—I know to be false. That's perverse, pointless. Like telling the punch line of a joke not last but first.

"You know," he says, "this beautiful mission came to life at the hands of a people in toil. Today we're going to get them what they deserve."

"Father, I—"

"God's children endured true pain for their heavenly rites."

The blonde has arrived, observing me as if I were a colorful anemone on the reef at the Monterey Bay Aquarium. With curiosity, yes, superior spinal cord curiosity. This close I see that her legs are crisp with blond hair, having recently changed her mind about shaving. Now she's straight barbarian/bohemian.

I sit up, shake my head out, rapidly blink to rejoin the world.

She shouts out, "And what is your purpose here?"

Verbal judo, just like I predicted. Father McFadden nods so I relax a bit, leaning against the rainworn pillar of the shrine. Her sign reads, HOY MARCHEMOS, MANAÑA VOTARAMOS.

I don't like her arrogance or the way she stands, with one hand on the high end of her thin hip, neck slightly tilted toward the same side, so I say, still sitting, "The sign is wrong."

"Excuse me?" she says, like a drill sergeant.

"That sign is wrong."

"What someone like you needs to understand," she says, "is that these people have a right to be here. They're working the jobs that people like you should be working."

"I've been employed by McDonald's," I lie, "for the last five years of my life."

She's stifled, can't say a word. I'm not an envious wino trying to pilfer from the cause. I'm just someone who knows how to win an argument. Genuine in purpose, I like to think, or hope, however disingenuous in fact.

I push out the McMuffin. "Bite?"

"I won't go near dead bovine."

"Is there another kind?" She exhales really loudly. "By the way, nice leather purse."

"It's pleather."

"My name's Paul," I say. "And you are?"

"Busy," she says.

Father McFadden says very politely, "This is Athena, Paul."

"I can introduce myself, Stanley."

Stanley. I never knew. I nod at the father to assure him that, despite my theological issues, I'm definitely not on her side. To prove it, I say, "Athena? Birth name?"

"Does it matter?"

"Sort of. I mean, if one takes the name of a Grecian goddess of wisdom and war, it matters. You know. Like if I called myself Zeus or Thor."

"I matter," she spits out. "And that's all that matters."

"Does conjugation matter?"

"You're drunk."

"I wish. But I'm only hung. Over."

"And vulgar."

"The sign's wrong, Madam Athena. As I said before. It should read HOY MARCHAMOS, MAÑANA VOTAREMOS. *Los verbos estan marchar y votarer.*"

The father nods. Spanish, a good Latinate language. Perhaps he remembers my parochial promise back in the day when I was an educatee of the Jesuit institution that wouldn't hire him because he didn't have the scholarly chops. But I always liked his intellectual humility.

The goddess is looking back at the paisas, then at me, comparing notes. Am I a Mexican farmer incognito? Too tall, too muscular, no cowboy hat, no accent, too American sassy. No chance, just like her.

"I guess you haven't taken your GE in Spanish yet."

The arrogance comes back, like rushing blood. "I will take care of this immediately," as if it's my fault for pointing out her error. I smile, she shouts, "Hereberto! Go get that marker for me, will you?"

I say, "I don't think he speaks your native tongue."

She says, walking off, "Don't go anywhere."

"Why would I dare move when you're all that matters?"

"I prayed for you and your troubles, Paul."

There is pity on the father's face. It's good pity, not condescending pity. I don't need it, but say anyway, "Thank you, Father."

"I was worried about your soul."

I feel the old smallness rise up in me. I'm not so sure it's bad. "Me too, Father."

"You haven't been to church in a long time."

"Probably longer than a decade."

"Why don't you come to mass this Sunday?"

What the hell can I say, *Tempi cambi?*

What the good father doesn't know is that I probably know the verse better than he does. I can now run the gamut of textual inconsistencies with too much ease, from book to book, chapter to chapter, mouth to mouth. St. James vs. St. Paul. St. Paul vs. St. Peter. Magdalene and the missing gnostic books. The insane Dungeons and Dragons game of Revelation. I went through the Bible twice in my life, once at a Jesuit high school (New Testament freshman year, Old Testament sophomore year), and later in a medieval four-by-eight cell in San Quentin, and it ruined me. Not happy about it at all. In both cases, I was surrounded by history and learning, but I never completely belonged or bought into either place. It was like education and incarceration touted the same book so hard that their irreconcilable differences left me with no system.

"Father," I say, "I suspect I'm in a lot of trouble."

"With the law?"

"No. Not this time, anyway."

"That's good, Paul."

"I meant with me, Father."

"I see."

"No disrespect, Father, but I don't think you do. I can't get any fucking grounding."

"Pray."

I don't say, It's gonna take a hell of a lot more than that. Instead: "Father, I admire you. I always have."

He smiles, knowing what that means: I'm not going to mass.

"Well," he says, "you'll remain in my prayers."

At the end of the day or the end of a life, McFadden is a kind man, and I think that's enough. I hope. I wish we could find a new start between us, wherever it might end up. Maybe we'd find an unequivocal key to this life.

Gotta give something back. "I'm gonna do this rally with you, Papa Mac. Okay?"

"Great," he says. "We need all the numbers we can get."

"Stanley!" says Athena. The goddess is back. "You're needed over there."

"I'm talking to my priest, if you don't mind."

"Oh, no. It's okay, Paul," says the father.

"That's right it's okay," says Athena.

I consider this odd couple. She came to the show singing Carole King in her mother's Volvo, he came mourning the fourteen stations in a hearse. She'd like to loosen the starch of his collar, he'd like to replace her beads with a rosary. She thinks we've come so far, he thinks we've lost so much. She thinks these poor, poor people, he thinks my brave, brave parishioners. She came down from the hills to kick it with the commoners, he follows the carpenter who died on a hill. Allies for a day, a political moment, no more, they are both ready to do good.

"Athena," Papa Mac says, "will you please sign Paul up here? He's going to join us this morning."

Athena says nothing.

"God bless you, Paul. I'll see you at the rally."

"*Mille grazie, padre.*"

She says, "So what are you really here for?"

"On this planet?"

"No."

"Am I allowed on it?"

"Here. Right here. Right now. Why?"

I'll give her one thing: she has eyes the alluring cobalt blue of Arabian nights. But I'm not fooled. She won't grant that a transient of her embattled earth has a halfway functional brain, despite the earlier tutelage in Spanish.

"I ain't homeless," I say. "I mean, sort of. I have a motel room I stay in."

"So?"

"But it was paid for by a fellowship. Which should upgrade my status a bit."

She looks me up and down. "Fellowship?"

I smile, nod.

"As in money for scholarship?"

"As in the Leroi Jones Hookup for Off-the-Hook Artistic Achievement."

"Okay, look, I—"

"Even went to school here once upon a time."

"—don't have the time for this."

"Let's be nice to one another, goddess."

"I will be nice"—liking the way she's been addressed but still detesting the source—"when I know what team you're on."

"That's what I've been trying to find out. Forever."

"Answer one question."

"Shoot."

"What are you doing here?"

"I don't know. I guess I just happened to be here. Think of me as an involuntary volunteer, how's that? Like an eyeblink."

"You better not waste my time this morning," she says.

"Or what?"

"You think this is a joke?"

"I think you can't speak the language of the people you're trying to help. Some might say that's the joke. And yet you think you're their leader."

She bites her lower lip, and I think she might cry. I immediately feel bad. She says, "I'm not sure I like you," turns, and strides off.

I try to keep pace. Don't know why. I might as well tell her I'm dying, call her *brother,* and twitch at every step. Might as well ask her for three dollars. Anyway, I just might.

I wanted to afford the happy crankster the same respect she doesn't give me, or anyone, but I just added him to a long list of people with whom the next encounter, whenever it happens, will be awkward; I'll end up apologizing, not out of fault or even misinterpretation but a need to clean the slate, as in, "Before we'd ever met, Mr. Crankster, sir, there were giant unclaimed sins between us."

It will be an attempt to repair the weathered, spindly, immemorial rope bridge strung between us time-bound mammals. It will be saying *sorry* for a life lived—not ours, mine or his, but Ours. That's it: Sorry about this story to which you and I indelibly belong. Simple contrition that we've had to cross paths in the first place under this cruel cosmos. Taking fate and physics and luck and all that shit and trying to claim it. A secular, interpersonal Yom Kippur.

Just atone for the blown deal and move on to the next apology.

We're alone behind the church in the mission garden beneath an old adobe cloister, restored, you can see, very recently. Vines of ivy branch and climb along the wall. Gardenias and orderly patches of impatiens and petunias line the walkway. It's a rainbow of petals, touched or kissed by some ineffable spirit that we hope came from the labor of the faithful but that probably had more to do with the tax-free designs of the well-endowed.

"I'm sorry about that back there," I say.

"Don't fuck with me," she says, squatting down to a stack of orange leaflets on the ground. They read, AMNISTÍA POR TODOS. UNIDOS VOTAREMOS. SOMOS AMERICANOS.

"Well," she says, "are they right, Mr. Translator?"

"Sí," I say. "Es A-OK."

"Now," she says, not missing a beat, "what I want you to do is take each of these leaflets and fold them like this."

She holds one out in front of me. All that you can see on the face of the leaflet is Che Guevara's tilted beret: the overused visage, the cliché for the cause. I copy the motion exactly, looking off at the church, folding it in half once and then once again. I hand it over and she nods but doesn't move. I know she won't let it rest. She has enough safety and enough time to expect perfection in her life, even in its most minute and elementary details.

She says, "Try again."

"I'll take care of it, don't worry."

"We'll see."

"Yes," I say. "Puedo hacer eso. Un perro puede."

"We need them ready in an hour," she says. "There will be people at the rally who are in-betweeners. Curiosity seekers. Some will be swayed to our side when they see the passion of the gente."

"The people."

"Others will pick up the banner after a speech that'll move them, or that they can identify with. Some will only be convinced by words in print. The *literatura*."

"Literature? Books?"

"What you have in your hands right there."

"Ah, yes," I say, looking down at the seven magical words in Spanish, "*Sí.* I see."

"I don't think you do," she says, and then she's off.

Though I feel a bit used, I'm happy to have something real to do this morning, which, I see on the leaflet, is the fifth of May. *El Cinco de Mayo,* a Mexican holiday celebrated here on the streets of San José, California, USA. A day that annually ends with broken store windows and burnt vehicles and a few beaten American citizens and millions of empty Corona bottles and segments on the local news about the beauty of diversity and a historical clip about the legacy of Cesar Chavez and how the city's first Hispanic mayor, Ron Gonzales, promises to end discrimination at once and us whatever we are still breathing in yoga deep this belief that all is right in our good land where the planet's inhabitants come at the end of the dream to camp between two identical strip malls made of staples, paste, cardboard, and lots of air.

4

Spring Buds

SPRING BUDS of the cherry tree ruffle like pink tissue paper in the soft breeze. Clouds even here in this oxygen-deprived valley are white as bone, pillowy, environmental eye candy. On days like this you can understand why a nation would push west to the Pacific coast. The Cesar Chavez chant—"¡Sí, se puede! Sí, se puede!"—doesn't seem to reach the undisturbed heavens, caught in a wind tunnel somewhere above our heads. All around us are signs of our own ephemeral heartbeat.

"¡Sí, se puede! Sí, se puede!"

Hundreds of cops are funneling us into checkpoints like cattle into the chute, waving us through the peril of barricaded intersections, beneath flashing red lights and suspended banners that say VOLUNTARIOS Y TRABAJADORES DE LA COMMUNIDAD, these uniformed men and women of the thick and faint mustaches, plastic toothpicks, and American-flag pins, hiding behind mirrored glasses and badges, then the bemused business owners at the doors of their establishments, unconcerned by a movement that won't amount to more than a dent in the local GP, tapping their thighs with rolled newspapers, munching on toasted onion bagels, draining bottles of alleged spring water, knowing their windows won't likely be shattered in this daytime deal of promised sobriety from Hispanic sources who know better than to give any chum to the cable media sharks, a helicopter with FOX News on its belly hovering overhead like some Grecian god chopping up the smoggy pollinated air of this place, a local news van docked at the corner of San Pedro Square and Starbucks, cameras springing out the rooftop, the sliding door, the backside, a mechanically mutated cockroach expanding its wings—and me, walking with a hand under my chin, unable even if I tried with everything in me to be a bonafide testament to the event, absolutely physically unable to join the chant.

"*¡Sí, se puede! Sí, se puede!*"

Athena is walking toward my side of the street. She's cutting across dozens of paisas and Chicanos, striding out, it seems, at a faster pace. I like looking at her in the gentle gleam of silence between us. I'd like to box her up and open her at my leisure, like a poem. Underarm hair aside, she is a beautiful woman, nearly my height, which in a crowdful of Toltec descendants is as statuesque as Gulliver. Trying or not, we both stand out. She likes it, I don't.

I shrink down, walk on.

"*¡Sí, se puede! Sí, se puede!*"

I try to get ahead of her so she won't open her mouth in my presence and ruin the peaceful new image I have of her. I look up at the turquoise jerseys of two San Jose Sharks of the week, Gok and Michalek, the smell of steaks from AP Stumps wafting across my face. It's loud as a college hoops game, and suddenly I hear her. Amost like she's shouting at me, but I don't dare turn toward the voice.

She's posted in my right ear, and when I finally look over, her wide-open mouth almost swallows me: "*¡Sí, se puede! Sí, se puede!*"

Five thousand people packed into Santa Clara Street, and she's found me. I nod, look forward again, try and pretend it's not happening.

"*¡Sí, se puede! Sí, se puede!*"

"Got it," I say, smiling at her, speeding up.

She speeds up with me. "*¡Sí, se puede! Sí, se puede!*"

"I know," I say, not turning toward her this time, mumbling to myself. "I'm not deaf."

"*¡Sí, se puede! Sí, se puede!*"

I turn and shout, "Get your ass out of my face!"

She retracts in horror, silent. Already she's walking back across the guileless crowd pumping their fists. She tugs on the back of some paisa's sleeve, and when I see the devotion on his face for this woman, good old prescience sets in and I try to make space, twist the hands of Fate to my pacifist liking. I gave the father a promise, yes, but I'd like someone up there to let me watch the rally in the veil of anonymity. Let me make a clean decision, unberated.

We march past the classical Hotel De Anza and Market Street, under and out the concrete bridge of highway 87, beneath the lean palms and long-trunked elms of Guadalupe Park, the flaky bark floating off the trees like ash. I don't want to look over, but I do anyway. She's displaying the geometrical skills of an airport flagger, one arm raised over her head to bring attention to herself, the exact point of the compass, the other aimed at me with a slight lead to account for my quickened step. If she had a slingshot and a dead eye, she'd squint her aim at me, let it loose, and I'd be finished.

Several paisas are in lockstep phalanx formation around her. Their wannabe proletariat goddess. I slide behind the cover of a paisa grandmother in a Mexican-flag muumuu, my right shoulder lifting ever so slightly to protect my chin.

We're separated by a forked barricade, the crowd divided to different sides of the stage. First dozens, then hundreds of people between us. That's good. Bye-bye. A gringo in a flea-market poncho has been strumming an acoustic guitar all along, rollicking side to side like a deadhead on the Haight, singing:

¡No nos moverando!
¡No nos moverando!

The air is warm now when it sits, cool in tiny gusts of wind. We move toward the music and take pamphlets from women in yellow shirts that say Trinity Episcopalian Church. We pass the booths of the United Farm Workers of Salinas and El Teatro Campesino, stacks of books for sale with Hispanic themes, Hispanic authors, American classics in translation: *El Viejo y El Mar, Las Pasturas del Cielo*.

We weave our way around the cabin of a truck, a burrito house called La Victoria handing out samples of its creamy salsa in tiny plastic containers, security guards in shades on the bumper of the trailer. The grass cut low for our arrival, the trail around Guadalupe Park taped off. Joggers with headphones and bikers in racer's gear share the dirt along the creek, paying no attention to us as we approach, pass, move on. The wind comes again and goes. The gringo's squeaky voice grows with each step, and by the time we reach the stage, five speakers ten feet high are beating on our eardrums. The chanting dies down now, tech claiming its audio territory. The crowd slithers onto the field, fanning out by the dozens, empty spaces right there, and then gone.

Native Azteca drums sound from the far end of the field. The gringo knows his cue and lets the song dwindle down, shouting, "*¡No a la guerra!*" as loud as he can.

Father McFadden and other clerics are climbing the stage. He's in his purple robe, caution in every step. His slumped posture evokes the veneer of holiness, of calm at the heart of chaos, Jordanian grace under pressure.

I want to call out, See, Papa Mac! I made it!

And he'd call back, Just like you said!

He's joined by a pale woman in a similar purple robe except that hers has yellow flowers over each breast. Youth and spring in her step, as if she's just gotten off a treadmill. She's followed by a brotha with a full-on 'fro, cool, smooth in his ascension, slight swagger up the steps, vaguely angry. A Punjabi Sikh in a maroon turban next, tentative, respectful, looking a bit caught in the net. And last up a Jewish cat in a pricey Italian suit and a skullcap, New York–sure of himself.

Papa Mac takes the mic from the gringo musician, the gringo bowing repeatedly, and commences to lead the crowd in a prayer. Everyone onstage, even the Sikh, has his right arm lifted at a 45-degree angle from his shoulder.

"In the name of the Father, the Son and the Holy Spirit, amen."

"Amen."

"I walked the streets of Watsonville with the great Cesar Chavez," says Father McFadden. "He was a man who loved his people and his God. He loved life. This is all that we aim for in the city of our friend: to go forth with absolute confidence in his mission. We met in the summer of 1967 at Assumption Church in a town called Freedom, where . . ."

I start to drift, just like I'd done as a kid at Papa Mac's homilies. I can't help but question the union on the stage, how far the groups stand from one another, how all the UN countries are represented except the delegate from Mexico. All the paisas are down below with me.

I want to shout out, What happened to all the Mexicans? Will they get a chance to *habla*?

Papa Mac drones on and the mind keeps wandering.

I sometimes wonder about strength in diversity. What I see around me today seems like new characters, same story. Power seizure, untapped discord. Too much disparate history and counterculture in the soup. It's all diluted, cheap base. No one from Mountain View, California, cares a lick about anyone from Lansing, Michigan, and vice versa. Hell: no one from Mountain View cares about anyone in Sunnyvale, its sister city two doors down.

It's not a matter of proximity; it's a matter of commonality, of being able to say that you understand what the fella to the left of you is thinking, somewhat. Of uniting under a story line. See what happens when you drop Davy Crockett into a conversation at Starbucks knocking back a mocha latte. Or, if you're a fifteenth generation American and therefore live somewhere in New England, try bragging at the next cocktail party that your kid's banished ancestors crashed at Plymouth Rock. They'll ask you, if they ask you anything, "Was that like Woodstock?" I'm more diverse than most, but it's hard keeping up with progress. Nowadays we Americanos need a working definition of the Khmer Rouge, a layman's understanding of the Hutus and Tutsis, and a steam-pressed kimono wrapped around the torso before borrowing a tool from the neighbor.

Just this month at a 7-Eleven on University and the Alameda I saw a fistfight in the parking lot between an El Salvadoreño and a Vietnamese patron over the last soggy donut under the yellow light of the heating lamp. The bearded, turbaned, hairy-armed Punjabi cashier whom I liked and was of course named Singh was shouting into the phone, "Jay-lee donut! Jay-lee donut!"

All the morning business people with their tanned crimson oiled heads and dollar-sign eyeballs and manicured nails and pearly teeth of bleach and Star Trek headpieces extending from ear to mouth jumped into their sloped aerodynamic cars that were silver as barracuda scales and left before having to bear witness. Before having to lose time. No one cared. I sat down on the spray-painted curb by a pay phone that probably still doesn't work, and watched. I hoped for knives, chains, guns. Cultural and maternal insults. Then I could step in between the two men when it counted, or mold a tourniquet for the wounded, have true utility for just a moment, feel real purpose.

Two good blows, a straight right from the lanky Vietnamese and a hook by the squat El Salvadoreño, landed dull, solid. It was a classic fight in framework, reach, power, a free ticket for a poor man's Ali–Frazier IV: the El Salvadoreño stalking and swinging for the ribs, the Vietnamese backstepping and keeping him at bay with the jab.

These two wouldn't quit, you knew it the minute they took to the lot; they had that old world determination seared by trying times. They had good chins, not because of some physiological attribute but because they'd been beaten by life, somewhere out there in the jungle, and weren't about to take the beatdown again. It was more than the fist connecting to the socket of the eye, it was history, faith in one's story; it was the future, the right to a new story.

Twenty-five seconds in, I'd say it was even. Hook, jab, body blow. A few wayward immigrants—Hispanic, Southeast Asian, African— stayed behind but fled when they heard the sirens. It looked like the Sharks and the Jets scattering over the walls, under the fences.

They had no clue where they were going, but they knew where they were at. By now, our 230th year, hyperintegrated America produced bad comedy at its best, B-movie material. Foolhardy emotion in the Silicon Valley, all over deep-fried, jelly-filled, sugarcoated American cuisine.

The police came but both men were already gone. Everyone but me and Singh, who had a good reason to be there. The cop asked me if I had any valuable information. "Yes," I said. "The terms of the Treaty of Versailles can be seen as the exact catalyst for World War Two."

He said with disgust, "Frenchman, eh?"

I shrugged, not seeing the difference in whether it was true or not.

Hooking his thumbs in his utility belt, he said, "I've been boycotting you assholes for nineteen months now. Ever since you people allied yourselves with Saddam. Won't let the wife visit Paris, see that Eiffel Tower. Stocked up on wine from the Napa Valley only. No champagne, no bubbly. Not on my watch. We buy and we drink American."

"That's right," I said. "We oughta go back to speaking the Olde English before those damned Normans arrived back in 1066."

"Yeah."

"Rename our kids Hrothgar and eat our mutton without mustard."

He was American and spoke a mongrel form of English, but he'd never read the first official tale in the language. Too bad. I got the sense that this one would have enjoyed the conquering exploits of Beowulf, precursor to the Schwarzenegger/Stallone epic hero.

"I've got the kids saying 'a burger with the works and freedom fries.'"

It took me a second before I figured out the culinary twist. "You mean french fries?"

"Freedom fries."

He didn't believe that I was a believer. He was, after all, an officer of the law: sharp-eyed, trained, a human retriever of men. And then also, for the first time in some time, I was laughing. He had a tan line over the bridge of the nosebone that he'd shaven, his Latin eyebrows so bush thick it looked like padding. His badge read LAFAYETTE, a strong Anglo surname.

Papa Mac's done. My standing daydream does not discourage me. When there's someone up there I don't want to hear, I can peacefully tune out.

The lady priest from the Unitarian church takes the mic like a rock star, leans in and smiles, her teeth the grimy yellow of day-old chicken skin.

"¡Sí se puto!" she screeches. A few people laugh at her error, but most are polite. She shouts, "¡Bah La Migra! I love you people!" and that's it. I look around. They're as bewildered as me, some don't even know what she said.

A child beside me corrects her: "Baja La Migra." Down with Immigration and Naturalization Services.

She hops off the front side of the stage into the crowd, and they give her plenty of room to land.

It's the brotha's turn, the pastor from Grace Baptist Church, the biggest holy roller denomination in the Bay. He's got a great voice, but he's using it on the wrong crowd. I can clearly see something he's missed: dropped cowboy hats, weight shifting from one foot to the other.

"And we must remember, my brothers, about the reparations owed to us and kept from us. We must never forget the profiteering that went on in our names because we didn't claim what's ours. . . ."

He's too loud for their liking, too pushy. This is a problem of style, not substance.

A hearty struggle coming to a theater near you: Black Power vs. *Sí, se puede.*

Look out, dog. *Mirale, ese.*

The brotha pastor puts a Tommie Smith fist up in the air. *Please please please don't shout Black Power,* I think. *Not here, baby.* Instead he gives us "Peace. ¡Baja La Migra!"

Scattered applause. Not really sure if this is an ally. Before anything can be decided, the Sikh takes the stage. He's cool, and I admire his spirit and guts, but no one gets a word he's saying. At one point or another, everyone is lost in translation in America.

I've always been caught in the middle of racial noise, factions trying to claim me. My freshman year in college, the head coach of our football team, a soft Irishman named Patrick O'Malley, didn't have the nuts to confront the brothas who'd decided to occupy the right bottom of the team photograph. Jersey number and height went right out the door. A few of the white guys, mostly linemen, were mad. I heard one of them say, "Are they clumping up by tribe?" Me, the half-breed Samoan, cool with both sides, stuck right there in the middle of the shot. There it was, the return of segregation, 1999 voluntary flouting of Brown vs. Board of Education, this on the West Coast, this in the Silicon Valley, right into the new millennium we go.

It feels sort of natural to observe life in neutrality: detached, cool, uncommitted. Nothing required of me, really, but to fill space, absorb an exotic dance, a foreign film. Whatever route my life takes from here seems fair in that it will happen; whatever I have to say about it is inconsequential, even my view of it won't last. How can it? There are six billion other bodies out there squeezing for space. But I, an American of this new century, am under the impression that no position is worth my life. Now I wonder if my life is worth nothing because I have no position.

The Sikh seems to be here out of confusion. Out of accepting a deal without quite knowing the terms, not knowing what he signed onto. He walks back to the rear of the stage, gets down on his knees. There's a microphone setup the height of a midget. He recites a Sikh prayer, though no one here can confirm that it's a prayer. Maybe it's a saying you share before dinner or a toast to camaraderie before battle, an anecdote about the dirt god.

The audience grows restless and fidgety, tuning out on this opera. I hear the Azteca drums starting up again. What pricks: right in the middle of the guy's tribute to their cause. The audience shifts and stands on toes to get a peek above the neighbor's shoulder. The drums grow louder.

The circle of Azteca dancers press toward the stage in ancient chant. Sounds like a powwow. They're shirtless, barefoot, brown-skinned in skimpy leather waistcloths, peacock headdresses higher than an NBA center. The feathers sway in the wind, splashes of deep blue and bright green, fast streaks of yellow, out-of-control spirals of red. They're dancing in circles, kicking out their legs, circle, kick. I get on my toes and see their feet: anklets of hay that look almost Polynesian.

Everyone seems to dig this dance. Several men whistle through their teeth, another dozen make barn animal noises. I bounce on my heels, feeling bad for the Sikh.

"¡Orale!"

Testosterone levels rising, racial pride in the air, energy levels up, a wisp of anger's scent, when I see her at about forty yards. Pushing her way through the crowd, separating parents with infants hoisted on their shoulders. The time to be reverential is over.

A couple of people point in my general direction, and to keep the hope of peace up, I look around me and find nothing out of the ordinary. Paisas, grass, the creek.

Then several eyes lock on me, almost like it's in me, whatever they're looking for. Pointing, nodding. A little bit of space opens up and I don't have to ask who's coming. That I didn't leave the place earlier says more about me than about them. The heroes of the ancient tales went down with the ship to save the women and kids and the old folks. I'll go down with the damned thing just to see what happens.

She emerges from the brown crowd, very white but very confident, fingering me, shouting, "That's him! Right there! He's the one!"

I don't know what she's told them. Maybe that I dragged her into an abandoned alleyway and accosted her, as I want to do now—*a tiny slap, please, one little pop*—or maybe that I flashed her my jimmy on the bus ride over. Maybe she told them that I said, "Mutherfuck chorizo, Acapulco, the state of Oaxaca, and Che Guevara." That seems more likely. The men around her are mad. They don't care about gender parity or even her directly, she's just the white conduit with tits.

I say, "What's up?"

She's hysterical now, screaming as if a life has been lost, "He's the one! He's the one!"

I see the cops at the taco stand drop their plates and start separating the crowd, moving into it. But they're too far off: this thing is about to blow up.

One of the paisas squeezes through the crowd and stops a yard in front of me. I've got him by five inches and forty pounds. He's got me by *La Gente. De la Migra.*

He says, "*¿Que paso, ese?*"

I can answer him in Spanish, but that would be a concession. I recognize the guy and his mustache from somewhere. His eyes are superior and bold, as if he too knows me. I don't like it, the familiarity between us.

I say, "Nothing much, dude," trying to sound as white as possible, Southern California, surferish, orange skin and bleached hair, eyebrow piercing, right off Hermosa Beach. Some of these cats think I'm Hispanic, and I want to remove that possibility fast. Not because I don't care for their race or would be embarrassed to be a part of it—*they're beautiful people, they're beautiful!*—but because fuck them, fuck these people. Most cats right about now would have it over with and shout, "*¡Sí, se puede! Sí, se puede!*" But a part of me doesn't like that these paisas know Americans are weak, will back down to danger.

What do they know about me, anyway?

I say, "What's up with you, dude?"

The paisa's looking over my shoulder with stealth. Someone's moving closer to my right. No drums now, the crowd is hushed. Amazing how the opiate of potential violence can make the masses go quiet. It's like one little peep could interfere with the rushing momentum toward death. I tilt my head to the left and the same thing's coming from that side.

Just like that, I'm shoved from behind and falling forward, right as I think, *Swing swing swing at the fucker,* and I do, connecting with the left eye in front of me. I know I got him clean because he's falling to his back, me falling too, atop him. I'm up on my hands at once and rip two shots off on his head and before I can let loose another I'm getting struck from the side the rear the ribs and I'm floating through the force of the blows until I reach out for the neck and choke the paisa beneath me whom the brain in its craziness has actually— *can you believe this?*—identified. . . .

Poom poom poom poom poom—jingle jingle.

I'm hit again but with too much power and anger and expertise, spun and lifted by my legs and backside of my pants and catapulted forward by six seven maybe eight hands. I land on my face and crumble with the force behind it, and just as I'm up on my hands and knees, thinking *these fuckers these fuckers,* I'm back on my face again in the grass, my hands being cuffed behind me. Suddenly I realize the true price of neutrality on this issue.

Off to the next little station of misinterpretation.

I hear, "Stay still."

English: didactic, uppity Monte Sereno accent. There's a knee digging into the middle of my back, at about the second lumbar, two hands at the top of my neck, then one hand, as the other rips the beanie off my head. Don't know how in the hell I could move. Until something other than my own muscles moves me, like the first grumble of the Apocalypse, I'm still.

"Stay still!"

Mounds of dirt and grass in my mouth, nose, eyes, I can't talk, smell, see; I'm still. *Okay?* Fucking still. Blinking, tearing up, now I'll move. I twist my head for oxygen and the hand that (I assume) stole my beanie jams my face back to the dirt and shouts, "Stay still goddammit!"

So I'll eat dirt for the moment.

Finally I'm lifted to my feet. I hear the weeping, the American histrionics. She's bellowing like a widow at the funeral. I know who it is and that the tears aren't for me so I won't look. I can't really see anyway. But if she can't handle the paltry mess she's made here, imagine the trouble we're all in when it really hits. Any recent exhibition of strength on my part, as in *I don't need to hire Huns and Visigoths to do my fighting,* is being erased with every marrow-freezing wail of Athena.

"That's him!" she's crying. "He's the one!"

"He called that guy a spic," someone else says.

"Yeah. A lettuce picker!"

"A greaser!"

"*El pinche puto alla.*"

I turn my head and it feels heavy. Off-kilt and oval, like a watermelon. My friend from Jack-in-the-Box, the paisa in the corner whose quiet dignity I was so taken by last night, is being cleaned with cotton, dabbed with rubbing alcohol, nursed with Q-tips. He's got blood crusting on his mustache and his neck is clawed and purpling where I choked him. No cuffs for the happy immigrant, just a gurney on wheels with clean white sheets.

I want to say, *Hasta luego, mi amigo,* but I can't move my face.

The world inside me and around me is blurring: yellow, brown, black, white. . . .

Buenas noches.

Good night.

5

You Think of Good Things When in Chains

You THINK of good things when in chains in the back of the van.

Don't think about the Motel 6 studio you've slept in for the past few weeks, native son living in immigrant squalor, iconoclastic neighbor to the resident transients, cranksters, molesters, sometimes all three in one body. Drive out of your mind the nicotine-stained bed beneath the golden western landscape (acrylic on cardboard) with the cowboy mounting his neighing horse. Don't ask why it seems so vital to write poems on the flyleaf of the Gideon Bible, on AA pamphlets left at bus stops, and other trite items of writerly deposit.

Poems, yes, think of poems en bumpy route to the land of incarceration.

Actually, I'd gotten the Motel 6 studio because of the poems. About half a year ago, I'd written some half-ass love sonnets for a rich Haitian lady named Beatrice La Dulce Shaliqua Schneck, after we'd made it on the Chinese silk sheets of her Desdemona chamber bed. She went wild over the words, started calling herself my Sponsor Lover.

I'd say, "Wow. What a deep paradox: a sugar mama who loves the arts."

Even at forty-nine, she's got the body of a Rodin sculpture. Not an ounce of fat on that sleek dark frame. Hindquarters that ride high on the hip from the side and bloom in absurd dimensionality from behind, a Moorish decathlete. It's like she came straight from the track and stripped, sack-hungry.

She drives me crazy. Any time she whines about her philandering Jewish ex-husband ("That puny techie is the antithesis of an African steed, my Samoan-stud baby boy!") and her own thwarted authorial ambition ("I coulda been the next Terry McMillan if I never married that rat!") and the aimlessness of her twenty-one-year-old kid I've never met or seen a picture of ("That *Cosby Show* nigga ain't got no mountain to climb in this life!"), I fantasize about throwing her out the bed. Sometimes my mind gets tangential in the late-night hours of her rambling, elaborates on the methodology of crime.

There will be time to murder, said Prufrock.

People are always debating the best and worst ways of dying—in the midst of fucking or entrenched in fire—and I could see early on that with La Dulce the best way for her to go was like her Italiano namesake: in fist-pumping mid-soliloquy. She wouldn't feel a thing at the bloody bully pulpit.

I realized that the processing of her stories, something that is reflexive in me (I'll listen to anybody), was pointless since she didn't want my input, didn't want any critical evaluation of her life. She sought blind and docile affirmation. I was a body two decades her junior, a fact that, when we'd fuck, gave her a beauty stroke and, when she'd talk, a wisdom stroke. She liked to play the old sage with the allure of the young vixen. But like many women her age, she felt stretched by the pulleys of time, aghast in her midlife crisis. So I learned to master the transitional enablers in a conversation. Whenever her pitch in tone resembled a question, or there was a brief interrogatory pause, or her finely stenciled Botoxed eyebrows would twitch in an attempt to raise the paralyzed flesh of her forehead, I'd hum, with as much bass as I could summon, "Ummmmm," like a Buddhist. Or like Yoda. This trick will give the impression to the narcissistic that the listener is being enlightened, and you manage to keep some peace of mind.

As we slept in postcoital bliss one evening in the Milpitas foothills, the wide-open sky steamy-strip-club lavender, she screamed out from her sweaty dream, all revelatory and betraying her Haitian mysticism, "You got talent, nigga!"

I looked around the bed for a beheaded rooster, and then back into her manic voodoo eyes and was suddenly fully awake, reaching for my still-attached root.

Minutes later she was rushing me off in her Beemer to Slam Poetry Fest in Oakland, California, an event she hosted in her ex-husband's absence. She introduced me to friends as "this century's Walt Whitman," which of course made her Emerson. She put me in the last slot of the lineup, and though I'd never publicly recited poetry before, I had done my penitence in prison long enough to memorize hours of Shakespeare and a few other Brits, plus my own personal effluvium, so what I did at the mic was plagiarize/ebonicize a little bit of each, apparently without anybody knowing, because by the end of the night I had a $1,000 fellowship called the LeRoi Jones Hookup for Off-the-Hook Artistic Achievement.

The reception was at an Americanized sushi joint called Yoshi's in Jack London Square. Someone other than my Sponsor Lover threw down some serious cash for a few rounds of Long Island iced teas between bluesy, soulful sets by John Lee Hooker Jr.

"It ain't fair!" Beatrice was shouting by the end of her second Long Island.

She wanted me, her intellectual stoolie, to graze at her feet. She wanted me to stop chasing the Long Islands with fifty-dollar merlot from Sonoma ("Just sip, fool, sip!") and ask her highbrow, exclusional, lisping friends about the enclave for artists in Villa Montalvo. She wanted me to weep uncontrollably at her generosity of spirit. But I played indifferent, the ingrate, pounding whatever liquor came my way, howling—*boxcars! boxcars! phonies!*—at her improprieties. I knew what authors she had on her bedside: She was the personification of a Latin mantra that I remember an English prof hanging over his office door: *Laudant illa sed ista legunt*—They praise good books but read the bad ones.

Anyway, by morning we'd made an arrangement that, rather than kick down the g she owed me, she'd offer unlimited stay at a Motel 6 parallel to highway 101 and a five-dollar daily per diem I could pick up at the manager's desk.

"Unlimited?"

"That's right," she said.

"No catch?"

"Only one."

"What's that?"

"You let me edit your book of love poems."

I thought I'd push the advantage, see how far I could take it. "No problem. The only trick is I can't ever see you again. That way I'll have access to true tragedy."

She said, "I understand completely, nigga. These be the mysterious ways of the muse."

"Totalitarian. Fickle trick."

"You get to work now. No cable TV, no honor bar, baby."

I just thought, *What the hell, something to see, something to do. Who knows what will come of this silly elementary school contract?*

But Beatrice kept her word and I tried to keep my end of the deal by earning my fellowship. I found I could write poems to Beatrice when I didn't think about Beatrice but of other women I'd either bedded or loved or both or neither. Beatrice in verse was a composite of my ex-love Sharon, of the daemon-driven purist Marydawn, of the street-smart stray cat Monina, of the vain and simpleminded Kisa-La, of the good-hearted plump-bootied Morisa, of the long-legged obsidian-skinned Sayo, of the holdover hippie Flower, of Rebecca, Leilani, Shikima, of Anne Sexton to prevent her pain, of Dickinson with honey from her bees, of Meryl Streep in *The Deer Hunter,* of Katie Couric in a bob with banana pancakes in bed watching clips of her shows over the decades, of Madonna the mortal, of several cousins at reunions with furtive glances, of the quirky smile and subtle skills of Reese Witherspoon, of some woman at a bus stop in Santa Cruz weeping into her crusty hands, of Jorie Graham post-fifty reciting Sapphic verse in of course the Greek, of the pleasant, cursed, undoubtedly virginesque university librarian who loved to look up and then hunt down my obscure, dusty, gilt-edged books of poetry on Tuesday nights, of for some reason Hillary Clinton, of specifically the backside of J Lo for a game of Pin the Tail on the Donkey, of the Bush daughters on the Persian rug of the Lincoln Bedroom with a bottle to be drunk and then spun and then whatever.

I was rotten, am rotten.

What I figured out is that only the women who can find themselves in the poems, whether true or not, actually like the poems, and only poets, true poets or not, think poetry actually matters.

My Uncle Rich, the one guy I can talk to for longer than an hour, is someone who falls into neither category, highly suspicious of verse. I don't know why, really, but I've wanted to persuade my favorite relative otherwise for a long time. Maybe to convince myself that I haven't been wasting my life.

"I mean, I can't see it," he's always saying. "What is the point exactly in putting all this energy into something you can't live on?"

After I won the LeRoi Jones, I gave him a holler with the intent of proving the point of poetry's utility. He told me, slurring his words, to meet him at a bar called the Redi Room on Saratoga and Moorpark and to bring no money, no credit cards, only my relatively healthy liver. With the exception of the credit cards, which I didn't have, I brought as much cash as La Dulce had given me earlier in the week, which was the five-buck per diem, and headed out.

I got there and waited for an hour. Johnny Cash was busting "Folsom Prison Blues" over the juke and these two Hell's Angel–looking cats were throwing darts in their sleeveless vests with sewed-on patches of red-winged chariots across their bulging backs. They wore those asshole shades with the slanted lenses and had stormtrooper helmets on the table with lightning bolts and eagle heads on the crest. I could smell the burnt gasoline and dirty oil from the door.

When my uncle showed up, he was sloshed. He grabbed the cock-tail napkin I was writing on and read:

> "The brain is its own engine,
> its own fuel, its own vapor, its own
> contaminant
> and it finally to its own amusement
> and horror
> breaks down in its own empty desert,
> without its own water,
> in the very heat
> that it itself has generated."

"Jesus Christ," he said, sagging onto his stool, the barkeep with a Cherokee ponytail and a dreamcatcher around his neck watching with folded arms at the end of the bar. "Why don't you just hit me in the face with a baseball bat?"

"I guess you won't be attending my next poetry reading."

"Nephew. You gotta stop wasting your time."

"As in coming down here to meet you at a dive bar?"

"As in do you want a job?"

My mother's only brother, Richard, whom she hasn't talked to in eight years, became a multimillionare the right way, if there is such a thing: hard work, frugality, sound investment. But he had a better story before he ever earned a penny: a nineteen-year old army medic who won a Silver Star for valor during two voluntary tours in Vietnam; later, a run with the ACLU as a speechwriter and troubleshooter for potential cases; a baby born during the first year of night classes for a master's in history. He started at the bottom of a small real estate operation on the Peninsula and within ten years was running the whole deal and within twelve, owning it—Santa Clara Real Estate West—adding eight offices across the Bay. Faithful husband to my lively Aunt Lanell, father to my older cousin, Nina, who'd be twenty-nine next week except she's been dead for thirteen years, a gun wound to the head, her hand, his pistol.

After Nina died, Uncle Rich would take me out to have a beer, even when I wasn't yet of age, and talk about any range of topics. I got the sense that he cared about me, if only because he was always dropping little suggestions I might consider about what to do with my life. He's the one that got me thinking about going to an all-boys Catholic prep school. He's the one that got me thinking about West Point. Ironically, he's the one who thought I had some talent writing poetry, although he was quick to point out that it wouldn't make me any money and certainly wasn't something to build a life on. But it would kill time. He was visiting me in San Quentin. I remember I said, "Everyone in here's a poet." Our conversations have always been pointed, he gets what I'm saying, and I get him.

"This country is dying," my uncle mumbled now.

"What about the job?"

"Pause means you don't want it."

"Right you are, uncle o' mine. Were saying?"

"It's too much, too much. Stuff."

"Here?"

"It's more than that, though. I could talk for days. You know what I just saw at a real estate barbecue in the hills of Via Santa Teresa?"

"Golden silverware?"

"Some show called *Survivor*."

"Yeah. Been around for a while."

"You a fan?"

"Hell no," I said. "I'll watch that show when they airdrop ten .44 magnums onto the island. See some *Lord of the Flies Redux* go down."

"We the people are weak."

"Suddenly survival has nothing to do with staving off death."

"No guts. Even me. I've gone soft. I was a kid in the bush back in 'sixty-eight who'd whip the man I am now."

"Come on, Uncle."

"Listen. That's the truth. Do you know that I live in the last region in San José with any natural beauty?"

"Of course I do. The Silicon Valley is L.A. minus twenty years."

"Trees, trails everywhere. They go up the hillside to the silver mines."

My Uncle Rich has got a pukka estate in New Almaden with a crew of paisas cleaning and trimming it, a vast and vacant guesthouse, an artificial lake stocked with trout and black bass, and three different half-mile driveways to the place, the south, the north, and the northwest entrances.

"And so every morning for twenty years I've started the day saying I'd climb one. The end of the day? Haven't gone out there. Twenty fucking years, Paul. Twelve-hour days."

"Too busy buying property, selling it. Need to appreciate poetry of the eye."

"I'd say your generation is even worse. Far worse. The most selfish buncha jerkoffs in the history of mankind."

"Don't remind me."

"The Me Generation. Hah!"

"I feel you, Uncle Rich. I can't talk to anyone under thirty."

"I love you 'cause you ain't like 'em, you know."

"Yeah."

"But I'm telling you, nephew. Don't listen to me and my sniveling. You gotta change it and go with the flow. You won't make it the way you are. You know that?"

"Let me take you home, Uncle."

"Let me give you a job."

"Come on."

"Listen to me! You gotta smash some of your antennae. Break 'em off at the root. You gotta turn off the awareness for a minute."

"I don't know how," I said.

The Beatles came on over the juke, that masterful last jam session of songs at the end of *Abbey Road* and their togetherness, and my uncle jumped off his stool and started drum-soloing on the air at "Mean Mr. Mustard," and I began to nod at the rhythm and the sadness of the scene—and yet I also felt compassion for my uncle who was nakedly sharing with me in his most pathetic state of existence, and then I was actually standing and singing at the top of my lungs, perfectly sober, drunk on the nuttiness of life, TVs above us behind us around us in this dark cave of Pabst Blue Ribbon on tap, some random brotha suing Nike and Michael Jordan for eighty million bones because his life as a warehouse foreman has been ruined by mistaken identity (he's five-ten to the six-foot-six of His Airness), another winner lacing his kid's dinner soup with prescription drugs to set up a lawsuit against Campbell's, a far cry from little Max coming back from his dream of where the wild things are to find "his bowl of soup still warm," the strange weather in one corner of the screen, the elapsing time in the other, a tape-thin line of steady clips running along the base and leaving forever, one in English, the other in Spanish, Sunni and Shia dividing votes, Brangelina giving cash, hugs, and birth, O.J. saying when or if I did it here's how, Rockabilly

Kim Jong Il with the bomb, Coney Island contest of hot-dog eating won by a 150-pound Japanese teen, starving Dinka boys decapitated by white-robed camel-mounted swordsmen called *murahaleen,* Hugo Chavez hugging Cindy Sheehan, a cell phone's disco tune in the wall-carpeted corner of the bar clashing with McCartney's melodic "and in the end, the love you take is e-qual to", a whore with no pimp or client in the other corner scratching her scratchy legs and playing electric solitaire on the house machine, and then my uncle, in tears over more than his dead daughter, a *Suicide Girl* gone bad, whose spread-eagle picture of gothic piercings is still plastered on a depraved Web site on the Internet, my uncle, leaning on me, whispering, "The truth is, nephew, I don't know a thing about this life. Each day it's less and less. Nina was like you. Always thinking, watching. I had a little more to believe in than she did. That's all. It's no good, no fucking good."

My mind wandered at that moment to the quandary of relativity. I questioned my uncle's suffering, I actually did. I considered mass suicide at Masada, the Chinese in Nanking, 1942; I pondered a rotting George Chuvalo, the old Croatian boxer who took Ali the distance in 'seventy-two and paid the price for his fifteen minutes of fame by playing a twentieth-century Job, losing son number one to suicide, son number two to suicide, son number three to suicide, and finally wife to suicide, not at once but over the course of ten years, '85, '93, '93, '96, his entire family, bit by bit, gone; there is worse out there, always, there is worse. Much much worse than my spoiled, confused, bulimic cousin of nineteen years of age who tried to seduce me once at a beach party in a Capitola cove, who thought she knew enough about this life to quit it, who was screaming for tragedy, or love, or something she never found.

Maybe the dead are lucky, for my uncle goes on, as we all do. Is he weak or is he sensitive? Is he in love with his daughter, whom he probably never knew like he wished he had the courage to know, or is he in love with his own story? Is that, in the end, what grief is? Love of thyself, of thyself in connection to the dead?

Clapped into jail by consciousness.

I don't know now in this goddamned police van and I didn't know then in that dead-end bar, so I just stood there and nodded when I had to, squinted my eyes when I had to, finally joined him in knocking back coal-filtered vodka without a chaser, wincing at the fire in my heart and my gut and my loins and my lungs, and when he called a taxi to return to the mansion in his idyllic untapped hills, I went back inside the Redi, told the wannabe Indian behind the bar, Fuck you and your fake-ass dreamcatcher for laughing at my uncle, offered the whore half a free bed at the Motel 6 I was "staying in for the night" (I didn't want her to know I lived there or she might come back the next day), and we left with a good yard of space between us, and nothing else.

6

They've Got New Machines Now

THEY'VE GOT NEW MACHINES now that prevent the messy process of having to stain the thumb and index finger with ink, yours and theirs. Now you just lay your hand on a transparent counter of lasers that looks like a Xerox machine without the hood and press it down evenly when the cop says, "Press it down evenly," and there it is, your epidermal ID. They can hunt you down anywhere in the world by a downloaded map of your palm. A snap of the finger, press of the button.

Eternally.

The American in me can't accept the suggestion that I've no right to an older, alternative method of fingerprinting. When the cop says, "Please place your hand above the machine and relax, sir," I say, "No. That's okay."

"Please, my friend, let us do this civilly like gentlemen."

That's a first: a booking cop calling me friend. He has a slight accent which I'll nail when he talks a little more. His tone has the decorous Victorian ring that a hooked-on-phonics tape evokes: *Hello there, boyo. And how are we today, chappie?* I'm getting excited in that region—southern, center—where it counts, and I wonder why.

Princess Di on the beach?

No, posthumously disrespectful.

A Spice Girl?

No, musically irrelevant.

I feel like I can test this cop, test the red tape, so what the hell, I'm bored. And though I haven't seen my face after the mess at Cesar Chavez Park, I can tell by how tough it is to keep my eyes open, the itch and scratch in my nose, and the mealy-mouthed feeling when I talk that I'm blackened and swollen and pulpy. That should give me a little leeway to say whatever I want.

"This thing is a hotbed of invisible cancer-causing lasers, officer, and I'd rather get ink all over my hands and face than get some radical cells going in my system. Already got millions as it is. I mean, I ate your institutional food for a couple years."

"You are on parole?"

"No, sir."

"You discharged your number?"

"I never was on parole." He wants to know how it's possible. I'm about to tell him. "I did my time straight through. They wanted to kick me out in a year and a half, but I stayed in and finished it out."

"I have never encountered that before," he says. "You are unique. Everyone accepts the terms of an early release."

"The terms mean you're still officially incarcerated. Same condemned status. And for another three years they do what they want with you. Send you back for sleeping in late."

This guy's got an educated, even elegant look to him, despite the crew-cut. And he's got self-discipline, you can see it in his forearms, which are veined and thick as a dairy farmer's. He's trim in the midsection, a runner, carved cheekbones and jawline. And were he not a cop, I'd say his posture suggests gentility, another first. I'm sure there are dignified cops out there, but I don't come across them as an arrestee. I suspect they're in the hidden offices of every jail and police station, polishing their boots, reviewing civic code, whistling

"Battle Hymn of the Republic" between contemplative puffs of a dry-leaf Cuban.

"Actually," he says, smiling, "you're quite right."

The hard-on is now raging in my pants and I wonder if it springs and eventually comes from the simple kindness of an unexpected source. Flattery from a dominatrix. Niceties from the executioner. Or someone granting what I've always wanted on every level: *You're right, my friend. Quite right.*

"You do have the right to be fingerprinted traditionally, should you so choose."

"Then, I so choose, sir. Might I exercise my right for the ink?"

"You might, my friend. Please wait here."

He leaves me alone, without cuffs. I just stand there, unwilling to turn around. No eye contact with the transient hooked up to the blue plastic chair behind me. I can hear him shuffling his feet, slid-ing in his seat to get my attention without words. He'll want me to snag something, a pen, a paper clip, an extra cheese and mayonnaise sandwich, anything to come up. The code of the streets is Machia-vellian and jail/prison is the streets times five/ten. You get and keep whatever you can, when and however. But I feel this strange sense of indebtedness to the cop, not so much for trusting me, although that's the thrust of it, but more so for slipping protocol, breaking rank and being human.

"Hey, dog," the transient says.

I turn, and his eyes are full of mischief. With evil. The smile cements it: I'm gonna have to fast for forty days in the desert to cleanse myself of this cat. His mouth is rotting from too many years of Dumpster diving. I can't tell from the weathering if he's Hispanic or white or a mixture thereof, but when I spot the bird on his neck, an institutional tag for peckerwoods, I know he's white. He says, "Pull the fire alarm, dog. It's right over there. He ain't gotchu in the com-puter yet, man."

"Why don't you do it, bro? That way they can get your pearly whites on camera."

"No, no, no," he says, still smiling. "Trust me. They won't know it's you."

It's funny, man. Too funny. Is this devilish arrestee offering me a pair of scissors to slice up the red tape I've just questioned in my head? Is it cowardice not to up and run if I can do it, get it done right now? If I were a lifer, heading off to High Desert or Pelican Bay, maybe. Escape or die in the pen. But then, too, the cop wouldn't leave me unattended. No: I don't like the idea because, whoever it's from, any kind of coaxing to me is like saying I didn't know the suggestion in the first place.

"Hey, bro," I say. "You see my face?"

"Yeah. That's right. I get it."

"You get what?"

"Go ahead," he says. "Tell it, man. Tell it."

He's fiending on the conversation he foresees between us. Vows of vengeance, a tale of treachery, the dawn of the dead. Vortexes and black holes and mosquito swamps of defeat. He's panting like a fucking dog. It's lonely looking for a co-conspirator down there in the gutter of sorrow.

I can't tolerate his scheming ill will. I'm going to punch him in his ear, get some blood going. Aim the right front tire of my street sweeper for his head. I look down at the fingerprinting station and by a herculean bidding of the imagination envision this hardened transient as a thin-skinned eleven-year-old, a Little League failure, a chubby right fielder with the dexterity of a manatee, the arm strength of a T-baller half his age, sipping on his melting Slurpee between innings, hoping that the demure brown-skinned Maria from Mrs. George's class will come to the next game to catch his team when he won't strike out three times—*whiff!*—won't drop a liner right in his mitt, won't boot a grounder that dribbled through the uncut

grass slower than a three-legged rabbit. He doesn't have to hit anything out of the park, he doesn't need to sit on anyone's shoulder
after the game, he just has to do something barely acknowledged by
coaches and team mothers and peers at the pizza parlor. Acknowledged through a greeting or inclusion in a conversation, a tip of the
hat, a little nod to his little heart of the seminal universal need to
belong. Anything that will keep the hope alive and give him the right
to return to practice tomorrow.

Now I can talk to him on the straight, no condescension, as little
ego as possible.

"Having your face bloodied up," I say, "is the first step to becoming a fashion model. Like the body making broken bones stronger
than unbroken bones. I'm gonna come out looking like a young Paul
Newman. The body's like the marines. You gotta get beaten down
before you can carry a gun."

"What kinda gun you got?" he asks, still hoping for a compadre.

The cop returns and I'm actually thankful. He's cradling a print-
ing kit in a giant Ziploc bag. The transient sits up, looks around innocently. "Okay," the cop says, "let us commence."

I put my hands out. "Commencing."

The name tag reads BEHBAHARI. My first guess is Afghan. I'll give
it a run. "What do you think about what's going on right now in
Kabul?"

He nods, rolls my thumb into the ink. "Very complex."

"Do you miss your family?"

He looks up at me and says, "Of course. With the supreme one's
favorable eye, most of my family made it here. Our twenty-fifth an-
niversary was two years back, thank you. I am not Afghan. Your index
finger please."

Iranian then, or Persian. And with language like "the supreme one,"
he's not Muslim either. One of the last descendants of Zoroaster,

maybe, or an up-and-coming new-age recruit of Baha'i. He probably got out in '79, or somewhere thereabouts.

I say, "I'm glad y'all made it."

Officer Behbahari nods. "Thank you very much. Ring finger."

"I once had a friend who was Persian," I say. "Name was Cyrus."

"Very popular name. Pinkie."

"I want to tell you about him."

"You be careful with your wounds now."

"Amazing guy, good old Cyrus."

"You have been beaten up very badly. You seem not to know this."

"Worked with him in a house of books. Wanna hear about him?"

"Not today, my friend." He snaps the fingerprinting kit shut, taps on my hand almost with compassion. "Okay. You are finished."

7

I Needed to Stay Out of the Pit of Solitude

I NEEDED TO STAY out of the pit of solitude after my girl left me in the spring of '04, and so I'd gotten a job at the Santa Clara Public Library shelving books. If you took away the people who ran the place, it was the best job I'd ever had. I loved pushing the carts down the aisles, flipping through book flaps for leads to a great story, alphabetizing the F–Gr fiction section. I loved sharing a favorite book with a patron, guiding some random high school kid to his first encounter with Steinbeck.

All the stuff that mattered in that place mattered most to me. I preferred the dead to the living in the library. The only thing redemptive I felt toward my pedantic, punctilious coworkers was sympathy for some kind of physical deformity they endured—*What's Eating Gilbert Grape?*—obesity, unthinkable acne, physics-defying limp, shocking facial tick, sanguine body odor. But I capped it there. I've never believed that an ailment of the body should necessarily lead to corruption of the soul.

They usually had their noses in some digital monstrosity and would meet on Friday nights at Chili's for amateur-hour karaoke with watered-down, umbrella-shaded, glistening drinks in big phallic glasses. They'd bring back laminated and framed photographs of their forgettable weekends—which were remarkable to them, of epic proportions, worthy of a novel. But I think they vexed my sensibilities mostly because they never read novels, or any books for that matter. They were ensuring that oddballs like themselves wouldn't have jobs forty years from now in a future where libraries wouldn't exist.

It's just that they were all so skilled in committing energy to events that didn't matter. They got off on tech logic and star gates of Dewey Decimal systems. They equated violations of library protocol with crimes against humanity, which drove them to the brink of frenzy. They were minutiae fiends, petty. The month-late book ("That'll be"—giddy-voiced—"let's see, ninety cents, sir"), the absconded DVD, the indignant patron ("Did you see the veins on his forehead when he said, 'I don't care what that computer says I returned the goddamned book last week I made a point to I always do!'"), the pair of smooching teenagers in the juvenile fiction section ("What's this world coming to? We were just getting into hopscotch, God!"). It required the tiniest phrenological literacy to read the text of my face: these people were wasting precious oxygen.

One woman named Robin, an aspiring third-grade teacher, made a point to follow me around. She had a designated *Sesame Street* sweater for Dress Down Day. That wasn't so significant in itself except that she was actually proud of it, proud of the sweater. As one would be of a child, one's own child. I think she ironed it.

Once she said, "Why don't you wait for us after work? You run out of here like you can't stand the place."

I was surprised by her perceptiveness. "I have to get back to the studio and check on the dog."

"You have a dog?" she asked.

"No."

"You should walk us ladies out of the building," she said, smiling.

I looked into her plain and pleading eyes, then down into the insane cross-eyed dots of Cookie Monster. "I think you'll be safe."

"What do you mean by that?"

"I mean what I say, that's what."

There was one coworker who kept me curious about the living people in the library, an old Persian man named Cyrus Rohan who patrolled the nonfiction section. Though he was always polite and overtly humble, you could see from a distance that he was immensely proud. He had the upright posture of a high school football coach, an old-school disciplinarian in some agrarian midwest borough, and his dress, while simple, was orderly, refined. If he wore a sweater, he pulled it down just above his belt; if he wore a collared shirt, it was tucked; every thread of clothing was ironed, and his shoes, a pair of Mervyn's penny loafers, were spit-shined. And his eyes: always watery, often leaking, the moon-gray iris afloat in a dead yellow pond, the top of the cheekbones marked by two deeply ridged frown lines.

I knew he had a story, a big one, and I tend to leave people like that alone. Though that's not totally true; I'll talk to a paraplegic as if I've known him all my life. As if we'd just finished elbowing each other in a pickup hoop game at the YMCA. All to swing against those good-hearted but ultimately lame people who use conversational tongs with the ambulatory challenged. They pull the same deal with the paisa at a Burger King drive-in, talking superslow, like, "That's . . . right. One . . . Whopper . . . and . . . one . . . onion . . . ring, por . . . fa . . . vor."

So it took me three months before I introduced myself. He was the only employee quieter than me, and I finally couldn't take it anymore. My opportunity came when I saw the old man stretching dangerously for a top shelf. I myself had slipped once, so I rushed over. He said no, he didn't need my help, thank you very much, walked past me and down the aisle of fat dripping fictive memoirs and other items of high-art bellybutton-gazing. He reshelved a coffee-table history book that was practically blocking the aisle and came back with a steel footstool. Passing me, he said, "Excuse me, thank you very much," and climbed upon it.

I said, "My name's Paul."

He fingered each poetry book—Lowell, Maio, Mehigan, his face inches from the texts—until he found the book, Millay's *Collected Sonnets,* its proper place. Then he stepped down, pulled a handkerchief from his pocket with his left hand, snapped it like a football player with a wet towel on a teammate's ass, dabbed his dripping eye and nose, repocketed the handkerchief, and shook my hand surprisingly firmly with his right unsoiled hand. He swallowed to liquidate his mouth with saliva, the right eye flickered like a dying lightbulb and the whole right side of his face winced in pain. He bowed in that kind of Middle Eastern consummate affirmation where the shoulders dip with the head.

"I am Cyrus. Thank you very much."

In the next twenty minutes, Cyrus went on to explain that he had been in the United States for over twenty years. He spoke a poor version of broken English and so I didn't say a word until I was sure I had his story right. I listened, made easily interpreted gestures. It pained him to speak, not figuratively but literally: he had to fight some kind of facial paralysis to talk, palsy maybe, I don't know. I sure as hell wasn't going to ask.

I decided to offer up a yes or no question so he could at least know I was interested in his life while not forcing him to articulate a response. I asked him if he'd read *The House of Sand and Fog,* and when he shook his head no, I said wait right here, please, ran down the center aisle, cut across the self-help 600s under the rainbow-lettered sign (BE LUMINOUS: FIND BLISS AND AWARENESS IN YOUR LIFE), out to the vacant fiction section, snagged one of the fifteen copies with the O on the cover, ran back, and urgently handed it over.

He nodded thank you very much and said excuse me, thank you very much, and plodded step by step to the expansive foreign language section and found an English to Farsi translation book, slid that and Dubus and the code of his card under the visible laser of the self-checkout station, a mandatory procedure which no employee ever abided, and came back to where I was standing, said thank you very much one last time, and then finished shelving the books on the cart.

A week later I went to see if the book had been returned and of course couldn't tell with all the other copies there, hogging the shelf. I risked encountering those evasively vague enthusiasms of someone who clearly hadn't read a page of a recommendation and asked Cyrus straight up if he liked the story.

In good faith, his dead eyes came to life. He swallowed for saliva and nodded even before he'd said a word. "This is my life."

I was so excited that my mind started to pedal its predictable little tricycle of imagination. I brought forth romantic images of the old man in his indigenous inaccessible land, a sun-browned youth with a scythe at his side, mounted on some ageless slump of a camel, gown flowing in the sandswept wind, an extra on *Lawrence of Arabia*. Then he was squatting on the floor in one of those mud-dried hovels, a minuscule pile of food between his humble feet, tea in hand, blessing something, maybe the food, the hovel, maybe someone, his wife.

My head returned to the book, which took place here on the Peninsula. Thinking on its cursed, displaced Persian protagonist, Colonel Behrani, I realized that Cyrus reminded me of this figment of Dubus's imagination. More than its kindred cultural element, it's why I'd chased the book down in the first place.

I asked, "You were in the army then?"

He nodded, shoulder, eyebrow, wincing.

"And you were a colonel like Behrani?"

"General," he said, with a trace of pride.

"General?"

He did not like that I repeated the word. "I am in charge of operations and field strategics," he said firmly. "Thank you very much."

That week he invited me to his apartment for dinner to meet his two sons. They visited Cyrus every Thursday night. Before knocking I kicked off my shoes in a respectful nod to their culture, one that my Samoan cousins halfway across the world also practiced, and when the door opened they smiled at my anticipation and I, in thick camping socks, smiled back. They both called me *bro* and had white wives with sun-whitened waist-length hair, both in teetering heels. The brothers were playful with their father, who, without any help from them, had prepared a five-course five-star (in my novice culinary book) meal.

We had *zereshk polo,* a kind of brown rice with dried cranberries, a dry flat bread akin to naan called *lavash,* roast chicken, a Persian cheese called *panir* that tasted like a wet feta, and my favorite, *tarig koresch,* potatoes crisped beneath the buttery drippings of the *zereshk polo*. I loved it all and paid tribute to Cyrus's generosity as host, his skill as chef, by eating everything on my plate the first time through and, sipping on tea in between, the second time through as well.

After dinner the wives left for home and the brothers cracked open domestic beers from microbreweries in Portland, Oregon, and I listened to their stories about showing up in St. Paul, Minnesota, one day before the American embassy fell in their birth town of Tehran. The boys had been whistled and honked at here, threatened at school, marginalized by teachers. This was 1979, hula-hooping kids were rotating their waists in T-shirts imprinted with Mickey Mouse giving the ayatollah the bird, folks pasted a WE PLAY COWBOYS AND IRANIANS stickers on the bumpers of their station wagons.

I mimicked Cyrus: polite, curt in conversation. "Were you worried then?"

"Hell no," the older, Sefidi, said. "We all knew there was nothing going down here that could compare to where we just came from. America's a cakewalk, bro."

"We were worried about our father," Qavi said.

Cyrus was sipping his tea, looking down at his plate.

"So he wasn't here then? You didn't come out with them, Cyrus?"

"No."

The brothers looked at each other and the oldest spurted, "He came out in 'eighty-one. All the brass except my father were executed."

"How did he survive?" I hated myself the moment it came out of my mouth, stupid prying American intrusion.

"I never mistreating my men," said Cyrus, face scrunched up, eyes aflame.

Sefidi refilled my cup, winking at me as if to say, *We know this is uncomfortable for your hypersensitive infrastructure, but just indulge the old man, won't you, bro?*

As I nodded back, accepting a sugar cube for my tea, the other brother came out with a framed black-and-white photo of Cyrus at twenty-eight, an officer in the Iranian army learning the latest avant-garde strategies at Fort Benning, Georgia. He had the photographer right there in his sights and the calm, confident, unblinking portraiture of a young president.

"We had to burn the other photos," said Qavi. "This is the only one that survived. Mother smuggled it in her bag."

"Very stupid," said Cyrus.

"And luckily nothing happened. I actually bought that frame for Mom when I got my first paper route."

"Did you?" said Sefidi. "Does she remember that?"

"I don't know. Ask her later tonight."

I looked at the brothers.

"Oh," said Sefidi. "You didn't know she lived in Fremont?"

I didn't respond, hoping he wouldn't answer any further.

"Yeah," he said. "Ma's had her own little apartment for about ten years now."

"Eleven."

"You sure about that?"

Cyrus stood up, left the room. Welcome to the season of divorce, the land of it. Sefidi winked at me again and Qavi started cleaning up the dishes. I offered to help and as Sefidi said, "No, no, of course not, it's cool, bro," Cyrus came back with a flea-market ghetto blaster balanced on his frail pointy shoulder and motioned me over to the living room. I went at once to show loyalty to him and not to his Americanized but very nice and polite sons, walking across the clean soft rug in my socks, feeling sad for Cyrus and yet good, full of fine, exotic food and clean tea.

I sat down at the base of the couch, the brothers talked and whispered and clacked plates in the kitchen, Cyrus plugged the contraption in and hit the dice-sized PLAY button. This woman's beautiful operatic moan came out of the box and I stood up and lay back on the cool white cushions like Daisy fanning herself in *The Great Gatsby* and followed the rhythm with an instinct I thought I'd lost. Or had killed. Floating in timelessness, mining the soul. I was humming a tune I'd never before heard and I could hear my heartbeat behind the moaning, and the minute I proceeded to measure the *thump thump thump* my treacherous mind snuck into the game and rendered a puny list of tangents loaded with sarcasm: could be an early Verdi, this middle-eastern Aretha, a Farsi version of Streisand, Ottoman queen of the song.

"*Gol-e baran. Gol-e baran.*"

Cyrus was sipping on his tea, nodding. I wished to God—even his God—that I could speak Farsi and give the old man a moment he'd remember. I was his half solution, interested enough in his story to visit respectfully and more or less keep my mouth shut, but with no capacity to talk history or politics or genealogy. I was the surrogate society, a trigger for nostalgia. I was, for the moment, just barely good enough.

"This sounds very nice, Cyrus."

"Sima Bina. A lady very much older than you."

"What is she singing about?"

"She is crying about love. Lost. You sang like a bird and go away. You fluttered my heart and leave it behind."

Both sons emerged from the kitchen. Sefidi put his hand out and I hesitated; I didn't want to leave. "Well, thanks for coming, bro. It's good of you to keep an eye out for Pops at work."

"Yeah. Thank you, Paul."

I stood and said, "Yes. Of course. I'll get my shoes." I turned to Cyrus and said, bowing, "Thank you very much, Cyrus, for the excellent dinner. Good-bye."

He said, "Thank you very much, good-bye," pressed the STOP button, unplugged the radio, hoisted it to a shoulder and walked back to his room, the cord dragging lifelessly behind.

Later that week Robin asked why I talked with Cyrus at lunch break and no one else. I told her a few talking points about his life and she yawned right through them. Didn't ask a single question. My coworkers forgave or ignored Cyrus his silences because of his age and immigrant status, but they didn't see anything worth investigation about someone who reported quietly to work, always on time despite catching the impunctual county bus each morning, who never took breaks or lunches beyond the allotted thirty minutes, was curt but polite with greetings and, at seventy-eight years of age, outshelved the lot of them every day with ease.

Robin knew how much I detested all of them, because the feeling was mutual. They cleared out of the way and fell silent when I'd round a corner with my cart. Unlike Cyrus, my tight-lipped approach to the job was offensive, arrogant. I was a native son of the Silicon Valley, however much I disavowed it in gesture and attitude, and I should have shown some silly categorical reverence to the other native children.

But how could I be expected to worship with a group of people who started a deal called the Sunshine Fund, a "strictly voluntary donation to ensure that every retiring employee gets a tiny yet dainty sendoff party"? This meant chips and dip and little pointy hats with rubber bands hooked under your chin that said, GOODBYE AND GOOD LUCK. And a few plastic kazoos. Oh, and it was voluntary, all right, but that doesn't mean it was private. In the break room, there was a plastic chart the size of a chalkboard divvied up into months with the names of every employee on it. Only the ones who gave to the collection were given a smiley-face sticker, and those who gave more than a dollar were given a star sticker to match. Two of the thirty-six employees were starred. I was the only employee of the library who had neither smile nor star sticker to his name, and when I looked for Cyrus on the chart I saw he wasn't up there at all. Either it was compassion on their part or just plain oversight. Either you're someone we just won't take money from or you're not someone.

When Robin pointed out my altruistic shortcomings, I said, "I'll give cash when you change the name to the Moonlite Fund."

"What's that supposed to mean?"

"It means y'all bring me down."

"What do you mean by that?"

"I mean: way down."

"You heard about the new building plans?"

I shook my head no.

"They're gonna double the size of this place, make everything state of the art. Air-conditioning and skylight windows in two years."

"How much you wanna bet the library collection doesn't grow one book?"

"You know, you have the worst attitude of anybody I've ever known."

"Yeah?" I said. "Well, I'm gonna make it worse."

"Impossible."

"How many times do I have to kick you before you stop chewing on my leg?"

"Jerk!"

But even without the flak—even on the best of days, when I wouldn't talk to a soul in that house of books and, ordered to shelf-read in the Poetry section, would just float amongst the best of our species and browse their eternal lines—I couldn't remove my peers from the shadow of the old man. I watched Cyrus work harder than the lot of them; I watched them let him work harder; I watched them recognize his steady diligence, his timeliness, his discipline as nothing more than mere factors mitigating their own need to be diligent, timely, disciplined. As young and fresh as twenty-one, they'd leave loaded carts in the aisle, knowing Cyrus would unbegrudgingly pick up their slack, as if they were doing him a favor, giving him something to do, keeping him alive. We had a two-star general with us, a man of importance, and no one knew.

Finally I went to the top and told the head librarian, a crater-faced woman named Benilia Blight, about Cyrus's story. As she was in charge of the place, Ms. Blight was doubly afflicted. She had red hair that stuck close to her skull in the cranial area of the head but was patchy and wiry and actually of a lighter color near the nape of the freckled neck. The texture was like a bad mix of sod, weeds and crabgrass. And there was a lazy eye over which she sometimes wore a pirate's patch, depending on the intensity of the sun's brightness. She'd married an Iranian accountant whom she'd divorced within a year after he'd spent half her life savings watching women a third his age strip at the Blue Noodle Cabaret Club. According to Ms. Blight herself, she was able to capably greet an Iranian in the native Farsi. But before she'd even finished saying "*Salam*," she was explaining to anyone in listening range the etymology of the word and its theological significance and why you, too, should pick up another language.

I thought she'd been unimpressed by the tale I'd shared until she made a rare appearance behind the scenes. I was checking in books with Cyrus, sorting them by genre. All of my fearless peers immediately stopped their conversations about nothing and put silent kisses on their obvious faces, saying, "Hi, Ms. Blight," in obsequious unison. She befittingly acknowledged none of them and, as she marched directly toward us, I began to feel a tangible guilt about shooting my mouth off. She'd come to address something: her lazy eye was nearly centered in the socket of her rage.

"*Salam*," she said to Cyrus.

"*Salam*."

Nearly all of my coworkers watched in amazement. How did this impotent old man rate the head librarian's tongue? And then: her tongue in a foreign tongue?

"Did you read the papers today?" she said to me.

I had, but said no for safety reasons. I didn't like the tone of her voice: it implied I was a sheet in a windstorm.

"Can you believe what happened at Abu Ghraib?"

I shrugged for the same reason.

She rolled her good eye and said to Cyrus, "They tortured those Iraqis. And one of the torturers was a woman. I'm ashamed of my gender."

I coughed into my hand.

"And I'm ashamed of my country." She was talking to her Iranian compadre now, not me. "Of my president."

Cyrus dabbed on his eye with the old handkerchief, swallowed, winced, and said, "Well. That is war."

"Yes. Well. You're doing a fine job, Cyrus, keep it up," she said, and walked out.

She didn't know what the hell he was talking about, but I like to think I did. His statement wasn't a contradiction. It almost wasn't even a statement. It didn't have anything to do with local or national or even international politics. Those were all sad things, too, terribly sad and beyond resolution, but somehow whatever he said went deeper and longer and probably hurt worse when it hit. It probably hit over a long period of time. It was closer in concept to the liquid constantly leaking out of this wise old battered man's nose and eye than some theory or punditry or flag-waving/burning. At the end of the night, Rush Limbaugh, her Antichrist, and Janeane Garofalo, her savior, washed each other out. They wouldn't say one kind word about the other side and that nearly invalidated anything they stood for. But this thing sat forever in your heart and guts, hooked like a thorn of barbed wire—*the horror, the horror*—and no position on any issue could ever dislodge it.

Beyond solution, beyond sense, beyond this place.

Cyrus and I were friends, but I selfishly wanted more. I yearned for him to see that despite my superficial inheritance as an American, I, unlike the others, understood him. I didn't care how he got out of Iran—bribing some hooded black-eyed merchant a million rials, whatever—I was just happy he was here and alive. I had some inner degree of peace in the goal that one day I'd prove my friendship to him, not through words but through action. Driving him to work listening to Sima Bina, leaving bags of pomegranates on his porch: whenever I could get enough money for a car or some extra food, I'd do it. I knew no one else would help the old man, just like they wouldn't help me, or even, if it meant their asses anyway, help each other.

One day, a cool and wet Tuesday, I was shelving photography books in paranoia. Everyone in the library had just attended a seminar on sexual harassment in the workplace, and as I either casually or ardently held many of the forbidden attitudes covered by the outsourced sexual specialist, a woman with a flattop named Jo, I knew it was only a matter of time before attitude birthed behavior and I'd be warned, probated, fired. So in order to keep my job, I'd have to be either criminally dishonest or so internalized that no one could read the blasphemy on my face or in my posture.

But I had a bigger worry, one of the spirit. I was surrounded by conversations that did not fundamentally matter, and if I, too, participated in that sordid practice, the weakness of climate would infect me through a kind of osmosis, sneak in under the radar of the consciousness, and I would, through simple science, thus mean nothing.

Like you are what you say.

I was walking down the makeshift handicap ramp of the employee entrance with that very conflict in my head and the doting Robin on my heel like a lost dog when I noticed a kid in a red bandanna spot Cyrus at the darkest end of the lot. He came up on him fast and I was already over the steel rail of the ramp in one of those feet-first cop-show bounds and as I shouted, "Cyrus!" he took a lump to the ear with a roll of quarters, fell to a knee, tried to get up, slipped on the silver pieces.

I landed like a stray cat in the alley, running the moment my feet hit ground. The kid maneuvered behind Cyrus and fondled his ass with vigor and at thirty yards from the scene I mumbled, *Fucking perv,* just as he ripped Cyrus's wallet from his back pocket and took flight.

I sprinted past Cyrus, who was mounting an attack on the air with his crooked and probably broken index finger—"*Mo-ney! Wal-let!*"— leapt the island splitting the rows of parallel spaces, and maybe fifty yards later, caught the mugger at the end of the parking lot. I came down on him from behind, clotheslining him in the neck. I shoved the jacker's goatee into the asphalt and then, in the slow time, had my first thought since the attempted heist, a purely American thought: *I want the old man to see this.*

I swiveled my body so Cyrus had an unimpeded view of me, and when the bully rolled over between my feet and was supine to the dark sky above us, I bent down at the waist, ripped the rag off his head, and went to town. I hit him once in the mouth, busted the nose like a ripe grape, slapped him across the eye, spit out, "You like jacking old men, mutherfucker, I'll fucking kill you," and slapped him again. I shoved my hand up under the scruff of the chin and drove the rear of his skull into the pavement, and that's when the second thought occurred to me, the more important of the two and tougher to abide: *Better quit it, champ. Best quit.*

I didn't. I stood up, kicked him once across the mouth, watched the eyes roll back into the head in a flaring pool of blood. In the gray of the lot, the blood was black like oil, shiny liquid obsidian. I reached down, reclaimed the wallet, and tossed it toward Cyrus without turning my body. The old man was flailing his chicken-neck arms above his weary head, limping like some frantic gimp in the easy suburban twilight, "You stop it, Paul! You must right now stop it!"

Before I cut out, I wound up like a striker on penalties and kicked him one last time in the rib cage. I heard Robin scream from the ramp. She hadn't moved the whole time.

I sprinted around the block, then slowed to a casual speed walk. An older Filipina in a flowery bonnet passed me on the street on a ten-speed. When she was out of range, I cut through the campus of a junior high school, boosted myself up an eight-foot ivy-strewn cement wall, landed on a hillock, and twisted an ankle. I reached down through the weedy grass to massage the swelling, looked up and read:

Feeling down in the mouth?
Come in for a faithlift!

A plastic billboard for The Neighborhood Church. I limped past the sign and, opposite a row of state-funded apartments, saw a dislodged window, just above head level, to the church. I pulled myself up off the good foot, crawled halfway through so I was positioned on the bridge of the sill, stretched out my hands for the rim of a toilet, dipped incrementally down until one shoe, on the good foot, crashed into the water. I stepped out of the toilet, put weight on my now swelling ankle long enough to grunt, "Shit," and then, as if I were in a fucking *Scoobie Doo* cartoon, covered my mouth. What a joke. I sat down on the toilet, shook out my dripping foot, dried it with a toilet seat cover.

I had no plan, no statement. I liked, maybe loved, the old man and I detested, maybe hated, the kid, whoever he was, that jacked him. But I didn't know anything about the kid, really, so maybe I just hated him at that moment. That's all I could say. Oh. And then I hated Robin in the moment, too, the cya observer, innocent and clean by uninvolvement.

But my lens wasn't trustworthy, isn't. I may have hated myself, too, just for the hell of it, and was only trying to save Cyrus in some crazy hope to get shot, stabbed, whatever. I cannot say. I like to think I was good, but I truly didn't know. Wherever I stood on the spectrum of humanity was a straight-up mystery. There was nothing to do in the relentless silence of the stripped church but contemplate problems infinitely bigger than my lowly self, so I lay down in the pew farthest from the pulpit, right under a sign that read SEVEN DAYS WITHOUT JESUS MAKES ONE WEAK, used a hymnal for a pillow, and fell asleep.

The cops came in the early morn and woke me up. It went down all right, no drama. I came out the church in cuffs and saw behind the menagerie of lights Robin nodding to a husky cop with a pen and a leather-bound notebook: "Yes, yes, yes, yes, yes. . . ."

When I got to court five weeks later, she embellished the case for the state by saying she'd once had a conversation with me where I'd admitted to having fantasized about stomping a man to death with a giant steel-toed boot while a vestal virgin looked on. I laughed aloud, and my attorney clutched my knee under the table. She was playing her crooked part, helpless, with the lisp of a little girl who just lost her front tooth.

Old Cyrus refused to testify against me. In fact, he refused to testify at all. The district attorney, a little red-faced baboon named Espaniola, decided to charge me not only with attempted murder but with trespassing and breaking-and-entering as well. At a downtown English pub called Trials, he tried to turn Cyrus's silence into a win when he told my lawyer over a black-and-tan that, anyway, he couldn't put a foreigner like that on the witness stand. He'd meant a man who spoke English that badly. They already had Robin and her healthy Freudian imagination. But it didn't matter if Cyrus spoke perfect English: he wouldn't roll on someone who helped him. I knew that and so did Espaniola.

I cut a deal where the DA dropped the trespassing, the b-and-e, and reduced the attempted 187 to assault with bodily injury. He offered two years in the pen, no second strike, so I signed on. Before I got shot off on the silver-bullet transport bus for Quentin, Cyrus came to visit me at the county jail. Our visit was less than a minute long. I didn't do any of the talking. Cyrus was dressed in an ironed navy pullover parka, the rim of gray hair on his timeworn gray head was greased and combed, and his beige work slacks flared just a bit at the ankles. He was dabbing on his eye and his nose even as he picked up the phone and nodded courteously, solemnly. He was an old man and I'd made him older.

"You are staying strong," he said, wincing. "We can no longer have the communicating. I was leaving Iran because of men like you. Thank you very much. Good-bye."

"Good-bye," I said.

8

Here Was Prison

HERE WAS PRISON: Keep your back to the wall, your head up, keep
the poisonous mouth shut, remain polite but never weak in gesture,
idiosyncrasy, or posture, keep the trinket of hope contained in your
pocket, never initiate a conversation with a cop, never say a cop is
cool or of some kind of worth or anything close to redemptive or even
necessary, never broadcast your crime as if you were the heir to Billy
the Kid, never leave a stamped envelope unused, unsold, or untraded,
stay with your own race at all times as you have a race indeed and
will be given a race if you're under the politically correct impression
that you don't have a race, don't play cards, eat, or shower with other
races, don't workout anywhere near other races, don't don't especially
don't cut a deal for contraband like weed, heroine, or crystal meth
with other races, don't look into the eye of a member of other races
unless you're in church, in which case you can with a civilian chap-
lain, keep your issues to yourself, keep your date of release to yourself, keep away from those cats who don't have a date of release,
always clean your plate, always drink your milk, always eat your hard-
boiled eggs just like your mother, if you had one, always said, try and
find something solid to read for the vacuous torturous twilight hour

like the harsh winter novels of the Russian masters or the pure struggle poems of the Harlem Renaissance and then finally take one incident that you'll find nowhere in the world but the mad slammer and laugh about it the many days you'll need it like the time a big steroid head named Rambo got knocked the fuck out beneath the pull-up bars by a brotha half his size named Droopy who, without his diploma, GED, or facsimile thereof, shouted, "I'll pop you like a balloon, you muscular dysmorphic mutherfucker!"—*pop!*—because he'd been studying obscure psychological conditions in his spare time.

9

This One Is Clean and Uncalligraphied

THIS ONE IS CLEAN and uncalligraphied, sufficiently lit for late-night reading, newly painted and, most importantly, except for me, unoccupied. I lie down on the steel bunk and try to nap, but my mind refuses the body its rest and starts up again. Cells, American cells, are often nice enough. This is almost my thousandth day officially locked up and I have no doubt that if life relegates me to another thousand for the present insurrection, I won't necessarily be casual about it but I won't bullshit about it either. I like that everything stops. It's a break. If you summoned every techie on the planet, you still couldn't convert this dead time to a video game, a virtual reality. You've just gotta sit back and look at the black screen. Suddenly your inner life, if you still have one, is all that matters. Your wants evaporate, every hour and day you wait and wait and wait and are finally provided through the power of another entity only what you need, sometimes not even that. All else you earn yourself in the hours.

You learn to appreciate the principle of deprivation: *When does the berry break sweeter upon the tongue than when one longs to taste it?* Everyone, especially cops and judges and politicians, especially attorneys and movie moguls and megalomaniacs on cable news,

PhDs, and the intelligentsia—would do well to spend a little time behind bars. Half the New Testament was birthed of a jail cell. Like an institutional retreat, a lock-and-chain sabbatical, you'll be right there with yourself, whatever's still real in there, pure you. Certain celebrities might survive by shouting out their broadcasts through the spaces in the bars, under the crack of the door, to the concrete walls, but they too might capitulate to the invisible forces at work against them, as they're right there in it when the lights go down, right there in the spook of themselves.

The irony I have to accept now or explain to family or future women I date is the charge of a hate crime against a minority, me with one-half Samoan blood, the quintessential American minority. Plus assault and battery and disturbing the peace. I guess I could file a countersuit of hatred, have an arsenal of ambulance-chasing attorneys running their *mulis* off to solicit my Polynesian *muli,* testify at the proceedings that the other party had said I was a "coconuthead," have cousins and aunties show up at the courtroom in garish *ie lavalavas* and colorful leis. When it comes to a jury, image is more important than veracity of story. Their ascribing of verdict is a bit like kids picking football teams on the playground. The blind lady in the flowing gown is losing control of the imbalanced scale in her hand, a goddess drunk on judgment.

Well, so be it. In these times, today's news is out the window before today ends. That'll save me, give me another breath of impure oxygen. I'll wear the scarlet A for a day. The minute they coax me into moral shame, they'll be ushering me out the door—or, rather, flushing me down the toilet for the next momentary load of waste. They won't remember my name. I guess I'm like anyone else out there: guilty. I harbor a capacity to hate. This time they're right.

To calm, redeem, or at minimum keep me busy, I pace for a while, reciting a few odes of Keats, get my persecution complex on and roll into a little street ditty by Tupac, thumping beats off the intransigent wall—*boom, chit, boom*—and somehow segue off that into "I've Just Seen a Face" from *Rubber Soul* of the Fab Four, the twenty-second piano concerto of my man Amadeus, recite a few lines of a Nobel Prize–winning speech, starting with "I feel that this award was not made to me as a man but to my work" and ending with "not for glory and least of all for profit," then stop at the door of my cell and look out the slit of a shatterless window enmeshed in chicken wire.

In the middle of the pod in the jagged shadows, the correctional officer: a big pink ball with a fat chaw in his cheek, leaning back in the swivel chair, two army boots kicked up on the control panel, a bulbous Copenhagen spitter sitting upon a layer of chin on the upper chest, zoning out to the evening news. I have a good angle on the television and can see two thirds of the screen. All the other lights in the cell block are out, but that doesn't mean anyone's sleeping. Along the second tier I see eyes in the corner cells, I see eyes along the ground floor where I'm at, I hear voices echoing through the vents.

The CO's fiddling with something. I can't see what it is, but my safe guess is: edible, processed, packaged, high in trans fats. I'm right: a family-size bag of Spicy Cheetos that the paisas (whom I, according to legal sources tonight, hate) straight-up love. The CO's pawing four or five at once and, without removing the chaw, is slamming the chips into the Antaean mouth, tonguing the fingers.

Is a display like this supposed to imply masculinity? Is that what we men are now: lethargic, overweight, brainless button pushers? A generation of emasculated Playstation fiends encrusted on couches across the country? There are still men out there—*right?*—digging holes and laying brick and pouring cement and driving truck and lifting weights at the gym not for the mirror or the *Maxim* recommendation on how to get women, but to—*what's this?*—be brave and strong in the endurance of pain and to dispense their masculine anger in a socially acceptable venue. I mean, right? We're still out there, us dying men, dying to die for our woman, our child, our cause, whatever it is, and if we can't, then just being strong for them, being strong period, imperturbable in this storm of life.

What a romantic idiot I am. The modern American alpha male snaps his fingers to emphasize a point, lisps his *t*'s and *s*'s, shaves his eyebrows and weeps on television, has three pairs of shoes for Monday. If he's even got a woman, he doesn't fight it out with the mugger; he doesn't whip out his cock and say, "Take a look at this, mutherfucker." The A-male now whips out his cell phone instead, his balls shriveling up into peas in his little tiger-striped G-string, dials 911, lets a cop in a squad car do his birthright duty. All to avoid the scratches on the elbow, the sweat and blood, the lawsuits.

The CO stands and decides to make the rounds. Late-night count. He's a bit shameless, this one, carrying the Spicy Cheetos as he walks, looking into the cells. Halfway down the first tier he stops, digs into the bag of chips, heads back to the control station. So lazy he doesn't even make a complete trip around the block: twenty-five cells, two tiers.

On my toes, I can see the television over the control station. Tonight the lastest scandal: Mayor Gonzales has pilfered funds, pocketed overflow. Took kickbacks from a garbage company meant to clean up the dirty city of San Jo he inherited. Council members are lining up for the kill, circling the blood, hyenas howling in city hall. And to spice up the salsa they're charging him with a felony, the homely yet sexy Carolyn Johnson of Channel 11 News says.

And then there's me—There I am! ("a man whom authorities say interrupted a peaceful march")—being dragged off in cuffs like a bag of potatoes. And there she is ("while we organizers were minding our own business in the quad"), the goddess of wisdom and war shaking her beautiful head at the depraved racism of her brother in peace, pleading into the mic for a better, brighter day despite the badness out there. And there he is ("the brawl resulted in serious injuries to one unidentified"), the nameless paisa on the gurney being wheeled up the ramp of an ambulance, a heart-shaped see-through oxygen mask over his thick mustache and smashed mouth, his hands crossed at the lap of what appears to be a truly relaxed—or truly injured?— illegal immigrant. I get my answer when he puts his hands behind his cowboy hat which, amazingly, is still on his head. The sympathizers clap at his courage. He's cool, kickin' it.

The CO looks back at my cell door and gravely shakes his head at me. Oh, I see. Suddenly we have standards, do we, Mr. Leviathan? Suddenly life matters? Get up there and slip on your soapbox, hypocrite. This guy should thank me for my insurrections with the law, he should treat me with respect: Without me and men like me he wouldn't get a fat-ass check each week cut by the Governator himself of sixty-five plus guaranteed g's a year for pressing buttons and counting sleeping bodies.

He's still looking over at my cell. Maybe his muscles have atrophied so badly he can't move his monstrous head back to its original position. Like everything else about him, there's a dinosaur age between movement. He points at me and then down to the ground. I know what he wants but I won't give it to him.

He does it again—pointing in my direction, then at the floor— but I've got my rights: I can more or less do as I please in here as long as it's not (1) flooding the toilet, (2) shorting lights, (3) smoking or slamming anything into veins, (4) shouting out threats, (5) sawing on the bars, (6) masturbating, (7) fornicating or fighting with my cellie, (8) blocking the window with cardboard from the lunches, (9) getting naked. I ain't sitting down. Just like him, I'll never get the fuck back up if I do. Plus I want to see him stand up, put the chips down, get off his fleshy backside, and do some work.

Just as he's pushing himself off the chair, I hear the outer steel door in the sally port slam, and that means more cops or more inmates or more both. Over the desk radio the confirmation: more inmates—the midnight cranksters and restroom perverts and barroom brawlers rounded up and herded in tonight in the city of San José and its flanking suburbs. He plops back down into his chair, forgetting me at least for the moment, looks back at the sally port and flicks a switch, which at the same time activates a buzz sound heard in every cell.

The doors to the block open, and in come five, six, seven, eight guests in their loose, saggy orange issues and dog-eared plastic sandals, all carrying the generous accouterments of the county: one mattress, one towel, one ten-cent shaving kit, one Tylenol. Trying like hell not to stand out, even at 2:24 in the morning, hyper aware of each other, of us ghosts behind the shatterless glass, looking like sheep in the field with their dirty noses in each other's asses.

He gives the new arrivals an order and they follow it, finding a steel chair each. One cat drops to the floor and falls asleep. He looks vaguely familiar. The CO says, "Hey." He starts to snore and another inmate with swastikas on his cheeks and forehead and over the bald white scalp puts his foot under the guy's chin and balances it on his toe, this Zinedine Zidane with his soccer ball. The CO watches, amused. The guy on the floor wakes up with his fists in a foist position, though he's still on his back, wild-eyed, the Nazi Zuzu's foot sliding up his face. It looks like the crankster I'd slapped in the Jack-in-the-Crack.

The CO says, "Go sleep your fix off in there, you burnout," pointing to my cell.

The cell door clicks and in comes my cellie. It's the crankster, all right, but he's got no clue where he's at. He doesn't know who I am because he doesn't even know I'm in here. Christmas-tree hair matted on his head, he's already starting to fall. The walls catch him. He crumples down right at the base of the door, his head smashes into the steel toilet, and he's out. I arrive upon an idea I hadn't thought of before when he hit me up for a meal: I don't want to get too close to the guy: hep B, hep C, West Nile, staph, avian flu, typhoid fever, consumption, the black plague, cooties—you never know what kind of rebellion some microorganism is staging in the sickly immune systems of our have-nots. He's breathing, and that's good enough for me. Tomorrow I'll walk around the cell with a shirt scarf across my face, the anti-germ Jesse James look. Maybe he'll have forgotten our little encounter. With cranksters anything's a possibility. If the CO lets us into the dayroom tomorrow, I'll read a book for the stretch, even a crock book from a crock writer, I'll play bones with the brothas, run a game of gin rummy with the Asians, sling a handball with the *eses,* all to avoid this bacterial breeding ground of a cellie and his unlikely memory recall.

But this ain't that bad: he's better than a cellie I'd have to talk to, listen to, convince myself each long minute of the long day not to whip into shape. And believe it or not, this guy is helping me, man, he's actually helping me. When someone is so high on life he's unconscious, it's like: What's the point? Don't break him down. Don't throw him into the bottomless pit of comparison. Who cares if he wakes you up and shouts, "Didn't you bitch-slap me once in the Burger King?" You just say, "I never been to that joint in my life, mu'fucker," and let him struggle with the image. Whatever goes down, so be it, it's going down, that's it. Maybe *way* down. I put my nose up to the humming vent so I don't catch any of his shit and take in the dusty cold air to my lungs, wrap myself up in the gray wool blanket, a human burrito, use the palms of my hand as a pillow, just like the happy paisa on the gurney, no complaints. Then I take my cellie's lead and convince myself—*just take it, man, and shut the fuck up*—not to think about anything, not even nothing.

10

I Am Dreaming About the Loss of Blood

I AM DREAMING about the loss of blood when over the PA in our cell a voice says, "Tusifale. Pack your bags."

I know I'm not OR'd, released on Own Recognizance, so someone must have bailed me out. And I know that with an assault charge and a hate crime to match, the bail had to exceed fifty g's. Neither of my folks would know where I'm at, and big sister Tali wouldn't put up the cash even if she had a million bucks. Her husband would, though. All anyone has to do to get old Gaelic McLaughlin digging into his personal stash is drop a few Samoan words his way and remind him of the integral unit of Samoan culture, the *aiga,* the family. All the guilt that McLaughlin has over not being Samoan would then rise to the fore and he can parlay through another strange day in his weird little world of cultural denial.

When I first met McLaughlin, I saved him. I was at an afterparty of a local *halau,* a hula dance-off between competing troupes of Philipinas, Portuguese, Puerto Ricans, and Tongans. I'm sure the Hawaiians, who weren't there, would have appreciated the very Polynesian get-together, both in timbre and proportion: much love and music and aloha in the air, much grinds and drinks and inflated stories about the islands to be bellied. It was all good three hours into the little *hukilau* when a cousin of mine, Aleki, arrived from Daly City in red rags and looped earrings, his homeboy, Lafa, tagging along, dragging his feet. They said, "Wassup, Paulo," we hit each other's knuckles, I saw the cloud of weed in their eyes, smelled the Olde English on their breaths, and they went inside the house. I should have left. But if I'd left I would've never met my future in-law.

McLaughlin arrived with another of my cousins, Malia, on his bony white arm. He had on an aloha shirt circa 1965, Don Ho, and about six or seven leis up to his nose and the bottom of his ear, so that his head was slightly tilted backward, like an old lord of the manor overlooking his labor force. He wore Bermuda shorts that betrayed his bony white knees and slippas that said SURFAH on the plastic loop. I'd seen his kind before, white people raised around Polynesians who deify being down for the brown. Who love the alchemy of a people who combine brute force with an inherently gentle and generous nature. It was a little sad to me. You knew they could never be what they wanted to be, it was impossible, like a blind man who idolizes fighter pilots. But you could see this guy was going to get as close to the jet as he could, even if just for a powerless ridealong where he could feel the torque of the g forces at work on his guts. My cousin, who wasn't the smallest of women (five-eight, 210 pounds), but was average size for a Poly, was nowhere near the doctor's chart for her height (145 pounds). She was throwing McLaughlin around like a raggedy doll—very much, in fact, like a copilot in the cockpit an F-15—and he straight loved it. He was on his way to romance with Malia, joint damage and whiplash.

Even that was all good until someone shouted out, "Go grab some grinds," and they went up the steps and inside the house to get a plate of *kalua* pig, *tako poke,* Hawaiian kimchi and mac salad. Three minutes later, McLaughlin was flying out the door, his body parallel to the earth, hands extended outward like some crash test dummy, the leis nowhere in sight; over the steps he went and down, tumbling across the cement, centrifugal speed sending him into a face-first collision with the mismatched planks of the fence. The cheap wood initially took the force of the blow, wobbling, and then in a long second where I could envision the ensuing scene, it toppled over into the neighbor's yard.

I knew what was going down. McLaughlin had just been body-tossed by Aleki or Lafa. I didn't know why. I'd watched Malia get down before and I knew she would have been on top of him a little faster. I would have heard her first. They all spilled out the house: Malia piggyback on Lafa, yanking on his neck in a headlock, Aleki pulling on Malia. They looked like a World Wrestling Organization special. In mid-choke, the severed leis in his hands, Lafa stomped toward McLaughlin. So it was Lafa who was probably interested in Malia, the Poly prize of poor McLaughlin.

He came from Los Altos Hills, a haven for old aristocrats, a place where the estates have no fences and everything down in the valley is disposable. Whatever's not thrown out is exotic. Malia took McLaughlin to Filipino cockfights, Samoan-Tongan rugby matches, overnight *umus* roasting pigs and turkeys and tritip underground with lava rocks, banana leaves, chicken wire, and soaked burlap sacks. When it came down to it, she'd protected him, or at least laundered him past the bulls of these parades. But I guess the noxious cloud of South City *indo* got in the way, and McLaughlin finally had to pay the price for his girl.

I don't know why, really, but I stepped in on his behalf. "*Fakali,* Lafa!" I said. "Calm down, man."

"I'll kill you, you punk-ass *palagi!*"

Palagi means white boy, though with a certain intonation of anger it's closer to cracker. McLaughlin jumped behind me and I said, "Hey. Lafa. Calm down, *uso.* This guy's harmless, man."

"Paulo! Step aside. I'm gonna kill this fool!"

"Nah," I said.

"Say what?"

"Nope. Sorry, *uso*. It ain't going down like that."

Everything stopped, Lafa and Fatu exchanged glances, I stepped forward half a step more, and from that point on I knew neither mutherfucker would ever say a kind word about me to anyone. Would call me half-breed, *afakasi*, and white boy behind my back. South City, Daly City, San Bruno, anyone on the Peninsula crossing paths with these cats would hear a salted version of my treachery. Not only that. If something serious ever went down and I needed a little help from my brothers, it wouldn't be from them. Even Malia was a little surprised. It was all good if she looked out for her lay, but me, blood cousins with one of the aggressors, to whom she herself was also family?

That kind of shit, her eyes were telling me, *will get a man shot up in this mutherfucker. You know that.*

I don't care one bit, I told her back with my eyes. *Not one bit about the lucky bullet.*

So after Malia right-crossed McLaughlin later that night for not defending her, I set him up with my sister, Tali. Six weeks later they were married. Six months later, they had little Toby. No one but me did the math: my little neutered nephew with none of poor McLaughlin's blood. What's strange now is that they dress the kid up in *ie lavalavas* at my sister's insistence, even though he's whiter than his considerably white father, even though neither he, the kid, nor they, the parents, speak a lick of Samoan, even though Tali, in behavior and personality, lost or forewent her Samoan blood long ago.

My father left this country with his fluent Samoan and never came back. You could say this country killed my father's soul, killed our family. But some people would say, and have said, that it was a just killing. The USA birthed it, the USA buried it, that's the way it goes. But I knew it would happen years before it did, I knew it as a nine-year-old hope-filled kid. Our family was always looming beneath the wings of disappointment. My father couldn't accept that there were many options when it came to behavior, that everything is up for discussion in America. Could be good, could be bad, could be neither. Each second he spent here was potential trouble. When he went back to Samoa during my seventh-grade year, a part of me was relieved. He's in the right place. My father being here was a mistake and maybe I, by inference, or by byproduct, am a mistake as well.

You know how it is with immigrants, I mean true immigrants from anywhere in the world except Western Europe: They calibrate all things by death; they come from places where the possibility of death, the likelihood of it, governs all action. Life was serious to my father, is. Now he's not displaced, his ideas aren't outdated. Every morning he wakes up at dawn and hauls his laundry to the beach to wash in the ocean water on the reef. Before he'd even shown up in America, the eternal bonds of death, God, and love were being put to the chopping block. But he married my mother under the auspices of all three: he didn't want the child, Tali, to die in the womb as all my mother's nipping American friends had wanted, he believed God would condemn him to hell if he didn't meet his duties as a man, and so he forced or forged love in his heart for a woman he'd only known for four weeks and a few days. That kind of purity of code gets diced up in the land of opportunity.

He lost everything with us. He'd come from a *matai* family of generational royalty, eight hundred underlings in the clan. When my grandfather, his father, died, five thousand people paid their respects over the course of a week. His obituary was in *USA Today*. My father landed in your average American suburb, the swallower of indigenous tales.

But this is not his story, or even the story of my mother. How could it be? They had their shot. No, this is my reluctant story, and I could give a fuck about my empty palms and pockets. What worries me is this empty heart, panicky muscle that's asphyxiating me softly.

II

The Cell Pops

THE CELL POPS, but before I step out the door I drop a flattened cardboard from a leftover box lunch on the chest of my KO'd crankster cellie. I hope he has the smarts to investigate. His upcoming time in jail depends on it. To see the one word I've written and retraced across the cardboard over and over, right there in waxy lead. I want him to feel the connection to life that I never quite feel when someone tells me they're sorry. I want him to wake up and feel like he's lucked into contrition for the weak, suspect, fucked-up condition we're all in, jail or not, addict or not, truly sorry or not.

I get processed out by a Japanese cop whose badge reads I. Kai and there she is: Beatrice La Dulce Shaliqua Schneck. She shakes her head and I smile. She's embarrassed and won't talk to me. It's a rather nice continuation of the silence that won't last.

"Now what's this shit," she finally says, as we hit the road, "'bout you not digging Mexicaners?"

I yawn right through it, lesson number one and one million from my last nine-hour gift of an anonymous cellie: Be a z-catcher in the face of the senseless.

"I said," she says, "what is this funky shit about you having racial attitudes towards my brown brothers?"

"Just what you said." I lean the seat back to partial recline. "Shit."

Suddenly she goes soft, takes my hand. "You don't like the little Mexicaners, baby?"

"Who cares if I do or don't? Are you a Mexicaner? I mean, what the fuck is a Mexicaner, anyway?"

"You the one charged with the hate crime, not me!"

"I mean, what are you, a Haitian hick? What the fuck kind of politic is that, girl?"

"We never liked them back home!"

"And what about now?"

"Now? Oh. Well. We tolerate 'em."

"Hah. Don't preach to me, bitch."

"Who you calling bitch? I just paid five g's to get your hate-criming ass out of jail! You better recognize!"

"Oh, I recognize all right. I hear Mr. Don King himself."

"Oooooh. I don't care for that electroshock-looking nigga."

"Only in America—that's his line—only in America will you find two-time second-degree murderer-Republican promo men like his black ass, white suburban crips raised in two-story houses with black-bottomed pools, Christian Jews, mainstream porn stars who wage in on politics, capitalistic Buddhists, a Haitian refugee bigot. Mexicaner? Sounds like a fucking combo meal at Taco Bell."

"Oooooh, baby! He back! My wild Samoan pony is back! Gimme some sugar! Some ten-dollar magic! Some dynamo!"

"What the fuck is dynamo?"

"Gimme some of that LeRoi Jones Fellowship, baby!"

"You lionizing me?" I say in my most ebonicized voice. "Okay. Hear me roar:

Life is but a walking shadow,
a po' playah who struts and frets

his hour upon the stage
and then is heard no mo'.
It is a tale told by Beatrice La Dulce
     Sh-Sh-Sh-Shaliqua Schneck,
full of sound and fury,
signifying nada."

"That's deep, love."

"I'm sure Sir Willie Shakes would appreciate the compliment."

"He a rapper?"

"Or the idiot would."

"Got a new place, baby."

"'Bout time you left that shit city."

"What's wrong with Milpitas?"

"Where you live now?"

"Not in Motel City, honey."

"Ouch. If I cared about what you said, little girl, I'm sure it would sting." We're approaching the border of Eastside San Jo, where La Dulce first lived when she moved from Miami. She never talks about Florida. It's like her life as an American started on the West Coast. "We going to the Eastside?"

"Please," she says. "I only climb, honey."

"What do you climb on?"

"You lucky, sucker, I'm even gonna let your dirty ass set foot in the estate."

"Estate?"

"So you wanna move in, baby?"

"With the esteemed lady of the house?"

"Who the fuck else, nigga?"

"Do I have an option, nigga?"

"Hell no you don't. You know that."

"Then absolutely."

I want La Dulce to stop the car so I can give the ungracious ho the old heave-ho: back to the ghetto you go with all your Mexicaner brothers and sisters! It's not that I'd celebrate her misfortune, if it in fact would be misfortune (she'd still be alive, she'd still have a strong and bouncy and well-fed booty, she'd have access at every streetlight to cutting-edge hip-hop shimmering out the windows of tricked-out lowriders and mini-trucks); it's just that this tapping of her bank account might behoove La Dulce in the spiritual realm: a return to the immigrant American pseudo-squalor from which she came could resuscitate some latent muscle memory of humility. She treats every human being that crosses her radar as if s/he's applied on a résumé to be a bootlicker, of her boots, and that the farthest you can climb up the tier of promotion is the midsection, her midsection, where you'd be tonguing the same task, king/queen of her sweet and sour mound of love.

I guess she's obsessed with me because I'm neither. She doesn't want to admit it, but if it came down to categorization she's *my* bootlicker—or slipper licker—as well as my midsection licker, not because I've asked for it or even sought it out (though it is nice at times, her warm wet tongue and plump Haitian lips working instead of talking), but because she's volunteered it, almost forced it into play. She's like a red light turning green: you walk across the street. Who knows where it stems from at her end? Some strange tendency of the slave owner to sympathize with the slave so much she hands over the whip for a day. I could do with or without La Dulce, and it destroys her.

We get off 101 at Santa Clara Street, right next to Five Wounds, the old golden, magisterial, Portuguese cathedral. They're all out there—about a hundred parishioners or so—with the maroon flags of Portugal snapping in the wind, dressed in Adidas slippers, Adidas shorts, Adidas windbreakers, maroon soccer jerseys with the names

Ronaldo, Deco, and Figo in yellow letters across the back, obviously not on their way to mass. And they're chanting. And seem to be drunk. It's only nine in the morning, you can still hear the birds.

Some firecrackers pop off in the lot across the street at the Prasad Island Market, where sometimes my pops would buy Samoan food—*fa'i, taro, ulu, povi*—from a little bearded Lebanese hustler drowning in an *ie lavalava,* who'd always yell out *Talofa!* when we'd walk in. I hunch, thinking, *Gunshots.* Cheers go up. We're at the stoplight to cross the bridge over the freeway. La Dulce doesn't seem to notice the festivities: she unzips my jeans, bends down, and licks my boot.

"Hey, hey, hey."

Now she's really going at it, but I can't respond. We're in the middle of a fucking Portuguese Pride Parade, for chrissake. A few soccer balls are being kicked around, and now I remember: World Cup, 2006. Portugal just beat someone on the other side of the world. Advanced to the next round.

I say, "It's a green light."

"They turn you queer in eight hours?"

"Yeah. Let me out. I gotta go find my street corner."

"You nasty," she says, sitting up.

"I'm nasty? It's fucking green. Just do your job and drive."

La Dulce rolls the window down and shouts, "This ain't Lisbon, you dumb Portugees!"

We zoom off over the bridge and down Alum Rock, its ruined lanes unreadable, and there are paisas at every street corner, on bikes, on scooters, at bus stops, taquerias with *futbol* posters of Mexico vs. Argentina over the door, signs diverting traffic around mounds of gravel that have been uprooted and left in the sun, *pho* houses stuffed with Vietnamese hunched over their steaming bowls of noodles and rice, and straggler whites using forks and talking (you can tell even from outside) way too loud, and beauty salons proprietored by women named Tiffany Le and Michelle Nguyen, their names in English and Vietnamese detailed in flowery pink paint on the windows, a Dunkin' Donuts with no one in it, a triangular eyesore still called Wienerschnitzel, Walgreen's, 76, 7-Eleven, the bright yellow foothills in the nearing horizon rising slower than the sun.

We get to Capitol Expressway and go right. We're heading out toward South San Jo, Morgan Hill, Gilroy, middle- and upper-middle-class suburbs. So much for my fancy of Shaliqua in the chains of poverty. I should have known better, this one's more than a survivor, she's a straight rodent. I kind of respect that about her: Whenever the big bomb hits, if you're still around, look and listen for Beatrice La Dulce Shaliqua Schneck and get fast on her hard-shelled heels. She'll find you water and shade and maybe even love before you've uttered a single word of complaint.

Now we're climbing the dry, quiet, colorless San José foothills, and somehow La Dulce has been infected by the ambiance. It sounds silly to say but it's nice, the silence—peaceful—maybe because it's unexpected with the present company in the present age. Isn't a cell phone supposed to go off somewhere, or a thousand of them, beepers, horns, Slim Shady's croaking voice from an eight-year-old's iPod? You suck it all in knowing it won't last, not with the likes of the Haitian hurricane sitting next to you. La Dulce is the embodiment of the old admonition in Proverbs: she speaketh words without wisdom. If La Dulce were eight years old she'd be the ADHD poster child, you'd hear her mouth on a six-mile radius. I've learned that it's better not to contemplate the intricacies of her quietude, just to go with it, in the same way one accepts a week of free cable television.

I hope. . . .

I hope. . . .

I hope she stays shut.

There are big two-story houses in grapevine rows on the apex of the nearest hill, all the same color, gray with dark brown trim, en-

closed by a mile of faux-concrete walls parallel to the road, eight feet
tall, or eight feet short. You get the sense that they could be higher
and, with eventual funding, will be. It's like these people are expecting barbarians for lunch. The alligator moat and the king's archers
will be the next topic of discussion at the Tuesday meeting. We reach
a left-turn signal and pull up under an iron placard: Silver Creek
Estates. At the tollbooth, a Punjabi in a turban and a Goodwill
security guard outfit stands. "Hello, Ms. Snake."

It's Singh from the 7-Eleven where the big immigrant fight went
down earlier this month. I lean across La Dulce's lap and say, "What's
up, Singh?"

He doesn't recognize me. Why would he? I just bought Chewy
Sweetarts two or three times a week from him for under a year. He
nods anyway, clearly not remembering our little chats. I know what
I was to him: our conversations about the Punjabi folk hero who'd
held his own severed head like a lantern in the dark as he cut down
a thousand invading Hindus were no more than an immigrant's
manner of talking himself sane at the end of a sixteen-hour shift.
And then, from my end, I hadn't thought about the guy's welfare in
a month. There was a mutuality of nil at play. All I can really say is
that his beard was a little thicker, a little longer, and it's nice to see
him moving up in the world, as that's what he'd no doubt wanted,
what he came here for.

"Hey, buddy," he says.

"Way to go, Singh. Dig the threads. Nicely done, bro."

La Dulce looks at me like she should be introduced and for just
that reason I lean back to my side of the car and say nothing. Turning to Singh, she says, "The name's Schneck. You ain't saying it
proper. You gotta get the *sh* in there, man."

"*Sh*," says Singh, nodding. "*Sh*."

"*Neck*."

"*Neck*."

"Now say it: Schneck."

He flexes his jaw muscles behind the beard. "Snake."

"No. Listen, man: Schhhneck."

"Ssssnake."

"All right, nigga. You call me La Dulce."

"La Doosh," he says.

"Goddammit!"

"Just call her lady," I say.

"Okay, my friend," he says, happy with the compromise. The orange-striped gate rises, he calls out, "Good-bye, lady!" and we drive through.

"That A-rab never gets my shit right."

"He ain't Arab," I say.

"Do I give a fuck, Mr. Hate Crime? Do I look like I care?" I slap the side of her ass and she perks up. "Hmmm," she hums, leaning toward her window and pushing it out at me.

We make our way down the vacant streets, each named after a local tree: Pine, Elm, Magnolia. Genius! Ours is the only vehicle on Pine, Elm, Magnolia, just as we are the only visible people. I know where all the neighbors are. The place is as hollow as a Hollywood set: you get out of the car, walk over to an "estate," lean up against the wall, and fall right through the paper. The streets are wide, clean, unused. There are no kids tossing Nerf balls around or skipping rope, no youths on bikes or scooters, no parents on the porches in lawn chairs, no barbecues at the sides of the houses, no one shooting hoop in the driveways, no Wiffle ball games. In fact, all the driveways are empty, not just of people but of cars, of oilstains. And all the garages are closed, every one of them. The private community of Silver Creek isn't new, but it looks new—or rather: untouched. It's like the silence I'd praised ten minutes ago at the base of the hill is now showing how it, too, can be ugly. Yet the citizens here have retreated to private quarters of their own volition. Everyone's inside the air-

conditioned "estate," keeping the contract to stay away from one another for a fat mil each. I haven't been inside one Silver Creek estate, but I know this.

"Real communal place," I say.

"I'll show you communal," she purrs.

I'm zoning again, tripping out on the strange place that is twenty-
first-century America, identical cardboard domiciles on a private hill,
when she hits a button on her steering wheel. Before us a countour
of blackness grows from the ground up, ending in a black rectangle
the size of a carport. We pull into the blackness itself, haven't even
killed the engine before the automatic door is closing on the sun-
light and the sheen of the houses in the rearview mirror.

So we're in the box. I know what's next: I'm in *her* box. We forni-
cate on the front seat of the car in the empty garage, thousands of
blind amenable eyes we'll never see surrounding us.

12

I'm in the House

I'm in the house for thirteen days, floating. Everything's so damned clean you wanna buy a four-legged pet to shit in the middle of the living room, just to mix things up a bit. You can't help but think of all the filthy images in your head—a greasy restaurant alleyway between Ginza and Gombei in Japantown, an issue of *Penthouse* magazine—almost with pride. Somehow this kind of sanctity seems ignoble. Every corner of the house is cool: wisps of refrigerated air tickle your feet, slide along the back of your neck like the first touch in a movie theater, swirl above your head. There's not a mite or a flea in sight. You can lie down on the couch, the rug, on the sparkling kitchen floor; you can lie down anywhere you want. You can eat off a plate, the floor, same difference. There are entertainment centers in the living room, on the patio, upstairs in La Dulce's room, hulking speakers on polished oak, miniature honor bars, everything designed to keep you inside the house forever.

Each day I wake in midmorning and she's gone off on some secret rendezvous on the other side of the Bay. She leaves me Odwalla tangerine juice and cold but cooked blueberry pancakes for breakfast, stationary notes with her four-name name in a fancy header that say, insensibly, *The muse wants some dynamo, baby,* or, *All work and no play makes Jack a dull boy,* a lipstick kiss as signature. Almost two weeks I give her nothing. I can't write a line of anything in this fluff. I've the house to myself, but most of my time is spent curling up in some hidden corner of the couch, sleeping in the buff for hours, or interviewing myself—Charlie Rose, Brian Lamb—on current political issues.

La Dulce is a woman of habit. When she's about to go to wherever she goes, she wants it. When she gets back from wherever she's been, she wants it. And it's always in the garage. I readily provide it, parcel it out with booty slaps and nasty lingo and slow draw. I'm like a steady server in a soup line. She loves it, she nibbles on my ear, shreds the skin of my back with her cheesy dragon nails. All the in-between time, we're platonic, though that doesn't mean we're quiet or in accordance. It just means we don't fuck. And that we're anywhere except in the garage. I have no clue what I'm doing here, though that's hardly a new state of mind.

Today I lose all the threads except for my *ie lavalava,* which La Dulce calls my Samoan skirt. She's almost home so I wash a few dishes, empty a trash can in the living room. I stretch out in what I imagine to be a version of the lotus position, wind down, and think of myself as a delicate flower in the breeze. The pads of my feet don't even come close to touching when I hear, "I want you to die, bitch!"

I pop up, jump to my feet. Don't know why—*I do know why:* If all the windows and doors are closed, if the garage is shut, if La Dulce is gone, someone else is in the fucking house! I walk toward the vast hall on the east end of the estate, realizing that there's a section I seem to have forgotten about. I walked through it the first day and never returned. It's furnished lightly—a hutch with faux china lining the shelves, a framed photo of MLK in D.C.—with the same white short-fibered carpet crawling through it. There are three rooms, two with doors open. One is a weight room with a Sears treadmill, dip/pull-up bars, and standing mirrors; the other a re-spectable library with an emphasis on black American authors. The place appears empty. That's why I haven't been down this way. I approach the third door, which is shut, and hear, "You whore! You goddamned whore!"

I put my ear to the door and don't hear any sound of struggling or argument: no one's being beaten. I do hear keys being struck, the kind of keys on a computer keyboard. Someone's playing video games or maybe answering e-mail? Should I wait for La Dulce to return? She never mentioned a boarder, a roommate, another body in this place. Finally, not out of concern, really, but out of the minimal curiosity that springs from boredom, I open the door.

It looks like a strategy room of the FBI. All three walls are en-veloped in graphs and charts and facial photographs and partially and totally nude full-body photographs and women like my dead cousin in creepy positions, their ankles behind their ears, looking back at me over their shoulders, some with disturbing trepidation, some with disturbing bravado. Upon closer investigation, the graphs are body parts with a number next to it: *tits 8, pussy 7, ass 4, face 6, stomach 4, legs 8*. And then there's another number, the sum of the body parts: 37.

There's a microwave in one corner, a hot plate atop it, at least thirty Mickey D's cheeseburgers on the corner of the desk, case upon case of Coca-Colas stacked as high as my shoulders. Top ramen packets, unopened, everywhere. An industrial-sized garbage can to my im-mediate right overflowing with empty cans and crumpled wrappers. The windows are shut, the blinds are closed, the rug is worn down in selective areas. The bed is not made, the sheets are yellowed. Musk. Stench. An opened door leads to the bathroom. There are cameras in each corner of the ceiling, hanging in midair like sleep-ing bats, the eye of each on the chair in the middle of the room where a young man sits, his back to me. He's slamming away on the keyboard like a novelist trying to get the scene out, every last word. He still hasn't turned, and does not even stop to look up when I'm standing right behind him, my reflection on the screen. He's written one message: BITCH. U R EVIL. DIE.

"Hey, man," I say.

He doesn't say a word, punches SEND, starts drumming his fingers with one hand, reaches out with the other, grabs a Coke, eyes on the screen, mouths the lip, lifts it, doesn't get a drop. There's a reason: it's not open. I feel no inclination at all to tell him. It's hard to discern his cultural background from behind: He's in a v-neck T-shirt and Donald Duck boxers and the skin that I can see looks like it's never been outdoors. A little bell rings on the computer, the screen flashes, and a new message appears: U R THE BITCH, BITCH. AND WHEN U DIE, I'LL JUST FIND ME ANOTHER BITCH. BYE-BYE, BITCH. (smiley face).

"Oooohh, that's dirty," he says.

He breaks open the Coke, which fizzles on the stuffy air, leans back, downs the drink, and tosses the can behind him. It lands in the general vicinity of the garbage can. He slams down on his keys, breathing hard during the task. The new message says: BITCH, I'LL FIND ME 20 BY MIDNIGHT 2NITE: (20 smiley faces).

He hits SEND and I say, "Hey. Why don'tchu open some windows, man?"

He says nothing, glued to the screen, waiting.

"The world's burning up, man. The Middle East is in flames. War and death are at the doorstep."

War?

Death?

He wouldn't know a thing about it. This is his war. This is his death. It's all in the brain: the unseen enemy, the cerebral whirlpool. Mind without culture.

Now he's chewing off his nails, spitting them out the side of his mouth as if they were seed shells at a ballpark. To the left of the chair there's a little pile of assorted chunks of epidermis and discarded or regurgitated food. I bend over to get a closer look and find fingernails, skin, uprooted hair of the wiry pubic version, pieces of (I think, hope) ground beef, pickles.

The bell rings again, the screen flashes, and there she is, a rear view of her spread-open backside, and nothing else, plunged into the screen. Close up the shadows of black and gray are almost entities unto themselves, a daguerreotype jawline, wings of birds, midnight roads, all leading to or rising from the darkest region in the middle of the screen. At the bottom of her bottom the message reads: TAKE A LAST LOOK, BITCH. HOPE 4 YUR SAKE YUR SAVE FILES AIN'T FULL. NEVER AGAIN (a middle-finger 4ever).

He immediately pokes himself through the urine hole in his Donald Duck boxers and starts stroking his boot which, in its vast girth and longness, shouldn't belong to an infertile mutherfucker like this, and as it finally grows to full capacity, he reaches over to another Coke can, pops it, mid-stroke, and takes a shot. I feel like a perv in a bathroom stall glued to his black peephole. I look over my shoulder, as if La Dulce is about to walk in and shout, "Aha! I knew it, nigga, I knew it!" As if there's a cop with cuffs behind me, or Singh of the housing authority and the Goodwill badge, shaking his head sadly at this latest example of American decay.

I see instead Olde English lettering over the door, cut in a slab of lacquered oak, an assignment from junior high woodshop: *The Babe Lair*.

I turn back around and he's at full throb, pinching the base so that the meaty knob expands like a wild mushroom. He fingers a few keys on the board, still choking the blood of his boot, and I hear the dangling cameras above coming to life. Suddenly on the computer screen there are four aerial angles of the boot, so exact in image that you can see the purple veins running through it, and he reaches out and hits SAVE, retucks the boot into his boxers, takes a sip of Coke, types in SAME GOES FOR U, BITCH (a middle finger 4 eternity plus 1) and hits SEND.

In the end, I heard tell, all the children will go insane.

From here on out, there's no going back. We're on a one-trek course to self-destruction. It's about the bile now, the fluid, the image. Make love? Romance? A bed in the tropics with vanilla silk sheets cloaked by fragrant petals of red roses? What's the point? The church was right: *Manus stuprare,* defilement of the hand, is the moral end of man. Of woman, too.

The Babe Lair? More like the Masturbation Station. The Embalmed Palm.

I don't know why, but I start to make vows of abstinence, of never touching another woman unless I've a heart-and-soul commitment, not only from her but of me. Let us spin back, my darling, *la mia ragazza bella,* against all those libertine hairballs on acid spinning their palms to the sky in the late sixties: true and total sexual liberty is a flopping fish choking on the oxygen. We're a decade away from permanent insulation, of never touching another body.

He's got his hard dick in a greasy hand again, a new erogenous zone on the screen, the chair on two legs, no real light anywhere to be seen.

I have a flash dream of stepping forward with gritted teeth and short breath, reaching out for a good grip on his light-brown locks of tangled hair, digging into the root, lifting his way-too-light ass off the chair. Half my torso and all his head on the screen, connected in cyberspace alas. Squirming now, his mouth in a bottomless concave of horror. He's returning to a flaccid state, and his scrunched-up eyebrows look like the crankster in the Jack-in-the-Crack but worse, as in: *The real world is so mean on the senses, isn't it?*

He doesn't turn around. I'm not here.

I walk out of the room, cross the flawless steam-cleaned rug of this strange *domitae naturae*. Open the door connecting the kitchen to the empty box of the garage and unlock and peek out of it as if there were goblins and fairies on the other side, and when the hot light hits my eyes and La Dulce pulls into the space, I step out blindly. The garage door is already shutting, the assembly-line hum and growing darkness womblike, and I lean into the open window on the driver's side of the car.

"There's someone living in your house."

She turns over and shows me her naked ass, looks back over her shoulder. Beatrice La Dulce Shaliqua Schneck's been driving around in the buff, big shock.

"Wanna play, Daddy?"

"No."

She lifts one leg over her head, almost kicking out the windshield, and says, "Are you sure, baby?"

"Yeah," I say. "I'm sure."

"You sure as shit," she says, suddenly covering herself as if I've walked in on her in the little girls room.

"That's sure enough for me," I say, thinking, *Beyotch*.

"Well," she says, fumbling with and sliding into a leopard-print g, "go ahead."

"Who's that freak down there?"

"Where?"

"Downstairs."

"That's my son."

"So that's him?"

"Yeah."

"He don't look Haitian to me," I say.

"He ain't. Willie African-American."

Here we go. Is he Libyan or Sudanese or Zulu or Pygmy or Moroccan? Does he speak Kru or Somali or Dinca or Afrikaans?

African-American? What a joke on our human cargo history. Every-thing is sensitively washed away—the residual guilt, the ancient suffering—by the encapsulation of an entire continent into one catch-all PC term. Same thing with our sweeping up the five hundred tribes into Native American. I prefer the term Indian: at least there the error of arrival is elucidated for debate.

I say, "Is he an Egyptian or what? King Tut's kid?"

"No, fool. He Willie. That's it."

I'm suddenly encouraged by a possible display of tact: maybe we fuck only in the garage because her son shouldn't see or hear that kind of behavior. Right? That's nice and retro. Maybe even a little motherly, a rarity for La Dulce.

I think about the harem of images Willie has in his head. "Aren't you concerned that he never comes out of his room?"

"We don't fight no more. 'Cause we don't talk. So the longer he stays in there, the better."

"I don't think it's for the better." I can see it hurts her to hear this. "How long has it been?"

"Nine months."

"What?"

"Same amount of time I carried him around in my belly."

"How is that even possible?"

"He got a door in the bathroom, leads to the yard. Buys fast food with a trust account his father left him. No school, no job, no nothing."

"As long as he stays in that room, he might as well be in Africa."

"That's what I just said, fool."

I lightly slap at the mocha globe of her ass, our lone connection. "How come we get busy in the garage and that's it?"

"I don't wanna dirty up the house. Gotta live in the damned thing. You want a little bit of that backside, my sweet Samoan pancake?"

"This whole thing is fucked up."

"Well whatchu want then, nigga?"

Where do I start? I want time to stop. Right here, right now. So I can figure one little problem out for good. It doesn't have to be a big one, but it needs to be definitive, it has to be something I believe in. That I don't question. That I don't debone in the meat grinder of analysis. By the time I'm finished with an idea, there's nothing to cook, eat, and freeze but air, and you can't cook, eat, or freeze that. It goes right through you.

Do I need permission from the mother to assault with great fury members of my gender like Willie who seize on the modern-day right to be a nonentity, a living zombie? His little mental stutter steps before the attack could cost him his life. I want to take Willie up into a C-130 and kick him out at five thousand feet like a package of C-rations over the hungry deserts of Southern Sudan. When he lands, awake at last, I want to brand his forehead—the Catholic cross, let's say, of Ash Wednesday—and slap a sign across his back that reads, YOU ARE THE REAL INFIDEL, OMAR AL-BASHIR, and rub alligator bait into his threads, then watch him scramble. Let him negotiate the world in its raw sick fury like some reject protagonist from a Cormac McCarthy novel fleeing the Antichrist. And whether he lives or dies as a wannabe Lost Boy, little Willie will have a story.

"You wanna hear some Shakespeare?"

She rolls her eyes.

"*Unnatural deeds do breed unnatural troubles.*"

"So whatchu want then?"

"Look, I'm offering you my free services."

"That's my loyal Polynesian lover."

"You want me to straighten that boy out? I'll take him down to the handball courts and let the parolees slap him around a little bit. They got tags on their faces that'll scare the shit out of him. Look like mutherfucking Maori warriors. Make him wish he never saw a sphincter."

"Damn!" she shouts, coming out the car, jumping in my face, right there in her g and a T-shirt.

"I'm trying to help out your family here," I say. "Your peeps."

"Family? Peeps? What you talking about, fool?"

"What's wrong with you?"

"Me? Me? Where the hell you been? You talking like you in another place. You forget where you're at? No one knows wassup anymore. Not your own son, not no one."

13

I Know What I'm Talking About

I KNOW what I'm talking about. It's embedded in me, too, that modern gluttony of the mind, that wild lewd greed. I'd ruined the only substantive relationship I've ever had with a woman because of the evolving sexual palette, the revolving nasty image. I was twenty-two, I was a walking hard-on. I crossed the busy streets of San Jo with my tongue out the side of my mouth. A sharp shift in the wind, an exotic accent, a gentle moment with a stranger, an idiosyncrasy as stupid as how one sips her morning coffee, had me tucking and repositioning and disappearing into obscure places for a stroke session. My poor girl and I would double-back beast twice a day, but she had only a partial understanding of the rotten nature of my organ. I was a demon. I should've been purged by fire, burnt at the stake. Or sent off to war.

In the beginning, Sharon was constantly making plans. Plans upon plans. She was like a kid building a fort in the yard. There were orchards and vineyards and beaches where our nuptials would be consummated, exotic locales in South America and New Zealand where our first child would be conceived. I bought a subscription to *Bride* magazine for her birthday, and she giggled. She considered the utility of certain friends ten years in the future, measured by who we'd be in the future: the Tusifales. That we could change and actually grow together, morph into some variable beyond our control, fascinated her. She was petite, blue-eyed, and thin-boned, but when she'd envision our future, Sharon inflated into a prophetic American genie.

Our pact was based on faith, on not cheating. For us it was a matter of driving toward the sanctimonious, of preparing ourselves for the carriage—when it came—of love. Every woman I'd dated before Sharon had been casual about adultery. "Just don't tell me about it" had been a common utterance. That meant, by translation, "I won't tell you about it either." They wanted to keep the gates open. For fun or just in case.

Everyone I knew had cheated, was cheating. Even my happily married sister, Tali, whose friends often say, "She was meant to be a loving wife," had had an affair with a brotha when she'd first gotten married. I overheard her telling a girlfriend named Tonicia about it at a luau, worried that she'd been knocked up and that the baby was gonna come out a little too brown for dove-white McLaughlin's tastes. "Poor McLaughlin!" the friend cried. "He got a sperm-bank son and a baby on the way that ain't his'n!" She'd asked for advice and the friend shrugged and said, "I don't know. Just keep the kid and that dude away from those DNA-testing scumbags!" I struggled with desire. I felt, somehow, sexually gypped in a monogamous deal, a fool on the stage. Like I'd been suckered into the narrative by a deceased Puritan playwright who was no longer culturally relevant.

In Sharon's daily absence, I started a ritual, the three-dollar three-minute run. Back then, 1999, 2000, I'd quit school eight classes short of a degree and was pushing a broom at the Mountain View Parks and Rec so she could finish up without worrying about tuition. She worshipped me for it, her parents questioned my ambition. That was tough to take: her mother was a swing-shift clerk at a Mervyns liquor

store and her pops was unemployed. He always enjoyed speaking to
the myriad ways in which he was overqualified for any job. I'd think,
*But you've yet to look into our burgeoning fast food industry, sir. You
could be so overqualified pushing chalupas and bean burritos that no
one would know the difference.*

Anyway, after work I'd catch the bus to the 7-Eleven in downtown Mountain View. Inside I'd buy a bag of barbecue Cornuts and
a peach-flavored Kern's nectar. This was the first step of the ritual,
getting the paper change (three one-dollar bills, each worth a minute
in the booth) from the purchase and making sure the store clerk (this
one a different Singh) wasn't suspicious. But he never made eye
contact, which was the way I liked it. Each visit I'd walk under the
bridge of the door determined to be inconspicuous despite the cus-
tomer beep announcing me.

On the day of my sixth uncaught month it all blew up.

I went behind the 7-Eleven alleyway and started toward the booth.
I kicked at a few broken stones of concrete. The air was Bay Area
cool, half an hour before sundown, mid-March, the sea blowing its
salty kisses inland. I was taking the half-breaths that I was used to
in the alleyway. In my Parks and Rec T-shirt, Ben Davis jeans, and
steel-toed boots, I was sweating profusely in the crotch and underarm regions, yet not enough to stifle the rising of arm and leg hair. I
was at the tips of my senses, alert for any interruption to the ritual.

I passed the back door of Delia's Cleaners, a few hanging racks
on wheels, rusting at the corners, discarded plastic. A bottle of Olde
English, unfinished by a golden third. Two more doors with numbers painted on the wall above, 223 and 225. There was a cardboard
box on its side between the two doors, popcorn filler spilled out the
mouth, the Styrofoam floating on the ground wind of the alleyway.

The back doorstep of Ga Bo Ja Korea Buffet was stacked with
empty kimchi bottles, the scent of garlic and soy strong. A penny-
bronze pussycat was digging through a box of kalbi bones. Sometimes

the cat would run when I came, but that day it just sat there and watched me. I didn't like what I imagined on its face of disheveled whiskers and so I hissed, "Hey!" and it scuttled into the restaurant. I could feel the excitement growing despite the stench of the alleyway. I reached down, still walking, and shifted my boot. I looked behind me and quickened my step.

The boot. The package. The wood. The johnson. The rooster. Used to call it the engine. I can remember the day when the engine would run wild on the cheapest gas, the oil dripping constantly. One shot of Elle MacPherson's nipple poking through the green latex fabric of a *Sports Illustrated* shoot—one nipple!—and it was running on empty for weeks. That photo would last in my head for a year, long enough for the next annual *S.I.* shoot on the beaches of Jamaica to hit the shelves by the millions.

I can remember, too, that primeval feeling I'd have when Sharon would walk into our shared studio, soaked from a two-hour workout at the 24-Hour Nautilus. I'd cross the limited space of our studio like a lion pacing his cage. Keen in the olfactories, watching her strip down, smelling the salt from her sweat-dried brown skin. The absolutism in my guts to fuck her absolute and hard feels now strangely foreign, almost out of body, the memory not even nostalgic. But I was losing interest even back then. A year into living together, I began to fantasize about Sharon's best friend, Susan, or Sharon's mother, Jan, the liquor store clerk, Susan's mother, both mothers, or a big messy sandwich with everyone involved.

That's the kind of deviant I was becoming at twenty-two, not even a father yet, a decade from a midlife crisis. Oedipus manipulating the images caught in his own head, wannabe orgy proprietor. I craved anything that would make the gasoline—Sharon, monogamy—not monotonous.

My straying mind was something I would try and hide from Sharon, but eventually I started dropping clues about the warped nature of my desire. Leaving hints at the scene. I had, for instance, placed a copy of Updike's *Rabbit, Run* on Sharon's dresser. I'd felt a kinship with the perpetually fleeing Rabbit Angstrom. After she'd read it as I knew she would, and said, "That was good," I offered her the next step-up with Updike, a tattered paperback copy of *Couples* that I'd bought at Recycle Bookstore on the Alameda. After she read it, I'd awaited a reprimand of some sort: adultery, philanderers, swingers, et cetera.

Instead, she'd said, "His picture sure doesn't fit a spouse swapper. He looks kind of New Englandy and bookish."

I said, "Okay, try this," and handed her *Tropic of Cancer*.

"Now this guy," she'd said, two days later, "he's interesting. Should we get a bidet?"

I soon discovered that Susan, the best friend, frequented a nude beach. Susan was muscular and somewhat butch, yet I found her very sexy. She had the quads of a gymnast, the bob to match, and the tattoos of a nineteenth-century swabbie.

I'd said, "I bet Susan needs some company in the sun, huh?"

"Nah. She doesn't want you going with her."

"No," I said, kicking my toes into the heel of the other foot. "I meant you."

"Are you trying to get rid of me? Susan says we don't talk enough."

"Well, then you should go. Talk on the beach."

"Not Susan and I. You and I."

"Oh."

"Anyway, I don't like the idea of old men watching. They hide behind the rocks and wait for Susan to roll over."

I said, "I'd be back there, too," and Sharon laughed. For some reason, I became embarrassed. "I'm just kidding."

"Really, Paulie. Sometimes you're so strange," and then, "Let's eat out tonight. Get ready to go."

So I started bringing *Playboy* home. I put the magazine on the coffee table in front of the television, a place where visitors would not only find it but find it first. Right between the framed photos of myself and Sharon pointing at the camera at Alcatraz, the other of Sharon and Susan hugging in Vegas. When Sharon had come home from her workout at the gym, she'd said, "What's this?"

"What?" I said.

Sharon was flipping through the pages and she'd already found the centerfold, an Amer-Asian with a bob. "Well, isn't she cute? She's got hair like Susan."

"Yes," I said, approaching Sharon, trying to find her scent, "like Katie Couric."

She pulled away. "Don't." She was studying each photograph. "So young."

"Nineteen."

"How do you know?"

"It says right here." I reached for the magazine and Sharon moved half a step away. I said, "It gives her basic bio. Ambitions, the kind of men she likes, a pic of her cheerleading days."

"What guy wouldn't want to do her," said Sharon matter-of-factly. "What an ass."

"What?"

"You might as well get a subscription." Sharon tossed the *Playboy* on the coffee table. It slid and spun. "Save some money that way."

"Really?"

"Yes."

"If you say so."

I was a little confused, having been prepared for a verbal assault. I was ready to take the discussion back to another century, touting the French Renaissance and its full-body models, or another decade and Marilyn Monroe—"the sexual avatar of class," I'd planned to say—or another memorized phrase: "The last artistic venue of portraiture."

I bought us tickets for the stage. Maybe we weren't getting out enough, maybe the studio was cramping our growth as a couple. A freak show might change that. On a Thursday night, I drove Sharon to downtown Berkeley to see an X-rated contemporary version of a Sophoclean tale, *Eddie Puss,* that was being performed by the Jugs-Or-Nuts, a traveling troupe of thespian transvestites.

I had a hard time taking the troupe seriously, especially since Eddie Puss was much smaller than his own mother. Yet when I watched for expressions of disgust from Sharon during key moments in the play, she'd either yawn or roll her eyes. Once she said, "How embarrassing for you men," and then turned her head to sleep. By the end of Act II, she was snoring so loud I had to wake her up with a nudge. I followed Sharon under the neon-lit sign and watched her toss the Eddie Puss ticket stubs into the first garbage can.

From behind I threw out a bone, something Catholic from my childhood: "Do you want to go to confession with me tomorrow?"

"Are you kidding? I'd be in there until next year! No sin booths for me!"

Nothing seemed to get a rise out of Sharon. Her basic attitude was instructive: on the second year of a relationship things plateau, especially sex; that's the way it goes for every couple. Like the dull commitment of lifetime service to the National Guard. Perhaps I had been looking for a fight, a spark between us, even if I'd lose the fight.

The spark that would make me feel alive. . . .

No sparks at the end of the alleyway, and I hung a left into the parking lot. Ivy was everywhere, feeding like a virus on the concrete and steel. Three cars were parked in parallel forty-five degree angles. I kept my eyes to myself. I'd learned my lesson during the first week of the ritual when I witnessed two people fucking in the backseat of a Toyota Camry. They had seen me coming and kept going. The shocks of the undulating car creaked like an old bed. They seemed encouraged by the idea of getting caught. I had picked up my stride and ducked into the back entrance of the bookstore.

I passed the three cars without incident and walked up the four-step staircase into the bookstore. This the worst part of the ritual, nodding at the clerk. He was just what you'd expect in a bookstore like this, truly filthy: pockmarked with the cavernous pores of alcoholism, lips smeared white with an anti-cold-sore cream that didn't prevent him from constantly licking his lips. On that day, he had on an Arco mechanic's shirt with the sewn-on name tag LOU and was shelving giant rubber phalli behind the counter—black, white, brown, red, transparent, striped—next to boxes of artificial vaginas molded in cold wax directly from the porn stars themselves. Then he was on his tippy-toes, stretching out for packaged Mardi Gras beads and the bigger version, a row of Ping-Pong balls on a string.

I slid past the counter, and he turned and said, "Hey, buddy. What did the ovary say to the other ovary?"

I didn't look at him, I didn't look at the items for sale behind him, but I stopped, my eyes on the ground. I couldn't believe my ears. In half a year's time, I hadn't exchanged one word with anybody in the bookstore, let alone Lou. It was a bad omen. I considered exiting the joint at once. But the image of Lou following me out the door, wondering if I was an undercover cop or a spy from another bookstore, kept me from leaving. And the thought of having to right-hook Lou on those plague-ridden lips before escaping down the alleyway was a trial I wouldn't put my fist through.

"What?" I managed.

His laugh sounded like the squeaky collusions of mice behind the wall. "Hey, there's Dick!" he said, slug tongue out of his mouth. "Let's egg him!"

The joke depressed me: my mind was fast to self-indict. When were Sharon's ovaries last drowning in my "protein fishies," as she used to call it during the early days? It was three weeks, maybe longer. Our sex was missionary, her head propped, my face to the side of her head buried in the pillow.

Sharon herself had started it. We'd lain down together, and she had stretched her neck to one side of the pillow. Automatically. When we'd first met, that meant nuzzle the neck, blow on the ear, nibble the lobe. But things had changed. My instinct had been to follow her lead and push my face into the pillow. There wasn't the slightest protestation from Sharon.

We no longer showered together. Sharon was invariably dressed before I woke up in the morning, no matter how early I rose. She'd also be dressed when I came home and dropped into the couch to yell at whatever demagogue I could find on cable news. And she'd been sleeping in a G-string, a knee-length Stanford T-shirt and black silk blinders that looked like doilies over her eyes. Sharon had loved Naked Thursday, a twenty-four-hour affair of mutual nudity where I was not allowed to touch her until midnight struck. That had been painful and rewarding, with a strong element of Catholic deprivation to it that I admired even then. By the time the moment of consummation came, I was desperate for contact. But no more prancing around our studio in the buff. Naked Thursday went out like a lot of Thursdays do, without note.

At the counter, Lou was now bent over a six-foot plastic doll, genially oxygenating it as if he were blowing up a raft for the kids at the lake. I walked past the desk to the gallery of both real and televised moans and all the way to the last unoccupied booth in line closest to the door (which opened into the lot for exit but not entrance), locked the booth, dropped my pants to the knees but no further, inserted a dollar into the pay slot, still standing, turned the volume down on the private screening, and flipped to channel eighteen, which featured Sapphic encounters, women feasting on women, violating each other in every conceivable way. My goal was to finish before I used up the three dollars, which gave me three minutes in all.

But the machine was not cooperating. Bad omen on that day, Aphrodite issuing a warning. It kept flicking back to channel thirteen. Each time I reached out and hit the flashing red button and returned to the isle of Lesbos, the screen jumped to two men in a steamy sauna with skimpy white bath towels around their waists. Finally the channel just stayed where it was, wouldn't move. And despite my efforts to mute the machine, it remained at full volume. Above their grunts and squeaky palms, everyone in the gallery could hear the conversation on the screen, my screen, and I knew that if I didn't find a fix fast, I'd have someone waiting outside my booth in seconds.

"You look like a big friendly bear, don'tchu?"

"Grrrrrrrr."

"And I'll be your little bear-er, won't I?"

"Grrrrrrr."

Then the machine went crazy. Flashing from channel to channel faster than an eyeblink, I saw silicon lips crying the Oh of ecstasy in mass libidinous excretion in the water on the streets in the gutter on rooftops in someone's sometimes many people's mouths, bubbling over like the froth of sewage on the shore of a stream outside an insidious chemical plant, and in the depleted well of romance in my head, I found the recurring picture of Sharon dancing through the bookstore. Prancing and pirouetting past that nest of Herpes at the counter, the only woman clothed, she did not belong in the filth, even the filth of my own imagination.

Maybe less out of sheer decency and more out of sexual survival, of keeping the images to themselves, I shouted, *Ahhhhh!* and opened the door, stiff-armed the besparkled chest of the queen of *qui tacit consentire* standing outside my booth, his bleached Levi's cut so tight and thigh-high that even as he was falling backward, I could see the outline of his boot like a map of Italia, and hustled past another royal queen awaiting escort on the carriage, ran out the door into the lot, the moaning ghosts hot on my tail, freed at last to feed on the virginal world.

I ran through the already dark lot and hit the alleyway practically skidding. A little lamp of light at the end of the lane. The moon, sitting in its own gray wash. Two Korean chefs in butcher aprons were smoking on the back step of their restaurant. They could see and understood immediately from where I came, or didn't come, and smiled, laughing as I neared. One reached into his pocket and pulled a cigarette from it, holding the unlit snipe out as I sprinted by them, right through their smoke.

I heard, "Need break, boss? Very tired?"

I remember thinking that each step over the sliding gravel and jumping rocks was like a cleaning of the conscience, an erasing of the past, a strike of six-o'clock weekday amnesia. As if my sprint would expunge the evidence of ever having been there in the alleyway.

I sped home under a blue-black sky dark as the inside of the booth, thinking on Sharon's goods, my greed. She was sloped like the silver line bisecting a Coke can, skin blown-glass smooth to the touch, men all across the city of San Jo wanted a piece of her delicates. She was beautiful. So many regions of Western Europe were in her face: Swedish down-turned pouty mouth, Irish sea-blue eyes, lightly freckled French button of a nose, prominent German forehead. A beautiful American mutt! Sweet as a teaspoon of sugar, salty as an oyster, everything ripe on her body for seed. And I was blowing it in my greedy head, or in my sticky hand, searching for whatever impetus out there I didn't have.

I decided right there that I'd no longer share myself with the channel-eighteen lesbians. They never existed. I would take it further than that. I would avoid the town of Mountain View for the rest of my life. Never drive through there again. A meaningless map dot removed from my head.

Mountain View is gone, my son, gone!

One purist sweep of the 48,000-population Silicon Valley suburb from my head.

And then all visual stimulation, the "body art" of *Playboy,* must also be erased. Showtime and HBO canceled, cable canceled—perhaps the television removed altogether. Out the door, signed off for donation at the Goodwill. No more Miller Light girls and Howard Stern whores. Walking the streets with Sharon, I would be a horse with blinders. And when Susan came to visit, or Sharon's mother, or any woman, it would be a cordial Hello, how are you, nice to see you. Retreat into the bedroom to read the poetry of Father Hopkins, SJ, keep it clean.

I'd read more selectively. All things promoting the mind to stretch, dulling the instinct to fuck, must go. They were the enemy of potency. Anytime I felt the urge for art, I'd drive down to the Carmelites and admire the architecture of the saints. And if it got really bad, I'd slip into a sin booth and try and confess through the screen. All for the consummation later with Sharon. That sweet whirling violence down below, the old gut flame of virility. I wanted to possess and be possessed. Sharon of Paul, Paul of Sharon. Body, mind, but especially mind.

At the apartment complex, I stopped at the fountain and put my hands out to catch the spray of the water crashing. Like it was holy water, blessed H_2O. I took a deep breath, prepared for a life of sanctity. Anticipating the baptismal romp with my girl. Just walk right in and claim my territory.

I got to the leaning wooden fence of our porch, unlatched the patio gate, and saw that the light was out, the blinds of the sliding glass door shut. I'd beaten her home, big-time lucky. Now I could prepare for her arrival. Light some candles, burn some incense, prepare the tub. Swoop her up when she walked into the studio, her arms loaded down with groceries, or, even better, dried with the salt of a thorough workout at the gym.

Right then a rhapsodic moan escaped through the cracks of the door.

It was Sharon. I knew the tone of her pleasure. I hadn't heard that voluminous pitch from her in almost a year. It picked up, like a car alarm. Or a booth back at the bookstore. *Jesus, God.* I stared down at the ground, Sharon's moan filling the little vacuum of hearing space on our patio. It was getting louder and I peeked over the fence into the neighbor's patio. All the lights were off. Bob, Jim, John, whatever his name was, probably had the bottom of a glass pressed to his ear, the shared wall between the two studios thin enough to rub one off in the darkness.

But I found a ray of hope in my image of our neighbor. Maybe Sharon was engaged in some self-manipulation of her own. Maybe the whole world was a private booth of self-indulgence. Maybe everyone, when finally alone, has a straying palm or a probing finger, and maybe the darkness was universal. Maybe Sharon had the lights dimmed, a silk sheet drawn to her belly, a glass of champagne in her right hand, the bottle in her left. Maybe Sharon's moans were uttered in the ecstatic vanity of solitude, a thorough celebration of self.

The moan came again, sustained, almost mournful.

So I'd been in the gutter for half a year, but Sharon was in the gutter too, or at least familiar with it, and that made for an even slate between the two of us. Rehab needed on both our parts, not just mine.

Then I heard something else. I looked behind me, held my breath. It was not true. It will vanish, just like the booth back in that nameless town in my deleted past. *It will be gone, gone, gone.*

But the new sound rose from under the door again, stronger. Then the exchange. A choral succession of lust. Pronounced in intervals by a tenor "Yes!" Definitely Sharon. "Yes! Yes! Yes!" A quickening of the pace and then the chaos of simultaneous guttural sounds. Each moan compounded by the other, two seals feeding on the pier.

I put the key softly into the lock and closed my eyes.

On the futon, their heads were deep in each other's midsection. I shut the door and Sharon looked up, still gyrating at the naked hip, moist lips pursed, the squint of pleasure in her Irish eyes widening to fright.

I sat down on a chair near the sliding glass door, eyes on Sharon. Candles were burning by the phone. Sharon was reading my face, looking for a sign. The whole time Susan, on her stomach on Sharon, neither looked up nor stopped. Mad with lust. She was as shapely as I'd imagined, and her breasts pressed against Sharon's belly were like little half-filled water balloons. She had a ruby-red-lips tattoo on her alabaster-skinned ass, and all along the surface in no discernible pattern were Sharon's handprints in fading blush. I was so close to the futon I could hear the wetness. I gritted my teeth, stood, and looked down on it all.

I said, "Get out."

Susan craned her neck back, eyes glazed as if in a dream, and said, "Shit."

"Get out."

She pushed herself up from Sharon and the futon. Proudly stood in front of me, muscular and naked, panting. She reached down and grabbed her clothes from the coffee table, stepped into her panties, looked up at me as she slid them up her legs, stepped into faded painter pants, wiggled them tight, buttoned up, and said, "Sorry, Paulie."

"Shut your mouth," I said. "Get the fuck out of here."

Susan snapped on her sports bra. "Will you be all right, hon?"

Sharon sat up. "Of course."

"Get out of here, bitch."

She was fully dressed. "All right. Glad to see you're in charge again. Leaving."

Susan brushed by me and I felt something uncontrollable respond and I turned and tried to drive the image of their coupling out of my treacherous head with a thrust. I heard from the futon, "Don't!" Susan crashed down to her knees from the shove and I stomped toward her. My hand reared back to strike the dyke hard and fast but Sharon's hands clutched me at the arm from behind and then slipped down to the waist.

Susan stood and turned with dignity. "Are you sure you'll be all right?"

"Yes."

"Get the fuck out of here!"

"Just leave, Susie."

Susan opened the door, "Don't worry, hon. I will be back."

She left the studio, the door wide open.

I looked down on Sharon. Both arms were wrapped about me as if she were riding hitch on a motorcycle. She looked up, nude in the middle of the studio floor, eyebrows lifted in unprecedented subservience. She wanted something. But I separated from her, and pushed her onto the futon. She fell back, crying, her knees curled into her chest, the dirty-blond mane sticky with sex, sweat dotting the inside thigh, brow moist. Fully blushed and passionate. I took a step forward and some life came to her eyes. "You dare put your hands on me?"

"Yes."

"You haven't made love to me in six months, you bastard! Fake purist bastard!"

"We did last month."

"You fucked someone else!" Sharon pointed at my eyes. "I know you've got a hundred harlots up there in your head! I know it!"

"Get out."

"You'd probably fuck Susie if I didn't! Wouldn't you? You sly bastard! Always on the sneak!"

"I said get out."

I reached down and grabbed Sharon by the elbow. She dropped to her knees and put all her weight in her ass and said, "What the hell are you doing, Paul?"

I dragged her across the rug of our studio amidst the cries: "God! Don't do it! Liar! Don't!" She felt remarkably light, probably from her carnal romps with Susan. Who knew how long it had gone on?

The door had creaked halfway shut and I slammed it open into its door catch, leaned against it for leverage, and tossed Sharon onto the porch like a UPS package. She fell and rolled, but lay there for only a second, glistening white in the moonlit shine, her wet lips shivering.

I piously shut the door, then locked it. Walked over to the candles and blew them out. The studio was black. I went back to the door, focusing on silence. I needed to calm down or she might hear my excitement.

I held my breath, my ear to the wood. The wind cut in and out the cracks. I looked into the peephole. Susan was kissing away the tears, wrapping Sharon up in a flannel. I unzipped my fly, gripped the engine. It reached for my belly button, filled with blood. Then suddenly, like a dying butterfly, the engine began to flutter: I discovered: whether I opened the door again or not, I was finally alone in the dark commodious booth of my head.

So I didn't see Sharon again, but within the month I was back in a booth, watching Janine Lindemulder take on a shiny hairless brotha named Lexington Steele. Not regularly now, no ritual for me, but casually, because there was no one like Sharon around to betray. This time without plan or consequences or even caution and usually out of boredom, I'd go in the front door while traffic on El Camino Real whizzed by, even after being honked at once by young highschoolers, mostly girls, it's like drinking in a dive whose patronage you disdain and to which you'd put a swinging wrecking ball with all of them, including yourself, in its dead center. Just when you're taking the shot of absinthe, fumes of dead wormwood singeing the hair of the nostrils and climbing upward through the nasal passage to drill holes in the walls of soft tissue—*Powwww!*—a big black ball of Lexington Steele right through the brain.

14

Today We Break from Custom

Today we break from custom.

Like the dutiful dog that I am, I've been pacing the garage for an hour in the late noon when La Dulce pulls in, says, "You just a lonely horny little thing, ain'tcha? Get in."

"What about the garage?"

"What?"

"Our daily tryst. In the garage."

"No."

"No?"

"We gonna go meet you some fellow *artistes*."

"Do you have to say it like a Frenchwoman?"

"I'm a Haitian, fool. Figure out the history."

"I don't like your *artistes*."

"You wanna keep your room?"

"What bait," I say, walking around the car.

We drive to Downtown San Jo in silence. I get the sense that she wants me to get all wide-eyed with hope. I mostly sleep, thinking about her beautiful backside bouncing around on my tip by the boxes and brooms in the garage.

We're entering the urban campus of the Silicon University of the Valley and I say, "Nah. Forget it. I ain't going back to school for you, for no one."

"You gotta keep your mind open for opportunity. You need some credentials."

"I'm kicking it with you. What more do I need?"

"I'm your last hope on the education front."

"You wouldn't know where to start."

"Start with money," she says. "Just like everyone else."

"Uh-huh."

"Don't embarrass me. These my folks. Without me, they got no program."

"You just go to these things to clean yourself up and act like a big shot. If they ever heard how you really talk, they'd ban you from the campus."

"Listen. Get your appetite on tonight. This MFA graduation party is your dinner."

The barbecue announces itself: there's a banner the size of a football field tied between the English Department building and the gymnasium. I can barely read the first few words without shaking my head: "WELCOME TO THE PRIZE WINNERS OF TOMORROW. . . ."

This special brand of *artistes* looks about the same as past gatherings. You've got your standard preponderance of berets and turtlenecks and all kinds of curious cross-dressing. You've got your bad dancing, bad acoustics. Today it's a lady whiter than her seashells doing a belly dance to a Ravi Shankar tune, the sitar played by a bearded prophet with one name, one letter: Z. La Dulce whispers this fact into my ear as if it were holy scripture. At a picnic table, a group of writers is playing Trivial Pursuit 2005, a game that has no data on its quiz cards before 2000. The Sphinx, St. Peter's, the Constitution? Not worth keeping in the long-term memory box.

I walk on, trying my best to feign non-judgment on my face, find another prize-winner-to-be perched in the branches of a small tree pontificating to the crowd of poets below about the essence of staying true blue to yourself and threaten to jump and (of course) not do it.

"Can you die from a sprained ankle?" I ask La Dulce.

"Shush."

"Shush? More like *shove*. Someone give the poor guy a hand."

"That's Swartie. He depressed."

"Better," I say, "than oppressed."

"He got his three-hundredth rejection letter this week. Carries them around in his backpack."

"Like a novel manuscript?"

"Have some sensitivity for once in your life. You only here because of me."

"That's exactly what I'm saying."

"Help me out a little here, baby."

"Okay," I say, "no worries." I take the bed of dead grass by the wall of the gym. It's shadowed by an unoccupied magnolia, the most ego-free area of this celebration.

La Dulce walks off to chat and I watch and listen to it all. Some bearded cat in a swabbie pullover is introducing himself to new recruits as Colonel Bobby Jameson. The Alpha Graduate. He has the entitled attitude of election. He's talking loud so that everyone, even me, can hear his loving elaboration on the creative value of oxygen bars in Berkeley. He starts up a debate with Swartie in the tree about whether it's better to write by candlelight or moonlight.

I hear from above, "I prefer to compose by Bud Light."

The colonel responds, "I prefer my bud lit."

And so on with the impromptu quips.

I hear tales of paper cuts told in weighty tones of limb severance, and this seems to me to be something of a story in itself, a bad vaudeville, where the characters are all by choice forcing themselves on one another. Everyone in great pain, everyone trying to be clever. The vibe of these people makes me worry about the arts.

Because it always happens like this, La Dulce interrupts my thoughts. "Baby, stand up and meet someone."

I do, wishing when I take his hand that I hadn't. It's palms down. I'm supposed to kneel and kiss it.

"This the colonel, baby."

"What's happening?" I say.

Arrogance all over the guy's face, like he wrote every poem that ever mattered. He traces with a manicured thumb the rim of his beer—a Bud Light—and watches himself do it, as if the act were deep as an oil drill, says, "I hear you're a poet?"

La Dulce says, "Paulie's got the chops, colonel."

"Is that so?"

"He working on a book."

"We are *all* working on a book, Beatrice," he says, bowing and softly patting her shoulder.

"He won the LeRoi Jones Hookup for Off-the-Hook Artistic Achievement fellowship."

"I see. I'm sure Gabby will offer him a scholarship before the night's over. Or a parking space. Whichever comes first."

"What about an office?" La Dulce says.

"So our poet is published?"

"No," I say. I've grown tired of hearing myself spoken about in third person. "But he almost killed someone once. Does that count?"

I smile full on, wide as I can, knowing not to look over at La Dulce's tortured face.

"Good to meet you," he says, nodding at me, bowing at La Dulce, ducking and spinning on his heels like an English gentleman. Less than half a minute passes before he's at the base of the magnolia, his head in the lower leaves, no doubt whispering to Swartie about my felonious history.

I look at La Dulce: *Why would you sponsor any of these people?*
"Did you have to say that to him?"

I don't answer La Dulce because, like a blessing, I'm offered a dog. No ketchup, no mustard, no relish, but it's cool. The server puts the paper plate down and stands before us both. He's in a tie-dye shirt that reads THE AVATAR OF AQUARIUS. I immediately feel a little bad for him, not only because his long handlebar sideburns have hairless patches that look like a mountain cat took a few paw swipes, but because his eyes exude a need for both pity and praise, the formula of the failed poet.

I say, "Thanks, bro."

Before I get or give a name he's telling me that the incoming poets are actually eating frozen leftovers from last year's reception, "Thus," he says, "saving us upward of a hundred dollars."

"That's pretty impressive," I say, chewing into my year-old dog. "You got one over on 'em. You came up."

La Dulce grabs my hand. "This Gabriel von Morley. He the dean here, baby."

Von Morley lets the fact settle into my system. I nod with appreciation and wonderment, he reaches out for my hand, the one interlaced in La Dulce's, and forces into my grip a thin, stapled, Xeroxed copy of a pamphlet. He nods, awaiting our perusal. La Dulce flips the words upright and holds the cover page in front of us like we were sharing a hymnal.

"*Impotent Yet Proud, Unknown Yet Grateful,*" she reads aloud. "*Twenty Poems on Pain*. A chapbook by Gabriel von Morley and Colonel Robert Jameson. Deadhead Press."

I add/read, "Thirty-nine dollars."

"It's a signed limited edition," he says.

"Cool," I say.

He's waiting for something. I don't think I'm going to give him this one, whatever it is. He puts his tiny hand out, palm up, and I smile, look over at my sponsor, the lucky lady with all the cash. "You gonna pay the man, baby?"

He takes the two twenties as if we're the ones getting the good end of a deal, looks over at the colonel, whose regal back is turned to us, pockets the cash without bothering to finger around for a buck change, says, "Somewhere in the middle of Nebraska, Jack Kerouac told me, 'Gabe, you gotta get some life into your stuff.' Forty-eight years later, I have done just that: an utter explosion of voice. Now there is an undeniable connection, I admit, to Ezra Pound, in that one starts at the base of formality and then, like Adrienne Rich— who is a dear friend—gracefully leaves it."

I nod. "Cool."

I can feel pressure on my elbow. La Dulce, fine woman, is trying to shove me along. I take her cue and step out, but he grabs my other elbow with his unctuous hand, pushes me back to my original place, and says, "I have tried to meet my writerly devoir, weaving blank verse with the chaos of language poetry, sometimes borrowing from the surrealism of the New York School of Poets, many of whom I knew very well, including John Ashbery. We studied together at the Squaw Valley Writers Conference. Iambic pentameter between terrifying runs down the snowy slopes. . . ."

I start to fade out from the soliloquy and I'm lucky, I guess, in one way: The guy can't see it. He doesn't need eye contact from me, nods, or gestures, he's content to go right on talking as long as I'm standing before him. What a trip: He's like a badly scaled-down version of modern American literary history through sycophancy. I reassure La Dulce with a hand squeeze that I'm not going to say anything rude ("Were you in the bombing of Dresden with Vonnegut?") and she kisses my cheek and promptly abandons me.

I used to believe in the sanctity of poetry—before I met anyone associated with it. I can remember what I felt poring over the lovely letters Keats wrote to his brother in the throes of consumption; I used to recite his poems to myself in the yard in Quentin. Who but the poet, I'd thought, stands on the doorstop of death and dares to ring the bell and not run? I may have been at the wrong hotbed of creativity, but the spirit of the greats appeared to be lost on these future Pulitzers, more interested in playacting and sipping wine spritzers than getting down in the pit with their demons.

But maybe it's good to enroll for an MFA so as to be daily reminded of what you don't like about people, what you don't like about yourself. After all, for every John Keats, there is someone like me, an intruder of sorts.

". . . wolfing down shrooms with Kenny and Hunter S. and a Hell's Angel named Scooter in the garden of death as midnight struck like. . . ."

Something ice-cold and wet is pushed into my hand. I notice that von Morley's students have put a ten-yard radius around us. Each of them, even the suicidal Swartie, knows that being anywhere in von Morley's vicinity means playing the prey for his big-name game hunting, and yet they stay at the barbecue, I guess, because they've bought what he's sold: the future, a $39 pamphlet copied at Kinko's, is in his hand.

I pop the can of beer, press it to my lips, the piss-water contents of Keystone Light tasting good for once, a matter of context, true relief.

". . . encouraged by an itemized note from Tennessee Williams which read, 'Yes, baby, I get a little lavish at times under the nipping influence of a warm brandy,' and thinking, *My God, heroin must do wonders. . . .*"

"Yeah, yeah, yeah," someone says.

This one's broken the radius. He's got on a white T-shirt that reads, in red letters, UKRANIAN POET, and his golden locks are styled into the hair-sprayed tsunami of a rockabilly. He hands me another beer, and I see a handsome tattoo of Johnny Cash on his forearm. The dean keeps the pace of the evening sermon, now commemorizing Thoreau and a woolen sweater hand knit on the shores of Walden Pond.

"No wonder they call you Gabby," says the Ukranian poet. He tugs on my sleeve. "You wanna get the fuck out of here, my bro?"

La Dulce is back, eyes closed, hands in the air, listening to the colonel read his poems. "Sure," I say. "Why not?"

"Follow me."

I leave Gabby von Morley there talking, and though with a new location and victim, I bet he'll still be talking into the early morning.

We make our way to Fourth and San Salvador without a word said between us. It's rather nice, I must say, after the glimpse of MFA nonsense at the party. We end up walking through a deli on First and San Carlos amid stares from the patrons and Mexican cooks, and then we step over several Vietnamese children playing hide-and-seek by a counter sagging with frozen fish, climb over sacks of white rice that look like stacked sandbags at a flood, and at last come to a door with a sign posted on it that reads, LUBIC'S DELICATES.

"My undercover bike shop," he says.

There's nothing in the room except six bicycles, a Ouija board, two candles in golden candelabra on either side of the board, and three books, *The Collected Poems of Czeslaw Milosz, The Book of Laughter and Forgetting,* and *The Giving Tree.* The bikes are flipped over so that each rests on its seat and handlebars, the tires in the air: five fifties-style Schwinn cruisers and a Bridgestone Trailblazer mountain bike. I can hear the noise from the deli, the walls thinner than the see-through wrap of a spring roll.

He says, nodding toward the door, "I hate those fucking people."

I crack open another Keystone I'd snagged from Dean Gabby von Morley, hand it to the Ukrainian poet, say nothing.

"They are very lecherous. I am only twenty-one"—here he crosses himself—"but I know about people. Especially rotten fucking people. You cannot be from Ukraine and not know what rotten is. We are stuck between two rotten fucking countries, one on the west, one on the east. Back and forth they are coming. Fuck it. First we are fighting Nazis, next we are fighting Soviets."

I say, "Well, then. You're kinda like the Vietnamese of Europe." He does not smile. "First the Japanese in the thirties and forties, then the French in the fifties, us in the sixties, Chinese in the seventies, the Cambodians and Pol Pot in the eighties. Now all of those nations gone, forgotten. Millions dead."

"And now!" he shouts. "Look at me. I am surrounded by jerkoff who think they are poets because they like to talk in the trees with birdies. And they like to make fuck like rabbits. Everyone there is fucking everyone else."

"Even von Morley?"

"I don't know the man."

"He's your dean."

"Nobody knows that fucking man."

"Never met anyone so heavy into nomenclature."

"What is that?"

"Names, man. The dean's a big name-dropper."

"My friend, the only thing he drop is fucking acid. Lots and lots of that, bro, trust me."

I say, "For someone who lives in the fifties, you sure have a dirty mouth, dog."

He raises his beer. "*Nastrovia.*"

I nod, pop the other Keystone I'd lifted, sip the bubbles, toast, "*Nastrovia.*"

Our cans crash together and after the first chug he lifts the beer high again and says, "Fuck it."

"Okay," I say, mimicking his actions. "Fuck it."

I sit there in the fuck-it-ness of his toast and look around at the nearly empty room with for some reason no despondence at all, wondering how someone who speaks such bad English can be working toward an MFA in Creative Writing. I don't say anything, of course, but find a picture behind a shattered frame of a slender Vietnamese girl arm-in-arm with—*guess who?*—the Ukrainian poet. She has stars in her eyes and, in the possessive apathy of a primadonna, she's looking at the camera, though he isn't. He's turned toward the girl, looking meekly at the top of her head, as if it's intrusive to have his arms around her in the first place. Before I can ask him what happened to the frame or the girl or his apparent fondness for a member of "the lecherous fucking Vietnamese people," he stands up and walks over to the frame, throws it against the door, and says again, "Fuck it."

Incoherent shouts in Vietnamese rise up from the kitchen, and several times I catch in a piercing voice, *"Du ma mai!"* which I know means *fuck you* in Vietnamese, and since we seem to be stuck on the crudest term in every world language, I decide to ask him if he's ever seen *The Deer Hunter*. I want to talk at once to show him that his temper tantrum doesn't scare me, which it doesn't, though it annoys me. He lives in an elevated range of the quietudes, which is to say his cynical head, and while I'm not sure I like what I'm hearing, I'm also not sure, from my own little island of cynicism, if I have that right at all.

He looks at me as if I've insulted him. "Why do you ask me about that movie? Only because I am Ukrainian? They are dumb Polacks."

"No," I say. "Because the Green Beret toasts De Niro exactly the way you did. They're at that big wedding and he lifts his glass to De Niro and says, 'Fuck it.'"

"Who is De Niro."

He's not looking for an answer. "Who is De Niro," is a statement in the way you'd say, "De Niro is a nobody," or "De Niro means squat to me," and so I gladly say nothing and return to my Keystone. He starts setting up this giant bong the size of an elephant trunk, and when he has the purple weed that looks like Russian cabbage packed tight into the bulb and lit, he offers me the first official hit. I like that. Under advisement from Mr. Shel Silverstein, he's gonna give me the green from his tree.

I say, "No, thanks, I've enough vices as it is, bro," and slam the Keystone.

We don't say a word to each other for almost an hour. He keeps blowing his bubbles like an eager bugler in the high school band, repacking and relighting, and I just keep finding more and more Keystones in my pocket. Finally he says, "You want a fucking bike?"

"How much?"

"No, my bro. Come on, man. It's free, of course."

I shrug. "All right. Sure."

He shrugs back—"Pick one"—and, leaving him the five identical gray Schwinn cruisers, I ride back to Silver Creek Estates on the Trailblazer, swerving through the streets of San Jo and shouting, *"Mea culpa! Mea culpa!"* I realize I forgot to give him my name, and that it's at bare minimum both our faults, though probably as a native speaker mostly mine, but because I won't ever return to his under-cover bike shop—or Silicon University of the Valley, for that matter—it hardly fucking concerns fucking me.

15

I Somehow Keep My Balance

I SOMEHOW KEEP my balance swerving up the driveway. Gotta be three or four in the morning. The garage is wide open. The Silver Creek Estates Socialist Council of Wellness charges $20 for this infraction if it occurs longer than five minutes; $50 for the misdemeanor of parking your car in the driveway; $100 for the felony of breathing too loud. I can see La Dulce in the shadows next to her parked car, spread out on a lawn chair reading a book.

I jump off, say, "Like my new ride?"

She doesn't look up. "Why'd you leave like that?"

"Let me see that thing," I say.

She hands me *Impotent Yet Proud, Unknown Yet Grateful,* and I walk over to the garbage can, listen to it tickle the plastic on the way down. "At least recycle it," she says.

"Some things are irredeemable."

She looks me up and down. "Tell me about it."

"You gonna owe these Silver Creek people a lot of dough if you don't close down shop."

"Shut your mouth and listen."

"At least you got some clothes on. That's a start."

"You didn't like the *artistes,* did you?"

"True."

"You could just as well do without 'em."

"As can you."

"You hate 'em."

"I'm like Bukowski beating back doom on his bar stool: I hate them all the same."

"You ain't beating back shit. You *feeding* it."

"Equal opportunity, baby."

"Your hate-crimeing ass don't like nobody!"

"Keep it down," I say. "I like a few people. Just that they're mostly dead."

"You crazy."

"They've been cleansed by *the long grains beyond age, the dark veins of their mother*."

"Why you talking that limey bullshit? In that stupid deep voice of yours."

"The oracular of my boy Dylan Thomas."

"Just answer the question, nigga: are you saying I gotta die before you take a shine to me?"

"Shine? Let's not use words like that. You from Haiti or Mississippi?"

"Just answer the damned question."

"I mean, what's next? Hoss? Gumption?"

"You don't even like me."

"That's not a question."

"Do you?"

"Let's not do this, lucky one. We'll destroy the fuckship in six seconds' time."

She snaps her fingers across her face. "Fuckship?"

"What else is it?"

"And what about *Beatrice*?"

I can't tell her the truth, that she is nowhere near the book. That thinking about her would destroy it, and maybe destroy more than just the book. And that it doesn't matter at all in the end, since the book is just a game. The image of a teenage Mishima clutching his novel manuscript on the tracks of the oncoming train does not here work. I'm just flossing my teeth, Q-tipping my ears, the creative impetus as thoughtless and abysmal as the wipe.

Instead I say, "I won't desecrate the terms of love—if it still exists—just to get into your panties."

"Oh, you one noble nigga, ain'tcha?"

"And if love dies with my generation, just like everything else, I'm not gonna make it worse by calling this thing we got exactly what it'll never be. That's like telling everyone you just won the Lotto when you ain't even bought a ticket."

"Well hell, nigga, how's this? I never liked you none, anyway."

"That's fine. We may have consensus for the first time. I'm not so sure I like myself, either." I slap her hard on the ass and say, "This is good-bye, La Dulce. Don't trip. You'll make out like a bandit."

She says, a little paranoid, "Well. Shit. Just one more for the road, home skillet?"

Vows of pointless purity out the window, out the garage, or what-ever. "Sure," I say. "Why not?"

She pushes a fifty spot into my hands, says, "You can get a couple motel nights outta this."

This means no more fellowship. "Thank you," I say.

"You all right."

"Just turn around, if you'll be so kind, ma'am, and put your hands on the hood. Don't take it personally, but I don't want to see your face in the arrest."

"Likewise. Ditto. All that mess." The garage door is going down on us. "Hurry your ass up and get in there."

16

I Troop Up the Steps

I TROOP UP the steps of the County Transit Line 22, say, "What's happening?" to the morbid-eyed driver in her long-sleeved sweater with a brand new red-white-and-blue county authority patch sewed to the side of the shoulder, drop sixteen quarters into the slot, and after they're all in the box the lady says, "That wasn't necessary."

"Yeah, I know. It's called a gratuitous pleasantry."

"No," she says, giving the bus some gas so I have to catch myself on the handrail. "The money."

"You people want more already?"

"Never heard of Spare the Air Day? All rides within Santa Clara County are free."

I could ask for my quarters back or get her name to complain later to some phantom bureaucrat on a 1-800 number, but instead I let off a dismissive stream of air that sounds like a deflating tire—*pssshhhh*—and head down the middle aisle past paisas, Punjabis, Nigerians, Laotians, Guatemalans, Tongans; preachers, derelicts, dealers; cheap, just-starting-out or environmentally conscious businesspersons; septua- and octogenarians with disapproval grooved into their dead faces; pungent transients clutching black plastic bags packed with clothes and blankets and all kinds of recyclable material; signs that say STAND BACK FROM THE DOOR and NO SE PARE JUNTO A LA PUERTA and DING DUNG GAN CUA. I take it right to the rear corner, farthest from the carbon dioxide of my fellow public transportees. It's hot outside, cool in the back of the bus.

Up Alum Rock we go in red-light green-light convulsions, the bus groaning past well-lit strip malls and 24-hour porn houses, over the concrete bridges and out the graffiti-war territory aka a city tunnel. At every intersection we're being officially recorded, the cameras perched atop the swaying streetlights like solitary ravens looking down on a million burrowing earthworms. No one in this city dare pull a fast one on Big Daddy, or Big Brother, or Big Mama Earth, or whoever.

"Smile for the camera," I hear. "You're a hell-bound superstar."

In the other back corner of the bus, this cat is writing in his journal. It's an old-school deal, cased in brown leather with a tie string thin as the lace of a moccasin, the pages yellowed and faded like a scroll from the Middle Ages. One leg's kicked up so his journal is resting on a naked knee, polyester French-blue shorts with 10 above the hemline rolled back toward his hip, a too-tight T-shirt, black, that says, ZYZZYVA, in white letters. The guy can't breathe. He's got a rough edgy look and dark Balkan eyes, an unlit cigarette behind the flap of his ear, a lit cigarette dangling from his mouth, a goatee gathered and twisted into a point under his chin, and a tattoo on his arm in Apple chancery cursive: *Maranatha*.

He lifts his pen and looks out the window at the traffic. The smoke fumes are drifting into a popped vent above us. The lady driving the bus is looking right at him and when he returns her gaze, her eyes dart to the street in front of us. I don't like mutherfuckers with this kind of sway. Before I can think on why, he says, "You wanna know what this is, don't you."

I'm the only person near the guy, but I don't care a lick about his deep thoughts. Highly doubt he's writing the sequel to *Notes from*

Underground, however nuts he is, whatever Slavic state he came from. I doubt he's even literate. If I wanted to listen to butchered Dr. Seuss rhymes, I'd turn on the radio.

"I'll bet you got no clue what I'm writing."

"You lost that bet," I say, looking out my own window.

"Well, then," he says. "I'm waiting."

"All right, bro. Are you and your big mouth ready?"

He ties up the journal and caps his pen, the cigarette right on the tip of his lips. I can see it, hear it: he's got some quixotic blood in his veins. Shit: looks like we're gonna either chop it up or have a duel.

"Okay," I say. "Here's the answer: Something of absolutely no consequence."

He smiles at once and I smile back and he looks out the window and says, "Well. You're right, of course. How strange that that's precisely what I'm writing about."

I say nothing: we'll see.

"But you will listen, of course."

"Why the hell not?"

He unties the journal, flips to a yellowed page, flicks the smoking cigarette stub out the window, pulls the unlit cigarette from his ear, lights it with a match that appears out of nowhere, reads:

> "In the end, the nature of this age, the entrapment of time, and the idiosyncrasy of locale are only variables in the constant formula of my ill-willed temperament, which set in at first polluted breath. In the end, I will have from these hands an account of punishment tantamount to each filthy exhalation of carbon dioxide put forth from the bacterial mouths of the afflicted inhabitants of this temporal planet. In the end, no one alive shall know it. In the end, the only people getting wind of my purpose are dead."

He's literate, all right. But I'm not happy about this at all. It's like I'm in the ninth circle with the archangel himself. I pop a window, put my mouth out for some air, focus for a second on the sturdiness of a deep-rooted oak, stay cool.

"Should I get off at the next stop," I say, "before you blow up the bus?"

"You can depart if you want. But that would be a waste of your time." He puts his hands up as if ordered by an invisible cop. "No bomb."

"Okay, then. I'll play this out. You're an Eastern Euro, maybe Russian."

"Pretty good."

"Raskolnikov's disgruntled great-great-great-great-great-nephew?"

"Pretty funny."

"And that's why I don't like you. You're an *übermensch*. You got too much pride. Deep down, Raskolnikov just wanted attention. To be the topic of conversation."

"And will we be talking about you?"

"No, no," I say. "I'd like to die with whatever grandiose ideas I have in my head still there. I don't want to add to the world's badness. My goal is just to float away."

"How sad."

"If I can manage it, my contribution to society will be no contribution."

"I sense trouble."

"Will we be talking about you?"

"You already have been, my friend. For a long, long time. Though I'm worried that you won't much longer. Legions come and legions go."

"You're full of shit, bro."

"No. I think not. You're familiar with Sir Shakespeare."

"Of course. I stole from him a few times to secure some cash."

He seems excited by the theft. "Yes. Perhaps you'll recognize the line and hence my problem. See, if *there is nothing either good or bad, but thinking makes it so,* I have to remind y'all every now and then to think. That's my job, I guess. And yours?"

"My what?"

"Your purpose."

"Shit," I say. "I can barely take the next breath of air without getting crossed up about it."

"I've met a friend," he says, putting his hand out.

I don't shake it. "No. It's gonna take a lot more than that, bro."

"We'll see," he says.

"As with anything."

"Let's have a drink," he says.

"I'm dry, man."

"You've stopped drinking?"

"No. My pocket's dry. I've got a bike stuck to the front of this bus, and forty-six bucks to cover eternity. Just dropped sixteen quarters into that fucking slot."

"Oh. But it's on me, of course."

"All right. I'll get you next time."

"If there is a next time."

"That's right, too," I say. "You remind me of a poem."

He waits and then says, "Well, let's hear it."

"*May you bite your lip that you cannot meet with God—or beat me to a pub. Amen.*"

"The title, please," he says.

"*A Curse at the Devil.*"

"The author, please."

"Sir Kerouac."

He reaches up at once to index-finger the slack cord, the bell in the front of the bus rings accordingly, and we shiver to a tenuous stop. Even as I'm thinking, *Who the fuck is this cat?* I follow him out the exit nonetheless, yank my bike off the rack as he continues to talk. We walk on with our heads down over broken white concrete laced with blue and brown shards of shattered glass. Right through the waste of the earth, the busted bottles of civilization, among the flashing grid of red and green lights controlled underground by the Morse code of some nameless engineer, right under the pendulant web of telephone wire, the crows looking down on us again with those ravenous eyes of infrared, he goes on and on with his stories.

For the first time in some time I don't mind. I listen. To his frustration. A red wheelbarrow of so much overflowing possibility stuck in his raining head, surrounded by glazed chickens upon which nothing and no one depends. Too much mud in his brain, clogging the pipes. He has a reflexive appetite for destruction, his own and anyone else in the way. He calls himself the bastardized result of absolute carpe diem, of forging destiny without limit. Ad infinitum. He flirts with passion. In the land of possibility, everything seems enticing and worthy of a lifetime commitment. All tangents shine like the sun. That's what he says. This guy at one time was a software designer for Oracle, a Triple-A baseball player, a deep-sea welder, a sociology researcher/documentarist, a porn star named Jude Lawless, and is currently looking to wed. His failed search for a calling has resulted in a network of acquaintances sold on his connection to their given passion. But the truth is, he became bored by each and left them before they could leave him.

We make our way out to the oxygenated patio of Rock Bottom Brewery: Tiki burners and five dozen yuppies in business suits or Dockers. The waiters of both sexes have spiked hair and pierced brows and wear colorful tattoos and gothic eyeshadow, always black, thickly applied, coats of paint on the canvas. Looks like they crawled out of caves. I lean back in my chair and place my line of vision straight above the establishment where finally a beautiful saffron mass of sky rolls west without anyone knowing.

"What do you think is my problem?" he asks, lighting the cigarette, lipping it.

I sip on my Hefe-Weizen, ponder the question, offer, "Sounds like you maybe have too much talent."

"I am admittedly," he says, blowing smoke, "a mess."

He's got sweat running down his brow, sweat down his arm. "Are you dying?"

"I may be."

"From what?"

"Neglect?"

"What do you mean?"

"No one cares that I'm alive anymore."

"What the hell are you talking about?"

"I may be on my last proud legs."

"Well," I say. "You got a woman?"

"Been dating someone."

"Will y'all marry?"

"Yes."

"Do you love her?"

He just smiles.

"You seem like someone who would marry only under the condition of love."

"Listen here."

"I've been listening for the length of a glass of Hefe-Weizen."

"I know," he says. "Thank you. And you're welcome. Here's the scaled-down bio of yours truly."

"Another one?"

"I've been saved my whole life by poles: tied to the post of family, girlfriend, job, or sport, whatever. Any time I got too wild in my meanderings I'd be yanked back to sanity like a dog on the fence, choking in his collar. But things changed. I don't know how, but I broke the chain, chewed through the rope. I don't know what to do

now with my freedom. I haven't had a sport since baseball, been job-
less for half a year, and my family—father, mother, and sister—have
fled five hundred miles east of San Jo to Lincoln, Nebraska. My ex,
Deidre, split after catching me inside a double-jointed gymnast at
her sister's wedding in Saratoga Hills. Nobody's left to keep me
moderately clean, see? I am alone on the infinite plane of desire."

"I'm missing something," I say. "I don't get why you'd marry then,
bro."

"Well. This new one'd kill me if she caught me in the coatroom
with a bridesmaid. She'd drop a pill of arsenic in my brew. I met her
in Kabul. My Muslim princess of Aryana."

"Uh-huh. What else?"

"That's it."

"Sounds promising."

"It is. I have to believe it is. I can't talk about it any further or I'll
start to break it down."

"Yeah. Well. Good luck."

He's looking toward the parking lot. "Let's change topics. Break
something else down."

"Like what?"

"Like that," he says, pointing directly behind me.

A kid the height of a fire hydrant jumps out of an army-green
Hummer and is led onto the patio. He has a collar around his neck,
and there's a five-foot leash attached to the wrist of a man with gray
wolfish eyes and finely detailed eyebrows. A woman in a diamond
cross necklace flashing like a Fourth of July sparkler trails the man
as if she were, despite the necklace, a dutiful Muslim. When they
take their table, the man tugs lightly on the leash like he's testing
the status of a fishing line, and the kid, fiddling with the gauge of
the faux-bamboo heating lamp, turns his head and skips to his seat.
He's no older than four, probably three, perfect age for experimenta-
tion. The man and the woman look like they've both been pollinated,

the tanned skin of beeswax. The patio is now full of Silicon Valley techies dropping in for the Thursday evening happy hour, yet no one but us has the nerve to even gaze.

My newfound friend shakes his head, splashes some Hefe-Weizen into my mug and then his own, and slams the pitcher on the table-top, his eyes on the new arrivals. His dilated nostrils look like the smoky twin entrances to infinitesimal black holes. "That's exactly what I'm talking about. I don't care how many abductors are out there. How the fuck do they get away with that?"

I sip my beer, leaving his thought afloat in the air, a kind of silent affirmation. I don't care how many abductors are out there either; just keep an eye on your child, like billions of other parents have been doing for the last four thousand years. At the table, the kid's sitting on the woman's lap and she's stroking his head like a kitten. He still wears the collar with the five-foot leash, rolled into a coil on the table like a garden hose, a rattlesnake fixing to strike. The man, already, is pinkie-crinkling a glass of merlot.

My newfound friend slaps my arm. It leaves a trail of warm sweat. "They taking the dog around the block for a walk?"

I take a sip. "Maybe he has Tourette's or something."

His eyes narrow into slits of cynicism. "Are they gonna throw a muzzle on him next?"

"Hey, I'm with you. Let him bite someone."

"Yeah. The kid ain't got Tourette's or anything else. He's just got bad luck. Look at him."

The kid's docile as a neutered dog.

"Lazy aristocrats. The kid's constricted neck is the price for his burger and fries."

I say, "Topic shift?"

"Yes, sir. I just got back from Afghanistan."

"Yeah?"

"I've had no one to talk to for a long time and so I'm a bit diarrheic. All I got was lean and brown from a yogurt diet and the lingering smog of war."

I sip my pint, ask, "What were you doing there?"

"Taking pictures."

"What part of Afghanistan?"

"Outskirts of Kabul. I'd stop at a tenement stuck to a hillside, sip tea on the dusty dirt floor. No running water, the blown-out walls in piles everywhere. Looked like ant mounds."

"Sad."

"It is what it is. The Afghans play house almost as if nothing has happened, no bombs dropped, no drone flybys. The family right there, fifteen people in a circle under the black speckled sky, no roof. We'd munch on salted chickpeas, smiling at one another. Toward the end, a week ago, I attended a luncheon with these Western media intermediaries. Bent on sustained U.S. funding. Contracts, extensions, that kind of thing. It was like being at the New York Stock Exchange. Oh! And I followed a herd of gypsy rug sellers called Kuchis. For two days. Here are the pictures."

The Kuchis are robed in flowing chestnut gowns, hair knotted like Rastafarians, leading camels heaped with salable goods, sheepdog trotting between the front and hind legs to shade in the camel's shadows.

I say, "They look like gypsies."

"That's what they are, nomads. Sell goods on the border of Pakistan." He pushes another photo toward me, sipping his beer, and there he is with a bearded Afghan, flanked by two men with RPGs over their shoulders.

"This guy a tribal king or something?"

"Close. Actually, yes. It's just we call 'em warlords over here. That's Ishmael Khan. He's the tribal king of Herat."

"Think I read something about this cat."

"You read evil stuff about him. He's refused to concede his region to Karzai. He had bodyguards everywhere. The only way I got in was by telling them I was a Canadian novelist writing about a warlord named Khan who's fighting off an imperial juggernaut. They asked me to prove it and I said, 'Fuck the Soviet Union.' They shook their heads like I was way behind the times or something, and I said, 'Okay. Fuck the USA, too.' I made a thumbs-down sign and they nodded and let me in. Khan told me I looked like an Afghan warrior in another life. That was a compliment."

"So is he a crook or what?"

"Sure he's a crook. All the warlords over there are crooks. It's a tributary system. He was so flagrant about his power that he gave me the lowdown on a laundering operation. Hinted at an upcoming coup against a rival warlord. It's a way of life that extends far beyond our little jiffy in time there. Whether we're dropping bombs or Wal-Marts in their cities, we better be sure about it."

"Yeah," I say.

He slams down his beer glass, squints, refills the both of us, says, "Once this old sage with half his face creviced by flesh-eating sand flies told me that the Afghan political picture is like the nine-hole Kabul golf course. He said the course was built in '73 by the Afghan king. Closed by the pro-proletariat Soviets for ten years. Reopened for several years after the Soviets fell. Closed again by the Taliban. Reopened in 2002 by an NGO. There is no grass, only sand and oil. The greens are called the blacks. No American will set foot on such a lowly course, for fear of irreparable damage to their skills. Very few Afghans have ever learned how to play the game in thirty years. Probably never will. But they liken the view to a peaceful plain, so sunbright with promise you can't even follow the ball."

"Well," I say, "if you don't remember that the sun also rises, you're gonna die internally."

It's the most I've talked to anyone but my uncle in a long time. I realize I may have made a mistake. Don't know why it happened, except it feels right to reciprocate the sharing spirit.

"That was a picture of you," he says, "in the *Mercury News*."

I'd forgotten about the bruises on my lip, the black eye. I resist the temptation to massage one or the other, sip my beer. "Yeah."

"Mr. Hate Crime."

"That's right," I say, and then, "but that ain't right."

"You look Mexican to me."

"Shit." The urge to clear my name to this guy seems heightened by the beer. I want a smidgen of truth to get into the discourse, so I say, "I might as well be Mexican. Those cops and that blond snitch haven't spent even a tenth of the time I've spent south of the border. Right here in San Jo: I grew up with *eses*. My best friend growing up was Mexican, my first lay was a girl named Dora Candelaria for chrissake. Those fools know nada. We used to cook carne asada in the summertime, pumping Vicente Fernandez's ranchero gigs on hot stereos."

"Clarify then why you assaulted them."

"I didn't assault *them*. They assaulted *me*. And the reason for that is they're no different from anyone else. They protect their own, that's how it is."

"I see."

"Just like anyone out there. It's a power play, from both sides, from every side. And that fucks with the notion of justice, with what's right."

"Or wrong," he says.

"Which fucks with my ability to act with conviction."

"So what you're saying is you couldn't decide who to support?"

"It doesn't matter," I say.

"But it does."

"Of course it does," I say. "We're born into this age with a Verifiably Committable stamp on our birth certificates. I mean it. I know it."

"So why were you at the rally then?"

"I don't know, man. For some reason, I keep hoping that life ain't as disjointed as it always seems to be. That there are more bridges than canyons between us. But I've spent the majority of my life keeping friends away from friends, family away from family, because they can't get away from some claim that defines them. And as all of these people and their positions are in me, by inference I don't mean a thing."

"Because you can't take a stance?"

"That's right."

"And you want to take a stance."

"More than anything, man."

He nods. "I told you I met a friend. This ain't a topic change." He looks over at the couple and their leashed child. "The question is: What about them? Is that their stance?"

He downs his Hefe-Weizen and doesn't look back over his shoulder. I've been watching the table, even in my rant: The kid knows the limits of the leash. In everything he does—rising from the woman's lap to look into the restaurant window, squatting down to play with the laces of his shoes, reaching across the table for ketchup or water or silverware to rattle, turning to embrace his mother—the leash gets primary consideration. He's methodical in his upper body movement, frugal in head movement. His right hand, subconsciously designated the save-me hand, always lingers close to the leash in case slack is needed. The kid's learning geometry at three, conceptualizing radius and circumference, a kind of physics confined to five feet.

"I'll let you have this one," I say.

"Well," he says, shivering as if it were cold on this warm patio, "those two parents on the cutting edge of what's hip are under the impression that life is theirs and theirs alone. You and I both know their notion of control is an illusion. Like anything else in this life, it can be smashed. And will be. It's a question of when; maybe—if you're a voyeur—how."

He lifts his pint and drains it, I follow suit. To hell with the happy yuppies and their errant flippant chatter. A slew of hot and slick twenty- to thirty-five-year-olds, this fake-and-bake crowd reveling in their temporary glory, their masquerade of fraudulence. The life force drawn from their Ayn Rand books of absurd objectivism, self-help gurus justifying their greed in a large-print book of clichés, the natural embodiments of Roman decadence, all on the verge of something huge: *huge* fake tits for the ladies, *huge* calf implants for the non-ladies, *huge* promotion at the place of employment, *huge* hierarchal notch up on the auto scale, *huge* trip to Cabo Wabo.

But maybe they're not that bad. It's just us, the reflectors. We must be a reminder of the exact kind of life they've been working so hard to avoid, a dual portrait of pariahood invading this warm safe plastic haven. What's strange now is how little it would take to be like them, to in fact *be* them, a tiny adjustment in the circuitry, the ousting of a glitch. Something has got to be turned off to survive in this century: not turned on, turned off.

I give the kid on the leash a quick glance, a safety measure: his teeth are too few and too dull to chew through anything. My newfound friend twists and puts an arm out. He and his index finger have ID'd the culprits for everyone to see, there they are. Right there.

He stays in this position for a long time, so long it pisses me off: not at him, at them. No one notices a thing, immersed in their own public private vacuums. A patio of mind-thy-own-business etiquette, let the authorities handle the problem. There may not even be a problem. I suspect we're the only two deviations who think there's something gangbusters wrong with this scene.

A waitress appears, the third in the last hour. I suddenly see the strategy employed by someone working the patio. There's a row of empty tables that have cleared out over the past hour and no one's filled them. So we've been sequestered off in the corner from our fellow citizenry.

She's nineteen or twenty, pierced in random spots across the face. You'd think by the light blond cilia on her arms that she'd also have blond hair on her head, but everything's dyed black. You can't think like that anymore, match up body parts like puzzle pieces. Now it's all just black.

She says, more sentence than question, "Would you like to close out your tab."

I smile and shake my head, my newfound friend squints and laughs out loud once, like a cough. She takes it as a yes. "I'll be right back with your bill."

He turns over his empty glass and says, "Did we ask for our bill? You act like you don't want our business."

"Well, we just want to make sure that—"

"We'll take another," says my newfound friend, handing her the glass.

"Would you like a pint, too?" she says to me, her perforated face starting to sweat.

"No," he says, handing her the empty pitcher. "A pitcher. We want a pitcher."

She walks off and we lower ourselves back into the conversational abyss. I tell him about La Dulce's virtually real son. He says, "In thirty years, no one's gonna leave the room. Everything'll be right there within arm's reach."

"I know it. Fuck. But we can't stop time."

"If only there were a reset button." His eyes are bottle-cap big. "We could start all over."

"You're talking like the Unabomber."

"Kaczynski was brilliant. I read his prison journals. He had too much vision. And commitment."

"Yeah," I say. "Mostly that."

He starts coughing into his elbow. It sounds bad. He strokes the ends of his goatee into a downward arrow and says, "Now I'm a little faded."

"As am I."

"But tonight you're gonna witness me trying to save this story."

"Oh. And I thought you were just spinning yarns. Being a good raconteur for your brothers and sisters."

"No, no. Tonight you'll get your chance to take a stance."

He stands and stretches and I immediately look to the kid. He's finished his dinner early and is pricking his palm with his fork. He gently pushes his plate forward, then jumps down off the woman's lap and carefully circumnavigates the table. He goes around three times, on his toes, heels, he's bored. Runs the slack of the leash through the palm of his little-boy hand like a rock climber preparing to descend the face of a mountain. Finally he stops, looks back at the blushing-of-wine man, who's either fully indifferent to the kid or totally absorbed in himself, and leans outward to test the pressure of the leash. No more slack. The kid's out over his toes, looking down on the ground, turning a little but smiling, a bona fide image of gravity. The turtlenecked metro wrist-taps the leash like an old stagecoach driver on the reins, and the kid obediently leans back in toward the table.

Before I can say, *Vayan con Dios* or *Esperas: ¿como te llamas?* my newfound friend's walking over to their table. The metro is swishing wine, holding the glass by the stem between thumb and index finger. The woman and the child stretch their necks out and around my newfound friend and find me. I nod assuringly, smile at the kid. His eyes are so big and unblinking that I want to comfort him, take him inside the restaurant away from all the heat of the patio and say, *Don't worry: on your side. Keeping an eye out for your future.* He looks up at his mother for guidance. The woman taps twice on her thigh and the little boy jumps up on her lap.

I can't hear what's being said, but I can see the face of the father. He expects a friendly encounter, briefly conned. His mouth is slowly opening. Finally, he's shocked. He recrosses his legs knee over knee and says, "Excuse me?"

My newfound friend says something else, and I catch *fucking* and *dog* and *block* and stand up just as I notice that the yuppies at the tables next to the kid have stopped eating.

I'm right behind them now. I see *Miller and Co.* on the customized collar. So it's manufactured in some makeshift warehouse, profitable 1-800 crap from late-night TV.

The dad says, "Why don't you mind your own business?"

"I'm gonna take that leash and tie *you* up so you can see how it feels."

"I don't exactly understand how that would solve anything."

"Hang you from the rafters of the Rock Bottom sign right there, so you'll understand that all things move toward the center of the earth. And the center of the earth is hell."

"You need some help."

"No, I don't. I'll do it myself right here and no one'll stop me. That's a fact."

"I meant," the dad says, his gray eyes rolling with contempt, "you need some professional help."

"What'd you say?"

"Hey, bro," I say, reaching out for his elbow. "Let's go."

The child is now being rocked heavily in his mother's arms, she's whispering a lullaby in his ear.

"Yes, I'd say that it's time to go," says the dad. "Why don't you escort your friend directly to the insane asylum?"

I feel a river of blood rising in my chest. *Prison makes the good bad, the bad worse, and the free all high and mighty.* I want to walk calmly over and line my feet up shoulder width in a linebacker stance, sturdy and implacable, bend at the waist to dust off the David Beckham rouge from this metro's cheeks, then get a good grip on his orange-skinned neck and choke his ass right there in his seat. It has nothing to do with loyalty to my newfround friend. I just would like to watch his flat gray eyes wane into humility, then I'll let him breathe. Yes, I want to rip the leash off the kid. In fact, that's first. And yes, I want to make all the Pontius Pilates of the patio at least passive witnesses of an active truth, to be the proxy signature of their names on the dotted line, have someone appreciate the meaning of present in body only. But mostly I want to put my head under a faucet and run a stream of ice-cold water, breathe in deep through the nostrils.

I say, "Forget about it, bro. Let's get out of here." The hue of the skin on his neck and cheek is clouding like an octopus on the reef: red, white, brown, purple. . . .

"You better take that leash off right now."

The dad's frown lines bunch up and he looks around. "Am I on Candid Camera? Is that what this is? Okay, okay, I get it. Hah-hah. Good one."

Someone from the crowd, a woman, shouts, "Can't you just leave him alone?"

The dad perks up, this show-off mutherfucker. He knows who's in the right with this crowd. Honor thy father and mother (or get choked). He closes his eyes, throws his arms up in the air as if he's about to embrace my newfound friend, and cries aloud, "Why can't you just mind your own business?"

Suddenly this little guy is standing next to me, his head high as my shoulder. I put it together fast: restaurant manager, Napoleon complex, law abider, police caller. He's so grossly violated my personal space that I have no choice but to turn and get in his face, or get in the top of his head.

"What's the problem, dog?" I say, feeling a little stupid.

He lightly taps, caresses my arm. "Your friend here is going to have to leave."

"That's cool, bro," I say. "We'll just finish our drinks and bounce."

"No," he says. "You both have to leave now."

My newfound friend takes a step toward the metro father and shouts, "You know what I'm gonna do with that leash?"

A lady from the circle shouts, "Just go already!"

"Fuck you!" my newfound friend yells into the crowd.

The metro throws his hands yet again in the air. "Why can't you just mind your own business?"

"That," my newfound friend says, pointing at the kid, "is my business."

The manager says, "You're going to have to leave."

"Yeah!" a sympathizer calls. "Leave!"

"Let's head out," I say, "while we can."

The midget manager is red-faced and worried but cool. "Please," he says to me.

"We'll cut out, man. Just relax. All right?"

The manager nods. I start to walk toward our table. My newfound friend's already there. I think, *That's good, anyway. Good.*

He picks up the pitcher of golden Hefe-Weizen, one last drink to finalize capitulation, looks over at their table, grits his teeth, says something vicious in what sounds like Russian, winds up like a discus thrower, and hurls the pitcher at the head of the metro father. It whips past the ear of the target and shatters the glass window of the restaurant. A woman screams. The kid screams too, is screaming.

"Right in front of the poor boy!"

I want to say, I didn't throw it, man, I didn't do it, but for once no one's paying any attention to me.

17

I Make My Break Backward

I MAKE MY BREAK backward, tiptoeing as if I were covering my tracks in the snow.

Now everything's slo-mo, drunk time under water, the betting lines are up. Everyone, even me, is looking at my newfound friend, several women sounding the siren in the early evening.

You better about-face, I think, *before the mace and guns get here.*

He nods at me as if he's read my thoughts, puts his head down, and jumps over the manzanita bush, already running north toward Mrs. Fields and Buca di Beppo. He cuts through an approaching crowd, dodging a biker in fluorescent spandex.

Keep on running, dog. Go, go!

If he makes it past the Bank of the West, his chances are good. Too many cars and not enough road to be chased by a roller here in the Pruneyard. Then it's ten seconds to the cover of two-dozen apartment complexes, where a potential witness will mix up the scene like a bag of Jelly Bellies.

I'm holding my breath, doing my damnedest to leave the air undisturbed. I'm the benefactor of that pedestrian tendency to ogle the accident. Not one patron of the patio follows me.

I jump on my bike, virtually clear of the scene, and he appears. Like a ghost out the kitchen. Untying his Rock Bottom apron with the subtle flair of a matador, macho aplomb foreign to these watered-down shores, the paisa cook with the two black eyes I'd laid on him at the rally tosses the apron into the crowd and gives chase to my friend. The son of a bitch. Is there square footage anywhere in the greater South Bay that this mutherfucker doesn't claim?

Okay, Twisted Fate: I'm in.

I bike down the lot behind the cover of seven straight SUVs, paralleling their path from fifty yards. I'm making ground on both of them. They're banking toward Barnes & Noble and Barbecues Galore, and I can't see them for three or four seconds. I pass the other end of the olive green bookstore and its monolithic display of a book whose cover—a blond leggy bulimic dominatrix—makes me think *Godless, Godless, Godless,* the book's exact title in blood red, and they shoot out across the intersection of Campbell Avenue amid honking horns, weaving and juking through traffic, the paisa at thirty yards from my newfound friend, zeroed in on capture.

I behold in my head the headlines tomorrow in the local section of the *San José Mercury News*: GREEN-CARD CHEF ON THE SUBUR-BAN HUNT.

But I'm gonna get to him first. He doesn't think anyone's trailing him and why would he? Who around here is desperate enough to take the risk?

¿Quien de los Americanos tiene huevos?

I reach the end of the lot perpendicular to traffic. My newfound friend veers right toward downtown Campbell, away from the triple canopy maze of apartment complexes. He's got one way to go now— directly down the artery of Campbell Avenue—and it all depends on me to see he makes it. I'm gonna trip the paisa up like a bad comedy, watch him slide into his new home base. Paint some strawberries on his knees and elbows before he's hailed a hero in a foreign land.

So you want to put your ass on the line, amigo? *¿Aqui?*

Okay. All right. *Ya estuvo.*

I put my head down and grind hard on the bike's crank, my heart-beat as rapid as a small bird's. The stricken streets of downtown Campbell are vacant. My newfound friend cuts to the right of the chevron-shaped billboard: WELCOME TO DOWNTOWN CAMPBELL: YOUR ALL-AMERICAN CITY. I accelerate past a four-stop-sign intersection, across the green grass of the county library, around skaters doing rails and ollies on the steps, up the alleyway behind Molly Bloom's Spir-its, diagonally into a hidden quad of dentistry, ferns and ivy hanging over the gutters, and hop off the bike, breathing hard.

Right then the message on his chest flashes by—ZYZZYVA!—two yards from where I'm crouching behind a plastic recycling bin. He ducks up an alleyway lined with dumpsters, Winchester Avenue on the other side, a definite out from this dead-end Dodge.

I wait. Keep my neck craned so I can see five yards from my po-sition, but the paisa's nowhere in the vicinity. I lean out a little far-ther and look up the walk and see nothing but empty storefronts and two kids playing rock-scissors-paper in front of Recycle Bookstore West. I pull back, wait another three or four seconds, finally step out of the alleyway.

At the corner of the street, the leaves of the elm trees are lit in patriotic red and blue. Two squad cars are angled into the sidewalk, and there's the paisa, already spread out on the hood.

I grab my bike and walk it toward the squad car. One cop is shuf-fling through the paisa's pockets, patting him down to the ankles, shak-ing his head. The other cop is listening to a citizen make her case about what happened. She keeps shouting it: "I saw it! I saw it!"

At twenty yards the paisa spots me. He raises his chin with re-markable coolness, and then he winks. Like: *This ain't nothing, puto.*

I don't know if he's recognized me from the rally or if he's just this way with anyone he doesn't like. I get on my bike and pedal slowly toward the squad car, neither of us looking away from the staredown.

"That's not him," the lady says.

The other cop torques a pair of cuffs tight around the paisa's wrists, and I nod at the green-card arrestee. *So how's that feel now, puto? On this fluffy cloud in middle-class America, you got taught a straight lesson about the hypocrisy of modernity, didn't you? Oh, amigo, we didn't mean for you to be that much of an individual.*

The cop spins him on his feet and presses him with one hand against the car door, turns, and puts a penlight in the witness's face.

"Do I gotta ask you for your green card too, lady?"

She's blind with obedience, dropping her head and saying, "But he's not the guy."

"Doesn't matter if he is or isn't, comprendamente?"

Oh, she understands, all right. She walks. I ride past the scene, nodding innocently at the cops, six Hefe-Weizens to the wind. Toward the town's safe corridors where triple frappuccinos are being sipped, cell phones flicked open, electric mice rolled across laptops, the good people of Campbell shut off to the stories around them. Maybe even inside them.

Well, now the DA's got a weaker case in *The State of California vs. Paul Tusifale,* a fellow arrestee to take the stand against me. That seems, for the moment, fairly just. At least acceptable. Lift up your latte in a toast. *Salud.*

I bike on.

The conversation has got me wandering again. Thinking. About the world sitting in its own red rage on the leash of a tilted axis, needing good and evil to spin. I cruise through side streets dark and cool as the deep sea, follow the light behind the trees, and hit Bascom, heading south beneath the tittering stars, the punctuation points of heaven, if it's still there. The American dybbuk,

Lennon's Nowhere Man, ensconced in hunger. Thinking on error. On my own. Our own. Everyone's.

Married to failure unto death.

I hear a click in my head and pick up the pace. Fly down Bascom past the partially nude strip club of T's and the full-on real deal of the Pink Poodle, left down San Carlos and past the old school Falafel Drive-In and around all kinds of paisas and cranksters talking to themselves on the curb of the sidewalk, and sometimes paisa-cranksters holding up for their lunch or five-bucks-cash big picket signs about discount deals at pizza places, liquor stores, and furniture retailers, under the hanging giraffe-necked streetlights, over the long bridge ten feet above the bumper-to-bumper rush-hour traffic of 280 and its aerial cloverleaf of entrances and exits, and then the merging vein of 17 and that purple haze of smog that rolls and swirls of its own volition, down into the shadow of the valley of commerce between the hill of Valley Fair Shopping Mall and the newly built mountain of Santana Row.

I cut up into the Row for the first time ever to save time. I'd always avoided the place. This valley went from the rowed beauty of apricot orchards to the borrowed architecture of Beverly Hills. Like there was a shift in the San Andreas fault line one day, and out sprang a haven of materialism. Everyone gets to be an aristocrat for a few hours: teachers, janitors, plumbers, 49ers, putting down Manhattans and mojitos in the bright afternoon. Forget about the Burger King, Big 5, and the other middle-class mainstays surrounding this place. The walls are built so high and magisterial that once you enter the corrida, you can't see out of it or over it. You're a done bull, as they say, *un finito toro*. You've got whatever's in front of you, whatever's behind you, and that's it.

I'm inside the chute on the main strip called Alyssum Lane passing high-end monsters like Crate and Barrel and fashion specialization shops with one-word monikers like Jacadi and Tumi and Furla, their gorgeous mannequins in suggestive poses on teak walls, done-up clients with spray-tanned honey skin, the same mucus-colored purse bouncing on their hips, posh art galleries with no more than four paintings on the wall, the proprietor in a kangol and woolen sweater ignoring you when you walk in.

Everywhere I look I see the smeared blowfish face my sister Tali used to make when we were kids. She'd press her palms to her chubby Samoan cheeks and pull them back toward her ears. Her eyes would bulge out and her lips would spread and widen and seemingly fill with blood or fluid or whatever. Women of all ages—twenty-five, forty-five, sixty-five—have the smeared blowfish face on the Row. A few men, too. They foot the bill to be wrinkle-free, but their eyes seem to strain with desperation, like they're trying to tell you something telepathically, like they're in pain.

I look up and across Alyssum Lane at the faux-bay windows of the decorative cardboard flats and at the nondenominational flags hanging like T-shirts on a laundry line, two sheet-large banners that read, DINE IN THE SEASON and LIVE IN THE MOMENT, and though I don't have any problem making a deeper trek into this happy hell without my Dante of an underground guide, in my beanie and befuddled frown I don't fit.

That I don't care is no big issue. Or no new issue. It could be just simple indignance, sure, but I'm cool with my same old story against these synthetic shoppers.

No. A bigger issue is three people I can see from fifty yards, sitting on a bench outside an eating establishment. Five feet from them, two men are playing stand-up chess on a giant board with dwarf-sized pieces. As I tentatively approach, they're being summoned into the restaurant: little Toby in the arms of my sister, Tali; McLaughlin trailing his wife a dutiful step behind. I catch them at the door and say, "Can we make it a party of four?"

All three turn around with no visible signs of excitement, not even from the kid. McLaughlin, however, grabs me by the shoulder and starts to pull me into the restaurant like a North African peddler strong-arming a mark into a desert tent of stolen goods.

"Well," says my sister. "Come on in, Paul."

As if this restaurant were her house.

18

No One Says a Word

No ONE SAYS a word as we take our seats, not even the kid, and as
the menus come, and Tali passes them to us one by one, I look around
at the restaurant instead. It's called The Left Bank. Of the Seine. There
are French flags and French ribbons pinned to potted plants and the
stiff collars of servers. Across the backside of the bar are multiple
framed renditions of the Eiffel Tower. Above the bottles of spirits: a
tributary black-and-white of a young mustached cocksure Hemingway
at Montparnasse. So far the Impressionists have been ignored in the
establishment, though I've yet to see the restroom. I'm sure I'll uri-
nate in front of a framed *Water Lilies* over the foldout bidet. There's a
terrace outside where I bet I'll find a miniature version of Notre Dame
cathedral. Like, for instance, in the center of a penny fountain.

Who said high art can't be transported in hidden drywall to a strip
mall near you?

And, of course, the enduring television has found its way into the
Chef Boyardee Franco-American picture, in this case six of them,
crisscrossing over the bar at different angles. On their faces a show
called *Adulterers,* hosted by a primadonna named Johnny Gecko. He's

wearing those black-rimmed glasses, the kind you see now on dispossessed species like poets and mimes, jet black hair chemically pulled away from his forehead, and a mouse, that smudge of hair under the lower lip. And he's sporting a black turtleneck, tight around the windpipe, cutting off oxygen to the brain.

So my options are to admire the little Eiffel Towers sprouting around, zone off into the world of adultery, join my hosts and stare down at the silverware, or head to the exit.

Tali says, "Daddy Kolu called while you've been gone."

I look to the door, inhale deeply, hope for the best, prepare for the worst. Right now I'm supposed to say, *And how is he?* but I don't. Daddy Kolu is a guy named Dimitri Taliafero. *Kolu* means three in Samoan. But Dimitri has no Samoan blood. He's Russian-Italian. Married my mother in 1992, her third vow for life. So Tali calls Dimitri Daddy Kolu in the same way she numbers in Samoan the other five men whom she claims as her fathers.

I say, "While I've been gone? Where have I been?"

"You tell me, Paul."

"Well," I say, "I haven't been spending time with Dimitri. Can tell you that much."

Tali says to McLaughlin, "Paulie didn't like to talk to his fathers."

Nearly twenty years later, it still sounds wrong. And this with the numbers having grown significantly: Mom is now on number six, a stout little Costa Rican named Culito, a retired dot-commer who hit it big in the mid-'90s. My mother left my father, or my father pushed my mother out; but however you look at it, we were your typical broken American family.

I'd like to clarify some things to Tali right now. That I don't, frankly, care. And I, personally, ain't broken. Or wounded. Or suicidal. I'm just nil. I was disappointed for some time, I suppose, but I got used to it. One less institution to believe in. By my early teens, I was functional in the flux of my mother's remarriages. It was like chang-ing the stage props for the next band.

I look over at Toby to try and defy our family history and get the conversation focused on what matters. He's so tame and lifeless that I reach out for his wrist, feel for the pulse and, relieved by the trace-able rush of the kid's blood, say, "Does my nephew talk?"

"To people he likes," she says.

I almost say, *I have never heard him say a word to his mother, sister of mine,* but somehow it would be like adding to why the kid doesn't talk.

"And who are you to ask that, Paul? You never said a word to our fathers."

"I used to talk with them, Tali."

"But you didn't like talking with them."

"That's not true. I used to rap it up with them about everything. Like with anybody I meet. I was cool with each one. They were okay guys."

"They were your fathers."

"Nah. We're split there, Tali. I mean, I think it's better to say that they were my mother's humpers. Or, I guess in number four's case—"

"His name is Spinos."

"Spinos. With the gargantuan peni—" I catch myself: little eu-nuch Toby needn't hear about Spinos's King Kong dong. Toby'll have enough problems learning how to put his first sentence together before hitting his teens. "That's right. Old Spinos. Cool guy. Loved to whip up a Greek salad in the summertime. 'Member he used to watch *Golden Girls* with Mom and read Alice Walker novels to her in bed? And he loved to pick out Mom's wardrobe at the mall. 'Mem-ber that time we caught him running around in mother's dress down-town? Anyway—"

"He loved our mother."

"I don't think we're in disagreement there."

"But you talk about them, Paul, as if they didn't love you."

"I don't talk about them. I don't really think about them, though I wish them well—as I do anyone. Even old Spinos. Hell, I hope he's kicking it in the Castro doing his thing."

"But I know what you think of them, Paul. You can't fool me. You feel like they had no right to care about you."

"No, I don't think so. No. If they felt it, more power to them, wherever they are. But I guess I'm sorry, too. Because I didn't feel it back. I think I just cut out the cancer before it could really hurt me. And since I made that sacrifice, no one could ever tell me that I didn't love Dad."

"Are you saying *I* didn't love Dad?"

"No, not at all. I'm just saying I didn't love your dads."

"Daddy Kolu paid for your tuition, Paulie, at St. Cajetan. Then later, Daddy Fa paid for the University of Alviso, which you quit five classes short of a degree."

"God. I almost forgot I was that close. How funny."

"Funny? It's tragic. All that money down the drain. All those years. Daddy Fa went to all your home football games. And he drove out to Utah once to watch you play."

"That was nice of him. Surely, I thanked him. Even now, I'm sure of it."

"Your problem goes back to your childhood, Paul."

Oh, God. Here we go. Spare me the new-age psycho babble, please. I'm trying not to argue, debate, bite back. Just trying to make me clear for once to you.

"When you couldn't find it in your heart to come home from the library or the mountains or the ocean and tell them where you'd been. At the Fathers' barbecue your senior year at St. Cajetan, you took some homeless guy you'd picked up on the street!"

"Not true. I picked him up in McDonald's. I told him to wash up if he wanted some real food."

"Whatever, Paulie."

"My teammates got a big kick out of that." I nod at McLaughlin. He doesn't nod back. "That guy loved the meat loaf and mashed potatoes that their spoiled asses hated. He got drunk on the wine and started calling me figlio mio. Then he was bragging to everyone that his son was going to be a cadet at West Point. He was great. I went back and looked for him later but never found him."

"Just like you, isn't it? You did more for a stranger than your own fathers."

"That's not true," I say. "I relinquished my Oedipal right to claim my mother. That was my gift. Believe me, I know I was a hindrance to them. Each one came into that house with the same look. They knew I was a threat to their territory. But I removed myself. That was my gift straight through childhood to our mother—who, by the way, wanted exactly that: no Sophoclean bullshit. That kind of old-world story she was getting rid of with Dad. He took all the honor and patriarchy of his heart with him when he went back to Samoa. So I tried to stay away amap and let them live their lives with my mother freely."

"Amap?" asks McLaughlin.

"As much as possible," says Tali, and reclaiming her theme, her childhood, her life, says, looking at her husband, "You didn't want to listen to them."

"That's not true," I say. "Whenever I was there, I listened a lot."

"So you did nothing wrong to them?"

"Oh, no. I'm sure I did plenty wrong."

McLaughlin's nodding encouragingly, hoping we can wrap things up and remove the tension. *Just get it over with and be wrong,* he wants to say. I want to say back to him, *This is only one half the problem, bro-in-law. There's still the other parent in the equation, living halfway across the world, from whom you take your discolored self-definition.*

"One thing I've never done is complain," I continue. "How could I? It was the kids whose folks *stayed* married who were the oddities. We were just like everyone else, with half-siblings they'd never met, weekend visits from a parent, eight last names. There were plenty of other little dreams to latch onto back then. I had a nomination to West Point for chrissake."

"And what about Dad?"

"You mean Daddy Tasi?"

"You know who I mean, Paul."

"Well, what about him?"

"Do you talk to him?"

"No. I prefer to write. Send him a letter once a month or so."

"I bet you make up stories about yourself."

"Of course I do. That's my gift to him. Dad knows, for instance, that I'm a churchgoing man, strong in my devotion to a virginal girl whom I'll only marry once the families have aligned. People respect me, sometimes envy my strength as a Tusifale. I am indebted to my brothers and sisters in American blood for life."

"So you lie."

"I write the opposite of what's going down in my life."

"You lie."

"I'm doing it for him."

"Yeah, right."

"I am. I don't care what people think about me."

"Well, I guess *that's* true, anyway."

"I just don't want Dad to ever think I'm so screwed up he has to return to a country he loathes to save me."

"And Mom?"

"We don't talk."

"Do you want to change that?"

"Change what? That's what she wants: me out of her business. I'm cool with it. I ain't complaining."

"You think you're so noble, Paul."

"Not at all. Not even close. But I can read the signs. I know what people want. And when they can take it without barking or biting back, I give it to them. You know that. I knew years before they signed the divorce papers that our parents were finished."

"You're selfish, Paul. You think you're over that time in your life, so you leave them by the wayside."

"Okay," I say. "Without arguing who left whom by the wayside, what do you want to talk about, sister? How we were caught in a crosscurrent of cultural miscommunication? The recent trend toward kid leashes? Hummers?"

"Paulie, I can't stand talking to you sometimes."

"Well, I don't mind sitting in silence."

I try to be cooperative, look up at the nearest television of the sixteen total, and read the words being transcribed across the bottom of the screen. Our conversation about Tali's fathers has bypassed all the frills of preamble and ushered us right into the meaty part of this show. We're observing in gray-and-white infrared what looks to be some kind of country-western nightclub. A big cowboy with a gallon hat, a T-shirt crawling out his overalls, is twirling and tossing a tiny cowgirl. He has his chin down in the two-step, serious, and she has her head up, laughing. Suddenly, the screen starts shaking up and down and then there is a rapid shaking zoom because the cameras are live and approaching the bar very fast. Big brothas in tight black shirts are sprinting ahead and fanning out along the street, and all along the bottom of the screen run the words of Gecko: "There they are. Block 'em in at the exit."

The crew of cameras reaches the bar and some girl points with her bottle of Bud Light, "It's *Adulterers!*" A sleeveless doorman commands, "You can't come in here," as the cameras whip by his crossing-guard palms and surround the two dancers. They're shocked and the cowboy responds. Open-hand slaps the main camera and for a few seconds I'm looking at the blackness of the ground. Suddenly another camera shows a different angle of the cowboy, carrying the girl underneath the crook of his arm like a rolled Persian rug. The man she's allegedly betrayed stays on the heels of the black-shirted Gecko, who's hard on the cowboy's heels.

Along the bottom of the screen: "Can you explain yourself, Trudie? Do you at least want to apologize to Littleton here who's been so faithful to you through the years? He was supportive of you through the death of your mother. He paid for your car insurance, phone bills, and breast implants. And you're making him pay now with a broken heart. How do you explain this?"

I say to myself, "This country is whacked out."

My sister, McLaughlin, and young Toby look up at the televisions. Tali breaks the silence between us, with barely restrained excitement. "*Adulterers!*"

I take a big long drink of water.

"Oh," she says, with barely restrained disappointment, "this is a rerun."

"You watch this show?"

"Of course. But I know you've never seen it, Paul."

"Nope."

"Now how did I know that?"

"Have you seen Mom on it yet?" I ask.

Tali immediately looks at Toby, as if the words are more damaging to his system than a life of silence. "Paul," she says. "There's a little boy at the table."

"I guess you'll have to wait for the foreign version of the show. When they find Mom in Siberia making whoopee in a bed of whale fat."

"Paul."

"Some barefoot Zulu with a nose ring will bust into the wickiup trying to find a target with his spear. All with this punk-ass Gecko at his heels."

"Paul!"

"She always did love variety. Was always, let us say, down for international cuisine." The waiter appears with complimentary calamari, apparently a French delicacy. I take one before he's laid it on the table. "Just like us."

"Are you ready to order?"

"Yes," I say, digesting my fried French squid. "Our order is to change the channel on the television."

"Excuse me, sir?"

"Paul. Shut your mouth."

It was a joke. Until now. "Turn around, sir."

"Excuse me?"

"I said turn around."

He does. He wants a big tip at the end. On the screen Littleton, Trudie, and the cowboy are looking down on a cell phone. Suddenly furious at what he sees on the screen, which is a blurred black-and-white picture of two people fornicating, Littleton is now punching at the air, as the cowboy hitches up his britches, Trudie begs her case, and Gecko placidly observes with a slight upward tilt of his glass chin.

I say, "You see. This show is like watching someone giggle in a mutherfuckin' funeral home. It's unnerving to think about having to ingest food to this crap. Don't you have some music from the Provençal or something?"

"Where's that?" the waiter says.

"Can you just turn the television off, bro?"

That wakes him up, if only because he's never considered the possibility. "Sir?"

"The TV: can you turn it off?"

"Uh—I—" The neurotransmitter in his frontal lobe is stuck, flickering in the gray-dead recesses of matter like a bug on a bed of cold clay.

"Well, can we at least change the channel? We want to watch something else. Like *Sesame Street*."

"I'll see what I can do, sir."

"*Merci*."

"Paul," Tali says, "what the hell is wrong with you?"

"How hopeless for us," I say. "We're done. Finished."

I look up at the television one last time. At least for the day. Okay, at least for the hour. Even I, its prime-time hater, can't control it. Spurned son of the visual medium. Everywhere I go I'm surrounded by TVs. Even in jail there are TVs, or the most bankrupt of dive bars over the tap of Lucky Lager and a skeletal bartender are five TVs, TVs on watches, on phones, in dreams, in space, everywhere are the images that aren't there, people that aren't alive and that I don't know and won't ever meet anyway, in situations that aren't real, though they're called real.

So Wes Cash, the big loyal lug in overalls, is digging into a toolbox on his flatbed truck, and when I think *What the hell is this cat doing?* he whips out a thin wand five times its normal length and points it at a big brotha in a tight black T. The brotha falls at once to the ground, like he was struck down by a heart attack. It's not the index finger of Zeus issuing bolts of lightning, it ain't magic: it's a god-damned cattle prod.

Oh my God! We're mad, downright mad!

He zapped him with a fucking cattle prod.

I'm holding my crotch with two hands, remembering the short story about the civil rights kid getting jolted in the loins by the cop with white man's penis envy. The boy writhing in the fetal position on the filth of the jailhouse floor. Everything has come back around, brave James, Mr. Baldwin, to mocking pain, this thing we call our lives over which you fought, or wrote, or died, or whatever.

We await, salivating, the created spectacle.

Now there's a fight between one of the brothas and the cowboy. Wes Cash spins him around nicely and throws him against the edge of the flatbed truck. The brotha rears a yolked arm back and, swinging at Wes Cash, knocks over a Styrofoam cooler. Two long, pink, skinned heads roll out. The meat around the bovine jaw is white and red. The dead cow eyes are looking up at me in this faux-French restaurant and I'm thinking, not laughing anymore, *It's all over. Forget about it.*

Across the bottom of the screen:

GECKO: What the hell is that?
CASH: Mexicans like to eat 'em. It's a delicacy.
BOYFRIEND: What kind of guy are you dating here, Trude?

(*Wes Cash and the boyfriend fight.*)

TRUDIE: Turn those fucking cameras off! Look what you're
     doing!
GECKO: No, Trudie. This is what *you're* doing. This is a
     result of what *you've* done.

I put my head down, finally, and opt to look at my silent nephew. Feeling the urge to apologize on behalf of mankind, I say, "Don't worry, kid. There's better stuff out there."

Then to Tali (who's shaking her head), "I hope this Gecko guy gets stabbed the next time he goes on the adultery hunt."

"He's already *been* stabbed, Paul," Tali says, like, number one, you need to emerge every now and then from the cave of isolation, Paul, and, number two, this Gecko guy whose integrity you question is actually willing to be a martyr for the cause, unlike you, Paul, whatever your cause is. Other than yourself, Paul. If you claim to love irony so much, there you have it, Paul.

"Good. If he ever gets the fatal blow I'll be sure to leave a rosary at his shrine."

"What?"

"St. Gecko, patron saint of entrepreneurial causes."

"I can't believe what I'm hearing."

"Death is what this guy wants, right? *Death, thou shalt die*. Okay. So let's hope he gets shot the next time, right in the gut. Guys like this cat have no reverence for anything. He doesn't even acknowledge the setup, that it's staged by his own greed. Think about it! He disclaims this circus sideshow as a medium of coincidence!"

Tali says, "Don't you believe in the sanctity of marriage?"

"I thought I already weighed in on that. I believed in it wholly while no one else around me believed in it and so I, witness of and surrounded by nonbelievers, don't believe in it anymore." I wave my hand around. "Not in this place, anyway."

McLaughlin says, "Gecko was on the gurney looking up at the camera, Tali."

That took courage. Not from Gecko, from McLaughlin. Tali's not gonna like this uncalled-for instance of treachery. "You say something, bro-in-law?"

McLaughlin nods, looks over at Tali for approval.

"Well, what?" I say.

"He said, 'This is the price I have to pay to help the faithful.'"

"Aha! You see?" Tali looks at her hubby like he's betrayed a bedtime secret between them. Oh, it's beatdowns for you tonight, McLaughlin. I look up at Gecko and over at the kid, curb my language: "What a piece of manure."

The waiter returns and says, "I'm sorry, sir. The televisions are preset to certain programs."

"All right, man," I say. "Just get us some champagne, will you?"

"Is Brut Napa okay, sir?"

"Just bring something that sparkles and is high in alcohol content."

"I can do that," he says.

"Are we celebrating something?" asks Tali.

"Yes," I say. "Do we have enough money?"

"*I* have enough, Paul."

"Okay."

He returns to our table with Brut Napa and a towel, plus some animated data about a riviera region in Southern France that he's going to fly out and visit for a *Playboy* party, and when I say, "Just pop it, bro," either the inflated head or the bottle, he does the latter—*poooomp!*—pouring three glasses, serving Tali's first ("ma'am"), then McLaughlin's ("sir"), mine last (silence). That makes me smile. But then: Tali is a lady, McLaughlin is a gentle gentleman, and I am admittedly insignificant.

I toast. "*Al morto.*"

"What's that mean?"

"To the passed." I say to McLaughlin, "You want the Samoan?"

He nods with death in his eyes.

"*I le oki.*"

No one repeats the toast, not even my pliable, docile, nubile brother-in-law, and I decide right there to drink only heartwarming champagne from here on out. Must avoid the dangerous mixture of drinking fire water (hard liquor), reading Patricia Highsmith, Poe, and Dostoevski (potential murderers who were curbed of the affliction by creativity), and watching anything by Quentin Tarantino (a video-store nerd who, never having been in a fistfight in his life, yearns to murder someone—anyone). With this wicked combination of liver and cerebral stimuli, my newly sprung fantasy to disembowel Johnny Gecko will no doubt come to life and though I'd no doubt get a life sentence for the act, I'm sure there's still someone out there who would know exactly why I'd done it, might pay me a visit in prison even, send me monthly stamps and nudie mags and other contraband, and that, really, when you stop and think the thing over, it was nothing short of amazing that no one had done the deed earlier.

19

When We Still Had Hope

WHEN WE STILL HAD HOPE, my father was working at the UPS ware-house, paying the bills so my mother could earn her doctorate. I was nine, Tali ten. Only one tale in a thousand tales counts, so this is it: Christmas, 1987, East Side San Jo. We'd been invited to a party at the house of one of my father's coworkers. My father didn't want to go for a reason I didn't understand then, but do now. My mother, in her goodness, insisted we go. She knew how hard he worked for her, and for us. What was merely duty to him was true sacrifice to her, because she'd never seen it in the American men she'd known, in-cluding her own father, my grandpa, dead before I was born.

When we got to the house, we had to drive past it and down a few blocks. The street was bumper-to-bumper with parked cars. On the porch we all kicked our slippers off in the traditional order of father down, adding to the dozens of primitive footwear already lost forever in a third-world mountain of worn leather and flimsy rubber, blessed by the lamplit porcelain shrine to St. Claire. We could hear a muffled rumble in some rear vicinity of the property, and even there on the doorstep the sour vinegar and musky soy odor of pork and chicken adobo collected under our noses like salty dew.

One by one, we wiped our bare feet on the welcome mat, which read ELCOM, from the left foot–right foot rubbing out of the first and last letters. Entering the house, we went from one plastic mat to another, my father in the lead, me last and watching everyone else, the mats connected like puzzle pieces throughout the living room and into the kitchen, a clear plastic walkway under which the clean, untouched bright-teal rug turned into a swampy green. It was like hiking along the cliff on the coast: you instinctively used caution. Between the wall and the edge of the mats grew thin strips of rug, like moss dividing brick and mortar. The chairs were also covered in plastic, though thinner. Over the armrests and down the legs of the recliner it also grew, over the arms and the seat of the couch.

It was a modern American nightmare, preservation prioritized before use, the postponement of time, the suspension of fashion. Even then, to a nine-year-old, it seemed something of a faulty formula, though I was to see it time and time again in the houses of other Filipino friends I grew up with: Ron Cristobal, Rubelle Bagan, Isidro Del Rosario. Yes, it was an appreciative gesture to keep the lavish furniture in tiptop shape for decades, yes, it expressed a successful campaign in crossing a hostile ocean for these American prizes, but alas, no, since I'd been trained from the womb to understand that nothing new in America is new for long. So whatever it is that gets you off you put to immediate use, even if it burns up old-world frugality and old-world story and even if it burns up your heart and your wallet. Whenever these good people would decide to actually deplasticize the house, sit down and live a bit, their protected rug would be in the same realm of cheesiness as a living room covered in plastic.

My mother was giggling at this fashion faux pas. She didn't get too far before my father said, "Shut up."

My mother shooed my sister and me away. She was about to confront our father. She was earning her PhD in Women's Studies.

We didn't stick around to spy on their argument. It was an old story. I said, "Let's check out the back rooms."

In a hallway we found a turquoise blind across a window, slid it open, and slipped through pretty easily. Our parents' bickering faded. We tiptoed across the porch toward a cacophony of shouting in the deep broad yard, as if both of us were on the same path in search of the same hypnotist. A fence between the two houses had been taken down and their respective yards, which were wide on their own, were combined into one. They'd left the centerboards standing, equally spaced across the property line, like the remnants of some washed-away pier. Rows of bamboo cages were stacked one upon the other, dark little UPS boxes in which darker, bright-eyed birds were hopping anxiously about, and it seemed to my virgin eyes that we were entering country on the other side of the wild world where no law existed save eat or be eaten. My hands were shaking and when I reached for Tali's hand I was comforted by how quickly she pulled her own back, tucking it into the other hand hidden inside the sweater pocket across her navel. The shouting was getting louder now, more precise.

We came upon an old leather-skinned man working over his cock. He whispered to it in foreign yet soothing tones, as if the bird were an infant, the thin, blood-purple, ashy immigrant lips kissing into the epicenter of blood-red wings flapping, and he stroked its smooth blue head in that gentle, somewhat rough manner of earnest, loving, possessive fathers, and the bird leaned back against the man's naked brown chest with trust and maybe even affection and seemed to rub itself calm, as if there were some secret magical balm secreted by the pores of this strange Melanesian wizard.

Tali reached out and I grabbed her hand. The man, now noticing us, put that same paternal gaze upon my sister, and she immediately responded, pushing me off and stupidly reaching out and in toward the cock. The bird murmured from the deepest reaches of its muscular chest and Tali, stroking it, was saying something like, "Good bird, beautiful bird, the colors of God," and then the man kind of nodded the both of us away and proceeded to put a cigarette to his lips, light it with one hand, reach back down and clutch tight on the bird's middle and pull back hard on one wing so that the bird, by reflex, pulled back just as hard, and he did this over and over again until I finally lost count. He switched over to the other wing and did the same. I didn't bother counting at all this time because the repetition seemed sinister and sneaky and something we shouldn't be witnessing. Then he reached into his pocket, pulled out a syringe and injected the bird, still coaxing it with words I didn't understand.

Tali and I headed toward two dim, barely traceable lights in the rear corner of the yard. As we neared, I saw that a giant tarp covered the lights and also the shouting, its volume growing as we neared. It looked in its obvious hidden designs like a sidetent for some hideous circus freakshow out of the nineteenth century. By the time we opened the flap of the tent and fell toward the crowd of shirtless bettors—all squatting like catchers behind the plate, all shouting, the crumpled fans of cash pumping in their tiny brown fists, Asiatic eyes alight, riveted on the two prize birds dancing one around the other in the ring—I was floating. I could feel Tali next to me. We were surrounded by incomprehensible sounds. A strange, nasal tongue I hadn't before heard, unrestrained tones, fired off rapidly. It sounded like the banter of chickens, human chickens, as if the bettors had taken on the linguistic traits of the very animals over which they themselves were lords, a weird case of reverse osmosis. Yet I wasn't surprised by what I saw. I knew, even at nine, that the world held darker, more primitive shades of life in its palm, and this was it. The noise, the energy, the secrecy numbed my very bones. I held Tali in her place.

The birds were beautiful. One was completely white, not a blemish of color on its virgin plumage, dove white even in the bowl of dust, the regal tail feathers twice the height of its chevron head so that my sister, a decade later in life, would mistell the story as a bout between a peacock and a chicken, ruining our credibility at a Filipino hula competition in Hayward called Hula Halau o Pilipine. The other bird was cobalt-feathered like a pair of Levi's jeans newly bought and its maroon head was the same color as the banner that sagged over the ring and read SABONG. Each bird had a blade tied to the heel of its right talon and then a sharpened bone lashed to the end of each wing, their cautious parry predicated by an avian understanding that the contraptions attached to their bodies were put there to expedite murder. Neither bird wore the scars of previous fights and it showed: when one hopped forward the other hopped back, this avoidance of combat happening three times over, until two bettors on opposite sides of the ring reached in with reckless haste and grabbed a bird each, contraptions and all, slapped their respective heads several times, and then threw the birds forward so they collided in an explosion of feathers midair above the ring, the crowd matching the collision with a high-pitched collective battle cry.

Now the birds fought. They moved like boxers, circling each other, moving in, moving out. The blue-and-red cock was more aggressive and as it hopped in to attack, its wings extended to their farthest reaches, a gesture of intimidation. A swift rush in and then a hammering peck with its beak, drawing blood from the other bird's muscular breast the third time through. The blood spot of a wound grew into a star-shaped crest across the clean white feathers, and the crowd, at the sight of blood, threw up more cheers. Tali was squeezing hard on my hand now as if to say, It's no longer pretty, Paul. You've got to save it.

I found myself caught on the first of what would be many destroyed bridges between two worlds: I wanted to jump into the ring and save the white cock but this was more than a matter of courage or cowardice. The red or the yellow badge. The problem was in the fiery eyes of the bettors themselves. I knew they came from a far-off place,

a place like my father's way out in the Pacific, and that the purity of
this moment had to do with their own performance in the dusty bowl
of the ring, and though I couldn't, at nine, articulate it for what it
was, I could identify the code, the story, no different in substance
than the springboard from which my father leapt one average suburban Silicon Valley afternoon, straight out the car to slap some
Mohawked kid with a KILL YOU LATER shirt who'd casually and a propos
of nothing flipped us off from the rolling sanctuary, or so the kid had
thought, of his skateboard. In the cockfight world my father came
from, a gesture like the middle finger was no more or less than a
prelude to death, my father's or the kid's; one or the other, someone
was going to die. That my father stopped short of killing the kid, or
even closing his fist on him, but only snapped the board over his knee
and ripped the kid's dog chains from his neck and winged both ob-
jects into the bed of the creek, was a sign of his worth here or of his
worthlessness there.

All through my childhood I would see it: the great divide between
first- and second-generation Americans. The children of immigrants
couldn't handle the blood and guts of the old world. Every horror
was buffered/negotiated/quelled by an outside agency, across the
glass table in the air-conditioned office of the designated bureaucrat at large, whispering our fears from the cloudy pillows of the soiled
couch. No gradation of suffering for the fattest people in the world.
Where afflictions were always self-administered and always, by the
law of relativity, absolutely horrifying. The craziest experiment in the
history of man has an orbit of its own, an all-consuming black hole,
yes, constantly increasing its mass, yes, its momentum, yes, everything spinning into nothingness, yes, no, it doesn't matter.

And there I was, paralyzed by the in-betweeness I felt, my ability
to see the promise of both shores from the bridge. These people were
ruthless but tough, and we were compassionate but weak. What to do
but jump over the rail and fly down into the rushing water, treasure

that one moment of freedom from thought. And then if you survive the fall, let the unpredictable tide take you to one side or the other.

It was too late. The white cock had lost the use of one leg, the talon dragging. The eye on the other side of the head had been pecked out, slimy fluid mixed into the dirt. The bird hopped crookedly about, desperately trying to adjust to both handicaps. When it found its balance, the other bird pounced like a cat, delivering a vicious peck, a swipe of the wing so swift it left behind blue streaks that dissolved like mirages in the burning light. Then the aggressor seized upon the eye socket itself, pecking at it once, twice, digging in a third time. The hole deepened. Blood geysered out crimson. The blue and red cock switched tactics, brushing its wing along the ground, severing the talon from the leg of the white cock, to lie in the caked dust like the rubber souvenir of a show-and-tell slaughterhouse. Neither bird made a sound. Even the bettors had gone quiet. The white cock took its last stand on one spindly leg, pivoting about in a jerky, almost out-of-body circle.

Suddenly I remembered Tali at my side. She was crying into her hands, covering her eyes. I pried them away from her face and said, "Go outside then. Get out."

She separated from me immediately and crawled out the flap of the tent on her knees, no one interested in her exit.

The white cock was no longer white. The blue and red cock circled. A few in the squatting crowd shuffled and repositioned their weight, but not one bettor whispered a word. The silver dust in the middle of the ring had browned into mud. The white cock extended its wings, a final salute, and the other cock sprang in decisively. It mangled the crippled white cock in a mad rush of feathers and blades, slicing one wing at the base, the last eye gone. The white cock, blind now, red in its own blood, collapsed on itself, and the crowd erupted. Everywhere in the tent cash was changing hands. Excited banter, praise for the victor.

The winning owner reached into the ring, petting and cooing his bird into calmness in the crook of his arm, removing the blades with the deftness of a surgeon. The loser, still alive, was convulsing in a growing pool of blood. Its owner sliced off the one remaining talon, the cigarette between his lips almost pure ash to the filter, and handed the spastic carcass over to the victor.

I didn't see the second fight. I was yanked out the tent by the elbow. I couldn't see the force behind it but I knew it was my mother. She dragged me across the yard. I was skipping along, my toes barely touching the ground. My father was waiting on the back porch with Tali cradled in one arm, her head on his shoulder like a baby six years her junior. I remember my father's face: expressionless, without contrition or even pity for Tali's condition, which I viewed as bogus. My mother saw this on my face. She grabbed my father's shirt and shouted, "You brought my children to this slaughter!"

In a flash I was sent reeling across the porch. I hadn't been hit, but my mother had. Her face was buried into her hands, just like Tali back in the tent. My sister was suddenly in my arms, pulling the back of my head down by the neck. My father stalked toward my mother, immigrant fury on his face, and I pushed Tali off of me. She fell to her knees, crying.

Does it matter that my father slapped my mother again on the porch, so hard that he bruised her cheek? Or that it took four clucking Filipino men to restrain him? Does it matter that the same thing would happen again elsewhere, repeatedly and worse: my father now determined to reestablish the patriarchal order that he'd lost in the house of his head, so distorted by the placid suburbs in which he held tightly to the old world code, my mother now increasingly secretive and dishonest, shit-talking him behind his back ("You're better than your father, Paulie, don't ever be like him. Promise me that, will you?"), suddenly intensely committed to charities of battered Muslim and African women millions of miles away, nosy now about the private lives of other men she knew, relatives, neighbors, how they treated their wives, their "infinitely better halves," as she'd say? Does it matter that Tali, despite her inability to watch the cockfight, would soon preach to everyone she encountered the merits of being "down for the brown," uniting herself with the Melanesian practitioners of Sabong? Does it matter that my parents would never recover from the episode at the cockfight, that the divide between them would only grow like a crack in concrete that widens from the force of surrounding structures intent on remaining uncracked themselves?

That each of us, however committed, good-hearted, and talented, however blessed, facile, and sharp, wherever we come from, whatever we are—each of us can only peaceably contain so much of the earth's molten fire in our core before we blow.

20

Just for the Record, I've Always Believed

JUST FOR THE RECORD, I've always believed that of course it matters. If either my mother or my father could have held their tongues in that plastic-lined living room, their marriage would have survived. Hindsight is twenty-twenty because you can choose what you want to see, but still it's so damned easy to psychoanalyze. To laugh at the story of the immigrant was to break my father's golden rule: *Never* mock the traits of those who suffered to get here, who've been hungry, who've seen and lived through death, who left family behind for the promise of America. To do so, to laugh at their trial, was despicable to my father. Because the trial *was* my father, immigrant by blood and experience, born of foreign dirt. And I, a little boy with no story then, agreed, the man with no story now, the same. When my mother started in, I was thinking the exact words my father laid on her. "Shut up. Shut up."

Understand, understand! Erect the bridge between the two worlds! Lay the foundation in the thunderstorm!

But my father also broke a golden rule, that of the modern American woman, my mother: Don't ever issue a canine directive.

Domestic decisions are made by a two-vote, equal-in-weight, equal-in-insight panel. To ignore this meant flouting centuries of suffering going all the way back to the caves and the club. That's the condition from which she and her sisters had triumphantly emerged to forge a new legacy, and nothing was lower than an attempt to reverse the course of progress, however brown and exotic you were to a white American girl raised on the Beatles and *Andy Griffith*. So when my father turned toward my mother, I held my breath in the impossible hope that he'd speak gently to her, cool as a summer day in Frisco, put an index finger to his lips, soothing whisper: "Please, baby."

Each time I witnessed the problems between them, I said to myself, "Don't do it, don't say it," but they did it all right, they said it, as if not just our family but everyone, the whole world, was on a churning riverboat that wouldn't dock so its passengers could stop and think about the ride they were on. Because there was an alternative outside the paradigm of their bankrupt nuptials. Maybe there was beauty on the ride, maybe the sights were worth it. I was bright-eyed in love with both my parents, hopeful as I'd ever be, but I knew as sure as simple subtraction that they were done. I was very young when I realized how poorly we manage our gifts.

At nine going on ten, I began the process of forgetting them together, as husband and wife, as mother and father conjoined forever. Tali is right. And if I lived up to the catechism of honoring thy mother and father by refusing to judge or indict either, I failed as a citizen of this nation by blaming the place that brought them together, the land where all things—good and bad—are possible. He wanted a strong-minded American beauty he could show off to his friends; she wanted a brown-skinned savage she could show off to her friends. They both paid for the simplicity of this sin, because that's what they got. Their circles never came together.

No one but the child figured out what had to be done, what needed to be conceded, what could be endured. The adult world said all should be abandoned, and so the story died. The father returned to Samoa to be with his people and never came back. The mother remarried for the first of who really knows how many times.

I was groomed for unfulfilled promises in the land of broken dreams.

21

The Interview Commences with a
Mickey Mouse Nightlight

THE INTERVIEW COMMENCES with a Mickey Mouse nightlight on in the kitchen. The price for my bed tonight. I don't mind. McLaughlin and Toby are both knocked out and Tali, sitting at the table with me, says, "So what have you been doing for the last two months?"

She's gonna ignore seeing me on television in chains. She won't lower herself to discuss such uncouth events. She's full of shit, that's what she is, but she *is* my sister and she does love me.

I say, "Just kicking it."

"Kicking it?"

"Well," I say, trying to think of something productive that I've done which doesn't offend her sensibilities, "I was working on a poetry manuscript."

"Poetry?"

The wrong topic. "Yeah."

"Manuscript?"

"Yeah."

"So how much will you make?"

"Make?"

"Money."

"None. I don't have it."

"You lost the money?"

"No. I used the money, lost the manuscript."

"So there was money?"

"I guess you could say that."

"Where is it?"

"The manuscript or the money?"

"The money."

"Oh. It's gone."

"The money's gone?"

"Yes."

"How can you get money out of a manuscript?"

"It was a fellowship."

"So it's unpublished then?"

"The money or the manuscript?"

"Don't screw around, Paul. Where is the manuscript?"

It's best to leave La Dulce unmentioned. Somehow, opening up the absurdities of our fuckship is more embarrassing than being slapped with a hate crime when half the blood nurturing your system is brown. Plus, Tali will automatically put the lucky one into the position of poor victim swept up by my aimlessness. From a certain vantage where you've removed La Dulce's eccentricities, I'm not so sure it's untrue.

I lie. "At a Motel Six."

"A Motel Six?"

A stupid lie. "Yeah."

"And do you have a title?"

"Yes."

"Well, what is it?"

The truth: "*Beatrice*."

"*Beatrice?*"

A stupid truth. "Yeah."

She's digging into her purse for her keys. She wants the manuscript. For me. "Can't you think of a better title than *Beatrice*?"

"Fuck that book. I officially disown it as a fraud. It was built on stilts. Toothpicks. I should have called it *Against Virtue* or *On Phoniness*."

"So you're just going to forget all about it then. Isn't that just like you?"

The final truth: "It doesn't matter."

"Does anything matter to you?"

"I mean it doesn't matter because I wouldn't have made money off it anyway." She looks up, puts the keys back into her purse. "Which is what you're talking about. I mean, it's poetry, man. Only Billy Collins, Billy Corgan, President Carter, and Jewel make money off their lines."

"Leave it to you to go into a profession that makes no money."

"It's not a profession. That's the point. And I don't care if it ain't lucrative."

"Is there anything you care about?"

"I think I care about people so much I don't care about myself."

"That's bullshit and you know it."

"You may be right. Let me rephrase that: I love our story so much that I almost detest the story's characters. You know, like they're not living up to the narrative."

"Whatever, Paul. Violence follows you around like a shadow. Everyone you meet you either fight or assault or castigate or undercut. Is there anyone you haven't gone after on this planet?"

"Yeah. Everyone underground before September 2, 1977."

"You have more confrontations in a week than I've had in my life."

"That's because you spend your time with handshakers."

"Paul. In a room of a hundred happy people, you still couldn't shake hands. You'd say they were all on Paxil or Prozac."

"No, I wouldn't. I'd just say they were handshakers. Only the ones who don't blink during the handshake are on Paxil or Prozac."

"Jesus Christ, Paul."

"And the ones who are stuck in the smile had their faces hijacked by Botox."

She puts a hand over her eyebrow. It hasn't once moved since yesterday. "Is this necessary, Paul?"

"And the ones who don't look you in the eye are either arrogant assholes or spoiled bitches."

"You're a misanthrope."

"I don't know. I don't think so."

"Why can't you just leave people alone?"

"Look, I have no intention of getting into it with anyone again. Ever. *Okay?* That's how it's always been. Seems like things just happen that way. Often."

"What about that girl?"

"Sharon?"

"Yes. Of course."

"I haven't seen her in years."

"Just like everyone else: ex-girlfriend, mother, father."

"You left out *sister*. Why was that?"

"You just do your own thing."

"Not just me. People don't spend time together anymore. They skip out before it matters. They just dress themselves up better."

"Yeah, yeah, yeah, Paulie."

"You dress it up the best."

"You have no right to say that."

"Okay. Well, how's this? Now that I think it over, you're right. Yes. I'd like to show how much I agree with you, how's that? Yes. I want to stay with you and McLaughlin, stay for a year, spend some real time with little Toby. Get him to talk, breathe."

She looks down into her lap, just barely, but just enough.

"Yeah," I say. "That's what I thought."

"We were talking about Sharon," she says. "The girl you didn't deserve."

"Deserve is such a cruel verb, but you may be right there."

"I am right. She was so pretty and nice. So giving."

"Well, that's about right, too: she gave too much. She gave it up too much."

"What the hell are you talking about?"

Her life on the isle of Lesbos. "Who cares?"

"Well, what about the others? You always have some different girl you're courting."

"That's a nice way to put it."

"Paul! Will you shut up?"

"Okay," I say, "that sounds about right. Can do."

We sit in silence for a three count, four count, five. She can't take it. She's one of these people that lays down a law whose terms she eventually can't accept. When everyone's lined up, happily or not, to get what she wants done, she cancels the edict on a whim and throws out a new one, sometimes totally contradictory in concept. All without apology, without explanation, qualification, remorse, contrition, self-interrogation, self-bemusement, self-concern, humor, or irony. Et cetera, et cetera. The bet is she'll blurt something out before half a minute's up.

At sixteen seconds she says, "Well, don't you have any friends?"

"Yeah," I say, "I met this guy on the bus who seemed pretty cool."

"On a bus?"

"Yeah."

"When?"

"Oh. Earlier today."

"Earlier today?"

"Around late noon."

She looks at her watch. The shiny real diamonds are damaging my eyes. She rolls her wrist a couple of times to finalize blindness. "Five or six hours ago? So what's this friend's name?"

"How the hell should I know?"

"*Lei loa igoa i le kama?*" I pretend like I don't understand a Samoan word she's said. I know she's only using her rudimentary skills to appear not only cultural but paternal. "You don't know his name?"

"I didn't ask him."

"Okaaay. . . ."

"I didn't think I'd ever see him again."

"And yet he's your friend?"

"Yes. It's one of the few things I've been dead right about in a while."

"So where is he now?"

"Either safe in a dumpster in downtown Campbell or in jail."

"Jesus, Paul. What am I gonna do with you? I'm calling Uncle, okay?"

"Nah," I say. "Don't bug him. He's got enough shit to worry about."

"He can help," she says. "I don't know why, but he loves you."

"All the more reason not to call."

"What does that mean?"

"It means why ruin a good thing?"

She's dialing the digits, not looking at me any longer. "Quiet."

"It's too late."

"He'll be up," she says, totally missing my meaning. "It's only eight-thirty."

I don't say, *Well, why are there no lights on in this place?* or *Why did your hubby hit the sack before his nine o'clock bedtime?* but, "Don't worry about it. It's no big deal. I'll just bounce right now and you get can back to your life. You deserve it."

"No. You stay. You sit right there. Yeah, Uncle. Hi, it's Tali."

Once my sister sets her mind to something, it usually works out. Success is based as much on scope as it is on ambition, and Tali would never waste an imaginative second believing she could affect her race through poems. Tali wants to conventionalize me. Her belief is that you've got to try to get in line, just like everyone else. Why? Because there are people out there who care about you. And it's not inhibiting. It's not bourgeois, mediocre. It's fair. But my metaphorical vision of life is like a picture of packed humans, randomly assembled, all looking around scatterbrained for something they can't find, let alone comprehend. Much like a kiddie cover of the *Where's Waldo?* series. My titular metaphor extends to *Who's Waldo?, What the Hell Does Waldo Want Amongst Us?*, and *Is Waldo Maybe Hiding for a Reason?*

Life, I'd once read, is a long preparation for something that never happens.

But for the first time since childhood I find myself agreeing with Tali. I feel like I've been running in a circle, chasing my own tale, a spectacle few people can stomach. I'd like to go somewhere, do something, anything worthy of my life. Gotta turn some lever of rebellion off, try to be normal, something in me has gotta die so I can live. I suspect that my only real skill is being critical. Finding the flaw in the day, the sun, its light. I could pick apart the heart of Mohandas Gandhi if you gave us thirty minutes of alone time.

Before Tali hangs up the phone, she's got a job lined up for me. Not even a second wasted on backstory. I feel grateful, I honestly do. She holds out the phone and whispers, "Don't forget to say thank you."

I nod and say, "Hey, Uncle Rich, whatup, how ya' doin'?"

"Good, nephew. You sure you wanna do this?"

I know that's his way of saying, *You're not gonna put me in a bad way, are you?* The little white lies of business have already started. I have no clue what this is, but so be it. "Yeah. I'm sure I wanna do it. I really appreciate this."

Tali smiles, less of joy, more of relief, and my uncle says, "Okay, old buddy. You got a place to stay?"

"Uh, not really."

"The guesthouse is yours."

"Nah, it's cool, Uncle. No big deal. I'll find me a vacant corner somewhere."

"Listen. That damned thing is just collecting dust. It's like an old art museum, a used bookstore. Move in tonight, tomorrow, whenever. The place is furnished, stocked. You don't even have to stop in and say hello to your Aunt Lanell and me. Just fill it up."

"Are you sure?"

"Yes. Now, listen. Tomorrow morning. Eight A.M. sharp, huh?"

"All right, Uncle."

"That's tomorrow, Monday. Just in case you've lost track."

"I'll be there, Uncle. I promise. See you then." I look at Tali and she's nodding like a delirious coke addict chopping up a lump for the first time in five months. "Looks like I'm back in the world, sister woman."

"Get some sleep," she says. "You're gonna need it."

I hit the sack scrunched up on a two-seat couch in the living room and lie there for an hour contemplating nothing. Then I walk down the hallway, find I am in none of the five dozen pictures decorating it, nor are my mother and father, and decide to look in on the kid to see if he's all right.

His room is empty, the bed made.

I walk a little panicky over to my sister's double-door room, slowly open it, and find the three of them asleep in the biggest bed I've ever seen. I don't dare wake my sister. Back in my nephew's room, I lie down on his bed, pull the Thomas the Tank Engine blanket to my chin, and fall asleep. . . .

The next morning I wake and put the edge of the razor to my face. No blood: the hair of the cheek, chin, and neck comes off clean. A good sign. Have to believe in this new deal on the horizon. There's a desperation in my faith that I'd rather not ponder right now. Self-inoculation: that's the only answer.

I sit down with my sister at the family-assembled IKEA table to a warm bowl of oatmeal topped with a swirl of honey and sprinkled with fresh blueberries. This morning my muscles feel strong, my flesh tight. I'm like an Olympic athlete. I breathe in deep through the nose and begin to eat.

She doesn't say anything. Watching me with the seriousness of a psych on call at a suicide watch, even squinting, putting an index finger to her beautifully fat Polynesian lips. Deep down, and even though she set the thing up, she deems this new sentiment of mine to be pure scam. The old attitude bubbles up in rebellion—or, rather, in support of her expectations.

"I gotta get in my antioxidants. That way I can take a dip of Cope during my first break, hit some heroin in the stall at lunch. Got any wheatgrass?"

She doesn't even smile. I feel a little pity for poor Toby and McLaughlin. Her two children, separated by thirty-one years. They're both nowhere to be found. And I can't hear the tiniest sign that they're back there in the house, sleeping, pissing, brushing teeth, weeping. I resume eating.

"I'm gonna give you some sisterly advice," she says.

I stop eating.

"Hopefully you'll take it in the spirit it's given."

"With condescension?"

"Don't start. You haven't even set foot in that place yet."

"I'm purging, *mi hermana*. Getting it all out of the system before I punch my time card."

"That's what I wanna talk to you about."

"Yeah?" I start eating in small spoonfuls. "Where's McLaughlin and Toby?"

"Now," she says. "I know how tough it is for you to turn that wild brain of yours off. No one's asking you to do that. Just scale it down. Trim off the excesses."

I look up, eating, "Like prime rib?"

"Now."

"Can you stop saying *now*?"

"Just listen! I'm gonna help you tie down your brain." She pulls from her purse a gift sealed in the green wrapping paper of Barnes & Noble. A golden sticker across the middle is shaped like a bow. Despite dwindling readership, the corporate arbiters of literature seem quite happy these days.

"Sister. You're kind and very thoughtful, but I ain't about to read your latest self-help manual by that dingbat Texan."

"Dr. Phil tries to help people."

"He tries to help *ladies*. And *himself*. He's a balding Alpha male who beats up every man that sets foot on his stage."

"Okay, let's not start the day out this way."

"He's like a big fucking phallus up there. The women just love to serve Daddy at the pulpit. Love to get lectured on how to cope after the parakeet dies. He's got them all over his knee, paddling their backsides. Oh, Daddy! Meanwhile his wife sits there at the sermon loving that all these women want her man. She's just bristling with possession. It's disgusting."

"Paul! Will you shut up? It's not Dr. Phil, okay? Jesus. Just open it."

I follow her instructions. It's a planner, my first ever. I flip through the pages and see that everything is organized in boxes: by time, by date, by activity. I smile and my sister says, "Do you like it?"

I can't tell the truth. "Yes."

"I thought it'd be perfect for you because there's a *Thought of the Day* section on each page. That'll keep you confined to one observation. One idea. That's it. And it's gotta be succinct enough to fit into the box."

How befitting. "Yes, thank you."

"Now. There's no excuse. Stop running around and wasting your talent. You've got to figure out a way to live."

I can't help but be a little skeptical about the redemptive qualities of a fancy planner. This is all I was missing in my life? Might we once and for all revitalize a flatulent American economy by mapping out our collective future in these neat little binders? Should we have Psych-Ops airdrop these babies into Baghdad like so many propaganda leaflets and untarnish our reputation in the region? The Kurds, Shia, and Sunni united at last around a little box of To-Do's for the Day, like Neanderthals squatting over the first flames of fire. I remember the old man Cyrus and his reflexive yet genuine expressions of gratitude.

His silence, his silence.

I stand up, nod. "Thank you very much, good-bye."

"Don't let us down, Paul."

"Speaking of us, where's McLaughlin and Toby?"

"Getting their rest."

I want to ask, From what? but don't. I'm out the door.

"Good luck!" Tali shouts.

As if I'm going off to war and there's better than a gambler's chance that the next time we meet I'll be blank-eyed, supine, harmless on the reused sheets of a casket.

22

I Arrive

I ARRIVE at Santa Clara Real Estate West an hour ahead of time. Take a shy peek into the tinted window of the entrance, but no one's in the office. Walk up a winding cobblestone path along a flowing stream and an ivy-strewn bank into the interior of the quad. The songs put out by the winged musicians in the knotty-trunked sycamores are fortissimo as I pass. There's a bench near a gushing fountain under the cool shade of the thick oaks, and I take it quietly, trying not to disturb the scene. The branches overhead have reached out to one another over the decades, intermingling into a polygonal enclosure, a virtual apse of nature. Early morning light streams through the cracks of the green leafy roof in the crisscrossing angles of a disco ball, blessed angels in some encrypted gilt-edged Bible of yesteryear floating down, kissing my skin, my brow, warming me. What beauty. Manmade beauty. Or man-fabricated beauty, bucolic farmed fish. What a beautiful, man-fabricated lie.

The truth comes when the people come. Does the place remain majestic when polluted by the presence of man? That is the question, the test. It's easy to fall in love with ghost towns, condemned strip malls, weed-laden Little League fields. When no one's around.

I could find beauty in the gutter, as long as it's empty of another heartbeat. Hell, I fell in love with a four-by-eight cell in the hole in Quentin for chrissake. Used to wake up smiling. And yet, I know it's people who make a story. No such thing as intrinsic story free of the forward-pressing fingertip of man. No Adam and Eve? Then no garden, no apple, no snake. No Noah or Gilgamesh? Then no ark, no flood, no beastly tandems. The very first set of eyes that claimed this place brought a thousand other inchoate stories to it. The fragrant mountains of pine and the valleys of towering elm and the untouched oceans and sparkling rivers were merely pools of oil, yet to be put on canvas, awaiting the order imposed by the artist, *tranquillitas ordinis,* the preservation skills of the framer.

Awaiting the redeemer, the destroyer.

But this morning no one comes. I spread my arms out across the bench like a free-falling skydiver, breathe in deep through the nostrils, listen to the orchestra of birds above and around me, trickle like dripping water into a dream.

It's a day twenty-one years ago in an elementary school classroom of second-graders. I am there in the front middle of the class, for one school year. I am in love with our teacher, a widow named Mrs. Garcia, whose brown eyes and short brown hair keep me awake. I follow her all day. I am her shadow, her one true admirer. I follow her at recess and she takes my hand and says, "Paul, don't you want to play with the other kids?" I say, "No. I'd rather help you." She is kind and lonely and I wonder how anyone in the world could ever be prettier. After class she asks me if I might stay behind to help her clap the erasers, and I say, "Oh, yes, Mrs. Garcia." She says, "You know I adore you, Paul, you're a wonderful boy," and I say, "Okay." I stay. She turns away from me in the shadows of the classroom, and when she turns back around she is taking off her blouse. There in her bra and cotton skirt, she walks toward me and pats my shoulder gently and says, "It will be okay." She sits down upon her chair and hands me a brush from her purse and I climb up on her desk and do what she asks. I stroke the bristles down her upper back in straight lines, my hand shaking, my breath so short in my throat I feel dizzy. She says, "It's okay, Paul. It's okay." The moles are dark against her fair skin. I pretend that I'm painting. The room is quiet like reading time, and out the window I can see the birds on their branches watching us. I am in love like never before and happy like Christmas morning all over again but worried in my stomach like the times when you lie and are about to get caught by your father, and when she is head down, crying into the bowl of her hands, I am saying back to her, "It is okay, it is okay, I will not hurt you. I promise, Mrs. Garcia, I promise." I know what they will do and I will not hurt you. I don't care about them, Mrs. Garcia.

I am awakened by a rattling of pots. I'm not sure what the dream means on my first day of official business, but I may get to the bottom of it if I forget about it. If it comes back under a different consciousness, which is just a fancy bullshit new-age way of saying *if it comes back later*. Without my knowing it. Without willing it into being.

Meanwhile, the rattling pots aren't pots. It's the heartless tinman's distant cousin in desperate need of a can of oil—*a clinking, clanking, cluttering collection of collagenous junk!*—the engine of a gray early eighties two-door Honda Civic hatchback that is sputtering into the lot. Once it stops, my uncle emerges—or escapes—smiling.

"Hey, nephew! Are you ready for the big adventure?"

I'm walking toward him and I realize I'm ecstatically nodding, nodding, nodding. I don't know why so much but I treasure the kindness in my uncle's pleasantry and that he's not ashamed to be seen by his peers in a little box that should have been diced up at your local chop shop way before we transitioned to the new millennium.

If I were to reciprocate the kindness in my uncle's voice I'd stop right here and now, U-turn down the cobblestoned path, and sprint. All to avoid whatever kind of hurt and disappointment I'm about to bring to my uncle's life. But I can't think like that anymore. Gotta meet the expectations of conformity, exorcise myself of the self-demon: *Out! Out! Out!*

I hope I stay shut.

"Morning, Uncle."

"Wanna take her for a spin before you punch in, bud?"

I realize the Civic jalopy is for me. I'd like to say, "No thanks, Uncle. Driving that piece of shit down the road will mark me as a target for the EPA's hit squad." I go with the truth instead. "I don't deserve this, Uncle. I don't mind catching the bus to work, honest. Even walking. I like walking in the morning when no one's awake. Plus, I don't want to put you out, man."

"Nonsense! Really, Paul. The deal cost me very little."

"I guess you're not the biggest realtor in the Bay Area for nothing."

"Listen, I didn't do a thing. Just drive it around, for Pete's sake, and see how it feels."

"Okay, Uncle."

"You gotta get around in this job. I have eight offices in the South Bay alone. And I may want you to do some work at a few of the offices on the Peninsula."

"Okay. Thank you very much, Uncle. Again."

He looks down at his watch, back at the car, hands me the keys, and says, "Okay, I gotta go. A guy named Chinaski is gonna be your supervisor. Now hear me out really quickly. You're ten times smarter than he is, okay? I want you to get used to taking orders from people like him. That's business. No way out. I'm telling you ahead of time, as a warning. You gotta smile your way right through it and produce. If you get through Chinaski and his bullshit, you can get through anyone. He's gonna give me a report after a couple weeks. Just think of it as business boot camp."

"You're prepping me for business war, Uncle? Corporate mergers and acquisitions?"

"In every little exchange there is war, nephew."

"Nietzsche."

"That's right."

"But what do you win in this deal? What are the spoils and plunder here? I mean, it seems very anti-business to hire someone like me."

He nods, looks down at the ground. "Well, it is. In business terms, I don't win here: I lose. I am committing myself to losing a buck. But I win elsewhere. Nietzsche didn't go much for the existential. But I do." He smiles at me, pats my shoulder. "I know this is a winner."

"Whatever happens?"

"Now listen. You're gonna do just fine. Don't let me get you all paranoid. You were ranked number one in your high school class for a reason. You were a candidate for the Point for a reason. You've got it, man. Just do your best not to think about the complexity of things. For eight hours a day, don't take the work to any level of intellectual depth. In fact, consider it a victory if someone at Real Estate West thinks you *have* no depth. Pick your qualifications on whatever you gotta say and then take it—let's say—a quarter of the way down. Stop and let the other guy get a word in. Shaking hands isn't just about being polite. It's about balance."

"Yes, Uncle-san."

"While you're at work, think about . . . hamburgers or something."

I smile, squint, look over. His eyes are back on the ground again so I put mine there with him, trying not to think on the sun sliver of promise breaking through the trees. I can ruin this whole thing not just with ease but with thoroughness.

I ask, "Hamburgers?"

He looks up at me, clutches my shoulder. "And don't say, 'How a propos, since we're all just minced meat in the grinder.' Rather, think about milkshakes. That's it! Vanilla. Okay? There's my ride. Don't worry, now, I believe in you."

A limo. Black. Long and thick. Of course. Hah-hah-hah. La Dulce's specialty. With vanilla milkshakes. Pretty good, Uncle.

He slides into one side of the backseat of the limo and a man ducks out from the side opposite. This guy's in a pair of ironed and neatly creased khaki chinos that are sagging in the ass despite the black leather belt. He's more than slightly hunched in the neck region, like a power lifter in the gym stuck in the trapezoid pinch of a shoulder shrug. His balding head is exacerbated by the comb-over. He's looking back into the limo where my uncle is probably sitting and twiddling his thumbs, and this guy's doing his M-i-c-k-e-y-M-o-u-s-e act, but with conviction. One of Uncle's devotees. He may as well get down on his knees, cross himself, and pray. I suspect this stoolie is Chinaski. When he turns from the limo and his kiss-ass face changes into sour despot at the sight of meager me, I know it's Chinaski.

I don't know him, sure, but I can tell you that this guy has that simple and stupid image of the world where everything right down to the brushing and flossing of your teeth is a metaphysical matter infinitely bigger than yourself. Whatever molars you lose over the decades, whatever slivers of rotten meat you loosen from your gums, all of it is tied into that larger scheme of the stars above. I haven't even shaken his hand yet and I know it. He's seeping with flustered ambition.

But there's something more to his equation on life and the constellations; I've seen it before on the faces of adolescents in high school hallways, drunkards in university barrooms, shot callers in prison yards: an earthly star awaits the proper recognition of his status. "Astronomers have discovered that between the Pleiades and Orion there is a bright flaming being that they've taken the liberty of christening Chinaski!" He's got fake greatness in his eyes, this guy's under the impression that each step he's taking toward me is the curtain-parting prelude to some big drama in the sky whereby all his cookie-cutter goals will finally be realized.

Trying to be stern-faced as a Nazi commandant, eyes focused on the building, he walks by me, says, "The name's Chuckie. Let's get to work."

I follow him into the building, and in less than a minute he's telling me everything about his life. The star of the hour. His ex-wife, their three kids, a home in Willow Glen. I don't say a word, just nod, nod, nod. And it turns out that the office is empty of people, a blessing, and not only that: the quad is empty of people. It's beautiful. So my peaceful morning with the crooning birds was facilitated by a struggling region in real estate. Everything's up for rent by Collier's International rep Erin Lagerman (408)247-3780, www.colliers.lease.space. Today I'm a desk mover, a file hauler; I'm cheap labor, a sturdy back and healthy legs, Chinaski's little beyotch.

The first minute starts with advice: "Keep your mouth shut and your ears open."

I tune out and think of the smoothness of vanilla milkshakes for some time, and when I tune in again, belly full of imaginary dairy, I see that two and a half hours have passed.

By God, it works!

Only five and a half more hours to go, four more days of the work-week. I have no recall of what I missed, but by the comfort with which Chinaski is speaking, I know I did well enough to play the hostage audience.

Now I hear: "Your uncle will be the first to tell you that hard work is not enough in this field." He taps his head, squinting. "You've gotta have it up here, kid."

I nod once, silently whistling.

"Do what's gotta be done, you do what's gotta be done."

"Lest you be the one who gets done," I offer.

"Remember that Rome wasn't built in a day."

In the spirit of historical cooperation, I say, "Pax Romana."

"Your uncle knows. I'm gonna keep an eye on you because when the cat's away, the mice will play."

I smile, try to look mischievous.

Big fish eats medium fish eats little fish: that's Chinaski's cartoon vision of the world, the unavoidable chain of life. And like most homo sapiens I've known, Chinaski now calls this cartoon vision his moral ethic. He has the right, the moral right, to eat me. And there's nothing I can do about it. It's like this amalgamation of natural law and Calvinist dogma: *I shall get eaten, as is predestined.*

But I can see through the formula's flaws. If I can avoid being eaten long enough, then before I know it—and to Chinaski's scorn—I'll grow in status, and we'll see who eats whom.

He looks down at his watch, over his shoulder, says, "Your uncle's gonna be in the Peninsula today, I hear."

This guy is going nowhere in this company; he can't even last three hours before he's moving on the rump roast of lethargy. Of paid worklessness and worthlessness. If he ain't decadence, I don't know what is. And the dream of Mrs. Garcia returns to me: Chinaski is the kind of person who'd hang Mrs. Garcia not out of justice or heartfelt concern for the kid: he'd do it to use her body as a stepping-stone.

"Lunchtime, good buddy," he says. "We gotta go socialize with the bigwigs."

23

We Relax

WE RELAX, sinking into the Fairmont recliners, Chinaski royally sipping his $13.89 Manhattan, me disroyally chugging my $9.31 pint of Sierra Nevada. I look around the empty ballroom but don't ask where all the business hotshots are. I have a feeling they wouldn't be anywhere near us, be it at a high-end hotel or the local Taco Bell. I take in the chandelier above us that looks, in suspension, like the bottom of a diamond spaceship. I'm not seconds into my appreciation of the cut of the scintillating glass or the bitter tang of the underrated Chico, California, brewery when someone says my name in an intonation I haven't heard in some time, not just my first name but my first and last name both, along with my high school graduation year, and the goddam name of the high school with it. I keep my head tilted back, my eyes focused on the crisscrossing angles of dazzling light.

I hear from one side—Chinaski—"You went to St. Cajetan College Preparatory?" and from the other, "How are you doing these days, Paul?"

"Yes," I say, and "Just fine," still eyeballing the roof and its hanging glittering appendage. The voice is a former classmate, a fellow alum of the prep that I vaguely recognize. "You?" I say in his direction. It is a him, I'm sure of that. Despite the blurring of gender lines this century, only unandrogynous boys are educated at St. Cajetan, a 150-year tradition under constant assault.

"I'm doing just fine," says the voice of the alum. "Might I be interrupting something?"

There's your cue, Chinaski.

"Not at all," he says. "Sit down and join us, friend. Chuckie Chinaski."

"Dong-hoo Choi."

Good old Who Dong. The first Korean valedictorian of St. Cajetan College Prep. So whitewashed by now he couldn't tell you where Seoul is. So whitewashed by then that each day at lunch he gave away the kimchi his parents packed for him during our freshman year. That was good for me: the more kimchi the better, I say. I've eaten fifty-two different kinds of kimchi in my lifetime, the last experiment being a rather chewy, cartilaginous, pickled manta ray.

Anyway, well before our freshman year ended, old Who Ding got it into his head that we were academic rivals. I always just looked at him as my own personal kimchi supplier: he was my hustle for peppered wonbok cabbage. But all along he was trying to bring me down, this Korean Iago. I think my indifference offended him: in his valedictory speech, I recall, he said that his journey as a varsity cheerleader was so rewarding that he'd come to learn that the success of the football team, from which he'd been cut three years running, was contingent upon his services and not the other way around. In other words: If you took the two teams off the field, the fans would not disappear; they'd stick around to watch a group of young men in blue face paint lead them in the school fight song.

No wonder Who Dat was top student at the prep.

Early on I had bought into the mission of the school: an all-boys Jesuit education in the center of the Silicon Valley, that theme taught to starry-eyed freshmen—". . . St. Cajetan Prep has been the heart and soul of this region for a century and a half"—in minor variation during the initial days of brainwashing. The school had a lot of pull, and anyone associated with it knew it.

I had been excited at the promise of intellectual exercise. But now, as a thinker whose logical skills were molded at Prep, sharpened later at Alviso University, and then splattered on the wall in the pen, I suspect that any blessing in life probably lies with the undiscovered thought or even the barren brain, the blessing of the idiot savant. What greater gift might one have in this Age of Information than not having to measure the value of a tidbit?

My freshman year at St. Cajetan College Prep, the world got bigger. Blame it on the reading. On Father Styron, that bald, old-school Germanic Jesuit who never exchanged pleasantries with you until you showed the talent, grit, and commitment to finish his course. Whenever he'd turn on the lights in class, he'd shout, "Lay down the darkness!" and, by God, it would.

One day in the middle of a chill blue fall, he ordered us to pick up our "plebian tushes" and follow him across the campus. We made our way over the slick green fields in silence, London's *The Call of the Wild* tucked under our arms, walking into the next minute of discovery—*all of it was discovery! all of it!*—which was ours for the taking. This was only the beginning. We gathered around Father Styron at the College Park Station, which was a wooden bench plastered with graffiti, four wooden posts supporting a bell-less belltower roof, and a condensed map of San José encased by inch-thick screws on a clear plastic bulletin board. The concrete slides and gravel trucks of Albanese Bros., churning directly across the rocky tracks, disappeared for seconds behind a silver Caltrain flashing by like moving pictures.

The father told us to sit. We dropped our plebian tushes atop our stuffed backpacks, and crossed our newly hairy legs, proud of this oddity. Our heads popped up automatically, like bobbers at the end of the line. Still, waiting, still silent. He opened his own beaten copy of the book and read aloud from the scene where Buck, Judge Miller's dog, was delivered into the traitor's hands.

"It happened right here," the father said. We said nothing, though some of us, myself included, let out a big breath of air. He said, "Stand," and we stood as ordered, followed him back to class, the same quiet path.

I looked back over my shoulder, thinking, *There? Right there? My God.*

We'd gone through *Inherit the Wind, To Kill a Mockingbird, Julius Caesar, Catcher in the Rye, The Crucible.* Under heavy bright light interrogation, in my deepest sleep, I could quote lengthy passages, first learned as a form of punishment in J.U.G. (Justice Under God), later as a habit, a self-imposed and acclimated discipline. I privately loved the lines more than I'd ever publicly claimed. Yes, they were all books by dead white men, but back then we didn't start a book with a qualifier. By the time I got to college I chose my own course: Dostoevsky, Faulkner, Wright, García Marquez, Oe, each book the proof of another choice, maybe a hundred choices.

In the classroom, I knew how to reproduce what a teacher wanted. I had an appointment from Congressman Norm Mineta to attend West Point by the end of my junior year. I was ambitious. Back then I had a flattop and a staunchly conservative outlook on life. I lacked compassion. I believed in discipline and country and prayer and envisioned a life with an equally principled woman. I perpetuated order all around me.

But inside I was all bollixed up, as they say in the South, wrapped tight in a straitjacket of what really was my sincere hope in the prescribed program. I was dying to break a rule, a law, someone's skull. But I almost felt that if I could fulfill the school's prophecy of world vision, a big load of future graduates would be free to follow its light without a moment's thought over what I'd endured for four years, and I'd at least walk away with a story. What vanity: I thought I could be their cashed check on goodness.

I was midway into my journey at St. Cajetan when I joined the speech and debate team. Dong-hoo, hearing of this, joined the next day. We went one and two in the state, he two, I one. I became a natural at the notion of rationalization, prided myself in finding both the strengths and weaknesses of an argument. I could not keep many friends since a friend required picking one side or the other of an issue. I couldn't find a girlfriend who required picking her. The latter problem I'd dismissed as a fairly obvious microproblem of attending an all-boys institution where contact between the sexes was diminished to chance encounters at bus stops, shopping malls, and birthday parties, but the former problem I worked at very hard for a while: I desperately wanted to make friends.

I eventually learned how to handle the preponderance of alone time that being a thinker, or so I'd called myself, necessitated. I identified with Nietzsche's assertion that the deep thinker prides himself on being misunderstood. I, thus, had no interest in leadership that connoted a clear and easily interpreted message to others. Conversely, I had no interest in following anyone my own age. Halfway through high school, my private goal shifted to becoming an avatar of solitude, to taking on Emerson's claim that *the great man is he who in the midst of the crowd keeps with perfect sweetness the independence of solitude.*

And yet the thinking itself seemed shifty, certainly not something to stand on. You cannot float on clouds in the face of the real problems—death, taxes, family—that life presents. Eventually you have to make a decision. The vacuum of the classroom wasn't even close to scale. But the real caveat was one's own self, the inherited I, the created me. I soon suspected quicksand beneath Emerson's claim that *what I must do is all that concerns me.* I tiptoed around the directive of *Trust thyself.* How could I do something as reckless as that with 150 years of screaming self-reliance momentum? I felt internally like a meteorite blazing a path through the docile sky, gathering energy for the inanimate object about to be taken out. And then: How could I trust anyone else? As easily as I could rationalize into existence a belief (which was just as easy, therefore, to destroy), I could see that the thinking was not something to build a life on. And yet I had a Habitat for Humanity work crew in my brain, fortifying its existence in the bedlam of thought.

No complaints but I simply wonder: At what point does the thinking end? Or rather: At what point is the thinker so satisfied with what's been thought that nothing else need be asked? Or at least that nothing else need be asked of a topic? Or at least that an answer you have gives birth to righteous action?

That's where the problem has always lain, of course: in those moments where I've chosen action.

In the beginning of my junior year, a vagabond had asked me a simple question: "Do you have any cans?"

I gave a simple answer—"Yes"—drained my Coca-Cola can, and handed it over.

The vagabond moved on to his next aluminum prize when the dean of men, Father Reeser, arrived beneath his little black-Irish Afro and said to the recycler, "This is a closed campus."

"But there are a hundred cans lying around here, sir."

"We'll take care of the cans. Don't be in the least bit concerned," said Dean Reeser, brushing the lint from the jacket of his Italian suit. He never wore his collar and you'd never guess that he was a priest who'd taken an Ignatian vow of poverty. "Now leave before the police are contacted."

"You wouldn't," said the vagabond, stroking his ratty beard. "I know you wouldn't, sir."

Dean Reeser reached into the chest pocket for his cell phone and looked up at the vagabond, one last warning. These were the days when cell phones were big as a car battery, a last-resort weapon. The vagabond didn't move. Dean Reeser said, "As God is my witness."

So much for "being a man for others."

It would have been smarter to have waited until a good amount of time had passed between that incident and putting a brick through the window of the dean's office. For the window incident was naturally blamed on vagabonds and an order was put up to Blach Family Builders to construct an iron-blue fence around the perimeter of the campus, "to protect the facilities." "Let's keep those bums out," I heard one drunken alum say at an auction fund-raiser for the fence. In the end, the last person suspected of the deed was the doer, me, still held in high esteem by my educators. But who knows? Maybe some of them knew. Or suspected. . . .

"So you two went to high school together?"

I remember now where I'm at, the kind of cat surrounding me. Chinaski says it again. "You went to St. Cajetan together?"

"Indeed," says Who Dere. He's smiling at Chinaski, not meeting his fawning eyes but rather the top of his head, the comb-over, softly but visibly chuckling to himself. This is why the guy irritated me back in the day. He's one of those people always shitting on the saps below him with pizzazz, under the impression that his defecatory act is one of generosity.

"And this was at Cajetan?"

"Yes, sir," Who Dong continues. "Paul was ranked number one in our class until the end of our sophomore year."

Jab number one. I take it lightly on the ribs. It tickles. I breathe in deeply and blow it away. Meanwhile, Chinaski is on the edge of his seat, excited by the all-around possibility of milking the boss's all-star nephew. "At Cajetan?"

"Yes," I say. "It was at Cajetan, okay? I went to Cajetan. I went to St. Cajetan and you didn't go to Cajetan. Though you probably wanted to."

"Oh, no," says Chinaski. *Oh, yes.* "I'm just curious, I guess. My mother wanted me to go there. All she did for the first fourteen years of my life was ramble on to anyone in her vicinity how little Chuckie was going to be the first in the family to attend Cajetan."

"Well," says Who Dong, "It was a fine school. Is a fine school."

I want to say, And where *did* you go to school, Chinaski? just to shut him up, but instead say, "It's in decline."

"Oh, I wouldn't say that," says Who Dat. "It's just growing."

"Exactly," I say. "It's growing beyond its identity. *An all-boys Jesuit educational enterprise since 1851 is now a community of women and men conjoined in its vision of growing an organic citizen to enter the world and brighten it.* I think they stole that from Alcoholics Anonymous."

"I went to Blackford and I don't regret one minute there," says Chinaski. Translation: He was one of the 1,400 applicants that St. Cajetan turns away each year. "Although I'd like to go back and watch a football game now and then."

"Have you been banned from your campus for some reason?" asks Who Dere, smiling with perfectly polite fakery.

"Blackford was shut down back in 'ninety," I say happily.

"One year after I graduated," Chinaski says sadly.

"Did you make the one-year reunion?" I say.

"Paul here," says Who Dong, "was the hero of our alumni game in 'ninety-six. Eight thousand fans were in attendance at Kirk Shoe Stadium. Paul liked to say that Kerouac should've lived just to watch that game and write a better poem."

"Who is that?" Chinaski says.

"Jack Kerouac," I say. "He wrote about watching St. Cajetan play on a Friday night in 'October in the Railroad Earth.'"

"So he's like a sportswriter then?" Chinaski asks.

"It was a poem."

"That's right," says Who Ding. "The book was *Lonesome Traveler*."

"Sounds like a downer," says Chinaski.

"Paul here made an interception with thirty-five seconds left in the game. Took it eighty yards down the sideline for the score. And the best part was that he did it right in front of the St. Dwynwen bench. They all just stood there, hoping Paul would trip. But he didn't. Not that time, anyway."

There it is: the second jab. *Let's get ready to rumble!*

"Oh, I've been tripped up a number of times," I say. I look at the Greek-potted ferns posted at either side of the piano, take in the faux-Doric pillars in earth tones at ten-yard intervals through this ballroom, watch a bellhop wheel a golden cart of luggage toward the Fountain Restaurant. Holding the hour in my hand like a crystal ball, I say, "But I'd guess that you haven't."

"You'd be right on that front, Paul."

"It's easy to see why."

"The usual talent, commitment, intelligence," he says.

"Not at all. It's the usual aptitude to recognize what other people want. You're extraordinary at that. And then you give it to them. You play the course out. Stay within the lines, the boundaries. You never ask if they deserve what they want. Or need it. Everything is navigable on your course, and you sprint through it with the feet-pumping pistons of Carl Lewis. Everybody loves you, but your vision is small, and their love is superficial. As is yours. Meanwhile, the truly memorable folks have broken off the course and are hiking . . ." (here I lift the Sierra Nevada and pound it) ". . . mountains you wouldn't go near. It's unavoidable that one trips every now and then when there's a snow-capped peak to hurdle."

"I'm sorry I took the valedictorian from you, Paul."

Chinaski's shoulders drop back down: a misfit like myself messes with his baby formula of: I (Intelligence) + C (Connections) = S (Success) = C (Cash) = P (Prestige) = F (Friend).

"A simple thank-you will do," I say to Who Ding.

"Thank you?"

I say with total confidence, "That's right. You're welcome for the VD, as I call it, that you were given by me. I checked out of that school before my sophomore year ended. There was nothing left for me to learn. Oh, the minutiae were there: the periodic table, the love sonnets of Shakespeare, Lincoln-Douglas debates, all that good shit, there's always more info to absorb, always more data. Even now, there's a galaxy of facts out there that I couldn't speak to with any authority. But the vision of the school is another thing. By fifteen, I had the hidden forces at work figured out at St. Cajetan College Preparatory. I was sure I didn't align myself with their vision, our vision, whatever. And that was the start of an endless journey yielding the same result over and over again."

"The big trip," Who Dat says, rolling his eyes. He does some delay tactic of his own, registering the skylights above us, way above us. "I'm unimpressed, Paul. I would have thought that by now you'd have a better rationalization for your recent failures. You were always so adept at arguing the counter to the counter to the counter to the counter."

Chinaski's brain is in remission. He went into A-wave mode when I mentioned the periodic table: he's sleeping with his eyes open, he's zoning out on the television, though (miraculously) there's no television here in the ballroom. Chinaski may as well be fingering his way through a bowl of extra-buttery popcorn, sipping on a $6 small Coke at the theater. Maybe it's right that he's shit upon: he's a borderline peasant who thinks he's an aristocrat. Even in his unconscious dream right now, he's issuing orders to a custodian.

I say, "The difference between us is this: You won't ever hear me whine about the raspberries and bruises on my knees. And I don't have to hunt you down and challenge you to feel good about myself. You and a hundred others offer a paltry remedy for the nothingness I feel in my head and heart. The problems I carry around would end a fragile bird like you. You wouldn't get out of the nest with my nihilistic inheritance."

"But I did get to Harvard. Then to Boalt. And now to Eismann, Lichter & Smith. With ease. And soon I'll get to partner. Where did you get other than San Quentin, Paul?"

"You were in San Quentin?" asks Chinaski, snapping awake.

"He was indeed," says Who Dere, sipping his drink, holding in a smile.

"That's one of the mountains I'm talking about," I say.

"Is there any doubt now which anarchist put a brick through the dean's window?"

"You were in San Quentin?"

"Listen," I say to Who Dong, standing, shaking out my arms, my hands, "aside from the fact that a punk like you would've been crushed up in that mutherfucker and aside from the fact that what I took from that place translates directly into this moment, right here, right now, in that only my *compassion*"—here I get in Who Ding's face, grit my teeth, eyes flaring like Tyson pre-fight—"prevents me from biting your fucking fruity cheerleader nose off your face"—Who Dat swallows, steps back, almost trips on the colorful man-of-war behind him, and I sit down, content with his concession—"the only thing you have to worry about is what I read in the latest issue of the *Cajetan Column*. How did it go? Ah, yes: Dong-hoo Choi, '96, invites all members of the Korean Alumni Association to meet at Ga Bo Ja in late December. Now tell me that ain't true. It's a misprint. I misread it, right?"

"I'm founder and president," he proudly parrots, before he sees his error.

"Hah! What happened to your anti-kimchi crusade?"

"I realized I was wrong."

"Bullshit," I say, "that's bullshit. I've got your game figured out, man. You're transparent as a snowstorm. Back in the day, you gave up your bloodline to curry favor with the haves. The enrollment of our class was ninety-percent white and they ran the show. So you went around and told everyone to call you Michael. But when it became hip over time to embrace your culture everywhere on the planet, you aptly identified the power shift and realized that a redis-covery of your former culture was politically savvy. So now you're back to Dong-hoo. Well, they may have forgotten your original white-washed position with a tidy donation to the endowment, but I re-member how readily you abandoned your roots. You had no balls. Still don't. It doesn't matter if you're here at the Fairmont every day, ringing up a fat bill comped by the firm. It doesn't matter what you drive, where you live. I'll destroy you, Who Dong, Who Ding, Who Dat, Who Michael, Who Whatever. I got nothing to lose."

He's silent, as he should be. I detest the guy, this master player of the game.

"I'll eat you alive." Chinaski is about to get up and walk off to the bathroom, and I can't help saying, "Sit down."

He sits as ordered, slumps back, shoulders hunched, whistling air through his lips.

"Let's agree," says Who Ding, "that you were always smarter than me, but that I will always be more successful than you."

"Well, I'm in accordance with that," I say, lifting my empty glass. "Here's to your stupid success."

He lifts his own half-full glass. "Here's to your intelligent failure."

Chinaski suddenly pops up, like a beaver out of a hollow in the earth, his four strands of hair tingling with the cerebral activity below: *Could it be true?* his shocked eyes are asking. *Does intelligence truly presage failure? Am I, Charles Chinaski, simply too damned smart for my own good?*

24

We're Driving with Bling-Making Intent

WE'RE DRIVING with bling-making intent out to North Santa Clara in Chinaski's apple-green '06 VDUBBUG, the Jesse James custom-built convertible, top down, the wind rushing through our ears, pumping Usher and Ja Rule, looking cool for all the girls who laugh with us, not at us. The conditions are a test for Chinaski's new condition: hair implants. I didn't say a word aloud when I first saw it, don't say a word now. It's a new beginning for the both of us: he's got a thousand threads of string growing out of his head, and I'm committed to the silence mandated by the elephantine woofers. This silence will carry me to self-sustenance in the Silicon Valley; as ordered by my good sister, silence is the new rule for me, not just today but all the days that I find myself officially a subject of "The West." For the past few days, I've been cast in the role of the fifties child who is to be seen, not heard.

The great techie capitalists sprang from the well-tilled soil of this valley, and though I've a relatively late start at twenty-eight, and though we are presently winding through the Silicon ghost towns of northern Sunnyvale and central Milpitas, their spirits having vacated the premises for the warmer, more fertile climate of New Delhi, and though I have a disposition that questions any possible direction my life takes, I'm nonetheless positive that my cooperative attitude ("Bend but don't break," advised Chinaski) will—a propos of the mad beats—Usher me into millions of bones in no time, which, as Ja Rule would no doubt point out at gunpoint, is clearly what's important.

WHY NOT GROW A HEART ON A YACHT? reads Chinaski's bumper sticker.

We make our way into the suburbs, this great classless society where there's no wrong side of the tracks. No plantation mansions with Italian names, no families with Borgian pull, no inherited social customs. And no character either, no life force. Everything appears even, yes, fair, but facelessly dull. The monotonous train of banal architecture needs no mason, "giveth no man a house of good stone." No Usonian vision could spice up this endless drywall of conformity, where the streets fill up with junk like its inhabitants.

One wonders why: there are no kids in view to enjoy the junk. The houses here aren't vacant: more cars than trees in the neighborhood. More cars than people. The rest of the world would build the most elaborate and sturdy jungle gym on the playground with our (metallic) scraps on the table. All through the merit of hunger and hope.

Consume, baby! Consume, amorphous beast!

I recall now the message of our good Prez one day after 9/11: Just go right back to what you're doing, *mi Americano hermanos,* don't let them change your lifestyle. In other words, don't let this travesty be a lesson. The meat of our economy, the good Prez was saying, driven by our lifestyle.

Our *lifestyle*? Our impermanent lifestyle—Impertinent lifestyle! Consummate insult to the world!

Where have we heard that before, Romans of the Seven Hills, Mayans of the Yucatan? I don't remember seeing silicon implants and weekly therapists and bathroom spas and *Dancing with the Stars* and cordless laptops slotted into Maslow's pyramid of needs, not even as a bottom brick. Just like my newfound nameless friend said, *we're gods on earth*, or so we think. We've elevated our wants, wants, wants to the status of needs, needs, needs, this Pillsbury doughboy society, us Pillsbury people, rolling toward our comeuppance day of getting baked in the oven.

But these are moot points now, I know, since my adoption of the mature American attitude of earning an honest buck. The capitalist's euphemism for Get it, baby, just get it. There's no more internal dilemma in me: I know the code: At all soulful costs, get it!

Oh, I got it all right: Chinaski pulls up to the newly erected house of interest, the acreage of dusty plain in front of us, ripe for rampant construction. Ninety percent of the homes are empty out here, awaiting the resident heartbeat. He opens his door, steps out, and reaches back into the car. I lean back accordingly with my straight right cocked, but he goes for some contraption that he's been sitting on the whole time: an inflatable red cushion, horseshoe in shape, the words *Roid Void* in creamy white logo across its hollow center.

There's no way that a guy with a droopy body like Chinaski's takes animal tranquilizers, human growth hormone, or crushed African tree bark. Even if he never worked out a day, there'd be some sign of strength in his frame.

When I realize that the shortened Roid has another meaning, he's already guiding me by the elbow (which calmly I keep trying to reclaim) up the lamp-edged walk, past the crucifix of a Santa Clara Real Estate West sign with an I'M PRETTY INSIDE placard staked into the stark green lawn. It's artificial-turf shiny, level as a bocci ball course, porous where the dirt has been punched out to oxygenate the soil. Its designed order reminds me of the hair implants on this drip of a Polish sausage, dragging me along with one arm, his customized hemorrhoid cushion tucked under the other.

"I'm gonna teach you how to prep a sale today," he says. "You just follow my lead."

He veers me under the door into the empty (but pretty inside) house. Two stools are positioned on the unscathed hardwood floor of the living room. He points at a stool and I take it. He lays the Roid Void across the other stool, which is nearer the kitchen, plops down, says nothing. I'm twiddling my thumbs round and round, and he puts his hand out and covers my little rotary. I let my hands sit there in my lap for minutes upon minutes, thinking of the rotten, stagnant, backwood home life this idiot to my left must lead—his poor neighbors, his poor banker, doctor, grocer—when she finally glides in, owning the house and anything in it.

"Shhhhh," whispers Chinaski.

She goes right to the window and slides it open, looks around the barren living room with a detached yet possessive air, sniffs, looks at us with disappointment, sniffs deeper, looks at us again, through us, above us, appearing to grow angry, walks toward us, her heels clicking like a bomb about to blow. Despite his sphincteral affliction, I can hear Chinaski nervously shuffling on his stool, and as she zips by without the least acknowledgment I feel a tug on my elbow.

"Shhhhh," Chinaski reminds me.

I nod, not knowing how the hell this cat got the authority to raise a single child, let alone many. *Just let us alone, Daddy! Let us alone! Knowing which hole to put it in does not a father make, Daddy!*

She's behind us in the kitchen flicking switches, closing cupboards, turning faucets and disposals on and off, tapping on Formica, her heels rapping on the floor in perfect count, suddenly saying in the most enunciatory voice I've ever heard second to James Earl Jones (*CNN* or *Cooome to the daahk side, Luuke*), "Yes, Mr. Gupta, I am presently awaiting your arrival. The door is open, and the lights are on in the West."

The heel taps get louder, and as she passes under the arch of the kitchen I hear a rapid whisk and I know Chinaski's been hit. I look over and he's violently coughing from the fragrance glistening on his face, as she pumps her Lavender Febreeze throughout the living room, heels a-click.

She's making her way into the back rooms of the house and I can hear toilets flushing, toilet seats dropping, windows popping open. Chinaski is still coughing but, since she left his presence, not covering his mouth, and at the precise moment I move my seat a yard or two away from my gagging one-up in the West, I am soothed again by Amadeus. His Eighteenth Piano Concerto now lightly flowing through the place, like a hovering hummingbird with chimes on its wings. Two miniature speakers hug the adjacent corners of the ceiling line, both of which I missed at my uninterested first glance.

Chinaski nods. "Yes. It's better if you sit there like we don't know each other. That makes two potential buyers of the house."

I move my stool yet another yard away, trying not to think of the absurdity of the bidding couple: Chuckie Chinaski and me.

The clicking returns, too fast. As if she's read my mind's latest disturbance, she deposits a handful of red, white, and blue prophylactics into our laps. Despite his taxed system, Chinaski already has one in his mouth. He's breathing in through his nose, filling the balloon with his CO_2. Staying in theme, they read, THE DOOR IS OPEN & THE LIGHTS ARE ON IN THE WEST.

I start to blow up my balloons (there are four in my lap), and she's right out the door. I'm silently excited by her exit and now work a little harder, which means I blow more hot air than before. I breathe in through the nose and out through the mouth, but not anywhere near the pace of Chinaski. I'm waiting like the proverbial crook for the pop of the picked lock, dying to hear the car start, signaling her departure. Little Engine That Could, *fire up, fire up, fire the fuck up!* Spontaneously combust with her in it, seat belt fastened. Nobody need tell me what it takes to be successful in this industry: presumption, trickery, slopes.

My hope for her parting graces is premature; she's coming back up the walk. Chinaski grabs the unblown balloons in my lap and starts in anxiously, expert lips first. She's got a grocery bag in the base of her bent arm and a pile of leaflets, no doubt Xeroxed articles from the free local papers about her recent sales, the top three in value highlighted (probably by Chinaski the stoolie), her résumé going back to the honors bestowed upon her at Realtor's Institute, her attendance five years running at the National Association of Realtors Convention, a bundle of business cards, plus a listing of community events and farmer's markets, cultural fairs and wine festivals. Pinched between her elbow and waist, a rolled newspaper.

She drops the grocery bag and newspaper on the faux-brick raised hearth, and Chinask slaps my arm.

"Not it," he says. "You're the crumpler, baby."

I join him on my knees at the fireplace, assuming that "crumpler" means the guy who crumples newspaper into kindling. I start with the front page, which is weeks old, and find an article of minor note in the Local section. There's a photo of me being hoisted in chains to the van. The header of the three-sentence article is ARE HATE CRIMES ON THE RISE? and the last sentence reads, "The suspect, Paul Tusifale, has a history of public violence."

I shake my head, add myself in handcuffed repose to the airtight ball of kindling, throw it in the fireplace.

Chinaski's carefully taking the firewood out of the bag. "Put it in the middle, Chicken Little," he says.

I almost say, It *is* in the middle, you idiot, but stay silent instead, reach into the fireplace pretending to move things around.

He carefully leans the logs vertically against one another, around the newspaper, a skeleton of a tepee about to go up in flames. I haven't heard the clicking in some time, but there's a new sound, just as mnemonic. It's a thousand flies. Not quite in my head. Not yet, anyway.

It's out in the street.

Chinaski stands up to look out the bay window and says, "Oh . . . my . . . God."

"Chuckie!" we hear from the porch.

Chinaski jumps at the sound of her voice, pulling at and tightening the belt of his pants, I strike a match, put it to the kindling, listen to the paper catch and the crackling wood speak its first words in the flame. I have no interest in what's going on outside. It's funny— or sad: we long for company in the dark corners of our solitude, and then when company comes along we aren't happy.

A cell with myself or a day of freedom with Chinaski?

Pick 'em.

I don't have time to decide. "Ms. Clannonite wants you!" he shouts from the door, the sound of the buzzing flies growing. Chinaski tosses me the keys to his car and retrieves his Roid Void from the stool. He passes both times as if I'm a statue in the park covered in dried birdshit, and then he's out the door. At the street he tosses the Roid Void in its place on the driver's seat. Then he trots off, a stalking jog down the sidewalk, ducking as he runs, his progress slow but determined, surreptitious as a charging rhinoceros. I shrug, pocket the keys, and head out the door of the house to meet our empress.

Ms. Clannonite is looking down at her planner, leaning against the passenger side of her four-door silver '06 Benz, a shiny bullet on wheels. I nod; she doesn't look up. I haven't seen her operate yet with her potential clients ("Everyone's a client of the West," I can hear her say correctively), but I'd hazard a guess that she gives them all the eye contact she doesn't give underlings like me. She's flipping through what looks like a series of portraits with PowerPoints, colored portraits.

"You're a good-looking guy," she says.

An illicit romp already? I think.

"You've got a hell of a future here in the West if you play your cards right."

I don't say anything. I anticipate a favor of some sort. Not *from* her, *for* her. She's a go-getter all right, a first-string capitalist quarterback. She knows I'm the big boss's nephew. If I were even a waterboy on the capitalist gridiron squad, I'd have the West already in my back pocket.

Suddenly she stops scanning and is intently reading one sheet with a photo of a couple at the top. From my view, the picture is upside down, but I know the couple is Hindi from the *sindoor* on the broad forehead of the woman. It dawns on me: These two dupes are the Guptas.

Meanwhile, Chinaski has disappeared down the block. The buzzing is returning behind me. So today the flies come in the form of your average suburban runt. A wild-haired, pudgy-faced, Hindi/Punjabi kid in a red Adidas windbreaker, iTunes line running from an ear to his unrestrained waistline, munching a hot dog with one hand, steering his scooter with the other, the bending aluminum frame beneath his obese type-2 diabetes ass making welder's sparks on the unscruffed blacktop.

I don't know if I should feel excitement at seeing an actual teenage boy enjoying what's left of the elements, or if I should be bothered that he needs a lawn mower motor to escort his shrinking frankfurter around the neighborhood. I can't tell his age: Is he a supersized thirteen-year-old bound for early twenties gout or a stunted seventeen-year-old still riding his Mickey Mouse scooter? He can't hear his own engine, hooked up to his top-thousand tunes. The vision of his passing puts a dent in one's hope for the future.

This junior porker is the soft result of winnerless-loserless PAL soccer matches on wet and foggy Saturday mornings. When one team scores, guess what? Don't worry, no tears, stop weeping, the other team scores too: 1–1, 2–2, 3–3, free yourself of the harness of competition, Peewee. Everyone's a winner. It's one big lovefest! Work ethic, athleticism, courage, decisiveness, savvy, precision—all merely foreign forces of an older, more savage age to whose dead rules we no longer need pay homage.

Line up at halftime, kids, for your combo meals from Carl's Jr. Or do you want tacos and chalupas, boys? After the game, we'll go to the video arcade aka our living room and loosen on a plastic button all that pent-up energy that wasn't spent on the field.

He's weaving down the street, he's tossing the bun into the bushes of this house, he's issuing us the middle finger, he's gone. I remember the transient at the county jail who required an imaginary Little League scenario for me to tolerate—just to look at—him. This kid's got the exact opposite problem: he's got so much parental compassion dripping from his pores that he's impossible to handle, like a manatee.

I see Chinaski emerge from the construction site, follow at the same slow jog the path of the scooter.

"I learned a lot from your Uncle Richard," Ms. Clannonite says, interrupting my thoughts.

I nod, shrug, smile to make up for the shrug. I'm determined to be just a good-looking guy. If only all the pimps and dealers out there could see how valuable their hustle would be in this field. If only a lot of things.

"He taught me how to farm."

I try an inquisitive look—"I didn't know my uncle was a man of the fields"—but I really don't want to hear it. The less I know about my uncle in business, the more I can hold on to a working relationship. Not a working relationship in business, a working relationship in life.

"Farm lawyers," she says, smiling assuringly. Her teeth are drywall white, purely lasered of plaque. "Farm bankers. Farm insurance agents. Build up five to ten each in your arsenal. Successful lawsuits, business foreclosure, home and life insurance referrals—all of it affects the real estate market."

Don't want to hear it.

"He taught me to know my product and then to jazz it up. This place you're looking at is not a three-bedroom one-and-a-half-bath house. I defy you to call it anything but a cozy top-of-the-line, modern American domicile on a ventilated six-thousand-square-foot lot featuring multi-temperature bath and showers, hardwood floors, custom-carved oaken cabinets, earthquake-proof granite countertops, matching washer and dryer, forced air and heat, insulated by hand-carved panels, and an all-weather fireplace, adorned by a warm reading room with yet-to-be implemented alcove stacks, an emerald-green yard, and a secure two-car garage with an ADT alarm system, a sky-high redwood fence, and pre-set peripheral-motion lights."

Translation: three-bedroom one-and-a-half-bath house.

"He taught me that you never forget past clients. Stay in touch. Send out birthday and Christmas cards. Past clients have family and friends in search of referrals. And eventually past clients get tired of the house you sold them and need a new one. Not just once. Not twice. Before the decade's over, three times. This is a valley of movers and shakers. And then: past clients get tired of each other. Your uncle taught me that divorce is good in this trade. It's healthy. When past clients go to court to finish their life together, you've got two new sales at opposite ends of the valley. There's no such thing as a past client. Even when dead, past clients will appreciate a visit to the funeral home where you can make their grandchildren into future past clients."

I look at the crucifix on the lawn: *Yes,* I want to say, *but are you pretty inside?*

"The past and the future do not shape me. The time is now. A sale starts with the confidence of attitude. Of not merely being *in* the moment but *being* the moment. You prospect for but don't hope for a better future. Hope means nothing. Your uncle is a *now* thinker. Do you know why you're moving all that office crap to Burlingame?"

I don't say, *Because I was told to and I'm trying to be a cooperative guy.*

"Because we don't have an office anymore. We have a weekly meeting at the Fairmont, paid for by your uncle. You see, he's a visionary. He saw that everything could be stored on some database on his laptop. That he could eliminate not only rent but a secretary as well. And he did." Here she smiles. "That's right, your Aunt Lanell. Whatever you lack in not having an office can be made up for on-site. Clients are interested in the house they're about to buy, not the office they visit. Your uncle understood this and—not one by one but all at once—closed each of his offices in the valley."

Yeah, sure. He was probably afraid you were gonna steal his files and torch the place.

"He taught me that it's about the five senses of sales: sight, smell, sound, touch, taste."

As I'm about to break my vow of silence from the gutter of my imagination—*Taste? Taste what?*—a stripped and beat-up Ford Tempo pulls up, blasting mariachi, and a young paisa emerges from the car, carrying yet another grocery bag up the walk of the house. I can smell the chicken tikka masala from fifteen feet away. The kid's about to speak but thinks better of it. She's already breaking him off a twenty from a roll of green bills, as if the sound of crisp papers separating from one another were rather a soothing way of saying *shhhhh,* the Esperanto language of love.

He takes it, bowing, and she says in perfect accent, *"Muchas gracias, Miguel."*

Suddenly I'm famished: for healthy servings of Indian food off the nude belly of the Godmother of the West.

So you're just yearning to be authentic Americans, Mr. and Mrs. Gupta? Okay. All right. Why not walk in on some Americana in the raw? Witness us being "in the moment." Observe the screw screwing. This is what your children will be doing on MySpace in no time anyway.

My fantasy is starting to get loose, and the beast from below is responding with surprising vigor, here on the edge of no-man's-land, when the lady of the private showing counts out five twenties—"*shhhhh*"—and lays them seductively in my palm. Before I can say that my services are worth a wee bit more than that, ma'am, she adds her business card to the pile: Kelly Clannonite. I look down on her flawless smile, the clean glare of teeth like a ceaseless reminder to visit the dentist, and say nothing.

"Today's clients will buy the place," she says. "Know how I know?"

I shake my head no, but inside I'm rolling my eyes. I can think of nothing I detest more than when supposed specialists think their acute observational faculties and marked experience equate to Nostradamus prophecy. This is the kind of romantic self-inflation that has gotten many a world leader into irreparable trouble.

"The Guptas just came from an apartment complex in East Palo Alto. Know what that means?"

I think, *That they've learned the vernacular of modern American West Coast gangs?*

"It means they're desperate for quiet. Now I ask you: What's more quiet than a half-built neighborhood with virtually no occupancy?"

Genius, I want to say. *But you've a little problem with the Punjabi porker.*

"Just keep an eye on him for the next five or ten minutes." My guess is she means Chinaski. "Often his motive to please gets the better of his limited reason."

That makes me smile. Definitely Chinaski. She takes advantage of my affable silence and walks off toward the human nest for sale. I, too, walk off, but in the opposite direction. Up the street toward the buzzing sound, empty houses right and left, behind me and in front. *Keep an eye on him for the next five or ten minutes* can mean any number of things.

I put up a soft whistle of the Mozart I heard back at the house, and before I've finished the ditty I reach the corner of the block, stop, and wait. Chinaski is squatting behind a fire hydrant facing the street. I step back behind a fence but I can see him through the gaps. He needs another fire hydrant to hide adequately. But no one's around; the brand-new houses are empty. Chinaski is breathing hard, as am I for some reason. I sense something twisted about this setup, I feel as used as a wet handkerchief.

Chinaski has his dress shirt unbuttoned and then—*what's this? Oh, no, don't do it*—he pulls the shirt over his shoulder and off altogether like a cheap stripper. His head pops out and he shakes out his spaghetti hair wildly, rock star extraordinaire. Thankfully he's wearing a T-shirt underneath, this one all green with a yellow Green Lantern insignia on the chest: the same superhero symbol that dangles from the rearview mirror of his green '06 VDUBBUG.

Chinaski's one of those grown men who camped out in the hailstorm at AMC theaters for tickets to *Incredible Hulk*. Braved snow and ice for *X-Men*. Making big bucks for the comic-book folks. Yes, it was the kids who dragged him out there. One likes to think that nurturing the imagination is a good thing—*Imagine all the people living life in peace, you-who-oooo*—but a position like that is no longer impregnable in this lame age: by what mutant superhero do I define myself?

Imagine all the people living life in orange polyester jumpsuits. Cuck-oo-ooo.

It's no wonder men are on the decline.

Well, I don't want any part of it. What else is new? I don't want any part of a lot. Of metrosexuality. Of militias in Idaho. Of peace marches in the city. Of absolute capitalism. Of (microscopic) ear-

and mouthpieces. Of celebrity mania. Of scrolling a screen for your
soulmate. Of SUVs and three TVs for the kids. Of psychotherapy
and Prozac nation. Of the Minutemen with too much time and land
on their hands. Of infantile Me-Gen authors. Of Sean Hannity. Of
Michael Moore. Of Cindy Sheehan and of whoever is her flag-waving
opposite moron: *I don't want any part of it!*

How could I sidle up to one side and call myself wise? There are
twenty-five answers to the question. Twenty-five more questions after
that. Then you can turn a single page of the twenty-five-volume
questionnaire. No answers in the back of the book this time, no all-
knowing master to guide us into the future.

Hell, while I'm at it, I don't want any part of Chinaski rising slowly
as the kid emerges from his house, a fat slice of pizza in his hand.
No part of the zealot at the temple, the cannonball-bellied cannon
fodder. I want no part of this "service." That's what this preposter-
ously is: a simple transaction with Ms. Clannonite, the Godmother
of the West: "Ask the kid not to ride his scooter for the next hour."

Chinaski steps out from behind the hydrant in a predatory crouch,
fists pumping like dual hearts at the end of his arms, and then he's
up the grass of the house, scooter now in hand, underneath him, fired
up, a simultaneous spinout and wheelie past the kid. Chinaski slides
down the grass and flies over the walk, down the street at full speed,
the steel on concrete a dragon tail of Chinese firecrackers.

I'm jogging over to help the kid and snitch off Chinaski to the
authorities when I stop in my cold hard tracks. The kid drops down
on his ass and bawls, "Mom! Mom! Help meee!"

I can't push out of my head the image of Cyrus fighting off his
attacker. This kid just watched it happen, a reality-show television
stunt. His whining pierces my eardrums, and I half turn at the sound,
pause at the sight. Can't help the kid up, just can't. He's got enough
soccer moms to patch up his boo-boos. If he's lucky, he'll learn to
live with this wound for a few years.

I U-turn and speed walk like the ladies at the track, as Chinaski leans into a turn on the scooter, his dopey pumpkin head hanging over the handlebars like the crude tributary bow of an ancient Viking boat, his thread implants flat across his head as if someone heavy has sat on them.

The back of his Green Lantern shirt reads THINK ENTREPENEUR: GET THE BLING. In his own warped and what-he-thinks-to-be-heroic mind, he's just saved civilization.

He rides up the construction site with surprising skill, swerving to avoid the pitfalls of abandoned housebuilding materials, and then he and his buzzing machine are gone, dust clouds in lazy chase. The idiot has found the perfect mode of seatless painfree transportation.

I expect that should count as "keeping an eye on him."

In the reflection of a corner window, I see the Punjabi porker stand up, still crying to himself, the lost child at the mall. If I had gone over to ask if he was all right, he would have shaken his head no, as if it were too awkward to move his mouth without a Whopper to masticate; he'd have asked me for five bucks to go buy nachos at the 7-Eleven. I would not have said, "Nachos are a buck and a half, kid," because he would have fired back, "I need a Slurpee to wash them down."

Naturally.

So I start to jog. To sprint. Yet again I'm on the run. But this time I've got a good out (the asshole in the Green Lantern shirt did it), a good escape (the asshole's VDUBBUG), no witnesses like Robin of the Cookie Monster sweater anywhere in sight. Even without Chinaski (*a father, he's a father!*), the Godmother of the West, and the kid and his scooter, I can't help but think of the exchange of property as something altogether lacking in seriousness. Something inessential here, something not real.

So what's new?

The apple-green hue of Chinaski's ride lures me in and—as I pop the door, wing the Roid Void down the street like a Frisbee, and drop down into the leather seat, wondering why it's so quiet and feels so empty—I look over at the crucifix on the lawn and see a SOLD placard swinging in the wind of Kelly Clannonite's hurricane departure. So it ain't pretty inside no more. Mr. and Mrs. Gupta got duped-a after all, hah, hah, hah: cheap joke, cheap sale.

I fire up the VDUBBUG, drive off, don't look back. Chinaski, Ms. Clannonite, and me: we each got what we wanted from this scene. Everyone in the West leaves with haste.

25

And So the Days Pass

AND SO THE DAYS PASS. Every hour blends into the next. *We measure out our lives in coffee spoons,* a damned good bard once said. The day is diced up by triple mocha lattes and harmless and hurtful gossip both and flatteries from down low and diatribes from up high and every form of fluffy communication in between, and incoming/outgoing calls and lulls in the day that are longer than an hour and eased by a flask of Stolichnaya and female dress in various stages of disrobe, and Altoid chasers for the aforesaid vodka and litigational summons the length, inconsequence, and antiquated Latin of a doctoral dissertation in Medieval Studies concerning which cut of mutton should be eaten on holidays and new cars on the cusp of the manufacturing year and Alhambra delivered on Tuesday afternoons by a paisa named Pablo with his lazy acquired American swagger and pepperoni-free (for the six employed Hindis), sausage-free (for the four employed Muslims), chicken-free (for the three employed hippies), vegan pizza at the vacant Fairmont and the public alliances of family, company, and GOP people staid in their stares and Bill Buckley theories and secret signs of swinging clubbers constantly whispering into each other's ears like wannabe Gotti mafia bosses, and rivalries at the racquetball courts and on the beachfront lawn of an eighteen green, and adultery of every imagined combination while all throughout these trivialities the region is bustling with lots of hits and dozens of barren semitoxic lots are sold for the highest overpriced bid in which legal yet ridiculous commission is made and spent on cats and tits and yachts and invested in hot or conservative stocks as I, looking up from my bottom rung on the corporate ladder of Santa Clara Real Estate West, reflect with deep Dalai-Lama nearly hallucinatory fervor on the richness of vanilla milkshakes.

26

My Uncle Is Waiting

My Uncle is waiting for me on the porch of the guesthouse, cross-legged on the cement, back to the stucco wall, the terra-cotta angel that he had shipped over from Calabria directly above his head. He's got a bottle of Jack between his legs, he's in a V-neck T-shirt and an old pair of faded Wrangler blue jeans, and he's got so much pain on his face that I can't look him in the face as I say, "Hey, hey, Uncle Rich. You're like a reservation wino in a Sherman Alexie novel."

He smiles. "Who the hell's that?"

"No one," I say, guiding him up the walk, "that you'll ever meet."

"Just waiting till you got back, nephew."

"Why didn't you go inside?"

"Oh, no. Nonsense. That's your little rental now."

"I don't pay a thing, Uncle."

"Nonsense, nonsense. Anyway, I haven't set foot in there in years."

I key the lock, open the door, say, "Well, come on inside your guesthouse."

He ducks under the bridge of the door as if he's entering a cave of deathly peril, that's how polite he is. I switch on a light and my uncle scans the living room: all my stuff—sleeping bag and pillow on the floor, three collared shirts, three pairs of pants folded on the couch, several stacks of books in the corner, and atop the highest book a plastic bottle with the Treetop label wrapped around its gut. My uncle walks over to the literature, scans the titles, says, "Why don't you give Achilles and the boys their own room?"

I look out the bay window and realize something about my stay in the guesthouse: there are two rooms in the back whose doors I've never opened. Through the window I can see the rows of magnolia trees and the furled hills and the man-made lake with the splinter of a dock, and I know it's more than just scenery to me: I don't want to be alone in a room without a view if I don't have to. It's not institutional either. I may have always been this way: anytime I'm enclosed by a box of walls, I'll go right to the window, pop it, let in the air, and breathe in with tragic relief this oxygen connection, probably fictive, that I have with the outside world.

"I don't like to be alone in there," realizing right when I say it that it contradicts everything I believe about the beauty of solitude. If I can find beauty in a gutter, why not an empty room? Why not a toilet?

"You haven't even gone back there, have you?"

"No."

"Either room?"

"Nah."

"For chrissake. And the head? You piss and shit by the lake, right?"

"Nah," I say. "I piss on the side of the house. What do you think I am: uncivilized?"

"Jesus."

"Can I have tomorrow off, Uncle?"

"For what?"

"I got court."

"For that thing you got into?"

I nod.

"Yeah. No problem. I'll tell Chinaski myself in the morning."

"He doesn't need to know about me."

"I'm the boss, nephew. I don't need to explain my decisions for anything. Not to you, not to him."

"True."

We're both sitting on the stools by the tile counter looking out on the significant corner of San José he calls his property. This is his, his, *his,* and no one else's. The concept is strange to me. The claim of *mine* starts with the Tonka truck at six, lunch box at nine, dirt bike at twelve, high school sweetheart at sixteen. Don't touch, or else. I mean, how much land does a man need? When it comes down to it, six feet by three feet, six feet deep.

My uncle puts the bottle to his lips, hits the Jack, gasps. "So what is it? Why won't you go back there?"

"I'm trippin'. I've been trippin' my whole life. I mean, I wanna see and maybe be a part of the world, yet I won't open up the doors."

"Because they'll slam in your face, nephew?"

"No. That doesn't bother me at all. *Success is counted sweetest by those who ne'er succeed.* No, I think it has to do with the other doors that have already been opened."

"What do you mean?"

"I don't want them to diminish in value. I want them to mean something. And they won't mean shit if I keep opening more of them."

"I know what you're saying."

"Everything'll get washed out."

"I get you."

"So you've felt that, too?"

"Sure. I mean, one of the things that's so attractive about business is that no matter how much time I spend there, I don't care anything about it. There's no purity there to dilute. It's a game. I don't see how it can be anything more than that. Math, numbers, luck. There's hard work, yes, but to me it's just patience. Tolerance. Who can put up with the most amount of people's shit? That's the question. And the answer is me."

"And that's good?"

"Sure. Well, maybe. I haven't had any kind of epiphany since Vietnam. Is that good? Again: maybe. I'm not saying I'm a prophet. I'm saying I can read the signs. Nina could, too. She knew. Like you. But shit, I haven't opened a door in three decades."

"Maybe you're worse off, Uncle, than someone with no ties like me. I don't have anything, but I'm mobile. You're stuck with what you've got, and maybe that destroys your soul."

"Nephew, I'm convinced that life in this place destroys the soul period." He offers me the bottle and I take it. "But guess what? Things are looking up. You're my first employee in over twenty years that matters to me beyond the bottom line."

"Who was the last?"

"Your Aunt Lanell."

I remember Kelly Clannonite's claims, don't want to go near his pain. Whether he caused it or not, why dig my nails into the wound? I don't ask him about Aunt Lanell; he doesn't ask me about his sister, my mother. That's the deal. "I'm glad I'm at the West."

"She was my best worker," he says. "She coordinated everything, a true multitasker. She could've handled eight kids with ease."

I nod. I don't know what to say except, "I guess I never really see her around, Uncle."

"Oh, I'll show you some other night. Probably when I've got a little more than this one bottle to drink. But let's talk about you, nephew. What is your big dilemma?"

I think it over. I want to be straight and to the point, honest, respectful of my uncle's curiosity and superior amount of planet time, yet no ad hominem attack on myself. I want to be evenhanded, like a Supreme Court judge. "My dilemma is I have no dilemma."

"Don't play word games with me."

"I'm not. I'm serious. I don't feel the urgency to do anything."

"What about the job?"

I look over at my uncle, embarrassed by his hope. "The job?"

"Yeah. Is it going okay?"

"Sure."

"Sure?"

"Going great."

"Well, once you get your stuff together," he says, "I was thinking about handing the business over to you."

I can't pretend any longer. "Give it to someone else, Uncle Rich. Someone who can appreciate the gift. All day long at that place I feel like I'm St. Sebastian post–arrow encounter. Please please please don't give it to me. You deserve a better legacy."

"And what about when you were locked up?" he says, not skipping a beat. My last statement hurt him, though I can see he's already resigned to rewrite his will. He's a businessman all right, unfazed, at least outwardly, by the day's potential emotion. "That must have given you something to believe in."

"Even there I was just walking around for chrissake, saying, 'Well, this is an interesting place, isn't it? What a brilliant social experiment.'"

"Yeah, well." He lifts the bottle, thinks it over. "It wouldn't be like that if you got hit."

"What?"

"If you'd seen the abyss."

I lean forward, smiling, and show him the forty-stitch scar across my temple. "Does this count?"

"Jesus, nephew," he says, passing me the bottle. "I had no clue with that silly beanie you're always wearing. How come you didn't say anything?"

"That's what I'm saying, Uncle. It doesn't matter. I don't say anything now and I didn't say anything then. When it happened, my brain

was ordering my hands to fire at the cat and I was definitely firing at
him—I got off some straight lefts and a hook, muscle memory of box-
ing back in the day—but I got this feeling that it was no big deal really.
I was leaking blood like a busted faucet. Then afterward when I was
lying there in the blood and my body was doing everything to keep
itself going, another part of me was just watching the thing go down,
not an out-of-body experience or anything religious like that, but an
in-of-body; I felt in order for once, it was actually antireligious, as if
there were nothing in the world wrong with getting cracked over the
head with a steel dustpan. I could rationalize why the guy would want
to do it; I could rationalize why I would fight back; I could understand
why I might die or, if I lived, why *he* might die, but I couldn't really
praise anyone, couldn't really indict anyone, and that's wrong."

"It is."

"It's fucking wrong."

"You've played too many roles, nephew. You know too much."

"'Cept I don't know myself."

"You don't have a self."

The only answer to a statement like that is to assault the cells of
the larynx with Jack, saturate the funnel of the liver in liquor, let the
eyes water and the nostrils flare, let the heart burn from the infernal
heat of alcohol fire, let the arms and fingers go numb. Don't think,
don't think, don't think on the accurate nature of your uncle's statement; get dumb, amnesiac. Don't ponder the mandatory nihilism of
the century, don't wonder about the future of the story you love, of
the species, this people, this place. Take another shot of Jack, anes-
thetize your head, and believe that nothing is finalized. Keep the hope
alive in suspension, in mid-float, against all the evidence you've heard,
you've seen, you've felt, and you know. And then take another right
hook from Jack. And another.

"When I was in Southeast Asia," my uncle says, and my ears
perk up. The camera is off me. I pass him the bottle. "I thought

I understood about life and death. And maybe I did. But coming back here ruined all that clarity. I'm not sure I'm a wiser man now. I know more, I'm positive of that, but I'm not sure I'm wiser."

I wait, reach over, take the bottle of Jack. I know something big is coming from my uncle, but for some reason I can only wait. I don't want to facilitate his pain if I can help it. If. To hell with the therapeutic sell of confession. I say, carry it around unresolved in your gut, and if it doesn't dissolve in the acid of the stomach at least you've got a wound to believe in forever.

"My unit was involved in the greatest battle of the war."

"Hamburger Hill?"

"Yeah. 101st Airborne. Screaming Eagles. Jesus. I can see them all as if it were yesterday."

"The NVA?"

"Well, I can see them too. But I meant my brothers. I can see my old brothers-in-arms."

"What were their names?"

He shakes his head. "They all died. They were just kids. Shit. Every medic I knew died that day."

"You were the only one that survived?"

"Maybe."

He violently takes back the liter of Jack, and some of the golden juice spills on its way over. He hits it hard, like a post-marathon bottle of Gatorade. A lot of time passes between us, so much so I can hear the tick of the clock on the wall I'd like to smash into a state of silence; I can hear my uncle's sluggish breathing; I can hear his sudden crying. It's so fast and blurry and anti-business that by the time I look over he's recovered. Just like a flash rain in the monsoon season of the very Southeast Asian nation he's mourning. If it has to happen, that's the kind of crying I like. Miss me with that stuff. I'm wicked as hell. I do my best to rebel against the next unholy thought, the one that's been sitting there in the fore of my brain for several

minutes thumbing for a ride: this shit is so trite. This theft of a John
Wayne moment.

Out, out, out!

"You know, nephew, I went back for a second tour."

"No, I didn't know that."

"The shit that affects us ain't ever that complex, is it?"

"I don't know, Uncle. Things seem to have changed."

"Yeah, let's not talk about that. Your fucked-up generation."

"Okay. More than fine by me. But why'd you go back?"

He hits it again and says, "To get killed."

"Yeah?"

"Honorably."

"Yeah."

"I chickened out at the Hill, see? I got sick on 'em. Faked it, took
to the bed. I was like that little punk in *Patton* who goes yellow. I
wish Patton could've been there to slap me. I would've given him a
commendation."

"Yeah."

"A fucking coward. I should've died up there with my brothers.
Like I was meant to."

I know better than to say, *No one's meant to.* So I don't say anything at all, though I do want a shot. But I don't reach out. I don't
reach out for it any longer.

27

The Judge Is the Son of Another Nation

THE JUDGE IS THE SON of another nation, but he's a proud American through and through. The Honorable Barrett Nguyen believes in the system. He says so, over and over and over again, a slightly detectable Mekong twang in his otherwise impeccable accent. He looks sharp, man: square head, square cut hairdo, square shoulders, square soul. The man is the consummate square. He has all the faith in the system that a native son like me was born to lack. He believes in the blind lady with the teeter-totter scale in her hands. If this guy has anything to do with it, I'm gonna get hanged.

He's talking about procedural matters with his clerk, and I tune out by observing the DA. A rail of a man, so thin in the neck that the Adam's apple looks extraterrestrial. Sandy-blond hair, a Doolittle mustache, he's attaching cords into several speakers like a kid plugging away at a puzzle. He's got a laminated photograph of a brotha with a 'fro from what looks like the 1960s, Black Pantheresque, and underneath it the words, *Shout It, Brother*. I can't figure out the political connection until he says in the voice of a tracheotomy patient, "Testing one, two. Testing. Can you hear me, Your Honor?"

"As usual, I cannot, Mr. Weil. You're indecipherable."

"Okay," the DA says, immediately fiddling with the volume on his amps. I get it: he's got the Black Panther in lamination to encourage squeaking out his loudest voice through the trial. That's funny. Has nothing to do with the politics. The DA won't look at me. That's funny too. I want to reach out and say, Don't worry about the problem with your weapon. I'm sure there are a few cops out on the streets terrified of their guns.

About sixty potential jurors are now entering the courtroom, appraising me as if it were court-ordered. Looking back at them once for good measure, they hardly look just like me, not that it matters. I don't know who would, anyway, not that that matters either. Mr. Weil makes a point to smile at as many as he can.

In my scan for kindred faces, I spot a young woman with wide shoulders and frizzy hair pulled back into a parishioner's bun. No doubt a Poly at minimum, probably Samoan. She'll recognize my Samoan last name for sure, likely know someone related to me or related to my father, back in the old country. Every Samoan alive is related to every other Samoan, alive and dead both. But this is where the guessing game starts. Any variety of behavioral possibilities exists with even the tiniest culture in the world, less than 500,000 members.

Does she have the crab-in-the-bucket mentality, pulling down any fellow crustacean trying to crawl out and see the rest of the world? Or is she of the pious ilk whereby a troublesome cat like me brings shame to the clan's name? A guilty verdict would publicly disassociate her from my lawlessness, slicing the bloodline between us.

I take a quick peek back at her. She's in the third row, ignoring not only me but the people around her. I fear the way she sits, chest out, chin out, inflated with dignity. I can see that she'll destroy more than my life: she'll wreck the metaphor in my head. Jump with all her weight on my little imaginary bridge between opposing worlds, send me right up the river.

Today my peers are techies of every variety and culture, Southeast Asians, Indians, Pakistanis, one memorable no-doubt-American-born kid with a Mohawk sprouting not from the forehead to the upper neck but from ear to ear, a new twist on an old upstate New York tradition of a near-dead tribe. Somehow this unorthodoxy strikes me as being not creative but boring. My peers are old folks of Portuguese, Italian, Polish descent who've brought tablets and pens for posterity. A brotha who looks like a teacher maybe and who nods at me, the only one. There's a man with a shaved head and a supercilious look on his face that I want to slap off at this, my trial for assault and battery. All kinds of dutiful citizens with closets full of bones, no doubt, their two-week judicial clout indisputable in time, in history, a true portrayal of man, of me, American drifter who never sticks around long enough even to be an apostate, the dropout who's still here talking—at least thinking—a big game.

This jury is a reminder, the official stamp, of my breakup with my fellow Americans. Today it's a half-breed skeptic before a dozen assorted donuts who couldn't say a word about me that matters. Couldn't speak to why I love Johann Sebastian Bach and Tupac Shakur at the same time, polar opposites in bio and attitude, brothers in passion and pain, why I see Democrats and Republicans not on an issue line but a timeline, the former being futurists, the latter nostalgists, both equally beautiful and madly in love with our story, both equally seduced by error, inflexibility, arrogance, why I love and detest this country both, why I want to live the fullest life, whatever that means, and yet somewhere in the marrow how I long for life's validator, the qualifier, the end. What could they say about me related to this joke of an event?

I'm twiddling my thumbs at the concept at hand, drumming my fingers at the core of the American way. Twelve peers just like you. Anonymous to be judicious. And things are getting better, they say. No longer Tom Robinson before a dozen white men.

I don't know. Maybe, maybe not.

What I do know is that money sings in this system. The poor get robbed in court on a regular basis. So the state's got the Robin Hood story in reverse: *steal again from which side to give to which side?* If you've got the cash, you can pay for a bigger lawbroker. If you don't, you can seize on your constitutional rights and have the state hire you a public pretender. No one can dispute that. When's the last time a fat cat accepted this free gift from the state? If it were worth it, a capitalist would hit it up for sure.

The judge says to the potential jurors, "Thank you for coming today, ladies and gentlemen. We shall begin with an overview of the day's schedule, and then I shall speak to some of the procedures. After that, the court will call you up to answer the questions put to you by both attorneys. Please hold your questions until the end of the session. The likelihood of my covering your particular problem is very high."

I tune out and look back over my shoulder and everyone, it seems, is paying close attention, all except my own attorney—who isn't here of course, whoever he or she may be at the moment. During the arraignment and then again at pretrial, I had three different attorneys assigned by the county, each one rushing into court at the last moment, to the irritation of the judge and the amusement of their client, me. Their representation took the form of some variation on three or four sentences transitioning their client—me, Paul Tusifale—to the next bureaucratic session. This system is as big as the Himalayas and as perilous. People are lost in it, people die in it all the time. You don't find their bodies until a few seasons have passed. I, Paul Tusifale (SSN 660-04-9116, case #D459293), never bothered to say a word to any of my attorneys, a gift each had taken without gratitude, as if I were not only inarticulate but comatose as well and thus unable to delve with any intelligible bearings into the complicated court proceeding I'd just witnessed, all three minutes of the preliminary stage that they, untested legal rooks or tested legal hacks, had been assigned by their bosses not to screw up. It's not only elementary but, when a life is on the line, inflammatory.

I make a decision: it's strong, pure, and maybe even right: I will forego any further complimentary samplers from the state. If I must, I'll represent myself.

I look up at the judge, confident now that my place here is clear, the lines of my life at last drawn, when he stops in mid-speech, looks directly at me, shakes his head, then looks behind me. For a second I'm miffed, until I feel a palm massage my shoulder and the judge says, "Nice to see that you are on time as usual, counselor."

"Dong-hoo Choi, Your Honor"—here he claps my shoulder, then begins rubbing it possessively with the kind of attention my previous attorneys lacked—"representing Paul Tusifale."

The judge does not nod. He, like me, wants to know what the catch is. The DA seems intimidated, fiddling again with his sound system.

"My most humble apologies for my tardiness, Your Honor. I assure you it will not happen again."

"I am sure it will not, Mr. Choi. Shall we return to the court's instructions?"

"By all means, Your Honor." My attorney sits and pats me on the knee.

I whisper, "Stop touching me, mutherfucker."

He pulls out a legal tablet from his briefcase, writes: *Write it.*

I take the pen he offers, write: *Stop touching me, mutherfucker.* He attempts to take the pen from me, but I push his hand away, write: *What makes you think I'm going to pay your outlandish corporate fees, you fucking jackal? You ain't even getting a bottle of kimchi from me.*

He takes the pen and taps twice on the desk, to hammer home whatever he's about to write: *This is pro bono.*

I write: *What's the quid pro quo on your pro boner service?*
You either flunked or forgot your Latin. I'm free. Your lucky day.

I look back at the potential jurors glaring at me, as the judge re-
cites instructions, write: *That has yet to be proved, counselor.*
Just treat it like another day at St. Cajetan.
Look at the nuns-in-residence?
He smiles. *Exactly.*

I zero in on the stenographer's desk. Upon it, a tribute to all things
leather. A name plaque—Ms. Dendela Dido—wrapped in leather,
a penholder encased in leather, the phone handle gripped with
leather, the base of her super typewriter enveloped in leather, a
photograph of the stenographer on the back of a hog framed in
leather. In theme, she's leathered down from ankle to chin, her arms
halfway around the global gut of the bad boy in the bucket seat, also
leather, before her. He's got no exposed skin except the tip of his
nose, everything covered in leather or hair. I find none of this odd or
even noteworthy this late into the game, until I realize that as she's
slamming away on her encrypted keyboard, recording every word said
in this legal hovel, she's winking at me and blowing kisses my way. I
shake my head, look down, look back up again.

The signals are fired off so rapidly that I give her the benefit of
the doubt: she has a nervous tick—yes, two ticks—made manifest
by the unconscious trials of labor; they're habitual, tied to performance like the trigger and the hammer of a pistol.

One of the jury members is explaining with unguarded passion that
he has no prejudice in his heart, absolutely none, not even against his
Pakistani neighbor who never says hello back, who beats his kids and
makes his wife cover her face with a scarf, they have the freedom, he
says, to be themselves in this country and that's what's great, he says,
and also, he adds, what sucks about it at the same time. As I look for
some potential jurors of Pakistani blood, hoping for some volatile excitement, I finally meet Ms. Dendela Dido's two ticks head on.

She adds a third signal to the mix: her tongue delicately splitting
the lips, in and out, in and out, et cetera, et cetera. She's so smart,

she's using me as cover, typing away and pretending that I'm the neutral spot in the distance upon whom—or, rather, upon *which*— she must focus to keep up with the dialogue.

The judge is falling asleep but nobly fighting it, Mr. Weil is revising his notes and stroking a lucky rabbit's foot dangling from the control panel of his sound system, my attorney is asking the prejudice-free juror if he agrees with the Don Imus firing, the potential jurors are tuning out, tired, annoyed, everyone except this breath of fleshy air, the leather princess. Everyone's indifferent, awaiting the entertainment or the end of it all.

I admire her initiative, wink back, curl up my lip and growl a little. She frowns ever so slightly. She's the kind of girl who takes pleasure in pain. My attorney sits, says, "Sure, we'll take him, Your Honor, why not?" and writes, *Archie Bunker over there is the last of his kind, ain't he?*

I don't write anything back. Obviously I haven't been paying attention. I tap on the pen and try to focus on the next potential juror, a techie in an Intel polo shirt and specs thick as telescopic glass. Still, I've got my mind on leather and all its usages.

Putting the mic to his thin lips, Mr. Weil asks the techie what he thinks about the new law across California prohibiting spanking, a question that makes the stenographer shift in her seat, frown, and look back at the judge.

The techie answers, "What no-spanking law?"

That earns giggles.

Judge Nguyen throws in some innocent humor. "I am sure you are glad that you came to court today then, yes, Mr. Thommavongsa?"

"Yes, sir!"

The stenographer is still puzzled. I want to walk over to her with the best debonair air I can summon, lean over the desk, and whisper in her ear, It's the kiddies, my little mistress. The kiddies can't get the paddle, baby girl. But you, a consenting adult who's been very, very bad—

My attorney takes the pen from me and writes: *Forget about it.*

I write back: *Forget what?*

She does that shit with every violent felon who sits in your seat. She's debunked half the county's tough guys that come through here in chains.

Who has? I write, testing, hoping, yet knowing.

I'm telling you: she has priors.

Who?

Ms. Dendela Dido.

All that means is she never gave you a shot. So what's she got against attorneys?

He writes: *What've you got against attorneys?*

Finally, some truth in this place. How big is your database? Got a list as big as the atom bomb. I'll destroy your world a hundred times over, counselor.

He tries to change the topic. *Don't you have any poems for me, Shakespeare?*

I put the pen to the paper and he seizes it, one admonitory shake of the head. A breech of courtroom etiquette? I look up at the judge and he doesn't have a clue about our dialogue, or so it appears. Who-dung writes: *I want a real poem.*

I take back the pen hastily, write:

> *the problem:*
> *the black of birth*
> *and white of death*
> *belie a life of gray*

Yeah, Who-dung writes, *you're the problem.*

No. YOU are the problem.

Is it really in your best interests to argue with your lawyer?
You can be fired any time, counselor.
Am I on trial here or you?
We're all on trial.
Yeah, sure. Write another poem about it.
I'll tell you a story instead.
Hold up.

A jury member with dark hair and darker eyes is recounting the sinister foster homes of his youth. I, for one, feel legitimately bad for the cat, as he describes his adoption into a family of usurers of the system, adding annually to their crop of kids to secure extra cash from the county. My attorney looks over at the dark-eyed foster home juror, says aloud, "He's fine, Your Honor, he's just fine," writes: *Let's hear your st*

"No questions, Mr. Choi?"

"No, Your Honor. We'll take him. Thank you."

The judge's eyes narrow. Mr. Weil reads the judge's suspicion for what it is and looks over at us, trying to incite the judge's wrath. Neither has a case this time: If we have no questions, we have no questions. You can't force us to be interrogative. Why I have no questions for my attorney during jury selection, however, is another matter. Now that I think it over, the reality just may be that I'm enjoying this little debate; it means something to me, amazingly, more than a verdict, which means nothing.

My position is simple: The law is not the truth; the law is a deal, an agreement to the way the story will be told, a simplification of life; therefore, don't attach haughty grandeur and flowery language like justice and *in veritas* to a handshake. I'll take whatever verdict they throw down and ride with it, no complaints, as long as they leave the sermonizing to some other quack on a mutherfucking street corner.

I write, *Heard the case of Pal Singh?*

Don't know. Let's hear it.

Met him on the inside. Punjabi. No. 3 Greco-Roman wrestler in the world. Came to compete for us in '06 Olympics but dropped into East San Jo. Cousin's a gangbanger. This cousin gets surrounded one day by rival gang, getting beat real bad.

He takes the pen from me, looks over at the jury, nods, smiles, writes: *I know this story. He cut off one guy's finger with a scimitar. Sliced into another guy's leg.*

Right. Everyone fled, cousin too. Singh calls the cops. Quoted in the paper, "Helping, very much helping. Man down. Hurting with blood."

My attorney writes: *Already know the tragedy here. He called the cops . . . on himself.*

Not even the bad part, I write. *DA offers Singh 13 to 15 years, attempted murder. Or one year county for two counts of assault.*

My attorney shakes his head. *DA was bluffing. Couldn't get 13 to 15 in Texas.*

Did my boy Singh know this? He bought the bluff, foreigner scared shitless by big numbers. Second deal was worse offer. DA split the cases, one per victim, so Singh gets two strikes. One for each scimitar stroke. Singh was the cleanest mutherfucker I ever met. Now one slipup away from a 25-to-life third strike. What do you say?

At the jury box, a woman of Hispanic roots is explaining how she believes the police are crooked. The lady next to her, mid-seventies, maybe also Hispanic is shaking her head at each mispronounced word. One denouncing cops, though maybe Mexico City cops. One praising our cops, or maybe just denouncing chilango accents.

My attorney stands, says, "Your Honor, we have no problem with this selection for jury."

The judge raises an eyebrow and says, "No questions, Mr. Choi?"

My attorney shakes his head, sits.

"As you wish, Mr. Choi."

He writes: *I say he got bad representation.*

Was the DA innovative or a crook with no heart?
Both.
Yeah? Let's flip the script: How many guilty clients have you gotten off the hook by technicality, because the DA didn't cross one of his t's?
Let me ask you this: Who between the two of us is more intelligent? The pariah who outlines the system's flaws or the insider who can outline the system's flaws? I'm alive and kicking. How about you?
Do you defend child molesters, rapists, snitches, murderers, thieves?
I defend you.
Rephrase: Do you defend clients that you know are child molesters, rapists, snitches, murderers, thieves?
I defend whoever I have to.
Tran$lation: You defend whoever will pay.

My attorney stands, says without looking over at the box, "Mr. Sandhu, have you ever known anyone who has been beaten in your native country?"

Mr. Sandhu stands to speak and the judge says, "You may be seated, Mr. Sandhu. You need not stand when answering Mr. Choi's questions."

Mr. Sandhu, still standing, doesn't move.

"Sit down, Mr. Sandhu," the judge orders.

He sits at once and my attorney says, punching a fist into his palm, "Have you ever witnessed anyone being beaten?"

Mr. Sandhu looks around with concern, as if he's the one on trial or the one about to be beaten.

Judge Nguyen joins the charade by punching his own cheek and taking the blow. "Beaten, Mr. Sandhu. Have you ever witnessed anyone being beaten?"

"Beating?"

"Yes, Mr. Sandhu."

"In India?"

"Yes, sir."

"Of course I get beatings in Punjab. Many beatings of all kinds. That is why I come here to America. Here, right here."

"Well, you're not here anymore, Mr. Sandhu," says my attorney, nodding with what I believe to be fake concern. "Thank you for your time. Not interested, Your Honor."

Judge Nguyen says, "You're dismissed, Mr. Sandhu."

My attorney sits, even as the judge is issuing an evil eye our way, writes: *That's right. I do.*

So you're the problem.

You're missing one half of the equation.

I nod at the other side of the aisle. *Fuck them, too.*

Precisely.

No. Fuck them. And fuck you.

Fuck you back.

Do they prosecute people they know are innocent?

How the hell *would I know?*

Why the hell *would you take a case if they only prosecuted the guilty?*

You're gonna have to come with something bigger than that.

All right.

I stand up, the pen in my hand. "Your Honor, I don't want this crook representing me."

The judge doesn't even look my way. Doesn't swing his seat in my direction. This sends me into a euphoric state which translates in real time into reckless, but absolutely liberating free speech. "I am under no obligation, Your Honor, constitutionally or morally, to accept representation from someone so thoroughly incompetent. My liberty is in jeopardy, sir, and putting it in the hands of an attorney, frankly, means entrusting my life to a precocious used-car salesman. I would rather lie, swindle, misrepresent, hyperbolize, and smooth-talk on my own behalf, Your Honor."

Again, the judge is calm, unrattled. The man could at least blink but he won't afford me eye contact, extending my status of persona non grata. Even the leatherhead stenographer has stopped typing and won't look at me. So I have said nothing. Officially. Somehow this cat knows that not acknowledging my statement is infinitely worse on my insides than holding me in contempt.

"Mr. Choi," he says, not even asking me to sit down, "in what capacity are you with us today?"

I feel two fingers loop inside my belt line, hear the whispered words, "Trust me," as I'm pulled downward into my seat, the counselor in question rising to his feet, smiling.

"Your Honor," he begins, "might I apologize for the outburst of my client? He has been under an inordinate amount of stress with the recent death of his Aunt . . . Liluokalani, with whom he'd resided for a decade and a half. He was Aunt . . . Lily's personal caretaker to the very last minute."

"Mr. Choi," says the judge, "your client's misfortune is of no relevance in this courtroom. In fact, as evidence by the testimony you no doubt heard today from our potential jurors, we are all under stress, sir. And I am sure your training and experience have educated you on the concept of legal pertinence."

"Yes, Your Honor, certainly."

"Okay, Mr. Choi. Then I am also sure you will not mind if this court holds you personally responsible for any future outbursts your client should have on behalf of Aunt Lily."

"Not at all, Your Honor."

"Very good."

I write on my pad for the insane: *Just when I think I'm out, they pull me back in.*

He writes back: *Trust me for once.*

Do I have a choice?

He begins to write, but I take back the pen and leap blindly into the litigational future: *Go ahead, man. My life is yours.* I look over at the potential twelve, whisper into his ear: "Those mutherfuckers are going to hang me."

He glances over at the box, nods at a random potential jury member, opens up his briefcase, pulls out a brand new yellow tablet, and scribbles: *Again: write it with a straight face.*

I take the pen, draw an arrow halfway across the page, *Those mutherfuckers to your immediate right are gonna hang me with straight faces.*

Impossible.

Don't flatter yourself, counselor.

Hangings were outlawed in this state over thirty years ago. You'd get an injection of strychnine or the chair.

Comforting. Going out with a freewill of choice of poison. Real democracy at work.

How many strikes do you have, Robert Frost?

One.

2+3 x 2+2

What the hell is that?

The time you'll get if convicted.

What's the first 2?

Enhancement for a prison term prior.

The 3?

Sentence for the assault.

Second 2?

Second strike enhancement.

Last 2?

Hate-crime enhancement.

Enhance these nuts.

That's what better happen if you go up for ten, Emily Dickinson.

Can you get us out of here for a bit? Maybe we should talk?

Yep and yep. We'll have lunch.

"And it's on me," he says, standing and nodding at the judge.

28

I Know This Whole Thing Sickens You

"I KNOW this whole thing sickens you," my attorney says.

I sip my Coke, look out the cafeteria window, and watch the jurors, litigants, defendants comingle as if they're all friends out here in real life, returned from the virtual reality of a courtroom. "It just reaffirms the way the world works, man."

"Let's talk about the law."

"Tablets of stone on Sinai?"

"Code of Hammurabi."

"Fourteen stations of crucifixion rock?"

"Magna Carta and the rights of man."

He's good, fast, rightly vocationed. I say, "What a sham this thing is."

"A snow job?"

"A dyslexic jow blob. *We nolo contendere the show, Your Honor, yo no contesto por que yo no understand what jou want from me, man.*"

He laughs and I smile and this exchange makes the Samoan lady from the jury pool raise her eyebrows suspiciously. She's at the table next to us: two sandwiches, two bags of chips, no guests at her table.

"The law says we're not supposed to be near any jury members."

"Don't worry about it," he says. "Happens all the time. Look, you can tune out in the courtroom, okay? That's why I came today."

"To allow my mind to wander?"

"To give you a break. Don't worry about anything in there. I've got something that's gonna shut the case down, so you can rest a little, all right?"

I look up and he nods firmly. It's kind of him, an affirmation of a different sort. "Why you doing this, man?"

"Look, I can't say I felt bad for you in there because you'll take it as pity. I can't say that it was wrong what happened to you because I work for the system that made it wrong. Let's just say I felt a little guilty for fronting you off back at the Fairmont."

The Samoan lady has somehow moved closer to us, is sitting now right behind us, spying on our conversation. My attorney reads my mind. "I'm *telling* you. Don't worry, okay?"

"So what are we gonna do for the next fifteen minutes: share stories about the bar exam?"

"We could talk about your second strike."

"This thing's a joke and you know it."

"Well, then, let's get Lincoln-Douglas on one another. Old times sake."

"Bring it, Dishonest Abe."

"So what's the beef?"

"We'll keep it on topic. Argue: *The three-strikes law is not a sham.*"

He knocks on the tabletop, closes his eyes, opens them, and says, "California's three-strikes proposition was put on the ballot in the mid-nineties and voted into law by the good people of this state. Landslide figures, my friend. There's a reason for this: The law is sound. Premised upon the idea that society cannot allow a violent felon to repeat a crime, or one of equal or greater value, more than three times, despite his background, his economic circumstances, his genetic predilection, or our pervasive and good-hearted belief in rehabilitation. In this pragmatic state, there is a statute of limitations when it comes to our faith in the corrective capacity of lawbreakers. We aren't magicians, but we aren't stu-pid either. Your floor."

"Pretty impressive," I say.

"We'll see."

"I'm used to standing."

"I'm used to DAs. Can't have it your own way all the time."

"I feel you."

"Stop stalling."

I smile, say, "Been some time, man."

"You'll be okay," he says, and raps on the tabletop for me.

"Well, here goes," I say. "In the mid-nineties, we purchased a good sold by the Wilson administration. They told us it would apply to the irredeemable worst: repeat murderers, rapists, et cetera. We good sheep of California, given to the romantic notion that the law, once erected, is unshakable, did not appreciate that the law, like a reef, is a living organism in a constant state of flux. It moves by case prece-dence, which is to say it moves by stories, officialized into existence by the cracking echo of the gavel. The three-strikes law, with thir-teen years of momentum, has now grown to include that most hei-nous of felon, the petty thief, the most demonic of maniacs, the piss-test flunker, the parole violator, the reefer addict, the domestic disputer, perhaps one night it'll even snag a wicked jaywalker. By now, fewer than half of "violent" third-strike lifers are even violent the last time round. Shear not this sheep, 'cause I smell a sham. I hear, Madam Justice, *a tedious argument of insidious intent.* Your floor."

He knocks fast, too fast. I'm a little worried, already thinking ahead to my next platform. "Make no mistake about it. The law has been successful. Overwhelmingly. Crime rates have dropped since incep-tion, this despite a tremendous population boom occurring over that same period. That is against the law of averages. Virtually ahistorical. If people out there are afraid of the three-strikes law, it's the right people who are afraid. Your floor."

The Samoan lady is now turned in her seat, watching us.

I tap on the tabletop with one finger, looking her in the eye until she looks down, and then proceed. "We've made American history, all right: we incarcerate the most people in the world. Now that's a statistic to be proud about. Of course, this is done by economic design. AT&T has a multimillion-dollar contract with the California Department of Corrections. The correctional officers' union is the strongest in the state; the Austrian bodybuilder in Sacrameento bows in deference to their will. Their salaries rival or eclipse street cops, firemen, and of course lowly teachers. Our new saviors of society are now legally state police. Can carry guns on the street. I am afraid. We all should be. Of them. Your floor."

He spins in the seat. The Samoan lady is nodding her head, chewing her sandwich, like, *Wow. He's a good talker. What kind of criminal is this?*

My attorney says as much without turning to her. "Aces, isn't he?"

"Stop stalling," I say.

Then he inhales, nods, says, "The common complaint against the current state of the penal system is that our recent prison growth speaks to a nefarious campaign of revitalizing a stagnant economy. Crossing into the golden state, a visitor might wonder why the greater majority of these facilities congregate in the central valley. I'll answer a question with a question: What, precisely, is nefarious about employing over forty thousand people, the greater majority of whom have families, in a region that was otherwise unilaterally agrarian and thus seasonally infertile? You turn the badness of criminality into the goodness of jobs. Sounds like socially responsible capitalism to me. A true rarity, we all realize, which makes my case all the stronger. Your floor."

The Samoan lady's clicking with her tongue, squinting approval at the way we're throwing around ideas. Suddenly I come from a good family.

She's on the second sandwich, awaiting my response.

I knock three times, close my eyes, say, "The question for the three of us to consider is rather one of comparative absurdity." I open my eyes. "In punitive terms. Any American of any political persuasion would denounce the Indonesian practice of chopping off the fingers of thieves, agreed?" Here I pause. The Samoan lady thinks about it, shivers, nods. My opponent doesn't, but I didn't expect him to. "In fact, in this modern world it is considered nothing short of absurd. Why is it, then, that a thief we incarcerate for life would offer up not only a finger but an entire arm as a bonus limb in exchange for a removal, or even a reduction, of his sentence? Wouldn't he, by the law of what is civilized, prefer the punishment that we, the civilized, render? The answer, of course, is of course not. And the reason for this is that it's more absurd—more draconian, I should say—to strike someone out for petty theft than to chop off that person's finger. What more need be said? When limbs are offered as punitive recompense, you've reached immoral critical mass. Your floor."

He looks at me, smiling. Nods, says, "Not bad, Mr. Lincoln."

I smile back, nod back.

"Let's go," he says, smiling at the Samoan lady. She now likes me, will maybe even throw up a not guilty vote. "I'm gonna get Nguyen in chambers before we start up again. Bet I can get him to make it a half day."

"And the case?"

"Jesus. Faithless. I told you: *Don't worry.*"

We get back to the courtroom, take our seats beneath the looming eyes of the jurors, and rise at the order, "All rise!" when Judge Nguyen reemerges from his courtroom office. As he's regally adjusting into his seat, my attorney says, "Would it trouble the court for a sidebar, Your Honor?"

The judge looks over at Mr. Weil, who's fumbling with his electrical equipment, and says, "Is this necessary, Mr. Choi?"

"I'd say so. Could save us a lot of time, Judge."

Still looking at the pyrotechnics of the prosecutor, Judge Nguyen says, "Any objections, Mr. Weil?"

"No," says Mr. Weil, his glasses falling to the tip of his nose. His sound system lets out a screeching whine. Everyone in the courtroom, including the judge, winces. I smile, squinting. The bailiff walks over, his keys rattling, and yanks at something under the table. The speakers pop and we have silence. The bailiff comes up with a plug which he stuffs into Mr. Weil's hand.

The DA mumbles, "Sorry, Your Honor."

"All right, all right," says the judge. "Is it off now?" I think I hear a "dammit" under the judge's breath.

"Yes, Your Honor," says the bailiff, shaking his head.

Visibly concentrating, Mr. Weil says with as much bass as he can summon, "I'm sorry, Your Honor."

The judge looks down at his watch and says, "Okay. Is it off, counselor?"

"Yes, Your Honor," Mr. Weil whispers.

"What we are going to do is end the day right here. We'll have everything in order by tomorrow. Each of us, myself included, is expected back here promptly at nine in the morning. You may check in at the office of the clerk where you will receive your instructions for the day."

"All stand!"

Again we stand accordingly and watch Judge Barret Nguyen slip slowly off his seat into a standing position. He pays no attention to anyone or anything in his courtroom, and as I wonder if he's ever tripped on his gargantuan robe, I think, *A graceful exit gives the final stamp of authority to the story.*

When His Honor is through the door and back in chambers, the multinational jury disperses. Mr. Weil passes me head down and farthest from the table as if I—or, rather, we—were toxic. My attorney says, "Here's where the game ends for you, John, twenty thousand dollars of a turntable to boot."

Mr. Weil doesn't respond, and I say, "I actually feel sorry for that guy."

"I don't," says my attorney.

"So what's up now, man?"

"Now it's over. You may as well leave. And don't come back."

"How?"

"He's got no victim, no witnesses. Unless the case is moved down to Chiapas."

"They got deported?"

"Deported. Arrested. Hiding. Benefit of a brouhaha with illegals."

"And what about the girl?"

"Athena Taj McMenamin of Monte Sereno, California?"

I nod. "That would be her."

"You sure?"

"Who could forget Athena?"

"I thought she was Catwoman from the Blue Noodle Cabaret Club."

"Nah," I say.

"Oh, yeah. May not have been of age either. Turn of the century. Will be happy to look into it. Athena's at Mardi Gras in New Orleans right now. Probably see her on a *Girls Gone Wild* video by the end of the month. I'm sure her big cause isn't bigger than her reputation, to which I wouldn't mind putting a question or two."

"You don't fuck around, do you?"

"If Weil wants to go to bat against me, I'm gonna k him in three pitches. Then I'm gonna beam him on the way back to the dugout. He isn't one tenth the attorney I am. I've got so many ears in his outfit I can't keep track. That's why you could've never been a lawyer, my friend. You'd try to be the next Atticus Finch: the loner, free of the filthy sleuth of his peers. That's only in made-up books, Paul. You'd quit before your first case."

"Probably."

"Definitely. This is a chess game where swindling is necessary."

"That's what I was saying earlier."

"I know you were."

"Well," I say, "we made a nice team for a minute, anyway."

He nods, zips up his bag, says, "I'm off to meet my maker. Debate you later."

I suddenly feel warmth toward the cat. As if he's a little brother on my heel. Trying for something, anything, I say, "I guess I'll stick around till you get out, Dong-hoo."

"Suit yourself."

The courtroom's now cleared out and it's just the bailiff and me for half a minute and then, with a nod that says, *Don't fuck around in my absence, lowlife,* the bailiff bounces too, grumbling something into the radio pressed to his ear. It's my trial, it's my ass, but I'm not privy to the hand jive that's going on right now "behind chambers," so I put my face into my elbow instead and slobber into a dream about the proverbial ideal woman who has never existed, and never will exist, but who is eternal and worth dying for nonetheless, and before anything gets steamy between us, I hear the harsh words of coitus interruptus: "You're dismissed, Mr. Tusifale!"

I rub one eye open, then the other, and wipe at the spit dribbling down my chin. "Huh? Where's my friend?"

"There is no one remaining in my courtroom, Mr. Tusifale, except you and me."

I slide up my seat, yet again recovering from an unfulfilled dream, and find a slip of paper tucked under my elbow. It's the official letterhead of the county of Santa Clara, office of Judge Barrett Nguyen, chief stenographer Ms. Dendela Dido, with the message, *Call me, Sexy, and let's make a leather sandwich.* Scribbled beneath that the digits: 393-0967. I ponder the possibilities and pass the prize to the judge, "Are you sure I have no friends, Your Honor?"

"Mr. Tusifale," the judge says, finalizing his squarehood by depositing the hookup late-night bootie call in the nearest wastebasket, "I am hardly interested in joining the word game you and your attorney were playing during proceedings."

"But you preside over the ultimate word game, Your Honor."

"You were very lucky this time around, Mr. Tusifale. You are coy, yes, but unfortunately that is not enough in this life."

"I know it."

"Not everyone in your position would be able to walk away from this scot-free. I suggest you count your blessings."

I've never had a talent for that. "I suggest you get the facts right next time."

"Get out of my courtroom."

"Gladly, Your Honor," I say, nodding, standing to his eye level, then rising higher to full height. "Not another minute in your judgment."

29

All the Talk

ALL THE TALK about incarceration yesterday has got me biking over to the handball courts at the Campbell Community Center. Tali left a message on my recorder about her man and me bonding. Somehow she manages to call when I'm not at the guesthouse. I understand. Why talk to someone who can aptly correct your facts and the false conclusions you draw from them? She wants to speak in that presumptuous older-sister tone where her advice is dressed up nicely without my interruptions: "I want you to be friends with McLaughlin. You need someone like him to show you other ways of dealing with things. He's got a good head on his shoulders, little brother."

If only my sister knew the true setup between us. That McLaughlin—the follower—is all mine. A kind friend to many, yes, the subject of sympathy, but alas a liability. She couldn't handle the irony. McLaughlin actually believes that being around me— childless by choice—will make him a better father on two fronts: culture, manliness. He thinks that the blood of his son, which he himself lacks, might figuratively be borrowed from me; the same goes for what he calls "an abnormally high testosterone level," which he also lacks and wants from me. Well, anyway, this is what he thinks. What he doesn't know is that if I, as a half-breed, feel a genuine sense of cultural unbelonging, what will his son, a generation farther along in the dilution process, eventually feel, if he feels anything at all? He'll be lucky if the kid can pronounce his mother's maiden name. And what McLaughlin has conveniently overlooked about my "manliness" is that the testosterone has caused more than a good amount of strife. There have been hours, days, maybe weeks where I've been seized by the boot-stomping destructive vices of Genghis Khan. I'm always amazed at the number of lives I've left uncrushed over the years.

I pass the ladies speed walking on the track in their loose powder-blue cotton sweats and then the waist-high kids counting out jumping jacks in their huge helmets and way-too-wide shoulder pads. The former junior high school is divided equally to interested parties: Campbell Parks and Rec, Campbell Pop Warner, the theater town troupe, and John F. Kennedy University, one of those indeterminate Silicon Valley pop-up colleges that occupy in full capacity a classroom, a Xerox machine, a Pepsi dispenser, and a Web site-in-process. I wonder how our thirty-fifth President, that wily yet well-read Hahvuhd grad, would feel about his regal name being attached to an outfit of higher learning whose campus you can't see from the road or find on foot without a two-page pamphlet from the Campbell Center Info Booth?

Beyond the fields: dual courts built side by side, sharing a middle wall, like two horseshoes welded together at the prongs. Designated for handball first, an ex-con's fantasy. Tennis, racquetball, squash, and all their posh participants need to find the end of the line. In the first court, three Norteños are playing cutthroat, an old prison game, their jukebox bumping about "Scrap Killing in Soledad." I sit down on the turf of my empty court and feel the old wash of institutionalization come over me. It's never totally purged from the head, in the same way that hope is never purged from the heart. I'm nodding to the wicked beat, lacing up and double-knotting the strings of my shoes, pulling my beanie low over the brow. The floodlights go on and it's just like a handball court on the prison yard.

I think back to the time when I learned the dubious history of this gang. Like everything in prison, it's a straight-up saga and seemingly pointless. Gotta jump back to the sixties. The Mexican Mafia was solid in San Quentin, membership spilling to the streets, spanning the lengths of Cali. This went okay for a while, until one M gangster stole a boot from another M gangster. We won't say here who was the thief, who the victim. That depends on legend, which depends on what part of the state you're from. We'll just say that one was from Norcal, the other Socal. The gang split somewhere around King City: Norteños from anywhere north, Sureños from anywhere south.

This also went okay for a while, okay not meaning that no one died but that nothing changed. Then Central Valley Norteños got tired of taking directives from city and coast shot callers, broke off, and formed the Bulldogs. Northerners lost half their numbers. By now the immigrants who'd originally started the gang had second- and third-generation Chicano kids who didn't speak a lick of Spanish, didn't ID any longer with paisas, the very farmers who were their fathers and uncles thirty years before. Illiterates in their indigenous tongue, they still used street words like *oso* and *frajo* and *wila* but could not use the words in complete Spanish sentences.

This meant that paisas slinging dope started kicking it automatically with Southerners, since Southerners, who were close to the border, had fresh access to their roots. The authenticator of language was gone from the depleted northern ranks; they took in a good number of whites, Filipinos, and blacks from the neighborhood, even a Poly now and then. Meanwhile, in steady wetback streams, paisas were getting far enough north to see what was going down in northern territory, squat on it, and call themselves southerners.

So these three cats playing handball on the court next to me in their 49er jerseys, red beanies, and black Ben Davis pants aren't exactly of the same cultural composition as the paisas who jumped me at the rally. There's hostile blood between them, they're no kissing cousins.

I can't see them but I can hear the plum-sized ball ricocheting off the slick surface of the concrete wall and the scuffling of their shoes against the turf, and when I look out toward the lot and see the pink-white kneecaps of McLaughlin in his *ie lavalava,* I'm a little worried, a little pissed. I don't have to guess why the ball stops bouncing in the Norte court: they're looking at my brother-in-law, asking themselves if this guy's for real.

"*Talofa,*" he says to me.

Oh, he's for real, all right.

I nod, triple-tie my shoelaces, pump my fists a few times to warm them up for the blood rush they're about to get on the court. I don't mean to be mean, but I want McLaughlin to see that while his loyalty to my sister and half of her culture is, I suppose, to be admired, his outfit for the most part is an indiscretion. When it ain't wrapped around the hips of a 260-pound brown man with thick arms and legs, a flat nose, and an Afro, an *ie lavalava* is an obvious invitation to shallow male ridicule. He's a mark.

My silence is successful: McLaughlin unwraps the sacred garment, folds it with the delicate and respectful mindset of a soldier with a flag at the tomb, and starts to stretch and bounce in his polyester tennis shorts.

I hear several pops of canned carbonation. The Nortes on the next court are breaking open beer, Budweiser no doubt. The city is asleep to the shit that's going down in it. I say to McLaughlin, "Let's go."

"What?"

"I said let's split."

"But I thought we came here to play a few rounds of handball."

"We did, but now we ain't."

"I don't get it."

The ball has stopped bouncing around the wall, a can is smashed, kicked. "You sure you wanna play, man?"

"Of course."

"All right." I'm nodding, looking up at him. I want to say, *This is what you wanted, McLaughlin, this is your life, so here it is.* What could possibly be more cultural and manly than hitting up a prison game monopolized by Hispanic gangbangers? Let's see some of that down for the brown now, son. "All right, McLaughlin. You wanna play with me, you're in it for keeps. You got my back, man?"

"What?"

"I said do you got my fucking back, bro?" His pause in response is all I need to see. Shaking my head, I stand, say, "Let's get the fuck out of here, man."

"Oh, no," he says. "I got your back."

"You 'member how we met?"

He nods, ashamed.

I want him to recognize what really happened, and that I haven't forgotten. "When you were flying out the door of Aulaumea's kitchen?"

"I remember, Paul."

"You know why you got thrown out?"

"Because I disrespected your cousin?"

"Nothing to do with that, man. It was because you were a white boy. That's why they put hands on you. I'm telling you the way it is. You understand?"

"Yeah."

"And you don't know what it cost me, do you?"

"I don't think I do."

"It don't matter what it cost me, you feel me?" I bounce the ball, throw it down the lane. "You got my mutherfuckin' back if some shit goes down?"

He nods, gritting his teeth, looking like a high school middle line-backer on Friday night, pre-game, mid-autumn. I say, "All right, bro-in-law. Let's sling it then, homie."

We start up our game, and I go easy on him for a few rounds so he can warm up to the idea of defeat. McLaughlin's awkward, two left feet, as they say, straight-tripping over himself. His arms are long and thin and he's got that kind of bend in the elbow whereby his hands are out at an angle away from his body. His hips are wide, his coordination poor, but he's got spirit. And his juices are flowing. I like that. It's good to watch, it kills time. Any time I see another human dance like nobody's watching, I don't ever laugh, can't. We're moving through the game, closing down at 10–1, when one of the inebriated *eses* decides to jump in and join us. He's on our court, our side of the wall, the guy didn't even ask us a question.

Well, that's not too bad, I guess; we got almost one whole game in before the bullshit starts up.

He says, "You gotta mix it around on the wall, homie. High. Low."

I say, "Thanks for your help, bro, but we got a game going here."

"Shit, homeboy, this ain't no game."

I say, "Eh, bro. You cut into our rally."

He starts bouncing the ball, he's not paying me any attention. He looks over at McLaughlin and I decide to push the bill, fuck him. "You wanna run a game, homie? You and me, one-on-one."

"Shit. You don't want none of this, homes."

"You got a twenty spot, McLaughlin?" He nods yes. I say, "I'll bet twenty bones to you going back to your side of the court that I'll smoke you by seven points."

"You got a bet right there, homie."

"You lose, you go back over and be quiet."

He stops and says, "You trying to say something, homie?"

"I ain't trying anything. I'm saying just what I said. You want the bet or what, dog?"

He's stopped to think it over but he can't back down now. It's too late: the other two homeboys have come over to this side of the wall. The taller one with tags on his face says, "What's crackin', Smiley?"

Smiley takes one last swig of his beer and then chucks it away from the court. I'm bouncing on my toes, looking at the wall away from everyone, swinging my hands at the side of my knees, cracking my neck. Thinking on the Greeks and their preparatory usage of sport: an alternate way to ready yourself to mass-murder Persians. You wrestle in a friendly forum of competition to eventually kill. You race in a friendly forum of competition to eventually avoid being killed. Sport at its most basic fabric is organized prep to kill, organized prep to survive.

My opponent's trying to use optic intimidation, to give me the *maka sepa,* as we say in Samoan: the evil eye of death. All right, Smiley. Schmiley. MacSchmiley. You dumpy mutherfucker. Let's switch cultural savageries. I respect your people so much I'm gonna steal from your people. Jump back to that war-torn society where old men were a rarity, shunned as cowards.

Gonna focus on the blood sport of the ancient Aztecan game of *tlachtli,* a deal so real and barbaric that the cost of a slipup by the ref was a limb. Where losing teams could be seen fleeing the victors and the fans and the understood price of mass sacrifice.

This over a pseudo-soccer game with a rubber ball?

Yes, your eyes are telling me. *This is what you need to prepare for, homie. This is me and my heritage. That's what this tattoo on my arm means. That time, those people are my story.*

Okay, Schmiley, okay. If I can't have a story then I'll have to dis- prove yours. Right now. Let's do this.

He looks at me and says, "You play three-wall, don't you, homes?"

I know what he's getting at. "I play anything."

"Okay then, *ese*. We're gonna play one-wall. Prison style, homes."

"Fine by me."

"You can't use the other walls, *ese*."

"I'm ready, man. Explain the rules to someone else."

He says, "Rally for serve," and lobs me a floater. I send it back off the wall right into his gut. His homeboys laugh out loud. I pick the ball up and say, "*Bola*."

He raises his eyebrows at the Spanish but before he can process anything *la bola*'s rocketing back at him and he swivels and punches at the air. The ball droops toward the wall so clearly I've got a wealth of placement options opening up before me and it comes back soft and without spin and I fire it at the right corner where he's gotta get on his high horse and run. He can't get it, he's about to fall down. It dies right there with his horse. A donkey. An ass. I say, "One-oh, *bola*," and start it up again.

He's slow on his feet, he's got no game. He's probably a closet X-box junkie. He's got a little kill shot that might work on another immobile *ese,* but not on a mutherfucker with feet like darts. I got excellent feet and a good arm, unimpaired vision, a healthy libido, and enough of a twisted experience and outlook not to give one up to this sucker. He's going down, bad. I send shots to the wide side to test his left arm. He ain't got one. I send shots off to make him jump in the air, and he ain't got any hops. I play high off the wall to see his overhand and it's average, go low for kill shots and the wind of the ball is tickling the ground, coming straight off to his feet. At 3–0 he's shaking out his arms, acting like he's just warming up, but I'm gonna smoke his ass and he knows it.

When the game's 5–0, my mind drifts to McLaughlin and his general safety, and when I look over at the poor guy he's nodding at me with faith, as if he were on an Acapulco cliff convincing himself to jump. I almost laugh but keep a straight face. *Don't look down at the water, McLaughlin! Gotta keep you from seeing your shaking knees.* I nod back, wink, play cool.

The other two *eses* now know enough about me and my skills to leave McLaughlin alone. I feel better and whip out a shot that whizzes by their homeboy's ankle, moves the game up to 6–0.

I call, "*Chonga!*" Means game point in prison-speak. We're already there, six minutes down, a shot away from a clean skunk. The silence behind me feels so damned good. I wanna bathe in their silence, I wanna breathe it all into the bottom of my lungs. I'm having some fun for once, I feel the bearable lightness of my being. I throw the ball out and he determinedly puts it into the air, a pretty good shot but not good enough. I'm already setting up behind him, waiting on it. He tries to block my way but I nudge him aside with my hips and wind down as if I were going to fire something high at his head. He starts upcourt towards the spectators at just the same time that I send it back, soft, with touch, so that it dies in a dribble, like a bubble in the air, 7–0.

"Damn, homes!"

"What the fuck happened, eh?"

McLaughlin is looking around, ready to defend himself, defend me, us. As if the poor guy could. I shake my head really quickly and he exhales, though still on high alert.

I say, "Good game, homie."

He shakes my hand, asks, "Where'd you do your time at, homes?"

"Avenal," I say. "Two-yard."

"Right on, dog," he says.

The Norte with the tags on his face asks me, "You a homeboy?"

"I'm an Other," I say. "I ride with *hamos* up in there."

Hamos. Samoans. Much respect from the hoods of the hood when you play the Poly card. All three cats look over at McLaughlin, holding his *ie lavalava* nervously across a forearm like a maître d' his first day on the job, still nodding.

The original Norte, the one I just trounced, says, "You Samoan, homes?"

Here comes their fear: I lift my eyebrows.

"Wassup, *uso!*" "*Talofa*, man!" "All right, homes." "How come you didn't say shit, *uso*?" "Wassup, eh?"

"Wassup," I say.

"You want a beer, homes?"

"Nah, I'm cool."

"How about your homeboy?"

I speak for McLaughlin, just like I should. "Nah, he's cool. Thanks, dog."

"I feel like I did time with you before, eh."

"Yeah, Smiley. I seen you before too, homes."

"Didn't I see you on TV, *ese*?"

I don't look away.

"You're the *vato* who slammed that paisa in downtown San Jo?"

I nod.

"That was you, eh!"

I nod again, know what's coming next: the crown.

"This fool fought five scraps, homie! I saw it right on channel 11, eh!"

"Mutherfucking scraps be getting crazy around here, *ese*! We gotta put those Southerners in check, homes."

I say, "Eh, we're gonna bounce, bro."

"Nah, man. We gotta party, homie. Celebrate, eh."

I hit McLaughlin in the shoulder. "We gotta get him home to the old lady."

"Well, you're welcome back any times, homes!"

"That's right, *ese*!"

"Stay up, man," I say, "Let's go, dog."

McLaughlin follows me and he's breathing hard, as if he, and not I, just played a 7–0 game against the wall. I don't know what to do with McLaughlin from here on out, but it makes me smile and sad both that he would've fought for me, however defectively, if it went down. That he would've gotten his head busted in for the cause. And it makes me smile and sad both that the hardest people in America will be kind to you after they learn from a beneficent beatdown that you're just like them. Or that you can be just like them. Or that you can act just like them. Or that you can excel at their games. Or that their enemies are your enemies. Or whatever.

But it only makes me sad that I did it while believing it wasn't me, that it ain't. Another stage performance, a role I can play well enough to fool the other actors of this set, soon to foreclose to the next jaded show, whose props are being erected even as I sputter out this sentence.

30

I Decide This Fine Morning

I DECIDE this fine morning to bike out to the all-weather track at Leland High School for a run and a few rounds of shadowboxing. I'm streaming with endorphins, all jazzed up. I pass the old Feed and Fuel, closed down forever, and make a left on Almaden Expressway back into suburban civilization and traffic. This Saturday morning the sun is high in its authority, undeterred by the trees and the houses, cutting right through the morning mist and alighting on the gray vaporous smog of early day. We like to say in the South Bay that our weather is temperate. We never say what that means in exchange. So here it is: We don't see the change of the seasons. The term *all-weather track* is just a fancy way of saying spongy synthetic stuff that's easy on the joints. By virtue of the moderate climate, all commodities of the Silicon Valley are all-weather.

I reach Radkovich, apparently a Serb who made a name in the town, and make a right turn at full speed. I don't get far before I run smack into hundreds of people filling the street, some moving at a pretty good pace, others not, some walking. Most are in runner's shorts, webbed muscle shirts, glowing tennis shoes. Ankle socks with cotton bells woven into the rim. They've got black numbers on white paper pinned to their chests or the hemline of their shorts and the more creative in the crowd have made hats like a fry cook's headgear, the little paper ships pointed full sail ahead! Some are tired, red-faced, pushing it; some not, casual, taking in the scene; some are talking with one another, bounding out in that ridiculous *Wizard of Oz* swing of the arm (*"We're* off *to see the wizard!"*), most quite happy. Even dutiful. Or so it seems. Is it because they all stay within the orange cones, the ones I'm zigzagging through at the moment? Boundaries for a race of some sort, a fluffy half marathon, 10K with an all-day limit on crossing the tape.

I'm passing the good people of the Almaden Valley, accelerating on the sidewalk. Every now and then, the combination of the strong glare of the sun with an especially thin polyester fabric gives me access to a dark G-string on a tight, tan, athletic, freckled ass, an Indian arrowhead, the upside-down chevron under whose point is the buried treasure, the curse and the cause of man. I'll slow down or U-turn on someone's lawn and come back around at a different angle of light, cruising this time, taking in the wild sights of the valley like any good citizen committed to the ecosystem.

Mostly women, blond, brunette, redheaded white women, being fit for a cause—breast cancer, AIDS—though there are some reps from my gender, blond, brunette, redheaded white men, who pay me close attention as I pass on my bike, though not that way. They think I'm a threat, dangerous. A lone wolf in the sheep pen.

Beware that mangy, red-eyed, crossbreed mutt in a logoless beanie who's got no house, earns a laughable wage, but is a fascist at heart! We all know how wet our women get at the sight of the whip and chain. Dying to be domesticated. For an evening. In our absence. Once or twice a week. On the other end of the valley. Some cheap motel of musky sheets. With a strobe light and Marvin Gaye on a ghetto blaster. Beware!

I round a corner blinded by ivy woven through a lawn-wide trellis and nearly collide with a parked golf buggy. Its occupant is a white guy in a safari hat. "Hey!" he shouts, as I pedal by ignoring him, over-turning orange cones, winding up the walk, driving on, "Hey there!" and I know he's setting chase.

Now a real race through the peaceful eventless suburbs of Almaden. I lean forward with my head at a slight downward tilt and work the crank as if I were a feline on the run through the cat delicatessen of Hong Kong. I pretend like demons are on my tail, I pretend like I am a demon, I pretend that getting caught will mean the end of my life, or of my wife's life, whoever she'll be, if ever will be, anyone but La Dulce. I pass house after placid house and turn hard right, then hard left, all the way up the street with the wind wet in my eyes. I pretend this is the last time I will ever ride this bike, and I press down on the pedals with all the power in my quads and hips, one to the other, hear the steady discharge of loose gravel under the tires and I feel so damned free and good on my imaginary run from the buggy authority that I'm off course, I've broken ranks, the race has gone on without me. I look back over my shoulder and the buggy is nowhere to be found, nor are there any runners.

I slow down, get my bearings, and head out to the high school on a back route to avoid the race. A marathon, half marathon, 10K, probably runs from Lake Calero out past Blossom Hill and then who knows from there. I'm excited: the chances of the track being empty this morning are pretty high. Many of the potential runners in the Almaden Valley are probably in that race, wherever it goes and why.

Riding behind the decrepit stands of the football stadium, I'm forced to slow down, nearly stop, my hopes for a running session in solitude dashed. The "all-weather track" is loud and packed as a carnival. Along one sideline and into the end zone are booths with big American flags taped across the rim, twirling down each post, army recruitment signs with alluring slogans like AN ARMY OF ONE, as if you and you alone were all that was required to vanquish a nation. There's a Leland Chargers Boosters booth with lightning bolts on its banner and a squad of stunning cheerleaders bouncing about on their toes. Next to them a PTA booth with mothers just as stunning, just as aware of their spotlight, equally naughty. Copeland's Sports paraphernalia is mainly footballs today, next to a National Football League booth with a thick-necked brotha in a purple tweed suit right off the shelves. A Jamba Juice booth is surrounded by pyramids of oranges blocking out the employees from the neck down, like they were readying for trench warfare with citrus the weapon of choice.

And everywhere the number 42: 42 on every booth, 42 in blue and yellow, 42 in cardinal red, 42 on football jerseys, 42 on shirts, even the finish line—for the race ends here, this is where it ends—has a gigantic 42 stretched across the track and is, upon investigation, marked at the 42–yard line. Just as I figure out what the cause for the occasion is, just as I look up at the stands and see the new name of the stadium painted across the beams of the coaches' booth, I'm taken to task for being here. My non-red white and blue, non-lightning bolt, stark black beanie, my suspicious crankster bike, my T-shirt unmarked by the holy number 42: I stand out.

"You know where you're at, right? He's ours!"

I nod at the assertion. I know enough by now to do that. A white elderly gentleman is steaming this morning, deep frown, squinting gray eyes, steam out the nostrils, out the ears. He's got an Uncle Sam goatee and I want to say: Are you mad you can't find Rosie the Riveter? He's one of the disciples of the valley's and the nation's hero, the posthumous reason for this event: Pat Tillman. He's standing at attention in the newly christened Pat Tillman Stadium, on the very track where Pat Tillman suited up for autumn football practice in the mid-nineties, in the very town that Tillman grew up in—Almaden—with Tillman's gridiron number, 42, on his blue and yellow Leland High School jersey.

I don't know why I'm so fickle, but I'm embarrassed for the old man and his outfit: Isn't it undignified to play dress-up at his age, whatever the cause, the occasion? Aren't the young'uns supposed to be sporting in honor whatever duds he wore to battle on the gridiron? Why isn't he in a Stetson hat and temperate suit with quietude in his eyes, the wisdom of old age?

Old man equals cheerleader. He shouts, "They think he's theirs! But he's not! He's ours!"

I nod again unenthusiastically.

"He's ours! What do you say?"

"I don't know. I say we should keep our hands out of a few honeypots in the world."

"What does that mean?"

The man in the golf cart is pulling into the parking lot, weaving through the hordes of SUVs, past the gate, bisecting the field, eyes directly on me. Alert as he nears, people step aside; he has some pull. Probably named his dog, his son, and his daughter after the man of the hour.

By now, everyone knows the story of Pat Tillman, the All-American kid with the movie-star jawline. A hard-hitting NFLer, he was so moved by the sight of the Twin Towers imploding that he bypassed millions of bucks to join the Army Rangers. Spent a minute in the friendly fire of media hype, and then was gone to the dunes of Afghanistan to keep the Taliban in check, a middle brother following his lead.

We went on with our lives and Tillman went MIA from our screens for a few tours, returning like a bullet through the brain to TV Land, reported dead in battle on the morn of April 22, 2004. A Silver Star for Valor. Undisclosed details, stay tuned, because everything comes out in the media, like spilled oil coalescing at the water's surface. Bit by bit, month by month, article by article, details get disclosed and Tillman dies again in (yet another) Pentagon scandal: Turns out the kid was killed on a dune in the friendly crossfire of his own team, aka fratricide. A cover-up by army brass?

And then there's the matter of his unbecoming-an-officer reading list: Chomsky, Thoreau, Hitler's *Mein Kampf*. A short stint as a young pup in county for assault and battery. An article from the other brother, the fellow Ranger, saying big bro Pat warned him of the powerlessness of being an army man. That they'd have to go and fight wherever ordered, be subject to the whims of the people. That the price of seriousness in a world of caprice could be their lives.

Another long-haired brother alludes to weed at the funeral.

What kind of All-American family is this?

In the middle of the big push for Tillman it became clear—to me, anyway—that this Tillman cat was obviously in search of some truth he probably never found, a ballsy cat, a put-your-ass-on-the line kind of guy. And he seemed humble. Not to be deified under the auspices of celebration. The kind of guy who'd avoid a gathering like this altogether. My guess by the look on his mysterious face is that he would've adamantly shot down being simplified.

Everyone here this morning is smiling and excited by the promise of Old Glory rising from the oil-rich flames, and I can see with absolute clarity that it's all for them and what's theirs, not for him, not for Tillman. It keeps them alive, keeps them going, and that's what Tillman's advisory words to his brother were all about. Our heroes now are too smart, too knowing, too aware of the hypocrisy of their role. They can see how paltry the heart of the people really is in the end.

So is this the story for me?

The point of it got lost a long time ago. Too many holes in poor Tillman's head. I say let the guy breathe in his grave. A dying breed in mouthy America, let him rest for chrissake. But it ain't gonna happen. You know what we are, how we do it: suck the marrow out of the kid's bones whether he's ours or theirs, alive or dead.

The man and his golf cart are here. He pushes his safari hat behind his head and its string latches underneath his triple chin. His flattop right out the fifties, Dick Butkus square. He wobbles out of the buggy, a radio pressed to his red, layered, hanging bulldog cheek, now looking away from us even as he's walking toward us, rattling off in some half-ass wannabe cop vernacular about my invasive presence on the gospel ground of Pat Tillman, digging under his belly to tuck in his shirt with the other hand. The T-shirt has a distorted peace sign in the middle of the chest, the word PEACE above it, the words THROUGH SUPERIOR FIREPOWER below it, the lettering in red, white, and blue. When he's close enough that his *Ten-four over and out*! shouting rattles my bones, I can see why the peace sign is distorted: it's an aerial shot of a B-52 bomber, the long wings spread across the peace circle.

Very clever, these idiotic pundit T-shirt designers.

I say, "Can I get one of those shirts in tie-dye, bro?"

He doesn't smile, he's pissed. With his stubby index finger and thumb he twirls down the radio volume, leaving the other party hanging on a sentence. "Ten-four," he whispers, assessing me as a drill sergeant would a new recruit.

"Well," I say, "it's been nice talking to you boys, but I'm off to an immigrants' rights rally."

"No," he says. "You're gonna have to stay here for a bit."

So the police are on their way.

He says to the old man, "Can you leave us alone here, Bill?"

Bill fires out, "Yes, sir! He's ours!" and then walks off.

"Let's just make sure everything's okay," the man says. "Can I see your ID, please?"

"You a cop?"

"I'm in charge of security here."

"I'll take that as a no, bro."

"You made a big mistake," he says, with a kind of seriousness re-
served for people like Judge Nguyen, "by running over those cones.
You'll likely be charged."

"With what?"

"Trespassing, destruction of property. You're going to laugh yourself all the way downtown. First and Hedding. The county jail."

"Eh, bro," I say, barely able to control myself, "let's start over."

He nods, awaiting my contrition. Guys like this guy make me sick.
One sentence out of his mouth and you can predict his every move,
articulate his peon political (dis)positions. He's like Chinaski, he has
a peephole for a soul. His window to the world is like a telescope
permanently connected to the very spot Neil Armstrong said, "A small
step for man. . . ." He's stuck in the heyday of the country, a time
well before his birth.

If I were to inform this provincial simpleton of my real feelings
about democracy, that its integrity diminishes the larger the constitu-
ency it serves, that there should be way less space between the vote
and the act, which means if you're gonna vote someone's ass on the
line be sure to volunteer your own ass first, he'll undoubtedly reroute
his energy from apprehending the suspect to executing the suspect.
And you can bet he'll be front row at the lynching, anything to catch
a splash of my commie blood on his B-52-for-peace T.

Should I be a humanitarian and save his simple heart from explosion by lacing my words with acquiescence, something like: *The
Athenians, after all, were marching up to the Acropolis and casting votes
while visible to fellow citizenry.*

Ignore the confused countenance of my audience: *The Acropolis? Duh. Ain't that where the Lakers play?*

Hell, I should just whip his ass for the sake of Tillman, the Athenians and—why not?—the Lakers too, bust him clean across the jaw,
test his John Wayne true grit. Sure, he's deified Tillman's number,

but by virtue of his sloppy need for a leader this follower is actually the Anti-Tillman.

In the same serious pompous tone he's mastered, I say, "Okay. Borrowing from the rebellious spirit of the honoree of the hour, Mr. Pat Tillman"—here I lift my beanie—"allow me to say that your wannabe cop ass oughta eat a big fat dick."

"Now that's not going to get us anywhere," he says.

"It'll get you not to talk."

He's quiet, thinking up a comeback. "I guess you're lucky it's not a crime to be a communist in this country."

"That's a pretty good one," I say, "for a security guard. Is that what your shirt means by superior firepower? Were you the speech-and-debate champ at the Esteemed Academy for Tollbooth Operators?"

"We're here today to champion democracy by celebrating a champion of democracy."

"Wow. Pretty impressive. How long did you practice that in front of a mirror? Bet it took a whole year. She sells seashells by the seashore."

The winner is a thin beanpole Caucasian with an I LOVE PAT shirt and a 42 headband. He doesn't bother putting up his arms; he just nods kindly and walks over to grab an orange at the Jamba Juice stand. I want to shake his hand for some reason, get away from this interim cop with his provisional badge, but I'm stuck until the real cops come.

The runners wind onto the track, five are finished, ten, twenty and—perfect timing—the lights of the authorities have arrived in the lot. I'm not fazed one bit. I want to test a theory today: After they've got their hands on all the evidence, which is far and away nothing, my bet is that Superior Firepower here will get stripped of his rank-smelling rank, dressed down in front of all his cronies. They'll all hide out in the shadows of the stands. I'm betting on the cops doing right by me this time. That I won't get screwed twice straight by the state's best funded lawmen.

And I'll help them out a little bit this time: I take off my beanie and tuck it into my waistline, brush my hair out. Flex my jaw so as to enunciate the ten-dollar Latinate words I'm ready to throw into the conversation to convince the cop that I'm just an innocent passerby, which I'm not. But I can't pass up this chance to play diplomat.

Hey, the rent-a-cop wants to say, Put your beanie back on your head and be the scumbag you were acting like seconds ago, but I smile and beat him to the punch. "I'm glad I was able to get all the expletives out of my system before I inform the authorities of my illegal detainment. Holding someone hostage against his will, et cetera, et cetera."

"Don't let him get you down," I hear, a familiar voice.

Superior Firepower jumps to attention. "Hello, sir."

I nod at Uncle Rich, roll my eyes as in, *But of course I find you here at the Pat Tillman benefit, Uncle. And of course you've barely broken a sweat in your jogging shorts. Of course.*

"Oh," I say, "I haven't heard anything but flak out of Officer Superior Firepower. Blanks, dud rounds."

My uncle says, "How are you, Lyle?"

"We thank you, sir, for joining us this morning."

"My pleasure. My honor to honor the kid."

I roll my eyes yet again as in, *But of course Lyle loves his war heroes: Tillman of today, my uncle of yesteryear.* Almaden is just filled to the brim with real men. The memory of Tillman, my barely winded uncle and Sergeant Superior Firepower are holding down the fort.

"Make the force yet?" my uncle asks.

"I can answer that," I say.

"Not yet, sir. I'm a reserve at the De Anza Junior College Police Department and a weekend volunteer at the police range in Sacramento. I clean the rounds and dispose of the targets."

"That's a two-hour drive, Lyle."

Lyle smiles and nods, as if it's a sacrifice of the Tillman caliber. I can't help but break this clown down. "That's a long ways to go," I say, "to pick up peanut shells at a ballpark."

"Well, good for you, Lyle. Don't mind this guy." My uncle grips my shoulder a little too hard, and I buck it a little too easily. "He has a tendency to get ahead of himself. Wherever he finds himself."

"Oh yes, sir," says Lyle.

"Why don't you teach me how to slow down, sir?"

"Let's go," says my uncle, and what the hell, I go, right past Sergeant Superior Firepower, who's confused as a walrus on skates, down to the track and around it, past the rows of booths, nod politely at the approaching cop who—*fantastic!*—nods back, slow-pedal through the safe and silly suburbs to be instructed on whatever's important about life in this place.

31

The Battle for Tillman

THE BATTLE FOR TILLMAN continues on the rickety dock of my uncle's man-made lake, a four-hundred-dollar imported fishing pole each between our knees, naked feet in the water with no straw to dumbly chew on, no raft with any river to conquer, no runaway slave to nobly go to Hell for. Our lines look like crazy string ending at the red and white bobbers ten yards in front of us, and the water's so shallow we can see the fluorescent gobs of Powerbait on the hooks. Not that it matters, but we haven't had even the slightest bite, though my uncle insists he stocked the lake with black bass and trout.

I recite:

> *"Not that it matters, not that my heart's cry*
> *is potent to deflect our common doom—"*

"No poetry, nephew."

"Even sexy Millay?"

"Even her. Whoever the hell she is."

"Excepting the artificial lake and synthetic fish," I say, "this hour is like an authentic Norman Rockwell painting."

My uncle says, "You know, he grew up right down the street from me."

"Tillman?"

"What a beautiful kid. An idealist."

"Yeah," I say. "They took the poor guy's idealism and ran with it like a football."

"I watched him score six touchdowns in one game back in 'ninety-four. That was the bravest effort I've ever seen on the high school gridiron. Didn't come off the field for four quarters. We named the stadium after him."

"Yeah. Probably rename the town of Almaden Tillman before the decade's done."

My uncle pours a shot of unidentified liquor he's pulled out of his makeshift tackle box. Not that it matters, but I sometimes wonder why my uncle didn't throw down for a roving barkeep on his property to satiate his palate and a leopard-spot liver. I don't wonder, however, where all the hired help went or why I haven't been inside his house since moving here: we have a symbiotic relationship on that basis: he hasn't been inside mine—which is really his—either.

He hands me a shot. I watch a dust cloud twirl lazily across the north entrance and then a car cutting through it. Glittering silver, long and thin like a shark, the four-door sedan accelerates down the winding path. I look over at my uncle, who can't miss the car, the only other sign of life on his property. When it slows to a stop at the southern porch of the estate, my uncle tenses up and says, "To Pat."

My Aunt Lanell climbs out of the driver's seat, walks around the car, up the porch, into the house.

When my parents split back in the late eighties, my uncle used to pick me up from school and take me to the San José Bees games. I can't remember a single player because he'd talk for seven innings straight about his life: how he couldn't connect with his daughter, how the deathless pressure of business seemed regressive after the theater of war, how it was the wife of a CEO who held everything together. The drag on those conversations was so heavy at that age that afterward, in bed, I'd have attacks of melancholy akin to hearing a eulogy that hits more than a nerve, that's so accurate and hard on the heart you can't breath. That gets beyond the corpse and reaches the people in the room who aren't yet dead.

I'd get dressed and walk to the park, the yellow-lined path glowing in the midnight moon, sit on the littered rim of the polluted creek bed and, alone, softly cry for my uncle, or myself, or whoever—for the dead fish and crawdads; it didn't matter—wondering what would hold the world together for another hour.

Aunt Lanell emerges with an athletic bag, shades over her eyes, hops in the car, speeds off.

Today I won't ask my uncle about his family.

"Here's to you, Uncle," I toast, knocking back the shot.

My uncle looks torn, the frown pushing down on his nose. "Well," he says, "I guess you're not on board with the Tillman thing, are you?"

She's up over the crest, the dust pushing toward us and then gone. "I guess not."

"Why'd you call him *poor guy* earlier?"

"Because," I say, "there's nothing worse than losing your life for a country that doesn't deserve it."

"I may regret this, but I want to hear your thoughts, nephew."

"Way before Tillman died, America had made up its mind that he was a hero. They praised him for bypassing six million bucks to go join the Army Rangers. They were shouting, *Look! There's someone who doesn't measure everything by money. Who actually puts his ass on the line for his beliefs, volunteers so that we don't have to.* He was the perfect symbol for all those corporate and political big shots who never send their own sons to the wars they sign onto."

"He was a hero."

"A hero? He died from friendly fire. How can he be a hero?"

My uncle says nothing, sipping his shot. "I know what you mean."

"There's no side of the issue that's right. His family was on C-Span with the fucking pink grandmas against the war. Tillman himself wrote a letter to his brother, warning him against joining up."

"Is that right?"

"Yeah."

"It was common in 'Nam," he says, "to hear stories about fighter pilots. One I'd admired had to do with how pilots with families would sign off before a mission. That if they got shot down, the lieutenant would make 'em KIA no matter what."

"Not following you."

"Well, their wife and children back home would be taken care of. Full benies under that classification."

"'Cause if they're MIA it means they're still alive?"

"Yep. There's a lot that goes on in war that can't be translated back to this place. I sympathize with what you're saying, nephew, I really do."

This surprises me. "Yeah?"

"Yeah. So here's what you're saying: We've got a hero who wasn't a hero get a medal he didn't deserve. Great kid, but that's an aside right now. We've got a family refuting the way they're told about his death, which nullifies the heroism, but not refuting the medal, which is awarded for heroism. We've got the pink grandmas on one side and flag-wavers on the other."

"That's right. With enough information, who in their right mind would pick one side or the other of his story? Tillman just added to the things you can't believe in anymore."

"As in this country?"

"I've felt this way for a long time."

"This is why you didn't go to the Point?"

"Honor, duty, country? I'd have been kicked out my plebian year like Poe. A matter of national security."

"You flatter yourself, nephew. You're not that important."

"I mean, how could I sign on as a cadet this late into our story? By 1996? Even back then I had a laymen's grasp of the horrors committed by this nation. Which is mainly to say who got squashed along the way to easy living."

"Yeah, well, someone afforded you the safety of easy living."

"I know, I know. I'm just saying one thing. This is the nature of man: you acquire power. Constantly. However much melatonin you've got in your skin, whatever tribe you're from, American, non-American. Until you've got so much power you don't know what to do with it."

"Why don't you give it up then?"

"It's not a good spot to be in. Everyone else wants what we've got."

"They're already getting it."

"Exactly. I'm saying, Uncle, that we're in decay. We've turned the scalpel on ourselves and are picking apart the monster—us—that we've created."

My uncle goes quiet. The lingering dust in the air makes me think of some far-off place in the Midwest, a family pressed to their living room window, eyes on the storm in the distance. I pour a shot of the mystery liquor, sip it, and wait for a bite, for a word from my uncle, anything.

"You know," he says, "I can see one night in particular. My second tour. We were on a hilltop somewhere, calling in air strikes. The sky was so wide open I felt warm almost, enlightened. Who knows, it maybe was nothing, but I remember thinking, *I'm on this side with these guys and that's it. This is the purest, realest, finest moment I will ever have.* Well, I been trying to get back to that place for a long time.

"I went to the rally today because he was one of ours. That's it, nephew, nothing more. All the stuff you're saying, while accurate, doesn't mean a thing to me. I drew my line a long time ago. I haven't always stayed faithful to it; I guess that's for me to figure out—to get right some day. But I went to the rally for Tillman, his family, and this country, whatever it is."

"Whatever it's become?" The dust cloud has finally lowered itself to this half-ass dock: I put my nose into my shirtsleeve, look over at my uncle.

"Yes," he says, nodding.

The last answer provides us with real silence, the kind that comes in places that this lake was built to emulate. The water is stiller than a corpse, we're stiller than the water, two patients *etherized upon a table*.

"Should we toss our lines out again?" I ask.

"What would be the point of that?"

"Getting a new start on a bite."

"Nephew, you only have so many new starts in this life before you have to live with it."

That strikes me as being true.

"Listen," he says. "I understand your crisis."

"Yeah?"

"It's like you live in this moon zone without gravity. Floating from position to position."

"*Eclectic* is the new chic word."

"That's just a cryptic fancy way of saying *everything*. You believe in and want and can understand and are not concerned at all about everything."

"I've been taught that all people are good and bad, equally generous and desirous."

"What does that really mean, nephew?"

"I don't know. Maybe that I'm a hyperempathist or something."

"Hyperempathists have no allegiance."

"There isn't anyone whose shoes I can't imagine being in."

"That doesn't mean you can really fill them."

"Let me put it this way: I view some guy from Sunnyvale in the same way I view some cat from Istanbul. I don't have any more or any less love for one person than the other."

"Yeah. Because you can. Which means you're allowed to. You therefore have no functional loyalty. And don't give me any of that *loyalty to the truth* crap. The key word is *functional*. You and people like you are living in a dream. You just can't imagine the fact that you have enemies in the world. Well, you've got them, bud, a lot of them. This place is so safe you can pretend you're at a cultural smorgasbord."

"I feel you, Uncle. Only I'm not pretending. Good or bad, this is my inheritance. I really am honest to God this way. And so are a million others of my generation. We don't hate anyone. We're detestable," I say, "but we aren't stupid."

The light wind around us fails to muffle the heavy whistle of our breathing. My uncle looks up at the northwest entrance, then over at me. "Says who?"

Just then I see a ripple in the water, oxygen tickling the surface, and whisper, "Hey, Uncle, sshhh, I think we got one," but he's up and gone, heading back to his empty estate at the prospect I offer of no prospects, his bottle of mystery liquor swinging and spilling over his hand, blind to the four-hundred-dollar pole pulled splashing into the clear water of the fake lake by a real bite, our first and last, dragged down and out into the deep by a fake fish we'll never catch to kill and fry—or even handle to release and save.

32

At Work I Have Nothing to Do

AT WORK I have nothing to do today but take a dozen defunct roller chairs and three scarred coffee tables to a Goodwill in Sunnyvale ("Get a receipt!" shouts Chinaski) and then unscrew a few file cabinets from the wall in the old San Carlos office. I finish up before noon, bypass Chinaski, and call the big boss man.

"Take the rest of the day off."

He sounds buzzed already through the static of the phone. "Uncle, I can help with something else."

"Nothing else for you, nephew. Go rest your back."

At the guesthouse, Tali has left the message CALL ME on a note under the door. Before I even walk toward the kitchen counter, the phone rings. I know who it is. Almost don't answer because of this knowledge, but anything to break up my weekday evenings.

I pick up the phone and hear: "Get dressed, little brother."

"For what?"

"Job interview."

"Got a job, remember? Two weeks ago you harassed our uncle into giving me one."

"Listen. You have too much time off. This job would be on weekends and a few days during the week."

"Do you ever ask questions, sister?"

"Look. I had to make some calls just to get the interview today. You've got to be there at three."

I almost ask, How'd you know I had a half-day? but I know the answer. Who wants to be reminded that a relation is checking up with your employer, another relation, like a probation officer?

"They're located at 137 Tully. Cross-street Capitol."

"That's East San Jo."

"Right."

I catch the bus out without incident. That's rather nice. Just for fun, or for torture, I count thirteen Starbucks on the way over, big ones, baby ones, all with customers spilling out the door. So much for strength in diversity. From the stop, it's a short walk. One block down and I'll be there. I pass another Starbucks hidden by the draping branches of some white-barked birch trees and decide in the shade of the cool elms along the street that it's best not to think about the world, about myself, about myself in connection to the world.

Hell, I just walk on, whistle it out, hum "Nowhere Man" by the Beatles, then a bluegrass jam I'd picked up called, "I Am the Man of Constant Sorrow," another tune entitled, "Thanks a Lot," by some Pacific Northwest country chick named Neko Case, play some soccer with an acorn from a wide-bodied oak whose apogee branch reaches clear across the street, fire a long-range shot into the leaf-and litter-strewn gutter ("Goooooooooooooooooooaaaaaalllllllllllllllll!"), and lift my arms into the chill air, eyes on the brown tinted windows of the commercial buildings. According to the addresses on the map, the people I'm seeking for help are in the offices of the Silicon Valley Chapter of the National Organization of Women.

I make my way over, spot the NOW unit and its mongrel American flag of rainbow stripes and a peace sign superimposed over the fifty stars outside the door, enter.

Immediately, I get slapped with a greeting: "We're not interested."

She's a thin-necked teal-eyed Nordic, teeth aligned like the rings dangling from her nose. I got the feeling that if she grew her prickly red flattop out to bob length, removed the fake African accouterments, and smiled, her world would turn upside down, and we could talk civilly. Maybe even flirtatiously.

Yeah, right.

"Can I help you?"

"Oh," I say.

"Oh?"

"Um, I guess I have—"

"Wait," she says. "Are you Paul Tusifale?"

I nod, hoping for the best, preparing for the worst.

"We've been waiting for you," she says.

"And you would be . . . ?"

"Follow me," she says.

I'm led past partitioned cubicles enveloping all kinds of busy ladies, one in brown hip-hugging cords, bare feet in Birkenstocks; another in a sleek business suit, her hair pulled back tight against the cranium. I try to keep my head up as I walk, to appear if not manly at least kingly, the despised despot. Cortez among the Incas, Mobutu and his Zaireans, Kamehameha with his Hawaiians. I have no clue how to hold my shoulders in here. It's strange: This is supposed to be the place where I feel the most vital, the most alive, where I possess something that the hostesses viscerally desire.

Ashamed to say it: I fear the gender zealotry surrounding me. I can feel my testes crawl into the most remote region of their shrinking sack, trying to defy gravity, avoid the void. Remain—if not potent—of use. I fear the clarity of the chirping women in this office,

frothing with angry, almost masculine energy. I'm zoning out, thinking of little Toby and his future under the whip, how he'll never get
out of the starting gate or even appreciate the metaphor.

"In there," she says, pointing to an office on a platform beyond
the cubicles.

"And you would be?" I say again, but she walks off.

Except for a desk with a framed photo, a few magazines, and an
overhead television, the office is empty. I don't dare look at the photo,
but I do it anyway, feeling my courage returning amid the natives,
standing, turning the collage toward me: it's a pantheon of feminism.
On the left, a black-and-white of Gloria Steinem circa mid-eighties,
looking, I must say, coital, fertile, and yet hostile; in the middle, a
Catholic print of Joan of Arc at the stake; on the right, Oprah Winfrey,
doctored up, slightly plump in green tweed. Three magazines: a *New
Yorker* from the last century, a *Vogue* with Drew Barrymore on the
cover, a lit mag called *PMS: Poem, Memoir, Story,* published, I see,
by the coed University of Alabama.

There's a newspaper at my feet, but I decide to angle my chair
toward the maze of cubicles behind me. I want to watch the women
walk about on their toes. They are strong, wide-shouldered, agile.
These are the breeders of yesteryear, sought after by all the bigwigs
with dough back in the day. Maybe our race isn't so bad off with these
women at the helm. Maybe one of these lovely creatures will row
her boat out to this manhole in distress. How much worse can they
do than the opposition from the other side of the aisle? I don't know.
But I do know they can't do it all, just like the opposition from the
other side of the aisle.

I pick up the *Merc*, at least to remove myself from eye-humping
my hostesses, and grasp the header on the front page: *Three Bum-
Beaters Charged with First-Degree Murder.*

There they are, the latest carbuncular-faced, testosterone-laden
Grand Theft Auto-playing, white boy misfit teens of clean middle-class

suburban backgrounds, terrified, bug-eyed, not quite getting what they've done to make everyone mad but on the undeniable verge of learning the concept of legal repercussions, the darkness of moral aftermath, the reality of hard time and *this is the price you pay for the life you choose,* yet even so still sitting in some virtual pocket of cyberspace they've become more than accustomed to creating, awaiting some benign button in the sky to appear so they may reset the game, having faith that they'll be all right, faith that the homeless Mexican transient they stomped into oblivion did not die or, à la Lazarus, will come back to life, as he always does on the Playstation screen, their thumbs and index fingers the fittest part of their flaccid bodies.

Oh, the places you'll see.

Marko Franzen, Mike Rude, and Thomas McMalley, lost children on the sea of virtual reality.

All three *enfants perdus* are being charged as adults, fifteen-year-old murderers in the first degree. Bastard fate: you couldn't have gut-shot a weaker target than Marko Franzen's frail mother. A part-time nanny, helpless, shocked, Mrs. Nineveh Franzen ain't gonna get through it, I know it. She's gonna break down like a jalopy in an Indy 500. Gonna get driven off the course, slammed into the wall, explode in flames: ulcers, heartbreak, insomnia.

I hate to sound callous but Jesus, Nineveh, you're on the front page of a national newspaper with a breathing apparatus stuck to your face, and your pleading eyes remind me of that crankster in the park in life-or-death need of his five-buck fix. You gotta fight it, Ninny, don't let them get you down. It's only going to steamroll from here on out. But she's quoted as saying, "My poor boy doesn't have a single hair on his chin."

I read the article, don't have a clue why. After the chumps at Columbine and the chimp at Virginia Tech and the five dozen hatchet jobs in between, we just get deeper and deeper entrenched in the

futility of this country, this people. Everytime a Boy Scout walks a
handicapped lady across the street, a gothic geek in black shoe polish has cut up three girls at the other end of the neighborhood: some
lame-ass in bifocals who grew up on slick inartistic bloodbaths like
Reservoir Dogs and *Kill Bill* and *Natural Born Killers*. The mental
chains of what's *just a flick, young man, just a film* have been broken, and he's now physically on the loose. Enacting mimicry. Not a
single book in his repertoire to counterbalance the sensationalism,
no poem to beautify this life. The Boy Scout's got no chance. He's
gotta escort a million cripples to erase the effect of his nasty coun-
terparts, do it until he himself is nearly crippled, blind, dead.

So this threesome came with bats and a knife and the hand-held
film of a cell-cam. Got the idea from a video called *Bum-Beaters*.
Caught their victim at the Palo Alto bus stop in the bushes, a quarter of a mile from the pristine, higher-learning halls of Stanford
University. According to other transients on a bus in East San Jo he'd
tried to get on the line 22 and pitch his tent but the inner sanctum
was already lined with sleepers. So he walked out the exit to the cold
outside, breath cloud rising to the heavens like a prayer. The three
kids hog-tied the bum and then wrapped him up in his own blanket.
No Christian compassion, no pagan compassion. When the cops
found the corpse there were twenty-six holes in it from head to toe.
Twenty-five were in the legs, arms, hips, and ass, and the last was in
the throat. They were playing with their prey, Orcas flipping the seal
with their tails. Sawing into the soul of man. The youngest, Mrs.
Nineveh Franzen's son/boy/man, wants to represent himself so he
can ask for the death penalty. Unprecedented legal stuff. By the looks
of his oily skin, he's supposed to be getting his permit to drive.

The victim has no family this time, at least no family in this country. Which might be the same thing. No one knows his name, uni-
dentifiable. But that doesn't mean there's no ancillary damage, right,
Mrs. Franzen? With appeals and attorneys and all those goodhearted

support groups against capital punishment now claiming your son as a cause, he'll live for two decades plus, get ready; with weekend visits to the high-walled nineteenth-century "Castle of Evil," Quentin's Condemned Row, get ready; with the years of denying the devil in your son, with the mornings and evenings ruined forever, with every social gathering, get ready; with the eyes of public pity that are yours for the taking like, let us say, at a fortieth birthday party, your sister's (to be gentle), or your own (to be harsh), there will be no moment from here on down that you will not think about him, get ready; what you did wrong in his rearing, why why *why* in the end he hadn't thought of you, or of God or the law or his country or shame, or of the life of another human being, get ready; your days will be the same in timbre and tone as your son, you may as well be there in the four-by-eight pit of concrete and iron with him, daily enervation on the horizon, get ready; guilt and terror and fear only because you clearly love him, ma'am, get ready to be eaten from the inside out, dear lady. Get ready.

Aw, man.

I don't want to think about this shit right now or these amoral assholes or—please bless him, *bless him*—the deceased Mexican bum, so I flip through the paper to find some innocuous news to scan or Little Caesars pizza coupons to use or whatever. Sports, Business, Local. I turn to the Metro in the middle of the fold and, as you might expect by now, find myself again the center of controversy, there I am, sort of.

I don't know how she did it, but I know why. I blink a few times and find the same thing still in front of me, the caption: *Who is this mystery poet of love?* The Os as hearts, the lettering in pink. And then the slanted image of a book with the imprint of kissed lips on its cover, the title *Beatrice,* the author, Anonymous.

I open to the article and find a photo of La Dulce reading an excerpt at City Lights Books in North Beach. At the podium, she's all gums and teeth, glamorous sparkles across her cheeks. I'm surprised she wasn't up there in a G, pushing her beautiful ass out at the crowd for a good *sasa,* as we say in Samoan, a good spanking.

The article notes: "Ms. Schneck is very careful to articulate that while she is the subject of the book, she is not the author." The University of California has published *Beatrice* under its Local Poet series, a first-book contest drawing hundreds of submissions. The book was selected as a finalist by a panel of national poets, then chosen as best in the bunch by the president of the NEA.

The citations are pretty impressive. With its "incomparable range" and "celebratory spirit of the beauty of Woman," the book is endorsed by local literati including the Dean of Creative Writing at the Silicon University of the Valley, Gabby von Morley; confirmed by the Poet Laureate of Pittsburg, Kim Maddodondia, with a plea to the poet to personally reveal to her "the fiery horizontal intent thronged in the body of these poems." Even the famed Shakespeare critic Herod Budoom has rung in from his lofty chair on Thermopylae or Olympus and afforded the book his highest praise in decades: "*Beatrice* is readable and decent and possibly worth the purchase."

I look up from the paper to process this onslaught of irony and the answer is not a joke: on the office television, already, Mrs. Nineveh Franzen's kid, Marko. Oh, he's finished now, up the river. Little Marko Franzen will be there until some other nutty kids copycat the cruel act somewhere in middle America and he's referenced as the trendsetter. Now his lifeless greasy face is in the corner of the screen, a still-shot yearbook pick of (of course) black eyeliner and black lipstick, with the cynical echo of his mother's quotation beneath it: NOT A HAIR ON HIS CHIN?

The show: *The O'Reilly Factor.* The host spewing venom. The television is in mute mode, but I can hear him just fine. *There's no art to find the mind's construction in the face.* He hates this kid, the ringleader. He would kill this kid, premeditatively. If he had a chance, he'd wring the kid's neck with his big Irish hands, rip out the larynx and chew on it. Maybe that's why he's so appealing to people: finally we have someone in the public eye who isn't afraid to demonstrate the senseless emotion, in all our hearts.

One of the host's shaking hands is virtually thrust into the hollow chest of Lomas Gerragos, his guest for this segment, the Franzen family attorney. The lawyer is taking the attack in stride, blinking and nodding respectfully at every jab of the opposing index finger, with a contented look that likely speaks to his own murderous hourly fees, and I have this urge to organize a mental outline of the ugly American issues on the silent TV when I hear, "I can't believe you're, like, watching that guy."

"It's not my television," I say, even before turning toward the direction of the voice. One watches what one has to watch. One watches what is around: the world at large. Or one closes one's eyes. And then there is also the matter of one's ears and one's mouth, the little monkey.

See no world, hear no world, say no world.

"He is just, like, totally wrong."

It's the girl at the door. She's looking down at a cell phone, the nose rings shaking from the fierce way she's punching in digits.

"Right," I say.

"The only thing, like, I agree with him about is Jessica's Law."

"Why is that?"

"Because these guys are taking advantage of innocent little girls— hold on."

The jingle from *I Will Survive* announces itself like a music box and she stops it in mid-jingle by pushing a button on her cell phone. She puts it to her ear, says, "Hello. . . . Can I call you back? . . . I know, I heard."

"I don't think they're all innocent," I say, quite loudly but to myself.

"Let me get right back to you, okay?" She looks at me. "These poor girls are getting taken advantage of, and it's time we did something about it."

I say, "Are you with O'Reilly that the Bum-beater Boys should be sent up as men?"

"Yes, I'm afraid I am." *I Will Survive* happens again. "Hold on." She picks up the cell, says, "Hi, Leticia sweetie."

"But how can these boys be grown men while these girls aren't grown women? Or vice versa," I say.

"No, no, no, sweetie, I'll talk to you about that later. Let me get back to you, 'kay?"

"And then," I say to myself, or O'Reilly, or whoever, "if you claim that these girls who get voluntarily naked are actually victimized by a society of hypersexualization, why aren't the boys victimized by one of desensitization to murder and violence? And what did you expect, anyway, from a feminist revolution that teaches girls to celebrate their bodies? Of course they're gonna get naked. A lot. Often. With many. The young, the old, either gender, doesn't matter. You're Everywoman, 'member?"

She hangs up, looks up, says, "Now, where were we?"

"We were on your penchant for little boys being men."

"That's right. Like, I usually don't agree with the guy." She looks up at O'Reilly, gasps, jumps at the remote on her immaculate desk, points up, and makes O'Reilly disappear. "I just can't stand looking at him."

Though it's an odd conflict (she likes what he says but not who he is), I say, "I can understand that."

"I hate his red face. He looks like a drunkard on Skid Row. And he's so, like, mean."

"I suppose so. But his show's a rigged game, you know that."

"What do you mean?"

"He's got the home-team advantage." I'm tempted to look around at the office for another kind of home-team advantage, the complete dearth of heterosexual men, but I keep talking. "A crew of brown-nosers working his fact checks. People think the story ends with the facts when, in fact, the story actually starts with the facts."

"Yes, like, that's so true."

"I read that somewhere."

"Great."

"See, this guy O'Reilly has structured his show masterfully. He makes the segments seven minutes long so he can talk for six of the seven minutes."

"Uh-huh—hold on."

I Will Survive has chimed in again but gets muted fast, and she says into the micro-mouth of the phone, "Good morning, sleepyhead."

I say, "And he solicits 'succinct' one-liner letters so he can beat you with the question, 'Where's your evidence, ma'am?'"

"Uh-huh."

"And if you make a good point, he'll say, 'You're being philosophical. You've gotta join us in the real world of common sense.'"

"That's, like, unbelievable."

"And he calls attorneys *counselor* so it seems as if he's the judge."

"Umm."

"And then he'll get other guests to shit-talk previous guests in their absence."

"I know! Okay? *I get it!*" she cries out, hangs up the cell, says, "I'm gonna put it on vibrate," and lays it on the immaculate plane of the desk.

She says, "And, like, that No-Spin Zone: what's that all about?—Hold on."

The little creature of a cell phone is now shaking, as if it were about to explode. It sounds like a dozen drumming fingers. You expect steam to come out its ears, wherever the hell its ears would be.

She picks the damned thing up, this animated CB, hits the button, and as she starts rattling on to the other party about matching pastels in the world of fashion and how torn she is about looking good in the world while still feeling good about herself inside, I say, "The No-Spin Zone? More like the Non-sequitur Zone. The Dingbat Zone. The Dead Zone. The End Zone. More like the Twilight Zone. A Hole in the Ozone." I stop to catch my breath, get another thread going. "A Hole in the Head. More like the Headless Zone. The Bonehead Zone. The Bone-Down Zone. The Down-and-Out Zone. The Outhouse Zone. I've never seen more loaded questions in my life."

"Uh-huh."

"That Gaelic prick's like a drill sergeant barking orders at Forrest Gump. Anyone who titles his memoir *A Bold Fresh Piece of Humanity* has some serious self-image problems. I mean, it makes me want to rush off to the head and lay a bold fresh piece of humanity."

"You're so right. Let me get back to you on that one, baby."

The beep of her postponed conversation extends throughout the office and she says to me, "But I don't know. I wonder: Why were you recommended to us again? What do you, like, do?"

"I write poetry."

"And you write pretty good?"

"Yes. I write pretty good, pretty well, pretty pretty."

"So you're applying to write grants?"

Sounds about right. "Yes."

"Do you have a résumé or something?"

I would have thought my sister had taken care of that. "Well." I can't believe I'm about to say this. "I have a book."

"Like, published?"

"Yes."

"You have it with you?"

"No." I can't believe I'm about to do this: "But I have something else." I hand her the article in the *Metro* praising the anonymous author of the book in question. She looks it over and shouts, "I love that book! Wait! Oh my God! You wrote *Beatrice*?"

I feel entrapped by the truth. There is nothing stranger in the world than the feeling of detesting, and therefore privately denying, a book you've in fact written. The story starts with the fact of your antipathy. I feel like a brand-new father whose secret gut reaction at seeing the infant for the first time is: *Whoa, there! That is one ugly baby!* But I have to own something in this world, goddammit, and I guess it may as well be this allegedly award-winning book of poems that everyone, especially women, seems to love.

At least it's mine, the new father reasons. *And I guess the baby got ugly from someone. You are a cutie, cute little baby,* he says, reaching out for the beginning of a new self-definition.

"I composed that book."

"You did?"

"Yeah."

"You wrote 'The Poet Will Be Uxorious from Here On Out'?"

"Yep. Composed."

"Really?"

It's a refreshing accusation not to be believed. *Excellent!* She wants the proper disposition of a poet, which is to write: one with visible depression. Or she expects the lover with pink cheeks enraptured by the Nerudan passion for women he cannot control. Or maybe she's troubled with the half-breed features. Despite her correct political rearing, she expected someone with angular Anglo cheekbones, ten-dollar words, and a regal air, like Teddy Hughes. And then she wants Silicon Valley evidence of the quality of the work; in other words, that I have no need to visit her enterprise strapped for cash. Yes, I disappoint this cell-phone princess: She's supposed to come to me, not I to her. It's always something of a letdown to meet the authors of books you love because the books, even the worst of them, are the best confection of what is bound to be a flawed human being.

I recite in my deepest oracular voice:

"The Poet Will Be Uxorious from Here On Out

You have used in our most recent days together
erudite terms like malleable, eclectic, aesthetic,
and with a wink of insinuation (the poet's right to be),
solipsistic. *(Don't you know by now*
that little jabs will never get by an ex-boxer?)
Between you munching La Paloma nachos
and your standard horizontal moans in our shifty
double-backed beast ("You know me—Oooh!"
you'd cried, "so pliably!"), I saw a picture of you
at the library, unfolding a book of "Brobdingnagian" length.
The Oxford *perhaps, or maybe* Ulysses,
something large to lend vocabulary.
I love you most for that generosity:
It isn't phoniness."

She has her cherubic little hands over her heart and the cell phone is shaking like crazy and I'm looking through the blue-gray windows of her eyes and finding nothing at all attractive about the growing tears there.

That's me, me, me! her crying is crying out. *That's me in that poem, not Beatrice!*

I nod: *That's you, you, you! Who the hell is Beatrice? Gimme some money.*

She says, wiping at her eyes, "I love that book. Your celebration of beauty makes me warm with life!"

Why should I mention how the book came into pornographic fruition, its creation myth of purging my head of filth?

"Okay," she says, nodding to herself over and over, eyes closed. I realize that she's building up strength. "I'm gonna go to bat for you.

I don't care what it costs me. But I need something to show the higher-ups. Do you have a contract or anything? Some papers I can, like, show them?"

I say, "Can I borrow a pen and a Post-it?"

She reaches into her drawer and pulls both items out, handing them over with the leery look of a gas station attendant giving out the key to the lavatory.

"Don't worry," I say. "I'm the poet, remember? I've a beauty obligation to fulfill." I point at the picture of La Dulce in the *Metro* article. "Here's this lady's phone number. Ask for La Dulce. She'll tell you what you need to know about the author."

"You, right? That's you."

"Yeah. Exactly. Me. But just keep that on the down-low, if you don't mind. And please don't tell her I talked to you. Is that cool?"

"Oh, for certain," she says, looking down at the triumvirate of framed ladies atop her desk. "But what if she won't give up the name?"

"She'll squeal like a piglet. So what's next?"

"Okay. If everything goes through, you'll get an e-mail in a week."

"I don't have e-mail." I don't have a computer.

"Okaaay. What's your cell number?"

"Don't have one. You can call the guesthouse of my—"

"Okay, like, how *do* you live?"

"Well. Should I call you?"

"Don't worry," she says, standing, "we'll take care of it."

I stand at once, bow to show deference, say thank you in a language she doesn't know—"*Fa'afetai lava*"—to appear mysterious as a poet should, and quickly get out of the National Organization of Women Silicon Valley office. I'm pushing my luck so hard I'm gonna snap soon like a schizophrenic in need of his meds, like, not tomorrow, like, not later, but, like, right NOW.

33

I Get Back in the Swing of Things

I GET BACK IN the swing of things midweek, work and vanilla milk-shakes coming together into one. Tali stopped by the guesthouse one evening and said three words: "Keep not talking." In the absolute spirit of her advice, I didn't say hello or good-bye. Today there are hundreds of lamps and desks to move from the San Jo office to a warehouse in Burlingame. I label them for later placement on eBay, tape a Post-it to the base of each item.

Chinaski, once I've got the truck loaded up, will be driving. He's sitting in the cab, apparently preparing for the long road ahead. I've got the layout of the inside of the truck loosely planned out when my uncle calls and says, "Oh, God, I hate this job. I'll be at the restaurant."

That means meet him at Original Joe's in downtown San Jo. It's not even lunch yet, but when the boss calls, you go. I don't know what to say to Chinaski except, "See ya," and not, "Do you wanna join us?" or "Isn't it funny how life works out sometimes? It's actually you who's gonna break your back today despite all those fake maps spread across your lap."

I get down to San Carlos and First, and the light of day dies the minute I open the heavy door of the old-school lounge at the rear of

O.J.'s. I squint and peer into the musky darkness, my eyes adjusting, and find my uncle at the end of the bar. He's in his work shirt still, but his tie is untied and hanging two-ended over his chest. He's already got one sitting there for me to his immediate right, along with a shot, both full, untouched.

"Listen, nephew," he says, as I sit, say, "*Salute*," hit the shot, chase it. "You've heard about the latest with the banks?"

"No," I say. "I don't pay much attention to that stuff."

"Well, you should. There's a hundred-thousand-dollar loan out there with your name on it."

"I couldn't get a fifty-dollar loan, Uncle."

"There's a house with your name on it, too."

"A moonshine shack?"

"No, the real deal. Three-bed, coupla baths, running water, nice yard, plenty of fenceline, civil neighbors."

The barkeep approaches. This guy's shady, he's got the meandering eye. Says, "So what can I get da two of yous?"

I don't say anything, just nod at our drinks. This restaurant, Original Joe's, an Italian joint founded eighty years back when the city's Italianos still spoke it, hires fake mobsters like liquor stores attract alcoholics. This guy's name—or so he'll claim—is probably Frankie or Paulie or Sonny. I don't know who's worse out of the South Bay: the one-sixteenth-Cherokee white boy who powwows for a Native American housing grant or the one-eighth-Napolitano white boy who thinks he's mafiosi because he's seen *The Godfather* and *Goodfellas* eighty-six times each.

In a nation with an identity crisis, you can be anyone you want to be. That's right, invent yourself. Sure, everyone'll laugh behind your back, but no one'll say you're a fraud to your face. Everything is so watered down by now that the authenticators are nearly extinct, anyway. All you gotta do is stay away from the reservations and casinos. Avoid the heart of Little Italy on your next New York vacation.

But even there no one'll say, That really ain't you, Kemo Sabe, the
pigtails and wampum don't cut it; nah, I don't think so, Collogeno,
the gold chain, hairy chest, and *Volare* ballad just ain't enough.

"So da two of yous is good?"

"We'll have another round," says my uncle. "Thank you kindly,
Luigi."

"Fuh-ged about it," he says, walking off.

"Get outta heea," I say.

"He's a nice guy," says my uncle.

I say nothing.

"He's just a little confused is all."

"Luigi's real name is John L. Smith the Third."

"Come on now, nephew."

"I trip out on all these poor-man Al Capones. They're everywhere
now. Luigi has got it ass backward. I mean, think about it: this guy
takes in a few Prohibition movies, likes what he sees, and proceeds
to worship an age and an image he ascribes to the race. I mean, if
you're gonna act Italian, why not go after the best and brightest of a
given people? Dante, Leonardo. This guy takes murderers and con
men as his idols."

"Last I checked, you weren't too innocent yourself."

"Hey! I don't want anyone idolizing me either."

"Let's get back to the loans."

"That fool reminds me of a line from Ferlinghetti:

> *Which one's my maybe mafioso father,*
> *which one's my dear lost mother?"*

"The loans, nephew."

"The salesman in you is coming out, Uncle."

"Let me have a shot," he says, "of getting at the truth."

"Salesman—truth. Bad mix."

"Cut it, will you?"

Luigi is telling a story to a patron, his mannerisms punctuated by his two Billy the Kid hands. He's got his fat little index fingers extended like gun muzzles, his fat little thumbs as hammers.

I say, "All right, I'll bite. But before you go off on your pitch, let's get the fuck out of here. Take a long walk to my car. I can't stand that wannabe goombah."

"Okay."

We stand and I say, "*Ciao, testo di cazzo,*" and he nods really coolly. "See da two of yous latuh."

"What'd you say back there?" my uncle asks as we hit the street.

"Good-bye, ball sack."

We make our way up First toward the ("One dollah!") Vietnamese sandwich shops and the Victorian halfway houses, the paint and scrollwork chipped, the porches and stairways packed with parolees. There's not a word between us. The city is loud. Fifty yards ahead on First and San Salvador, a near accident: sounding horns, diatribes. The endless racket of La Dulce returns to my head. I try to drive her out by taking the light wind tickling my ear as a trigger to romance: Sharon, nibbling, love.

We're passing the intersection and the two cars are still there, despite not having collided. The epithets are getting personal: "Asshole!" "Gook!" Lives are threatened. The traffic behind them swells like a wave about to roll over on itself. Sharon evaporates, who I was with Sharon goes with it.

My uncle is awaiting my full attention. The potential didactics of this situation concern me. But to show the spirit of neutral cooperation I'm learning to master here at the West, I volunteer a return to the earlier topic that has made my uncle what he is.

"Now: how can you land me—of all people—land, uncle?"

"Okay, look," he says, happy that I've jumped back into the arena of instruction. "I'm gonna give you an accurate rendition."

"Of what, your climb to glory?"

"Of the extremely recent history of no-interest loans in the Silicon Valley."

"That's a hell of a qualification, Uncle."

"No-interest loans are a hell of a thing."

"No-interest loans sound almost anti-American."

"Sounds that way."

"Like pre-profit Catholic Europe. Pre-usury. Benedictine monk stuff."

"Now hold up." He pulls out a cigarette, offers me one. I shake my head no. "Jesus. Don't go all historical and Euro on me. We're in this century, this continent, all right?"

"Okay. Shoot."

"Now. Somewhere along the line the banks and the real estate agencies realized they could work together. They were missing out on a pocket of profit."

"Which is just a nice way of saying they found a new way to put the screws to the suckers."

"Just listen."

"Uncle, I don't have a dime to my name."

"Well, you're the target. Precisely." He's blowing smoke out his nostrils, a nicotine blanket being pulled up over his face. I think about switching sides to avoid the contention with this last bit of blood who will talk to me, but I don't want to disturb his train of thought. I'm worried, though; dread, an overfed bird, sits on the fence between us. "Listen. This thing's contingent upon your not having a dime to your name. Everyone else out there in the Valley is stacking up their Legos, so why shouldn't you?"

"I don't think like that, Uncle. Hungry or not, I don't covet my neighbor's property."

"Okay. Better put: Someone in your unenviable financial position. Now just listen to this: They give you a one-hundred-thousand-dollar loan to buy a house. You pay no interest for the first year. Doesn't that sound nice?"

"Yes. I guess. But I'm suspicious of the philanthropic integrity of my brothers and sisters out there."

"Yeah, well, you should be."

We pass Circle-A Skate Shop, where five youngsters are doing rails and ollies on their custom boards. Each one is fashionably filthy; the torn punk rock shirts in faded black and the loose Dickies slacks with chains growing from the pockets haven't been washed since the purchase. I remember in the pen where the only thing every race and crew agreed upon other than *Fuck the Man* was the need to wield clean threads. As if a starched collar and stiff hemline would flush all the shit of that place away. Then you get outside and discover that there are kids who are striving to be as dirty as you used to be inside. The principle seems different, but it ain't; only the context has changed. The urge remains the same: to escape the context.

In our business collars, we're initially unnoticed. One of the skaters detaches from the group, skidding past us along the concrete walkway. She lifts the nose of her board, swirls to a stop, drops down on her ass and I say, "Looks like we're gonna get a break-dancing show."

Her dark eyes on my uncle, she lifts her palms in front of her chin, eyes to me, then back to my uncle. Is she serious? She has too much energy to be a panhandler. But maybe her filth is not a fashion statement and only the blind vigor of youth gets her through each day. I pull out a Fuji apple I've saved to devour after the drunken talk with my uncle and hand it to her as we pass.

"So the loans, Uncle." We make our way up the street. "You were saying about the loans."

"Well, the—"

Just then a zipping object explodes in front of us against the base of a magnolia tree. I know what it is even before it breaks up into a dozen white chunks on the ground and I'm already turning and walking toward the agent of delivery, the bomber, who's back up on her feet, slapping hands with her dark-eyed cronies, the nose of her board pointed at me like a schoolyard challenge.

I've got the attention of one, who shouts out, "Wassup, bro?"

"I'll show you wassup, you little punk mutherfucker."

My uncle steps in front of me. "Nephew, nephew."

I stop, regain my business sense: this is my boss, the chief exec.

"Let's go," he says. "This is a public place."

"All the better. Expose their asses for what they are."

"You touch her and she'll sue. Let's go."

I think, *Sue me? Fucking absurd. Because he's right. It's absurd because he's right.*

They're skating in a circle, derelict pack of fake wolves, offering a vast range of lurid gestures. Casually, in obscene safety.

I shake my head out urgently. "All right, let's go, Uncle. Come on."

Suddenly we're speed walking up the street in the opposite direction, making distance on their mockingbird calls, and he says, "Why do you let them get you worked up?"

"Why do you let them not get you worked up?"

"All right, all right," he says, flicking the snipe of his cigarette into the air, its ash spreading red-orange then gray-white in the gutter of the street, fumbling into the pack for another coffin nail, lighting it, dragging it, offering it my way like an earnest, pestering peanut vendor at a ball game, my easy refusal, his disappointed *pssshhh.* Would I get the capital P *pssshhh* if I shunned his business acumen in the same way? I wonder.

"I think you just missed five clients, Uncle."

"Let's get back to the topic at hand."

"Okay. So what's that catch you were talking about?"

"Oh. Well. You're paying the interest."

"You said I'd pay no interest in the first year."

"That's right."

"Then how can I be paying it at the same time?"

"Well, let me put it this way: you *will* be paying it. I should've used the future tense. I'm conditioned to using the present tense in this trade. You remember our motto?"

"How could I forget? *Santa Clara Real Estate West: Bend over and we'll screw.*"

"Come on. Stop fucking around."

"All right. 'Jingle, jingle. The door is open and the lights are on in the West. Jingle, jingle.'"

"Not that one. The one on our T-shirts."

"WE WORK THE ANGLE OF RIGHT NOW."

"Yes."

"Genius," I say.

He flicks the cigarette, which isn't a snipe, lights another. Is it uncool to smoke a cigarette longer than a minute? Yet another example of American extravagance? Or is it his weird way of convincing himself that he's saving his lungs? If that's the case, he's missing the sixth-grade arithmetic of the habit, a return to fractions, dear Uncle: $1/3 + 1/3 + 1/3 = 1$. No break in between, so no difference.

He says, "Anyway, at the start of year two, the balance of the loan jumps to one hundred fifteen thousand dollars."

"Okay."

"And the interest jumps to seven percent. On the whole hundred and fifteen."

"That's a big jump."

"Yep. And you know what happens next?"

"What?"

"Some people can't pay it."

"They fold?"

"Of course."

"So why do the banks give out the money if they ain't gonna get the money back?"

"Let's say you came at me and said, 'You can have one of two situations with these no-interest loans. Either (a) you can make ten loans, in which case ten are paid back or (b) you can make a hundred loans, in which case ninety are paid back. Which do I take?"

"The first."

"Wrong. I take the second."

"Don't get it."

"It's better to be big and fairly inefficient in this market than small and purely efficient. Or, rather, better to get bigger. Growth is the goal."

"Even if the growth is artificial?"

"Those ten loans are paid back five times over by another ten loans over a five-year period. The bet is that the house of cards won't fold because of its size. You assume the system can eat it, *it* being loss. The whole thing's about the short term *now*. Or, rather, about the short-short-short term *now*. They're pushing this thing to the limit. You know what's gotta happen."

"Too much air in the balloon?"

"A few soothsayers have said it's gotta pop. And it will. Something's gotta give. Let's hope it's confined to the valley and doesn't hit the macro level: the NYSE, the Dow, and all the rest. Too many people around the world are relying on our word to be good. But you wanna know the worst part of this trend?"

"Gets worse?"

Another cigarette flicked, another lit. "I was one of the principal engineers of the idea."

I'm about to say, *Yeah, Ms. Clannonite told me all about you,* but don't.

"Monster real-estate mogul," he says.

"You're all right, Uncle. Seen worse monsters at the Motel Six."

"That bucket of fleas?"

"Yeah. This flea included."

"You won't go back ever again."

"You never know. Even a big shot like you could find yourself in a place like that."

"No one wants to be there, nephew. Not even you."

"Wasn't that bad. I had my own little jail cell to myself." For some reason, the image of Chinaski on the stolen scooter whizzes through my head. "That was nice."

"Well, don't sham yourself into thinking you're living a life of decency because you don't mind squalor and solitude."

"Okay, Uncle. You tell me then: Can I find truth in that cheap pitch to the bidding suckers: *The door is open—*"

"*—and the lights are on in the West.* That's right."

"What do you gain by seducing me to your ways?"

"I never gain anything in business terms with you, nephew. I've everything to lose. Which is about as truthful as you can get. When I talk about the marginality of the real estate market and the fluff of these no-interest loans, I'm fingering me. And you."

"Indict yourself. I move desks and chairs for a living."

"Listen."

"Have been."

"Your weakness as a businessman is feeling bad for the loser in the deal. But someone always goes down for the sake of someone else coming up. That's not only life, that's capitalism. Profit couldn't exist without loss. Conceptually impossible. And just the same, capitalism can't exist without profit. It's self-sustaining by the concept of wealth and poverty. You'll never have one too many rich men out there that the system can't sustain. Even when it cashes out like in 'twenty-nine, it was merely a cleaning of the slate. It was basically the United States' turn to be a third world nation. Someone else out there was having for the sake of us not having. It doesn't matter that

there wasn't much to have. What matters is that however much there
was, we had less."

"Or not enough."

"Same difference. Because here's what you and Mr. Marx can't
accept. Based strictly on the instinct of getting what you don't have,
the best businessmen out there are amoral."

"So Karl Marx was a moralist? Don't think we disagree."

"Let me put it to you another way: the earning itself is the morality. Think about it. Everything else exists only because of and for the
earning."

I'm a bit frustrated that my uncle has either (a) forgotten that I
was making these very points at the lake during my dissertation on
Tillman, (b) he took the unpatented argument so deeply to heart that
he's now unwittingly stealing it, or (c) consciously stealing it, or (d)
he's now merely flipping the point about, attaching it to his issue
and using it against me. I'm not certain whether it's better to be the
originator of an idea or the last to use it. Or the loudest to use it. Or
the oldest with supposedly more experience to use it.

He says, "Are you with me?"

"Yes," I say, uninsulted. "Of course."

My uncle holds the cigarette out in front of me again and this time
I take it, drag it deep into my lungs, blow the smoke right back in his
face. We've stopped in front of an Afghan liquor store, two homeless cats sitting under the pay phone. I wish I had that Fuji apple
now.

My uncle says, "I can see you don't believe me."

"Oh, not at all. I believe you, all right. I know you're describing
the true nature of business. And the justification is that you're getting at the true nature of man."

"That's wrong. I don't need a justification. The whole world follows this paradigm."

"I know, Uncle. I ain't all eyes and no sight."

"Then see this: I'm breaking it down as a mere courtesy to you."

"Well, thank you very much."

"And listen here." I can see the two transients watching our exchange amusedly. "I'm gonna shut your elusiveness down for good."

"Gonna bear-trap me?"

"You old enough to remember when Exxon came out with the that big environmental ad program back in the early nineties?"

One of the transients digging his nose is smiling.

"Well?" he presses. "Why did they do that?"

"Um, pressure? Maybe lobbyists? A greener youthful generation making demands."

"Demands? Who the fuck cares about demands? It's just talk. They don't have to listen, and they won't. I assure you that wasn't the reason."

"Okay then, Uncle. What was it? You tell me."

"I will," he says, blowing smoke right back in my face. "It was because lobbyists and that greener youthful generation were affecting their profit base. The talk only mattered when it affected the demand-supply curve. Those people were simply variables. If they were reps for the tobacco industry or the Tennessee Home Owners Association it would've been the same difference. If they were reps for your kindergarden's sandbox. The question is this: Is our profit base affected?"

"I get you, Uncle. Just take it easy."

My mind provides an image antithetical to the transients' life: they sit quiet as aristocrats at a symphony.

My stiff-arming of and high stepping over being pinioned to a permanent position truly pisses my uncle off. I don't blame him. If I could get outside of myself like a twin Dostoevskian shadow, I'd probably join his cause and hurl stones at me. His eyes are saying, *You think you're worldly, punk? You ain't shit.* Sardonic yet affable interrogation only brings out the ugliness of his and what he'd hoped would be my

profession. If he's neck deep in this morally bankrupt business world
for three decades at 40 to 70 hours a week, obviously that bankruptcy
starts to invade the organism itself. It's not a hostile takeover, no coup
d'état. It's an outsider moving into a room of your house one day and
taking over, square foot by square foot. And then before you know it,
you're about to drunkenly defend the system you've so skillfully de-
cried because the system is grotesquesly yourself.

"I don't care enough to see you get mad over it, Uncle."

"Well, then, let me tell you something else."

"It's cool, man. Let it rest for a minute. Jeez."

"The only reason people started paying attention to the lobbyists
and the greenists was because the *Exxon Valdez* went down off the
shore of Alaska."

"Meaning what?"

"Meaning that dead birds and dirty water are the same meaningless variables, one ripple removed. Come on, nephew! What the fuck
are we talking about here? It doesn't matter until it matters fiscally.
All kinds of birds had died before that damned ship grounded. We'd
had dirty water in this state for decades. What's the matter, you don't
like what I'm saying?"

"I guess I don't."

"Well, don't guess anything, because that's the way it is. And you
have no place in this world, goddammit, if you don't cede this point."

"I agree with that view, anyway: I've no place."

One of the transients pipes up. "We've no place either!"

My uncle pays him no attention. "It doesn't matter if you do or
don't agree, get it? And guess what, big shot? You too are a variable
on someone's spreadsheet."

I look at the two transients, who must take great offense to the
stupid academic conversation they're hearing about what is in fact
their lives. As if my uncle and I were authorities on the matter, joust-
ing in an unpoppable bubble where we won't have to fight for our

words, for the air we breathe, for our lives. I want to walk on, at least respect their sordid little square on the sidewalk, respect their gone-bust story, but my uncle grabs my shoulders, holding me there.

"What do you know anyway? Where do you plant your flag, nephew? What is your stance?"

He tries to push me against the phone, but I twist my feet and, with better leverage beneath me, shove my uncle down the street, which he takes to, stumbling off. The two transients are standing now, riled out of their cloudy realities, mumbling curses and threats. I offer conciliatory words worth at least my uncle's flight, but if I have to fight alone again in this frivolous city on the edge of America, I'll know this go-round will be for no other cause than the hell of it.

34

We're Coasting Down

WE'RE COASTING down 85 blasting *Brandenburg Concertos* and not talking. Swerving a bit but it ain't too bad. Or my uncle ain't too bad. He came back with my car to get me at the liquor store, tossed the transients a fifty and no words of wisdom, which was kind of him, and now seems very focused, pushing the two-door Honda Civic to the limit. I'm writing a poem in the planner Tali bought me as a business talisman, each day filled up with a stanza.

He floors the accelerator, I can hear the engine cry out like a dozen angry pigs about to be slaughtered—*zeeeee!*—and suddenly the weight of the car feels light in the wind of the highway. Like it could tip over at any moment. I feel alive, too, and then, as often happens, I don't trust the feeling. Or I don't trust the person in control. I use my leadership skills and turn down the radio.

"*Finito,*" I say. "Wanna hear it?"

"I'm not into the oral tradition." I kick out Johann Sebastian and press in the slack-key slide of Gabby Pahinui, the old *ki ho'alu* master himself. He goes into his Hawaiian cowboy yodel and my uncle says, "Who the hell is this?"

"Who cares? He makes good music and he's happy."

My uncle picks up the CD case, scans the cover, says, "That's 'cause he smokes more marijuana than the country of Jamaica. What the hell is he whining about?"

I turn serious on him. "It's called *paka*. And what are *you* whining about, losing fifty bucks to a homeless guy?"

He doesn't say anything.

"You know," I say, "he's just gonna buy a forty with all that cash you kicked down."

I don't know how he does it, but I can feel his disdain in the silence.

"Well," I add, "about fifty forties, anyway. Stockpile a makeshift bar of King Cobra behind a Dumpster."

I want to say to my uncle that if I were one of his true recruits of the streets I'd have knocked the both of them down and taken the shoes right off their feet. All in the name of SCREW. And then, I want to say to him, I would've knocked you down, too, Uncle, same treatment, no distinction, your generous nepotism aside. Or, I'd say, if they were smart free-market capitalists like you, they'd use the Ulysses Grant you gave 'em to buy some crystal meth, which they could then sell double or triple to some frat punks at Silicon University of the Valley. But just to really fuck with him, I'd like to say— in fact, officially announce—that it was a very nice pseudo-socialistic gesture on his part to give up fifty bucks for the cause and I'm proud of him.

Instead I say, "But hopefully they'll get a little food into 'em."

Still nothing.

"So where we going, Uncle?" He doesn't look over at me. I say with force, "Did you hear me?"

"We're gonna make a visit to the hens." Still looking straight ahead.

"What?"

"The pheasantry."

"What's that mean?"

"The Blue Pheasant."

The Blue Pheasant. I remember coming across the place in the *Mercury News* a few years back. Some poor lady got so badly raped in Cupertino that NOW came out in numbers and called for a citywide curfew in honor of the victim. There was a lot of chanting on television and calls from various women to reclaim the night. The cops traced the victim's steps back to the Blue Pheasant. It turned out she was there with her swinging husband and they were recruiting players for the evening. The last anyone at the bar saw of her, she was leaving in the arms of two Afghan cats, her husband trailing behind, keys in hand. When the cops came, the wife was hysterical, hurling silverware at her husband. He'd been there through it all, hiding out in a locked closet. She picked the door with a hanger and stabbed him with it. So I remembered the strange name of the place because I more or less decided after reading the story never to go in it. But there was something bigger about the article that I can't quite pinpoint. Not something sinister, really, but something laughably odd about the place, an eccentric frame to the story.

I say, "You know about that big rape case?"

"It's all history, nephew. History."

I swallow at the thought of history, of yesterday vanishing in a sentence, reach out and blast the slack key so loud my uncle gasps, uncool, ugly.

We trail off of the 85 and De Anza exit and make our way up Stevens Creek. We're going away from the lights, away from civilization, toward the black hills. We pass houses and houses and more and more houses, and in the interlude of the white-lined road we await the next string of houses, which always appears. If I cared who sold them or who owns them, I'd ask my uncle, who'd know both answers.

I don't say a word.

Finally the trees grow in density and width and it feels as if we're going up an incline when—zeeeee! cries the engine—we descend a slope with an aerial view of the Blue Pheasant. At the bottom is a miniature canyon, phone wires of lights zigzagging across a lot. They hit the establishment at the roofline and run along the rim. Looks like the flashing grid of a computer chip. We can see it clearly, as could any passing plane, any airborne bird. I feel like I'm entering into the Tenth Circle of Hell, yet to have been invented during the good bard's age of tricks and cuckoldry.

I'm about to say, You ever seen *Apocalypse Now*? when I remember my uncle's recent confession of cowardice at the hill. I'd like to say, This is like that scene where they pull up into that coastal village. You know, with the lights and firecrackers and explosives going off. Ten minutes later they're done for. Too deep into the jungle. Once you're in, you can't get out.

That's what I want to say as we pull into the parking lot. But I don't say a word. I watch, listen, look around. The marked and un-marked spaces are packed tightly with cars. Cadillac Sevilles, Oldsmobiles from the eighties, the kind with the spare tire on the trunk, pop-up outline, silver trim. Suddenly I remember: This place is for geezers. According to everything I'd heard, visitors to the Blue Pheasant were at, past, or well beyond a midlife crisis. The poor lady who'd gotten raped was a grandma of six.

We pull to a stop at a platform of steps leading into the joint. Three gray-haired men, all balding badly, sixty and up, each with skin baked crimson, are on the stoop. The one in the middle has his sleeves rolled to his deltoids, the shirt wrapped around his torso like an Olympic swimsuit, ivory-white teeth. He slaps the shoulder of the man closer to him, lifts his red head like a beast of the Serengheti, and howls. He's mocking my ride, this geezer who spends his idle afternoons in a tanning booth.

"I'm not going in, nephew."

"Why?"

"You wanted to ask me about your aunt, didn't you?"

"Well, yeah. I guess I did."

"Get out of the car and go see her then."

I don't know what to do except look out the window at the three elderly fraternity brothers, and I don't know what to say except, "What the fuck is wrong with us?"

"This is it, nephew. I'm sorry."

"Not just us, you and me." I look up at the Glory Days threesome. "But *us*."

"The end of the line, nephew. Hop out."

I slowly open the door and put a foot on the pavement, feeling this eerie inertia centered somewhere in my knotted guts, lining the winding road of my intestines. My tongue is paralyzed, a slug in the cave of my mouth. The earth has stopped revolving, or so I'd think. This is the time—*right now*—to say something of conviction, something worth my life, something human. Not for myself so much and not for my uncle's sake, but for those of us in need of a lasting divinity, which is to say all of us, of something outside the empirical calibration of business, science, and tech, that heartless twenty-first-century trinity.

Now is the time, now!

And if the word still falls within the cursed purview of these corn-fed gods, at least give me something that passes undetected beneath them, some little bubble of mystery they miss. Something that escapes the prying scope of their cyclopsian eye. Let me give my uncle a golden line that is officially between us but somehow seems bigger than every breath of air we could ever take. *He must face eternity, or the lack of it, every day.* Is it still possible? We need to be convinced that our lives matter, not finally matter but firstly matter. The old assumptions inherent to the old equations no longer fly.

Convince him, convince me, convince us that this earthly blink of
the eye matters.

"Uncle."

"Step aside and step back, nephew. And shut up. This thing was
way done before it ever started."

"Uncle, I have to believe that this life is of the purest, realest,
finest—"

"I know, I know, nephew. I heard that song. I wrote it. But I can't
sing it anymore. You stay right where you're at and live it. And remember: there's more than enough hurt in the world without you
throwing in your pennies of pain. The suppression of suffering can
be achieved."

"Are you firing me, Uncle?"

"Let's just say it's time to quit."

"Are you taking this car back too?"

"Let's just say I am."

"You're my only ride back home."

He explodes into waves of laughter. Hilarity. Nearly lunacy. I don't
look around and I don't smile because I'm embarrassed and it's not
funny. He's coughing out this high-pitched whine akin to the heck-
ling banter of hyenas at the kill. This attack of laughter is an attack
against me, an easy target—when it comes down to it—of ridicule.
He's hunched over, two hands on his stomach, forehead pressed into
the ancient steering wheel.

There is no home, he's cackling. *And do you think I'd let you back
into this '82 two-door Honda Civic once you've set foot on the soiled
grounds of this place? You're defiled forever.*

Finally he stops. "You'll have no problem getting a ride, nephew."

"Uncle."

"A final word of advice: Try staying on the ride as long as you
can."

He speeds off, and the passenger door slams shut in the acceleration. He's not fifty yards before he's sliding into a bank in the lightless end of the muddy lot. I'm thinking, *You're stuck, you're stuck,* even as he spins out of the pit with grinding tires, sputters up the house-infested hill, and is gone.

Maybe I'll hail a cab. I have enough money now to do it. Instead I take to habit and start the long walk back to New Almaden. I like when the fresh night air swirls into the hollows of my nose and my mouth and I'm forced to use the moonlight as guide. I never know where I'm going but I always hope it's somewhere good. Everything ends up being at least tolerable, though all that means, really, is I'm still alive. When it gets intolerable, I guess, it will no longer matter.

A small crowd of geezer swingers near and pass me in a cloud of combined fragrances, Brut and Sunflowers. One of the ladies smiles. She has a spiked bob with highlights, a turtleneck sweater over a leopard-print dress, and those knee-high Eskimo boots you see on leggy Scandinavian runway models. Her earlobe is lined with studs of jewelry. I cough into my hand, head down, when a man with chains up to his chin, a purple polyester shirt fanned open to the sternum, and a stark black cowboy hat materializes from the darkness and slaps me on the arm. "Hey, hey, hey, youngster."

It's Chinaski. Who the hell else would it be? I try to keep walking as if I haven't recognized his desperate voice and fat face, but he spins me around and shouts, "We gotta pay our respects to the elders, youngster!"

I look back at the Blue Pheasant. In a crowd of twelve, I see a lady in white limping up the steps with a cane, the outline of her panties halfway down the leg of her skintight polyester pants. The three men give her more space than she needs. I say, "You mean pay respects to the dead?"

"Now, now, youngster," says Chinaski.

Chinaski thinks that our mutual aversion to greetings means mutual embarrassment. That it might affect our fate at Santa Clara Real Estate West to be caught in such a lowly establishment. It's like screwing your own cousin: neither party can say a word because both parties will be equally crucified by family, friends, society. Against the universal urge to share bed stories, you both keep your sin to yourselves. But Chinaski has no clue that I could care less about the incestuous hoodlums of the West. You can screw whoever you want to in these free, unrestrained, morally relative days.

Now he's popping spearmint Tic-Tacs, playing cocky. What would he say if he knew how close I was to being his boss? He'd start calling me Massah, Boss-Pa, Mr. Trump. He doesn't know it, but he was one minute removed from hard labor. If the Civic had stalled in the Blue Pheasant parking lot, Chinaski would have had to rip off his shirt again and push my uncle up the hill.

I say, "You're a regular at this place, aren't you?"

"Aren't *you*?"

"I've never been here."

"Me neither," he says, too quickly. He's about to hide his face again. Says instead, "Guess who I just saw?"

I'm afraid to ask.

"Your Aunt Lanell. On the arm of some muscle-bound hotshot."

It's irritating that, between us, he's seen her last. I shake my head and try to remember good things about my aunt. From Vermont. An old WASP. Dark green eyes that turned brown in the evening. Habit of tapping her nails against her coffee cup. Loved old Jimmy Stewart movies. Laughed a lot.

Yes, a nice lady overall whom I never really knew.

"Don't frown now, baby. We all need love."

"We all need rocking chairs. I'll see you later."

He grabs me again, almost bear-hugging me from behind. "Where you going?"

"Away."

He spins me and I can't help but turn my face to the street. His body deflated, he's slumping like a stand-up comedian whose jokes have all died at the mic. "Please come in with me. You're handsome enough to get a crowd of ladies. I just want a little take-home plate for the night."

"A doggie bag of dentures?"

"I'll buy you a drink, youngster."

"I ain't going in there. And stop calling me youngster."

"Please, young—Sorry, sorry. You don't understand: I'm begging you. You're as close to a sure thing as I'll ever have here. Gimme the leftovers, that's all. Just for half an hour, no longer."

No wonder he gets fed upon at SCREW. His flesh is dripping weakness. But I'm going to go in there with him—*why the fuck not?*—and I'm going to get drunk enough to forget the past, up to a minute ago, and not think about the future, about a minute from now. And if both happen at the same time, even better.

"All right, look. Just stop calling me youngster."

"You got it!" he shouts, hugging me, I hope for the last time.

I think about the Punjabi "youngster" he'd stolen from at the SCREW property site. "All right, all right, take it easy."

"I'm putting in a good word for your two–week eval tomorrow."

"Whatever," I say.

He detaches and asks, "Did you drive here?"

"No."

"Of course you couldn't drive here." He snickers. He's clowning my car, this coward is actually clowning my car. "I'm just joking."

"That's right you're joking." I'll make him pay for that cocky gesture, make him pay for the whole night out.

"Let's go! The ladies are waiting!"

As we're walking toward the establishment in question, my miscreant superior is handing me bathroom mints and generic wintergreen gum and half a pocketful of banana-flavored willies with bumps for her pleasure and offering tidbits of sophomoric advice about the shady nuances of the soon-to-be vanquished elderly ladies of the club. I look over and say, "Only a half hour, Chuckie."

He fires a canister of Old Spice in my face that makes me gag briefly at the base of the steps and says, "Come on, man, it's not mace," moves up the steps.

I look up through the mist and see the old lobster bouncer smiling down on me in the soft light. I'm close enough to see his arms, shaven like a triathlete, and his teeth, so white they make you squint. It's like he never put anything edible in his mouth. He's glowing with extraterrestrial pizzazz, radioactive.

I nod respectfully at my elder, this sixty-two year old doorman in the muscle shirt about to OD on Viagra. *Be sure to contact your physician if your hard-on lasts for longer than sixty-two years.*

He says, "No hats, man."

It's an inconceivable directive: I'm not wearing one. My beanie's in my pocket. He's a little nervous with all the horse steroids flowing through his system so I look down at my slippers to give him reprieve. Despite all the investment with the local Vietnamese beautician, his features—close up—still look older than mine. He's wrinkly at the neck and there's a sag in his chest that may get worse during my temporal stay at his establishment. He only has so many more years to stop juniors like me at the door for infractions of fashion.

I pat his shoulder. "Can I go in now?"

"You have a good time, bro," he says to me, a meaningful nod at Chuckie of the cowboy hat, a patron he obviously recognizes.

The place is one big heartbeat. Chuckie's shouting in my ear, his head bobbing to a growing pulsation, something about the electric-ity in the air and that he likes the jam. We get to the bar, which is packed with people, and for just that prompt registry of the miraculous, I'm shocked. That's saying a lot these days. I never thought I'd see a dance floor of quinqua- and septuagenarians freaking to the mating calls of a 50 Cent slam. But there they are, as tangible as time, pushing their hips to the physiological bounds of agility, hands in the air or on each other's (age-appropriate term here) *derrieres*, faces plastered with desire. A separate clique in the corner of the dance floor nearest the bar is shouting in synchronicity to the ghetto beat of 50, "Heyyy! Hoooo! Heyyy! Hooo!"

I close my eyes to try and find peace behind the void of my eyelids: follow my uncle's advice. Perhaps it will work. But I know better: it won't. Can't. The thumping of the rap song and the deep streety mumble of 50 betray me.

At the club—*boom-doom-boom-doom-boom*—at the club.

I am truly tired of myself. The clock has yet to strike midnight. I shake my head out, rattle its contents, open my eyes, reregister with reality, say, "Jesus Christ."

"Told you! Told you!" shouts Chuckie, tugging on the sleeve of my shirt with naked vigor. He throws his hands in the air. "Heyyyy! Hooo! Heyyyy! Hooo!"

I almost shove him. The gold around his neck is heavy and doesn't move. For some inexplicable reason, I put my index finger in his chest. "I'll have a Guinness!"

"Okay! okay!" he shouts, his hands still thrown up overhead.

I'm a little lost. "And a shot of Stoli!" He nods. "Black currant!" Nods again, waiting for further instruction. I withdraw my index finger, walk into the crowd and, all eyes on me, spot a booth.

I slide in, sit down and scan the floor for my Aunt Lanell. The mystery woman. Unless she's had some major reconstructive surgery— and that is, I suppose, a very real possibility—she's not here. So she got lucky early, like Chinaski said, and is already heading out

to her hook-up's house/apartment/dorm room. The image makes
me a little queasy, so I break down the dynamics of the place by
gender.

When it comes to the ladies, there are two kinds in this place.
The first is white, older, powdery and flat-assed and led by sloped,
Catwoman eyebrows, held together in the middle—you can see it
faintly—by a tube of girdle, hungry for sex. This would be my Aunt
Lanell's category. The second is Southeast Asian or Melanesian,
middle-aged women, prim and serious, internationally uppity, tight-
figured in svelte black dresses and bodysuits, just slightly gaudy with
the jewelry, foreign translations of money-speaking lips. The two
enemies are here for the trade: the first pack gives up their wealthy
limp-cocked husbands in exchange for the second pack's broke
boner-ready boys. Each can deal with the loss. They wouldn't be
here otherwise.

And the men, symbiotic to the equation, are either old loner sugar
daddies or young horny foreigners—mostly Afghans and Persians—
in twos and threes.

You look at something like this and almost feel responsible for the
mayhem: so this is just how far the tentacles reach? It goes across
the country, over the pond, right through Europe, and into some
Ottoman village; or it stretches back across the Pacific and drops
into an impoverished Filipino borough. And then it goes backwards,
too, suction-cups some lonely baby boomer into the now. These
geezers are really victims—*that's what they are*—the sacrificial lambs
of sensationalism, white noise, speed, and immediacy. Bling-bling,
Rock the Vote, and Microsoft. They've set themselves up like pins
to be bowled over by my generation.

Chuckie puts the shot and the beer on the table, and I waste no
time. Before I take another breath of air, they're both down into the
system, liquid fuel for illusion. I look around at the quick blur, lis-

ten to 50 wind down. The DJ is a young Southeast Asian in a black fade, sunflower shades over his flat head. He's elated, life spilling out his ears. America, America. He mouths his mic, bellows, "Are you weady for the mother of gawd?"

"Yeah!"

"Are you sho'?"

"Yeah!"

"Get on that dance flo', potty people, 'cause it's a holiday up in this place!"

"Yeah!"

The wolves circle. Madonna's techno-squeak filters through the joint—*dunt, dunt, dunt, dunna dunna nunna nunna, dunt, dunt, dunt, "Holiday!"*—as Chuckie, smiling, swaying, shouts, "Want some more juice?"

The loudness of the place puts you right on the brink of ecstasy. I fight the need to shout above the noise—*dunt, dunt, dunt, dunna dunna nunna nunna, dunt, dunt, dunt*—which seems wrong, almost perverse. I grab Chuckie's shoulder hard, dig into the muscle.

"Juice?" he shouts.

I nod.

"The same?"

I nod again.

Chuckie crosses the room in that high school hallway swagger, and heads turn from both packs. I realize something I missed before. I didn't give Chuckie enough credit, but he's a wanted man in the Pheasant, and it isn't just the hat. Marginally young and marginally rich, he transcends the mutually exclusive terms, at least for a night.

We walk through the leering eyes of the ladies. They can spot subservience with or without the afflicted vision, can connect the dots—*Chuckie's his bitch*—and they're right. If I claim it, I can have any woman I want tonight. The ultimate flattery or the ultimate insult.

I finally disregard personal safety and make eye contact with a lady a couple booths down. Not true: she makes eye contact with me. I can feel her stare for the eternity of seconds. She's twirling an olive on her tongue, nibbling it, enshrining it on the straw of her martini. It's the lady from the lot who smiled at me. Sitting down, she doesn't look all that bad, but who knows what kind of gravitational forces will take over once she stands up.

An eighties song starts into the refrain—*When the walls . . . come tumbling down*—good old John Cougar.

She looks like she's in her late fifties, early sixties, but you can't get a clean read on it with all these perfectly positioned, cavernous pockets of shadows. It's like they hired a Hollywood lighting techie as interior decorator, an airbrush for the flesh in the flesh.

Beneath this post-pubescent mating ritual, I see something that disturbs me. I flash back to childhood, Scott Lane Elementary School, Xavier Lumabacoda: he was the nerd on the playground looking for a friend. That look each day scared me into complicity. She has it now: despite her boldness to peek over at me, deep down she's expecting rejection. She knows I can do without her. She's taking the risk that I've been kind to nerds for decades. And she's right: I have been. I'd give Xavier Lumabacoda an ear, at least, if not the heart. I'd indifferently hear him out. But tonight I feel the urge to set something straight in this henhouse.

I lift an eyebrow, kind of half chuckle, look away at the dance floor, chuckle again, look back. As if I were sitting on a throne of gold, a twenty-eight year old emperor of the sun. The transmission hits home. Her facade implodes. She's fragile as a fossil, this woman. What's worse: she stands—*tumbling down*—and walks off to the bathroom.

My liquor sponsor for the evening has moved to the dance floor.

Mid-eighties George Michael kicks in. Or is it Wham!? The sights interfere with my ability to track the pop chronology. A woman in vertically striped spandex is humping Chuckie's leg. He's got his stubby arms over his head, my drinks in his hands. He's on rhythm, keeping up with the crazy beat, his brain sloshing around in the cranial pocket, the big electric sponge for titillation. It's like the cowboy hat's just holding everything in, midwest head dressing for the wound of unfettered hedonism.

She rips off her shirt and—a tribute, no doubt, to modern history—there's the black sports bra, *S.I.* cover shot of Brandi Chastain on her knees at the World Cup, two straps each digging into a shoulder. She wraps the T into a ball and throws it toward the booths, indisputable American victory.

Someone shouts, "Yeah, baby! You go!"

Temptress, invitation: she takes Chuckie's hat and pulls it down low over her brow. Her stomach and back are spilling over fabric and his big, slightly sloped, long-lashed eyes are glazed with desire. He throws me a thumbs-up. I point in the direction of the restrooms. They're right before the exit, and Chuckie panics. This is his place, his cash, and yet he can't freak an old fogie without me. He twirls his partner, steals back his hat, and heaves her off deeper into the crowd like a folk dance. Before I can get past him, he's at my side.

I grab both drinks, take the shot, chug the beer, finally shout the truth: "I can't stand you!"

"Come on, youngster, just stay another hour!"

"Stop calling me youngster!"

"Lighten up! The ladies are waiting!"

"I! . . . Don't! . . . Like! . . . You!"

He finally hears me. Guess what? He doesn't care. That's how lonely he is. Guess what? I don't care either. He shouts, "Come on! The ladies are waiting!"

The airwaves zoom into the late-eighties. I hear, "Hammer time!"
"I gotta use the head!"
"All right, youngster! I'll have juice for you when you get back!"
"Do that!"

I sit down on a bench outside the restrooms. Behind me is a din-
ing room of glass tables, the lights off, framed photographs of 1920s
New York on the wall. Skyscrapers in black-and-white, team photo
of the Brooklyn Dodgers, a shot of Ella Fitzgerald at the NYC Down-
beat. So the place doubles as a restaurant during the day, a modest
feeding zone in its quieter hours. There are a couple of potted plants
guarding the exit, two young ferns whose fronds extend across the
double doors, head high. People walk right through without knowing they're being touched by something born of this new millennium.
Tickled and blessed by photosynthetic youth. Thinking back on it,
I'd ducked into this place like I was entering a haunted house.

My lady friend comes rushing out the bathroom, right through the
fronds, and exits the Blue Pheasant. I follow her down the flight of
stairs, bound across the lot. I put my hand gently under her elbow
and she stops without turning.

I step around, face her, and smile. "Hi."

We're right there under a kaleidoscope of color, the electric maze.
A nightlight from the street accentuates the deep crow's feet under
her eyes. She does have beautiful eyes, though, luminous pools of
blue and green. I'm waiting for her Blanche DuBois moment, shading her wrinkled face from the trueness of light. She inhales through
her nose, the nostrils flaring. I cannot think of what to say except,
"Can I get you a drink?"

"I'm leaving," she says. She looks off into the lot, without moving
her legs, her shoulders, or anything.

The words come out too fast to control. "I mean at my place.
Would you like to have a drink there?"

She looks down at the ground, over at the street.

"I have olives."

Her gray roots mingle nicely with the golden shimmer of the high-lights. It's visual alchemy, sparkles in a starlit sky, good to look at. I hope she says yes. She raises her eyes, smiling, and—just barely—nods.

I say, "You gotta drive. My ride's inside."

"Okay."

She takes my hand and guides me away from the middle of the lot. We walk along the periphery of the Pheasant in leftover light and struggling moonbeams, not a word between us, no name exchange, no cheesy raison d'être. There's an honesty in the silence, and it's nice.

We get into her Beemer, and before she starts the car we're all over each other. Her mouth tastes of peppermint and cherries and the skin of her neck feels leathery, dry like the epidermis of some desert lizard. I slide my hand underneath her sweater and she hunches her shoulder, gasps, but in an instant relents, giving me access. I reach around with the other hand and make her seat horizontal. One breast comes out and lies flat across her ribs like a pancake. I close my eyes and dive down and tongue the areola, a hungry infant, paramedic on the patient's mouth. CPR of the nipple, erogenous zone rejuvenation. I reach down, palm her across the pelvis, slide a finger into her dryness. I put my mouth out for the other breast and nothing's there, not even a nipple.

I could stop and look up and say *Did it hurt you when they cut it off?* or *I'm glad you're alive and here with me tonight* but I recover gracefully in the act of discovery because I can hear in the held breath above me her fear and shame of exposure and I want her to know it's okay. I move right over the dime of keloid down to her trembling ribs and, to prove for good that I'm unrattled by the flatland scar of breast cancer, I up the sexual ante: "I'm gonna kiss you down there," as I probe with two fingers.

"I have lube."

"No," I say. Tonight she's gonna get a chance to shun the pause, postpone the end, WD-40 the rust, and shine in use. "I want to please you, baby."

"Okay then," she whispers, and there is hope in her voice. "Yes. Yes. Okay."

I move down onto the floor of the passenger seat, and she caresses the top of my head as I wind her G down the thighs, past the knees and surprisingly muscular calves, ankles, feet.

"You have beautiful legs," I say. "You must have been a runner."

"Still am," she says. "I like your olive skin."

"It's just the light."

"Are you Italian?"

I think it over. "Human."

She lifts the leg nearer me and I tell myself, *Don't don't don't think on it. Get Sophocles and Oedipus and Freud out of your brain. Be patient. Don't assess the ironies. Don't—by God—don't enter the figure of Aunt Lanell, pinned somewhere in this suburb recalling her exploits of yesterday to some Afghan youth. Just pet the closely tended, acid-blonde landing strip. Kiss the glistening at the long, gray mouth of the groin.*

Bring this poor woman to life.

Well, I think, *I'm ready,* but I know right before contact that it's just about to end.

I'm in, in, in, then out. In, in, in, out. In, out. In, out. Out. Down. It won't happen. Can't. I push myself up, wipe my face across the forearm and wrist, plop into the bucket seat, sticky hamstrings on the velvet, say—*what else?*—"I'm really sorry."

She spins and twists, buttons up, thrusts her hips forward, slides back into the G. I'm amazed by her dexterity: I'm sitting limp as a corpse, and she's already in the fucking lot, leaning against the car, the placid eyes of a mortician.

"Make sure you lock the door," she says.

Then her own side slams, the car fidgets, and she's headed back into the joint. Another round of eros at the Pheasant.

You know how this kind of stuff goes: I'd like to chase her down a second time, whatever her name is, nuzzle her neck and kiss the word into her ear: *Sorry*. But deep down, everyone understands why we're here. The whole thing's anticlimax. I mean, if there's such a thing as a victory lap, then there's a defeat lap, too.

35

I Wake Up

I WAKE UP filled to the throat with corporate bile, my larynx and the lining cilia clogged with shit. I wake up spitting, like some vile reptilian creature of the jungle. On the rug, in the sink, out the bay window, right into the oval eye of the mirror. I run down to the lake, unleash a string of phlegm that wings into the water's edge, run back up the hill, gagging.

You know how this goes: the apocalypse has arrived: judgment, aka evaluations. Today I get "eval'd" by a man who named his dog Boy Millionaire, whom his coworkers call Glory Days behind his back and his kids Upchuck to his face, who pumps Pink and Eminem in the company lot as if he were prom-bound, who drops a perverse twist of a presidential adage into any conversation within a higher-up's hearing range ("The buck stops with the buck"), who hid in an empty stall of the men's room to see if I washed my hands (I purposely didn't after spotting him in the reflection of the paper towel dispenser), who nonetheless has kissed my ass for half a month running in the hopes that the word gets passed along to good old Uncle, his boss and self-made hero, the goal he'll never reach: this guy is going to play the Man today?

Yes.

Assessed by a peon, the heir of Willy Loman: he's gotta find something substantive enough to say I'm not quite there yet (the slap) and yet (the stroke) that I'm doing much better than expected. He probably got back from the Pheasant last night and poured drunkenly over ten-dollar words and Hewlett-Packard How To books to get the language just right.

So this morning I'm hyperattuned to every sound in the world, even the commentary contained in my own head. I can't keep it down anymore; it's like an earthquake of observations; I'll "eval" the world right back. I knuckle at the collar of my shirt, walking—*click* goes the bathroom light, aftershave slap of a palm across each cheek, smooth as a good deal gone down, out the door of the guesthouse, a step down the walkway, stop (*goddammit*). Back up the walkway, forgot to lock the door. I'm inside the guesthouse and (*goddammit*) forgot to lock the back door. Free-for-all for any thieves tough enough to hike the hill to the estate. Fuck it, can't be late. U-turn in an ugly bitch of an knee-twisting pirouette, limping cursing right out the front door, which swings open by its hinges and keeps swinging like the double doors of an Old West saloon.

Limp right down the walk, snag the keys from the pocket of my ride which is miraculously there, and—*click*—the lock pops, shrug open the handle, slink into the seat. Start the car, a little too hard, go right to the madness of Don Amadeus and his tribute to the planet of Jupiter, see a hummingbird buzz from the gutter of the guesthouse to the juniper bushes of the lane, blurred fast-forward, rewind. I'm pounding on the thrashed dashboard to the fury of No. 41, accelerating down the hill of my uncle's property to the outer world.

And now the race: straight up Old Almaden like a corpuscle of blood through the vein, California-stopping through stop signs, rolling through lights so yellow they're red. I hit the expressway and cut off anyone slow enough to get cut, Darwinian principles in the midst of concrete and glass, the evolutionary Gallapagan birds and bugs of the Silicon Valley in steel-boned, rubber-mouthed, leather-feathered sedandom. Whipping through time, doubling the efficacy of predecessors, even with the dollar down and Persian Gulf gas rates on the rise. Bumper stickers on the older beat-up models as if to say *I'm still alive, I've got some personality left, see? I'm still around. Vroom, vroom.*

Already at the 85 West entrance looping around, people trying to pass with no available space, drivers stretching, reaching, putting up palms and fingers and faces of at minimum a grimace, maybe more. Coffee cups and routinely brushed-on makeup and Egg McMuffins flying past my true civil advantage of stoicism. Of professionalism. I—*click*—snap out the borrowed cell from Santa Clara Real Estate West, hit 85 West full speed, thumb the number of the first superior on the corporate ladder, the author of my unpublished eval, squeeze a shoulder to the ear, say, "Chuckie."

Nothing worse in the white noise vehicular chaos than silence. "Hey, Chuckie."

The eyeballs are bouncing from object to object to object to object.

Finally: "No, I'm fine. Great. . . . Yeah, I'm gonna be a little late. . . . What's that? Already late. Trust me, won't happen again. . . . I'm on the last rope of hope? I know, I know, no excuses."

Green light, yellow light, red light above, cop car whirling blue and red in the rearview mirror.

"Oh, you shithead—no, not you, Chuckie. Fuck. I'll call you back, man. Promise."

Hazards on, lane by lane, slowing, stopping, shift into park, leave the car running. Finger the—*click*—dropping glove compartment, finger the insurance and registration, finger the electric window down, feel the warm-wind breath of passing cars, driver-side elbow out, biceps over the lock. Be a storyteller, obsequious, the whole spineless nine yards. Pretend I'm twelve, just a boy, begging uncle for tickets to the game. Think about uncle's lecture on the ways of the world, the price to play. Curl up and debass the voice, remember the red and blue lights behind you brightening, remember your rap sheet and the three-minute stint on Channel 11, eradicate the rebellion spurred by testosterone and personal history and the easy lure of self-destruction.

"I'm *so* sorry, officer—My kid was throwing up this morning—Everything he'd ever eaten came out his mouth—He couldn't go to school—second straight day—happens again tomorrow, he's off to the hospital—And the wife wouldn't let me leave—said it wasn't fair—I felt bad—I stayed and hugged her for half an hour—Ran out, tripped, and tore a ligament in my knee—My life is going so shitty, officer—and now I'm late to work—And now a ticket—or a felony—or jail—I'll—"

"Just relax for a minute and turn off your car. Let me see your paperwork."

"I don't want to go to jail—I don't want—"

"Are there any warrants out for your arrest?"

"No, I just don't want my kid to have to visit me at the—"

"Are you on parole or probation?"

"No, sir. Absolutely not. Oh, my God, what have I done?"

"You're not going to jail, Mr. Tusifale. That's not how the system I work for works. Now listen to me."

"I just can't—"

"Listen to me."

Now the waiting, the unimmediacy of a powerless moment. Tech and modernity and salary going right down the gutter. The race is being lost: SUVs, trucks, vans, sedans, jalopies, mopeds are passing, me curled up gelatinously in the best furniture-moving clothes there are, T-shirt and jeans.

"Yes, sir," I say, "I'm sorry."

"Do you know what the fine for driving in the diamond lane is?"

Diamond lane?—Fuck. "Two hundred—"

"—seventy-one dollars. That's what that sign says, now, doesn't it?"

"Yes, sir. Two-seventy-one, sir."

"Now, I'm just going to give you a warning."

Just a boy, get the tickets, just a boy.

"Any other officer would cite you. And some for not buckling up."

Who the fuck has the time to wear their seat belt? Just a boy, just a boy.

"I usually do, officer. Always do. Was just running so late. Worried about my—"

"I know." Registration and insurance are handed back, the ticket bought, only the lecture left. "I've got a boy, too. We got hearts inside. Now. If what's important to you is your child, you've got to start prioritizing properly. Understand?"

"Yes, officer. Yes, sir. You guys are good people."

Probably'd ten-on-one me if I made a peep. Rodney King redux.

"If you get into an accident, where's that going to leave your son? Or your wife, for that matter? Or you? Or the people you've—God help us—injured? You see where I'm going with this?"

"Yes, sir. I have to stop thinking about myself."

"Exactly. Every day I pray I don't have to zip up another body bag at work."

In this lustrous part of San José? Gimme a break. Just a boy, just a boy. "Just a boy."

"What was that?"

"Nothing, sir. Was just thinking about my boy."

"Well, that's what I'm trying to tell you. Get your priorities in order. Are we straight on that?"

"Straight, officer. Straight."

"Have a nice day."

I start the car, gently this time, pull the seat belt down when he looks up from his reports. Wait for him to pass, nod and wave when he looks over, indicate the blinking reemergence into the race, into the infinite bustle, stick the arm straight out for emphasis. Look over the left shoulder, move leadenly into traffic as if I were in an Amish horse and carriage, thoroughly lose the race until the black-and-white's taillights are gone. Then pick up the pace and use the goddamned rearview mirrors like they're meant to be used. Pop the cell—*click*—finger Chuckie's button—*beet-doot-doot-doot-deet-doot-doot*—wait for the pickup.

"Chuckie. . . . Yeah, sure, I'll hold."

Nothing worse than the computerized rundown of the morning's plummeting Dow Jones backed by—*click*—*Eine Kleine Nachtmusik.* They should turn off one or the other. *Business and art, together, never run smooth.*

"Chuckie. What? . . . Yeah. . . . Well, that's exactly right."

Nothing worse than a punk-ass superior like Glory Days guessing your alibi, which this time actually happens to be true.

"Why would I lie, man, and to you of all people? . . . Nah, nah, this cop just gave me a little warning and a sit-down. I'll be in in ten. Don't worry. Or nine now. I'll be there in fucking minutes. I'll be right there."

Click—the cell snaps shut, both hands grip the wheel like a driver in training for the German Autobahn. New freeway now, north to the formerly known Barbary Coast via 280, "the most beautiful freeway in the world," whose untouched rolling hills and ridiculously wide lanes are so out of place in this valley you've just got to speed, high on the unfamiliar. Acceleration and whine of the engine and then— brake, downshift, brake, downshift: bumper-to-bumper traffic! Stop-and-go for a mile. Five minutes. Shit. Long time. Lose time. Lose money. Lose self watching the instinctively aerodynamic v-flock of birds soar over the most beautiful pollutive artery in the world. The uncurling fingers and palms return into gesture form, out the window, the last free space left on the freeway. Private-public boogie sessions going down with a brainless house DJ. Unfazed, generic, thoroughly entertained Americans. Everyone gets along if they're shut off in their own house, sealed up in their own car, the visors twisted to block the right and left view both, an idyllic *American Idol* in pump on the system.

"Fuckin' cop," I say, twisting the rearview mirror toward myself. I meet my eyes and wink. Calm, cool, but white as chalk, whitening with every blink. "He wouldn't make it a day in the business world. Lecturing asshole. See a ring on my finger? I don't think so. A tanline on my finger? What kind of investigating asshole are you? Do I look stupid enough to be a father? Or a husband? Asshole."

Traffic spreads at last, and I pick it up and slide into place. Stanford exit: three miles. The movement again, good illusion of movement, revolution of tires. No squad cars anywhere to be found. Time is rolling now as fast as time's inhabitants. I straighten the mirror onto the car directly behind me, too directly behind, but not for long.

I speed up but gain nothing. Ascend a minor incline at the Foothill exit and coming down it the cars in their lanes look like beads on the strings of an abacus. A 2006 Hummer two lengths ahead is slowing down. Shiny spit-black coating, tinted windows, tank on wheels, white nonchalant elbow out the window like a flag of fleshy bone, a statement: unperturbed by the rush, not late for life.

I move into the sacred unused diamond lane, remembering the last Hummer I'd seen, or had registered, the modern American family of the leash, remembering my newfound anonymous friend, his sprinting through the shadows of Campbell, accelerate past a (last year's trend) Beemer and finger the passenger side window down. The Hummer is so high off the ground I have to lean all the way across the seat to find the driver.

"Hey!"

Salt-and-pepper-haired man looks over slowly and then down, speeds up. I stay with him at sixty-five miles an hour.

"Hey! We're on the most beautiful freeway in the world! It's all ours!"

He snickers at me or at my car or at both me and my car. The son of a bitch.

The engine on this relic's about to blow up, but I don't give a fuck. Not any longer. He pretentiously raises his eyebrows, and I shout, "Join the army if you wanna drive a fucking tank around town!"

The monstrous Hummer's wheels sound like it's in an invisible wind tunnel of its own.

"You Schwarzenegger wannabe! You ain't no Terminator! You got nothing!"

He tilts his head with amusement and pulls his elbow flag in, as if his skin is being corroded by my words, the Rolex shining against the darkness of his tightly wrapped leather interior. Condescending eyeblink, effeminate purse of the lips, tinted window rising.

Before it's sealed shut he veers over and cuts me off, his bumper tapping my front end. I swerve left to avoid an accident, shouting, "Hey!" as the door kisses the divider, then seems to be stuck to it, grinding into it, steel on concrete. His tank rapidly shrinking into a black dot as I slice back across the lane to regain equilibrium but go airborne instead. All this in an instant.

I know, suspended in the silence, that it's all over.

Time has finally stopped and will finish itself off. . . .

Then the world slams a palace door across my face and I'm spinning through the wash cycle of—"arrrrrrrrgggg!"—two-hundred-and-seventy-one dollar diamond-lane pavement of the most beautiful freeway in the world until—*click*—everything in the 1982 two-door Honda Civic goes black.

36

The Tup Tup Tup Tup Tup

THE *tup tup tup tup tup* of slowing vehicles. Their labyrinthine undersides like the roof of the mouth. The wiry tread of tires straight-lined in the spin. Then the exhaust. No one stops. Only the vehicular slowdown occurs, sand lining up for the middle of the hourglass before the freefall. Above my head, behind my body, a hundred feet past the 280 North exit, the race resumes: my spill means merely minutes lost to the masses, nothing more. It's like a *Godfather* hit: it's not personal, it's just *tup tup tup tup tup* business. I too have lost minutes before, have lost a lifetime of minutes.

I am thinking of the middle-aged man in the Hummer. I do not think of the feeling in my legs, which I twitchingly amazingly still have—and would certainly be thankful to have—had I thought for even a moment of the alternative. I do not think of the alternative. That's how I've been taught: everything is an alternative. Nor had I thought of the *tup tup tup tup tup* of my beating heart when I'd first awoken and known, in a widening pool of my own blood, that the tractor tires of the Jeep Wrangler treading 3-D into pavement would flatten any part of my body not flattened already.

Am I a stain in the road? A drop of bird shit on the roof? A dead branch shed by the manzanita bushes lining the side of the freeway? Am I, at most, worth someone stopping?

I cough *tup tup tup* the blood curdling in, up, and out my throat like an angry Nevadan geyser. The tractor tire and the swerving Jeep Wrangler gone. Two other Jeeps just like it, gone. Mine, the 1982 two-door Honda Civic, done. A smoking heap of uninsured junkyard scrap metal. Yet still, despite their horizon-riding, fading-vision gonedness, more cars come and come and keep coming, climb out the opposite horizon line of the Fremont Hills. Jeep Wranglers, Ford Rangers, Volkswagen Bugs. Lexus hatchbacks, Mustang convertibles, a juiced cherry-red '62 Impala. Buses and utility trucks. Sixteen-wheelers. Motorcycles and, somehow, the beehive buzz of a moped. I cough *tup tup tup* again, so spasmodically that my cheek kisses the pavement, a quick chicken peck.

No one stops. My eyes are on the undersides again. Eyes wide, head leaking, supine. Between the flash of automotive arrival and departure, the pink stuck diaphanous sky. Now the cry of nearing sirens, their cry a distant song of death, whose death I do not know. It cannot be the death of the prim and proper middle-aged man, gone forever into the squeeze of the undulating traffic.

I, Silicon Valley native ingrate, Donkey Kong king at age four, bastard child of the Data Generation, am conditioned to the flashing thoughts of my own head, the flashing photos from a satellite, the flashing lights of an intersection, the flashing international news briefs, flashing billboard commercials, flashing Hollywood films, flashing clocks, flashing perverts, flashing finally boring heroes, flashing, flashing, flashing your regrets of the past.

That's what it is: The middle-aged man has something you don't. A verifiable past, a measurable yesterday, and thus a verifiable future, a measurable tomorrow. He had known, too. He had salt-and-pepper hair in the way that salt-and-pepper hair says, I have a past. And this is the result. *Hey, asshole. I have a story.*

But I have one, too. It's just that it's cut right down the middle of everything. I am a half-breed American man who can claim the brown pride of Polynesia or the white wisdom of western culture, land on opposite ends of the valley. I have been the best and I have been the worst. I am smart and yet I am tough, or reverse it. Walking through the hallways of decorum and posing in shiny ambition or sludging across the swamps of gutters and tiptoeing about in rocky prison yards. I know the mermaids on the bed of seaweed and I know the barnacles on the bottom of the boat. I have loved God and lost him and I have tried to regain him and failed. I have tried to love in an era of lovelessness. I have ridden both the GOP elephant and the Jeffersonian donkey both and have been tossed from their saddles through no poor handling of my own. I have written poetry in a hallway of charcoal portraits and have walked across the street to spend ten bucks at a liquor store on porn. I am beautiful and I am ugly, noble and depraved, I see too much and am therefore confused as hell; I am trying desperately for the rights to a story, something that lines up, goddammit, that lines up.

But there is only the *tup tup tup* of the tires on the speed bumps of the divider like the *tup tup tup* of the blood in the throat and the piercing song of the ambulance sirens rising. What is it that makes no one stop? That pushes forward onward outward upward? What plants this carnal chaos, the swallower of reflection?

I must stop now and think. For good, goddammit, for good, or my head's gonna explode. Feel an urgency I've never quite felt before. Linked—and what's this?—to the *tup tup tup* of the final moment.

Cars again!

Cars always again!

Not one square inch of pavement gets a rest, pavement serving over 99 billion miles of tire tread!

Dread the day the piston-pumping came and kept coming out from the horizon and over the hills and down through the fertile plain of my head to ride it, electrodes, tendrils, cortexes, smoke like clouds out the ears and nostrils and even the *tup tup tup* gurgling mouth. Dread the day I walked into Wendy's and ordered nothing, burning for a five-star meal. Dread the day this life destroyed my laughter, my fear of loneliness. Dread the day, the first one, where I had no discernible thought of bedding down a woman, all the yearning gone. Dread women, dread men. Dread the *tup tup tup* of my throat, my fucking throat. Dread what I am and what I see, dread what I hear, what I think I know.

"Can you hear me?"

I *tup tup tup* say, "Middle-aged—"

"Don't speak. Don't say a word."

"—bastard."

"Don't speak!"

They are latching on to me in all ways now: strapping devices to my arm, a wind-cold mask over the mouth still *tup tup tup* spurting like a fountain. Everyone is touching me in every place except the pockets, and then even that.

"Here's his wallet. Do you have any relatives? Don't speak!"

"How about this?" someone says. "*You* don't speak, rook."

"Hey! I've been on this job for eighteen months!"

"Act like it then."

"Hell with you!"

"Yeah, that's right. Let's get pissed off and feel proud and good while the poor fuck dies."

I swallow the *tup tup tup* ensuing argument and realize that I am the poor fuck of fatal reference. It hits me like a car crash. I have not been prepared accordingly. I am like a medieval bride on the baptismal eve she sees her very first cock: I am shocked. I have seen it at a distance so far off that the word, a breathless, ubiquitous, dark-eyed foreigner, has become less personal than business itself. I haven't pondered the word in ages, not since Cowboys and Indians with BB guns on the rooftops of Scott Lane Elementary School. In the last half month, the insouciant web of the Silicon Valley mocking its very existence: "We killed 'em, boys, knocked 'em *tup tup tup*." Or, "That deal was *tup tup tup* in the water before it ever begun." And, "Better alive than *tup tup tup*."

It has been there all along, hovering behind the cars on the horizon, as pink and living as the sky, the tender abscess of the sun.

Maybe, I think, *it is the sun. An old wound. The moon's eye. It is all that filth up there gathering for the big boom.*

Apocalyptic energy blurs my eyes and someone yells out, "We're losing him!"

But I will not go. I need to figure the sky and the middle-aged man and my evaporating life out for good.

I will not go.

I levitate onto the cloudy plastic bed and then I am rolling. I can find resilience somewhere within beneath the *tup tup tup* gurgling blood where I've heard words like soul spirit faith hope love take *tup tup tup* residence. I am lifted high off the ground by the thought of the words into the inside quarter of an ambulance. I am floating on plastic and then dropped into hygienic sanctity, everything inside these walls orderly and clean. Heavenly middle-of-the-cream-puff white. The faces youthful, angelic, the prodding massaging fingers, the coaxing words—"*Come on, baby! Don't give up, baby! I got you now, I got you!*"—selling me into believing, even after all the mess, that I'm worth something.

I see the *tup tup tup* of the intravenous machine sucking into itself, plastic-hearted prune, looking down on me like a streetlight.

I will end with this *beeeeep*—

"Give it a go!"

"Go!"

—thought: I am unbothered that Chuckie Chinaski and La Dulce and Tali and General Cyrus Rohan and Sharon and my eternally split-up parents and six daddies and torn Uncle Rich and the middle-aged bastard in the Hummer or whomever the fuck *beeeeep*—

"Again!"

"Ready!"

"Go!"

—won't visit. I've been frilled and prepped like a wedding cake for this day.

Death?

Well.

37

Of Course

OF COURSE, I live.

Three days down in this sticky hospital bed. Yesterday I got my mouth back, can painfully move it around to speak a few words at a time. My tongue feels like a fat slab of raw tri-tip in my mouth. I've got oxygen tubes stuck up my nose, but the doctor said the X-ray showed that I'm recovering. My own quiet room may be a long hike up the stairs. Nobody came to visit me in the darkness, no one comes now in the light. Not even my uncle, the crossed-up old soldier who went back to the war for more. Tali called, but her maternal, disappointed tone made me say, "No . . . I don't . . . want . . . to see . . . you." It's just like the freeway: everyone busy during these happy days of our lives.

I didn't expect anything different. You have to give to receive with this deal, an aphorism that seems to work fairly well for others. For me, I've just never really known what to give or to whom, so I've given everything to anyone in my vicinity and haven't asked for a damned thing back. That way everyone's covered or at least can shut up. There's more to it, of course, always more, but I'm fair: got no complaints. No celebratory dances either. I mean, I'm always expecting at the end of these messes to be dead, and the only real problem I foresee whenever it happens is that there will be no means to express my wholehearted gratitude.

The nurse says, "Here's your discharge papers, hon."

Between watching her flitter in and out of my room, I reread an old tale, the only book on the floor worth reading. The protag's unmentioned problem, a missing body part that he wouldn't talk about, should make me appreciate the scale of my own problems. I have a few lacerations on my face, across my neck, my chest and abdomen are swollen, a lung is partially collapsed, but I didn't go into shock, my heart didn't stop, I have no concussion, no internal bleeding, and I am not, after all, Jake Barnes, with the worst war wound you could walk away with as a man.

The nurse is above me. She detaches tubes and yanks out needles with the speed of a pit crew changing tires at Nascar. Probably helps that she doesn't give me any eye contact. She's thoroughly unimpressed by my story, the hairy chest, the little boo-boos.

To get by today, I should abdicate Hemingway's belief that a man can be destroyed but not defeated. Head and heart wounds aside, he'd pass me up as a potential protagonist for a story. He'd review my bio and general disposition and discover that I lacked the fierce clarity of his fishermen. He'd walk past the tiny Filipina nurses and into the clean well-lit room with a greased and thick-stocked double-barrel shotgun tucked tightly under his arm and pump a .762 German-manufactured shell into my chest. That's how he'd read me: a shivering foal with a broken leg sprawled on the hay-scattered floor of the barn.

He'd say, *You got no follow-through, son.*

I'd say, *Well. Nothing out there worth following through on, Papa.* *Nada y pues nada really truly means nothing now.*

I remember when my sixth-grade teacher, Mrs. Silveira, pulled me aside one autumn afternoon, the light tinted in gold like some antiquated Byzantine mosaic, and said, "In my twenty-eight years of teaching, you have the best chance of all my children to be president someday."

I'd thought, *What a nice lady,* and told no one what she'd said.

Later that same day I threw in *ignorant and desperate* as I watched her ignore the foreign-born Vietnamese, Mexican, and Filipino non-hopefuls for the White House.

Congressman Norman Mineta believed in me too, signed my papers for appointment to West Point. He was very sad when I failed the physical and even sent me off to a doctor specializing in spondy-lolisthesis, a degenerative back condition whose symptoms I'd fished up out of a medical dictionary while awaiting the army physician. He never knew, the poor sap. Hours before the examination at the Presidio, I'd read about Mishima faking insanity to avoid flying a kamikaze jet, a paradox I still don't get to this day (*You have to be sane to fly your plane into a ship, Mishima-san*) and I thought, *He loved his country but loved his life more and I at minimum question both.*

"Any conditions?" the army doctor'd asked.

"Spondylolisthesis," I'd said, without blinking.

This was an hour after I'd whipped out fifteen pull-ups, topping the list of my group of candidates. Two hours after the facilitator had noted my foot speed on the shuttle run.

"I see," said the doctor, nodding.

He may as well have said, *You don't believe in anything, do you?*

Back then I would have said with pride, *No, I don't,* but now I'd say, *I'd like to.* Or borrow a line from Brando: "What've ya got?"

My current physician returns for the check out examination. She's a lovely Hindu named Dr. Patel, whose kindness reassures me that under all the body of knowledge there's a caring mother, a sister, or at least a daughter in there. Early forties, weary-eyed and wise, traits that seem to co-exist too often. I can tell that she's seen a lot of life's shit even before entering this ward of death.

She smiles, adjusting her gadgetry. The steel of the stethoscope jolts my heart, and she says, "Sorry there. Just for a little bit, okay?" I can smell curry on her breath, her doctor's jacket, her hair. "Deep breath, Mr. Tusifale."

I take all the spices in, wanting to say something nice. I manage through the wincing, "Are you . . . doing . . . all right . . . today?"

"Yes," she whispers, still investigating my body. Her hands are magical, so soothing that I want to sleep. In the interest of what she'll say next, though, I stay awake. "Now, you have been in quite a hassle, Mr. Tusifale. I am a bit concerned, you know."

I nod, look up at her with what I hope is tenderness, a reciprocity in spirit and goodwill. I don't know why, but I care that she cares.

"Am I . . . okay?"

"You are asking me?"

I blink yes.

"Well, let me say that I am encouraged. You are strong. And you have made a good recovery in so short a time."

"Okay."

"Now I want you to get some rest at home."

"Okay."

She nods, smiles. Something big is coming. "But first I must ask you a question."

I blink in the affirmative again.

"The paramedics reported that when you went under, you said you wanted to die."

Hearing this makes me lose my breath.

"Do you want to maybe talk to a volunteer about it?"

"About . . . what?"

"Well." The gentleness behind the wiry gold-framed glasses makes me feel almost shameful. Taking up her time, needing her expertise, involving her in my confusion. "What you were talking about in the ambulance."

"No."

"You are sure?"

"Yes."

She pats my knee. "I will be back, okay?"

I close my eyes to rest. Open them a few seconds later and find again the lifeless machinery and laminated posters of knees and joints found in any office of Western medicine. The stuff that works without thought on the body, the gadgetry and knowledge that helps load the dice in our favor for a while.

I stand to see what life is going to feel like after the crash. I'm a little wobbly, but I don't need to sit down. It's as if the accident occurred from the inside out, not the outside in. Amazing the kind of punishment a body can take. That it was built to forgive you of forsaking it. I'd leave right now if it weren't for the wisdom and kindness of another human being. The doctor putting out for the cause, retying her profession to its original purpose of healing.

I open a drawer and find alcohol swabs and ammonia capsules and soap packets. Needles sealed in see-through plastic and a dozen different kinds of Band-Aid. When I slide it shut, the lock clicks like a fingernail on formica. Above the counter the cabinet is also open and I investigate, not knowing what I'm looking for, but somehow knowing that I'll leave it where I find it. The moment I have this thought I come upon a framed photograph, face down beneath a stack of carbons.

She's young and she's happy, surrounded by Indians at an outdoor market, the eyes, nose and mouth of the swaddled baby in her arms centering the photograph. Bringing it peace. My breath catches again. Second time in five minutes.

I put the photo back and drift, intent on tapping this emotion, all the content that matters. The gold in this office, the real fuel, the story of a life. I imagine the worst reason for the picture being hidden, that core fear of all parents who watch the infant sleep for the first time, and she's back.

I slink onto the patient's bench. "I'm sorry."

"Not at all," she says. "A doctor's office is more boring than most think."

I nod, smile, I wonder.

"Well, thank you for waiting."

"Yes."

She sits down on her doctor's stool and rolls slowly toward me. She leans forward and squints, as if trying to better make out the lashes of my eyes. Then she pulls back, upright now, and says, "Do you mind if I ask you again?"

"No. It's . . . okay."

"Do you feel," she says, reaching out for my hand, "as if you're going to hurt yourself?"

I swallow the dryness in my throat, look down. She's holding a pink slip of some kind.

"No."

"If it is not too much before I sign you out, could you repeat to me how you feel, Mr. Tusifale?"

There must be things to do, and reasons for doing them. People to find, and reasons for finding them.

"I want . . . to live," I hear myself say. "Of course."

38

I Feel Some Kind of Liberty

I FEEL some kind of liberty in my bones and my blood today. If the job from NOW comes through, I'll take it, heal during my first week of work. This morning I don't know what I'm going to do except defy the doctor's orders. Because rest can wait. Somehow keeping the rules would be disrespectful to life.

I take to the road on my own, the Bridgestone Trailblazer beneath me, heading south from Old Almaden Road, breathing the dry air deeply through my nose. My lungs are hot at first, but not burning, and when the mind takes over less than a half mile into the ride, I settle into the pain okay.

The tall brush of the yellow, distant, unadorned hills is pushed by the hot wind into rows of diagonal lines. On the road ahead are farmhouses with wide lots and double entrances separated by a home-made batting cage, an outhouse on the lawn, stacks of hay bales. Storage barns and water towers and horse apples in the driveways. American flags and political stickers on the old school mailboxes at the edge of the street, a hundred yards from the houses. The plots of land stretch out in no particular pattern because these homes were built one at a time.

The oaks and acacias thicken. The shadows from their careless branches widen over the low-shingled farmhouses. I see a white-backdropped banner in red letters over the road up ahead:

NEW ALMADEN
1854

It hasn't changed much by virtue of space, perhaps—it's small and not conducive to carpet-bombing construction—but I'm sure its day will come. This valley has gone through worse facelifts than wiping a quaint town off the map.

But still I hope for this time warp of a town, if only to provide a reminder of something, though I'm not sure what. You feel as if you're in Yoknapatawpha County, 1929, crawling along the yellow lines of a giant storybook. The post office has one door, one room, one window, and when I bike up the little wooden walkway it creaks under the tires like an old Victorian. I pull back onto the main road and pass two little outlets with wooden bridges over a shiny stream. Get suspicious glances from ladies in scarves watering their vegetables on their knees.

The houses out here have names and copper plaques. You pass the Randol Family House and the Robert Scott Home and La Casita de Adobe, and if you go far enough down the Alamitos road there's a ranch set deep in the woods with a wrought-iron fence at the entrance and the words *A Day's Lovely Glen* welded across the bars of the gate. A restaurant called La Foret sits aside a lush creek of pine and jasmine. No set schedule for business. I watch a bobcat big as a groundhog scuttle up a precipice of ivy with raw meat in its mouth, the domesticated cats crouching on the porches in fear and jealousy. A family of turkeys crosses the street with confidence. Every now and then a car comes, often a Ford truck with tires high as the rooflines.

I ride on decidedly, my lungs still warm, feeling almost undamaged.

At the end of town I enter the Deep Gulch, a tunnel through the green that reaches up the hill like a giant brown arm. I start the mile-long climb to the Rotary Furnace atop Silvermine Plateau. Manzanita huddles in the crook of the branchless cedar trunks. Ivy covers the base of every tree, like the first line of defense, green soldiers, green battalions. In the shine of the morning sun, the leaves of the cedar branches look like snowflakes, like glitter, stars in a mild sky. Moss shrouds the skin of the trees, fluorescent as seaweed, easy on the eye, a dress shirt for the body and arms of the wild oaks. I can see the shoe prints of the steeds carrying their overfed rangers, the zigzagging prints of anxious dogs caught between instinct and yielding to the loud biped with the leash. Everywhere the organism of the surrounding wilderness seethes with animal scent. I am doing my damnedest, like the dog, not to think too much. To stay on the trail and let the greater force that I can't and won't understand drag me along.

Let me bike up this damned dirt trail in peace, safe from myself and my own corrupt heart, hopeless soul, let me be clean of the connection to anyone else, let the tang of each sour step *quicken me all into verb, pure verb.* I'm closing in on the silver mine, escorted by the low spreading silver clouds, the path barely visible. If this is as close to heaven as I'll get, it's just enough to make the next blind bend in the trail, and then the next. The cool mist of the nearing hilltop collects at the tip of the nose and—*You can say it, man, say it!*—how good the clean condensation feels on the insides this early morning.

But think on none of it, just follow the long winding road up to the sky, breathe in, breathe out, one more revolution on the crank.

Already at the crest of the hill in a bath of light: the promise of a new day, a better vision, of regeneration. The big sell, the big purchase. My lungs open up to the molecules of untainted oxygen left in this valley. Whatever has survived the onslaught of toxins and emissions and ejaculations must be here at the end of the trail, farthest from the exhaust of man, this sequestered, green, natural, orchestral hall where the birds have made their final flight.

I pedal beneath their position and they don't scare but sing stronger for the sake of the last song, which may come now without warning (though we know there were warnings: this life is one big declarative warning), this irreversible slalom to the void, to the nethers, wherever we end up, however we end, whyever. Whether we began with an incoherent evolutionary grunt—*ugh!*—or a seventh-day kiss on the forehead from the deity—*smack!*—what we are now is too much, too vast in scope, too covetous of knowledge, too close to the mystery of this thing. *Reckless spirits yearning in desire to follow knowledge like sinking stars beyond the utmost bounds. . . .*

We're about to pull the green curtain on the magic of the wizard and discover that we're all just sniveling dogs.

I'm nearing Hidalgo Cemetery, and I put one hand up to shield my eyes like a horse with blinders. Deny, deny, deny until you die. I ride past death and its weed-laden cement house of bones. The birds are now fully aware of me. I step off the bike in the beauty of a morning's silence, breathing in, breathing out.

Here under the wooden beams of the silver mines that have rounded from the rain of a hundred and fifty years, discolored, frail, eaten, I remember two lines of a western poem from the last century— ". . . *the great deep mine, emptied, seeping methane, employing no one . . .*"—and then I see the body hanging listlessly in the shadows, dividing the dark hole into the dank mouth of the San Cristobal mine, wet from the soft rain of yesterday, the head collapsed on the collarbone, the limp palms open against the hip, the hiking shoes dangling heavy from the knees like ripe fruit.

I knew this would be his end. Just as I knew as a boy that my folks were stuck at the starting line, just as I knew that I was lost from the first little squeak out my throat, just as I know that this country is finished. I have no inclination to cut him down or look him in the dead-yellow jaundiced eyes and cry out, *Why? Why? How could you do this, Uncle?* For once, this place makes perfect sense. I turn from the sight, mount my bicycle, and head blazing down the path, the gravity of the real fake world in which I live too strong to brake against.

39

Nowhere to Go

NOWHERE TO GO in the dead middle of the day and so I bike slowly out to my former place of employment, a house of unread books, the last spot of bloody infamy with good Cyrus. I think I'm fine. On the ride out to Santa Clara, I battle the inner part of me that doesn't care if I am or not.

My uncle would have liked Cyrus. He would have understood the loneliness, he would have seen sadness where others hadn't seen a thing, he would have related to the lifetime restraints of backstory, the pride of leadership, of assuming the mantle of protecting your brothers and sisters from thinking about the grave. Maybe I should have brought them together to keep my uncle alive another day.

The library is huge now, twice as big as the old building. It looks like a cluster of colorful Legos on steroids, all blown up out of proportion. You wouldn't think that the yellowing leather-bound books inside are collecting dust. It's like they spent money on a new stadium for the same team. You still lose the game.

Plenty of people here, mostly kids. The rack is packed with all kinds of bikes, so I park next to a tree, leaning it upright, not locking it. I can't lock it because I don't have a lock, never thought to buy one.

I walk over to the pay phone, dial Tali's number.

"Hey, sis."

She tells me two things—"NOW passed you over" and "Uncle left something for you at the U.S. Air terminal at the airport"—and hangs up.

I drop two more quarters into the pay phone, thinking that efficient people are sometimes not prudent, and dial 911. "Yeah. Silvermine Plateau in New Almaden? There's a good man who needs burying up there."

Yes, my uncle had heard my spiel before from superior sources. Heard it from his own head and heart, dual forces far greater than old Me Generation me. This flunky of a project, his last ars poetica. What a setup. The nonbeliever as would-be heir to his misfortunate fortune, his daughter's flustered replacement.

How could I have convinced him that cowardice at Hamburger Hill was exonerated by a second tour, by his two Bronze Stars for Valor, by a Purple Heart? He'd have said that the deal, nephew, is a life for a life—Old Testament rigeur—and anything shy of that is merely rhetoric. Well, I could've said, if you'd had died in battle I would have never gotten the chance to know you as anything but an abstract face that looked halfway like my own, someone connected to my mother's childhood but hardly connected to me. We would have never had the chance, Uncle, to be friends.

Maybe it required the end of our friendship to keep him alive. That I'd gotten cruel with the truth: "Don't get down on yourself and your thirty-five-year-old fatal flaw because nobody cares any longer. Kids don't play Cowboys and Indians anymore. And as far as Cousin Nina goes, this beautiful inclination of yours to examine memory is probably the same stuff that killed her."

Maybe I should have given flippancy a shot. Ordered him to come inside the Blue Pheasant, drink a beer, drink ten, all night, black out, crawl into the corner of the gutter. If your wife is here, don't get angry, don't get sad, say hello instead, buy her a drink and watch her dance off out of your life, don't let the weight of failure kill you. Why not get as numb and as pulseless as the masses, dear uncle?

No cause, no utility, that's me. The conundrum of being alive today: In an era where an intelligent being won't give up his life for anything, how might that same being maintain intelligently that his life has value? Does he have passion? A reason to use pure reason? I don't want to go anywhere near using 8 percent of my brain. The 7 percent has provided enough confusion as it is.

I enter the library and immediately spot the Cookie Monster in front of the circus of an info desk. It's not even reason enough to smile, but at least I know what day it is: Dress Down Friday. Been two and a half years since I last saw Robin in her favorite outfit. I drop my head so she can't see my face, and then I decide against it. I've got to ask her a question.

The Southeast Asian patron before her speaks such poor English that his mispronounced gutturals and fricatives sound like he's chewing ice. She has the look on her face of an enlightened despot, such that his question is obviously stupid, yet she's blocking his path to the vast antechamber of the library because, the eyes say, her duty first predicates nonjudgmental service to the serfs.

Same story here.

"Upstairs," she says. "Second door on the right. You cannot take unchecked books into the lavatory."

He nods appreciatively and walks off. She takes her place behind the desk, surrounded by stacks of rainbow pamphlets in rubber bands, city-sponsored flyers, matchstick pencils sharp as needles. Every answer about the library is, if not in Robin, behind Robin and her sweet-tooth brute from *Sesame Street*.

"Where's Cyrus?" I ask.

I can tell she knows it's me, but she's gonna make me wait.

"Cyrus," I say.

"He doesn't work here anymore."

Oh, no, I think, panicky.

"He's the nonfiction shelver at the Franklin Mall branch. Can I help you with any—"

I walk off immediately and climb the wide, carpeted, stately steps to the second floor of the stacks, recovering from the fear I'd just had, wicked split second of speculation: *A man like Cyrus only stops working for one reason.*

My eyes are watering a bit from the relief that he's still alive, that he has another day, hour, minute. I pass the workstation overflowing with on-line patrons, their eyes mesmerized by the shine of the screen, faces blue from holding their breaths, and calmly enter my old haunt, the Poetry section. Maybe I'll find a self-addressed one-line note I'd tucked away in some ancient text to keep the game going: *Hello. You're still here. Good-bye.* Then I can incinerate the note in the flame of a 7-Eleven lighter or crumple it into a ball and swallow it and write myself a new note for the next cyclical yet futile rediscovery of self: *Hello. You still here? Good-bye already!*

This spacious house of learning has plenty of dead, unused books to liberate. I seize the only copy of a flimsy paperback—*Beatrice,* by Anonymous—and head over to the men's bathroom, take the book into the handicapped stall, rip out the silver sticker that alerts the lasers at the library door and toss it into the basin of the toilet, kick the handle with my foot, look over my shoulder, and find the janitor with a plunger in one brown hand, a spray bottle of Windex in the other, LA Dodgers cap pulled down low to the nose.

He says, head down, *"Necesito limpiar el baño."*

His Pancho Villa mustache is gone now, but the dark brow and serious eyes are the same. It seems like a lifetime ago, someone else's life, when I busted him good in the nose. Now there isn't a word to share between us. I broke him off, he broke me off right back, the law broke him off again, and now he's gonna clean up after me, though this time there's no mess except a soon-to-be-stolen book on his watch. I walk right by him, don't say a word, don't wash my hands, right out the door.

I get a few steps out past the cinderblock books on Congressional voting records and change my mind. I freeze, turn. He exits the bathroom, pushing the utility cart with cleaners and solvents on it, plus brooms, dusters. He puts up the little yellow tent of a warning sign, rolls the mop bucket out of the cart, and starts to mop without looking up or over, though he knows I'm here.

A woman nears, stands less than a yard to my left. Jesus. She's watching me as I watch him, another honorable citizen in this safe, lifeless Silicon Valley city. Is she gonna get out her camera? I hope she'll leave. Pray she does. She doesn't.

"It's a shame, isn't it?" she whispers, nodding at my old compadre with the broom.

What does she want me to say? We can't Pine-Sol our own shit-encrusted toilets, we can't pick our own crops, we can't bury our own bodies. In less than two seconds, I'm nearly driven mad by the vagary of her question.

I turn and say, "Everything in this place is a shame, lady."

I walk over and approach the paisa. He nods and I stop right in front of him. He's got a wee bit of leftover shine from the rally, permanent shading under his eye, that I'd missed in the dull glow of the stall. I look back at the lady, but she's already gone.

I say, "¿Me recuerdes?"

He shakes his head, not stopping on the mop.

"No?"

He looks up at me, back down again, pushing the mop harder across the surface. "No."

"You don't remember me?"

He looks me in the eye, says, "I don't know what jou talking of."

I say, "*¿No recuerdes cuando peleamos?*"

He picks it up. But the lady's back, this time with a security guard. "That's him," she says, as if I'm miles away from her.

The security guard is a dark black East African, probably Sudanese, as he has a Catholic cross around his neck and a wicked scar starting purple at the temple, slicing diagonally across the brow, over an eye socket, across the bridge of the nose, over the cheek. It looks like someone wheeled a pizza slicer across his face. He says, deep voice, perfect equanimity, more than a trace of weariness in the steady yellow eyes, "Everything is okay?"

"*Sí.*" The paisa pats me once on the arm. "*Es mi amigo.*"

I look at the woman and smile. She frowns. I want to apologize to this Lost Boy security guard for bothering him. I can see he doesn't buy my innocence, but the voucher from another immigrant stumps him. He says, deepest voice I've ever heard, "Okay. Please you will call me if you have to call me."

My amigo nods, the lady shakes her head, I wave her away, turn to the paisa and say, "*Gracias.*"

He nods. What luck. I finally know exactly what to do with myself. Commit a single act with the clean conviction of conscience.

"*¿Quieres dinero gratis?*"

He shrugs.

I shake my head, insisting on the scamlessness of the offer. Lightly slap his shoulder, "*Soy nada mas que un arbol de dinero.*"

He shrugs again. There's no such thing as that genus of tree where he comes from. This may be the land of milk and honey but not even the maddest Canaanite like me knows how to make a tree grow money. He looks up at me and shakes his head with fleeting yet sincere and maybe even sympathetic thankfulness, never stopping the pendulum motion with the mop.

"*Paisa,*" I say, "*eso es la verdad.* The truth."

"*Sí.*" He shrugs.

"*No me gusta eso lugar.*"

He looks around the building, as if I'm going to set off a bomb in his *biblioteca*.

"No," I say, pointing at the ground. "*Eso pais.*"

He agrees, "*Yo, tampoco,*" yet shrugs again, mops.

I joke, "*¿Pero estas saliendo tambien?*"

He looks at me like I'm crazy. He's here for a reason. Offers the mop to me, I nod, don't take it. His profession prevents a return to his birthplace in the foreseeable future, wholly and by extension. That's what he's saying in pushing the broom out, *el pinche futuro:* You want some? He says, "No."

"*¿No regresas al Mexico?*"

"*No ahora.*"

"Not now?" I ask. "Not ever. *Nunca. Eres en los Estados Unidos para bueno. Por vida.* This is it."

"No," he insists. "*Mi corazón esta alla.*"

"Sure," I say. "Your heart is there but your ass is here."

"*¿Que?*"

"*Nada,*" I say.

I watch him go back and forth, working, listening, trying to get the job done. Unless there's another paisa around cleaning windows in the Ante-Meridian, he's probably talked more with me in the last three minutes than he has with anyone else during the week.

I point to my ear. "*Escuchas, amigo. Necesitas hacer dinero, no?*"

"*Sí.*"

"*¿Para tu familia?*"

"*Sí, claro.*"

"That's why you came here. *Eso es el razon.*"

"*Seguro,*" he says, stopping for a moment. He takes a quick look behind me. The questions about his family paints me with guilt: anyone can be INS, even Canaanite nuts.

I say with hyperbolic disdain, *"No soy La Migra, amigo,"* waving
the idea away with my hand. *"¿Recuerdes cuando ellos me traen a la
pinche pinta?"*

He doesn't say anything. Looks behind me again, turns around
and eyes the library, back around again. I still love the hell out of his
indignant suspicion, his mission of self-/familial-/cultural preservation here on the gringo side of the border. He couldn't know it, but
his own grandkids will be the very people he fears now, despises. All
it takes is one little minute, amigo, with your feet kicked up on the
couch, remote in your hand, ignoring the Girl Scout at the door, to
lose everything you are in America. You came to this country for its
gold and riches, totally unaware of the toll for admission: you lose
your story, *amigo,* the story that makes you who you are. You lose
yourself. No more adios. It's bye-bye now.

Bye-bye.

I lift my shirt up to show him I have no badge, no gun, no cuffs.
He doesn't move. I do the same again, but spinning so that he can
see the entire rim of my waistline.

"Baja La Migra," I say.

"Sí," he says, smiling. *"Baja La Migra."*

"Bueno," I say, reaching into my pocket. *"Amigo. Usas eso dinero
para tu esposa. ¿Tienes una esposa?"*

He nods once, nothing more.

"¿Como se llama ella?"

He nods very seriously, as if he's about to reveal top-secret data
related to national security. "Juanita."

"Juanita. *Bueno."* I write down the digits of my account as well as
directions to the nearest ATM. *"¿Y tu, como te llamas?"*

"Santiago."

"Santiago. *¿Ellos te mandan al Mexico?"*

"¿Quien?"

"La Migra."

"*Simon. Tres veces.*"

"Three times they sent you back?"

"*Sí.*"

"But you always return, don't you?" I nod, say, "Okay, Santiago. Fourth time's a charm, amigo. That's an American saying. *Tu tienes una mas vida aquí. Esos son los numeros para mi cuenta a la Banca del America. Todo es tuyo.*"

He nods, takes the paper, says nothing.

I say, "*¿Me crees?*"

He looks down at the paper, looks up at me. I meet his eyes and won't let go: I want him to know the truth: It's his, all his. "*Sí.*" Then he flexes his mouth, frowning. "Jes." He nods, "I know you are *muy* truth-speaking, *señor. Es* in your face, *tu cara.*"

I smile, satisfied. I pull my cash out, six twenties and a few tens, my ATM card, hand everything over. With the g I've saved in the bank, this cat'll do all right: he can liquidate it wisely, stupidly, frugally, lavishly, whatever. The point is: he'll use it, he'll do it. I say, "Oh, wait. *Esperas.* I need maybe a twenty and that's it."

Somehow, that bit of English gets through and he hands over an Andrew Jackson. I nod, say, "Well, man, we're straight. *¿Pero me entiendes?*"

"Understand jou?"

"*Sí,*" I say. "*Yo.* Me. You believe me, but do you understand me?"

"Oh, no, *señor,*" he says, encircling me with the mop, not one wet string over the top of my shoes. He leaves me standing there on an uncleaned island, surrounded by slick, shiny new-age tile and the yellow too-bright SLIPPERY WHEN WET sign.

"No, no, amigo!" he's calling out, loud this time, American loud. "I no understand jou!"

40

The End of the Day

THE END of the day comes again like a warm brown stream of gutter water on the last ephemeral evening: cloudy with debris, filled with filth, flushable. I take a taxi driven by a dark-chocolate five-foot Cambodian named Samsay to the Norm Mineta International Airport, pull out my wallet with everything I own inside it and leave him a tip twice the five-dollar fare, pick up my care package at the US Air terminal, a paid-in-full e-ticket overseas—*Rest in Peace, Uncle, I love you*—think of a line I once read that went, *It's a part of morality not to be at home in one's home,* stroll past the lumpia-sharing, Ilokano-speaking Filipino security guards at the X-ray checkpoints, let momentum push me down the accordion-walled chute into the plane, smile past the stewardess and down the narrow aisle, pull out the book by Anonymous in my back pocket, take my assigned window seat, lower the blind to more clearly see the blank-screen visions of struggle and faith and purity and courage and hope and love and limits and beauty and, with no baggage, leave America for good.

Acknowledgments

ALLOW ME to introduce four lovely ladies, a literary hit squad of sorts, inviolate in their commitment to this book, and thus very much a part of the good fight:

The wife.

Who tempers the cerebral undercurrents of a certain novelist, which is to say tempers his nuttiness, who's so down for this novelist she's way up on everyone else, who's listened on two hours sleep at 3:13 A.M. to eight-thousand word chapter excerpts while the novelist masticated barbecue Cornuts drunk, who on their first real date in downtown S.M. not only tolerated but actually enjoyed the novelist's constant reference to his novel-in-progress, which he kept pulling out loose-leafed from his backpack to finger, explain, and finally read passages from, and who, when this novelist pressed, "You do think someone will take it?" not only said, "Yes," but added the season ("This summer."), which of course it was, whose beauty is unparalleled, who will return, with the novelist, to her West Virginia horse farm to groom her Arabians if the novelist ever earns enough bones, who always stays, whose longing eyes remind the novelist that his reason for writing is to keep the story of the species alive.

The sponsor.

> *An incident of wisdom and generosity, unheard*
> *Of in the hallway-long annals of academia, occurred*
> *One summer: a fellowship (Juanito, big dog) was conferred*
> *Upon a wanderer so committed to the Word,*
> *He was degree-less by a class or two. The passive-aggressive*
>   *nerd*
> *Who thought it mattered had no choice. He deferred*
> *To your authority, Madame, which meant your bank*
>   *account. I heard.*
> *Thank you for your faith. Consider me, like your old friend*
>   *Algren, spurred*
> *Onward.*

The agent.

On a Sunday evening on a Park Avenue street corner, first time in the biggest city in the world, springtime, we meet.

I get five traits (witty, wise, erudite, cool, confident) in five sentences. You position yourself so that I have to look at you when you talk. I like that. I'm from the West Coast but I imagine that on this island of ruthless competition you call this "balls."

"I want this badass on my team," I think.

Less than a month later, you inform me that I'm gonna have to file taxes for the first time in years. A deal cut for your newest client, who once decorated his walls, like Bellow, with rejection letters. (The ceiling also counts as wall.)

It gets better. You get me the very press that calls itself "a family" and started the concept of free speech. Perfect karma for this loquacious benificiary, daily prima facie case of that right.

"You keep on doing what you're doing," you say. "This is just the start."

The editor.

There are actually people in the world nuttier than we weebit writers, miraculous creatures housing the truest of known contradictions: a data-processor brain and a human heart. Somehow this not "in conflict with itself," the thought and the feeling as one. And somehow the slush hardens into something with form, the transformation given to the slowest of motion. All along she dusts and steam-cleans in preparation for the moment she can sit down in the peaceful space of the desk, word-sword of a pencil sheathed behind the ear, kind chin on the platform of interlaced fingers, and watch the book ascend to its place on the shelves.